MW01268105

DEADLY
DEFIANCE
A Stan Turner Mystery

Dedication

To my father-in-law, Herb Mello, a kind and generous man that I have been privileged to know and love for over forty-five years.

DEADLY
DEFIANCE
A Stan Turner Mystery

Volume 10

BY

WILLIAM MANCHEE

Top Publications, Ltd.
Dallas, Texas

VOLUME 10

Top Publications, Ltd.

Library Edition

ISBN 978-1-929976-87-4
Library of Congress 2011927403

Contents

1
Rollerblades

February 20, 1995

One of the most difficult events in a parent's life is when their youngest child leaves home. This was particularly true for Stan Turner's wife, Rebekah, when Marcia left home to attend Texas A&M University. For twenty-two years Rebekah had been a devoted mother, friend, nurse, confidante, and personal taxi driver. She'd spent every waking hour tending to their needs, worrying about them, and encouraging them as they grew into adulthood. These motherly duties, although demanding and tedious at times, kept her busy and fulfilled her as a person. It was good that they'd had a large family as Stan's law practice had been quite demanding and he hadn't spent as much time at home as he would have liked. Now, with the kids gone, Rebekah found herself alone with little to do.

It was a difficult time for Stan financially, too, with two kids in college and one in law school. Stan suggested to Rebekah that she might want to go back to work to help out with college expenses, but she adamantly refused. Stan didn't quite understand why that was. She was an RN and could have made good money working at a hospital or for a doctor, but she argued she'd been away from it too long and forgotten most everything she'd learned in nursing school. In reality, Stan figured it was more likely the trauma she'd suffered when she was arrested for the murder of a patient, Sheila Logan. Stan and Sheila had been lured into a relationship by Sheila's husband who wanted Sheila dead. He had murdered Sheila and made it look like Rebekah had done it. She was subsequently cleared of the charges, but she'd never gone to work after that.

Stan wasn't the type of person to force anybody to do anything they didn't want to do, so he didn't press the issue with Rebekah. Fortunately, in the legal profession there was plenty of money to be made if you were willing to put in the hours and could take the stress dumped on you on a daily basis by overzealous opposing counsel, irritable judges, and demanding clients. So they had enough money to get by without Rebekah working.

It was a Monday morning; Stan had just walked into his office and was sipping a cup of coffee as he went through his phone messages. The offices of Turner & Waters were on the seventh floor of one of the Park Central office towers and Stan had a nice view of Medical City Hospital and downtown Dallas. It was a mesmerizing view and he often found himself daydreaming, or in deep contemplation, as he liked to call it.

Off in the break room he could hear his law partner, Paula Waters, and an associate attorney, Jodie Marshall, talking. Jodie was like a daughter to him. She had started out as his secretary when she was just nineteen, worked her way up to a legal assistant, and then associate attorney when she finished law school and passed the bar. Stan couldn't believe she'd been with him for nearly fifteen years. *Where had the years gone?*

His intercom buzzed and Maria, his secretary, advised him that his 9:00 appointment had just rolled in. "Rolled in?" he asked.

"You heard me," Maria said, stifling a laugh.

Curious as to Maria's choice of words, Stan got up and came out into the reception area where he found an attractive brunette, in a white sweatshirt and blue jeans, carefully removing her Rollerblades. She had exotic eyes, a trim body, and looked to be in her mid to late twenties. She looked up at Stan nervously. He extended a hand.

"Hi, I'm Stan Turner."

"Hello, I'm Maureen Thompson," she said as they shook hands.

Stan noticed her hands were cold and clammy. He could tell she was scared and nervous.

"Did you skate all the way here?" Stan asked.

"Yes, my car was repossessed. It was the only way I could get here."

"Oh, Jesus. Where do you live?"

"Oak Cliff."

"Gee. That's what—five miles from here?"

She nodded. "That sounds about right."

He took a deep breath. "You should have said something. We could have sent someone to pick you up."

She shrugged. "It's all right. It's good exercise."

"I suppose," Stan conceded. "Come on back to my office. You can leave your skates there. I don't think anyone will bother them."

Maureen grabbed her purse and a backpack full of papers and brought them back to his office. She dropped the backpack into one of the two side chairs across from Stan and collapsed into the other one. She looked tired, pale, and depressed.

"So, tell me what's going on," Stan said, trying to seem upbeat. "What happened with your car?"

She sighed. "My husband left me about three weeks ago and I discovered he hadn't paid any bills for the last three months."

"Oh, wonderful. Nice guy."

"Yeah, the love of my life," she said bitterly.

"What does your husband do?"

"He's a home builder."

"Self-employed?"

"He has a company, Thompson Construction, Inc., but he's the owner."

"So, do you work?"

"I'm a hairdresser, so I don't make a lot of money and I have two young children. There was no way I could catch up on everything. It was either the car or the house."

"Right. It must have been very difficult for you."

"I tried to work something out with the bank but they weren't at all sympathetic."

"No, they usually aren't," Stan agreed. "So, what's the damage? How much in the hole are you?"

She started sifting through her stack of papers, and Stan made a list of what she owed. It turned out she had about five thousand in medical bills, thirty-five thousand in credit card debt, and an auto deficiency of seventeen thousand for a total exceeding $57,000.

"So, there is no way you'll ever be able to pay that, right?" Stan asked.

She shook her head. "I don't see how."

Maureen's story wasn't at all unusual. Bankruptcy was a fact of life in the current credit-driven economy and Stan knew the first casualty of insolvency was usually the marriage.

"So, tell me about your marriage. Is it over, or do you think your husband will come back?"

"No. He won't be back. Not this time. The IRS is looking for him."

Stan cringed at the mention of the IRS. He was painfully aware that if a husband was dodging the IRS, more often than not the innocent spouse would end up getting stuck with the delinquent tax bill.

"How much are they trying to collect?"

"Almost a hundred grand."

"Tell me you filed separate returns," Stan asked, holding his breath.

"No. Our accountant said we'd save taxes if we filed jointly."

"So, you signed the return?"

"Yes. Rod told me he was sending a check in with the return. I watched him write the check and put it in the envelope. "

"So, what happened?"

"An emergency came up and Rod withdrew the money before the check cleared. Three weeks later I got a certified letter stating I had thirty days to make the check good."

Stan shifted in his chair uncomfortably as tension started to build in his neck and shoulders. This often happened when clients began unloading their problems on him. There wasn't any satisfactory solution for Maureen's predicament. Stan told her she could file bankruptcy but that wouldn't solve the IRS liability since a government agency like the IRS had a priority debt.

"You mean I'll have to pay the taxes?"

"Not necessarily. If we waited to file for three more years then you might be able to get the taxes discharged."

"So we'll wait, then," she said.

"We could, but eventually your creditors will start filing lawsuits against you and defending them could get expensive."

"Damn it! Isn't there anything we can do?" Maureen spat. "I'm going to kill that son of a bitch for leaving me like this!"

Stan sighed. "I didn't say there wasn't anything we could do. I just said it's a complicated situation and we'll have to consider what options would be best for you. In the meantime I can write letters to your creditors and keep them from harassing you."

"Good. They've been driving me crazy—calling at all hours, at work, talking to my neighbors."

"Well, we can put a stop to that, but I can't keep them from suing you."

Maureen shrugged. "What about your fees? How much will this cost me?"

"I don't know yet. It depends on what we end up doing. A bankruptcy is $1,200. Defending you against creditors is $200 per hour."

Maureen's mouth dropped. "Twelve hundred dollars? Jesus! Where am I supposed to get that kind of money?"

"I don't know. Can you borrow it from friends or family?"

"Maybe, but I'll be totally humiliated having to do that. I can't believe my life has come to this," she moaned.

"I'm sorry. I wish there was a simple solution."

"Rod's got a half million dollar insurance policy. What if he should die? I'd get the money, right?"

"Ah, not if you had anything to do with his death."

"But how would they know?"

Stan looked at Maureen and shook his head. He couldn't believe how often clients would suggest an illegal act as a way out of their problems. He often wondered what they would say if he agreed that was an option.

"Okay. Don't even go down that road," Stan said sternly. "If you kill him you won't get the insurance proceeds and you'll end up in prison for the rest of your life. You wouldn't want your children to grow up without their mother, would you?"

Maureen shrugged. "So what do I do, then?"

"If you pay me $200 I'll send out letters to your creditors so they'll leave you alone. Then in a week or two we'll get together and come up with a long-term game plan. If we decide to delay filing bankruptcy for three years, you'll have plenty of time to raise the money."

Maureen didn't seem too thrilled with Stan's consultation but she left her papers with him and promised to send him a check for $200. Stan gave the papers she'd left to Maria to make a file. He offered to give her a ride home, but she politely declined the offer. When she'd gone Jodie walked into Stan's office with a grin on her face.

"Did that woman skate to our office?" Jodie asked.

Stan smiled. "Yes, her car was repossessed."

"Oh, my God! The poor woman."

"That's the least of her problems. The IRS is after her for almost a hundred grand."

Jodie shook her head. "So, that's why she didn't look so happy?"

"That and the fact that I couldn't come up with a miraculous solution to her problems in five minutes. I don't know what she expected from me. Her situation is pretty much hopeless—at least right now. In time I think we can resolve it."

Jodie smiled sympathetically. "Well, it looks like you've got a busy day. There's a crowd of people in the reception area waiting for you."

"Oh, really," Stan said, grimacing. "What do they want?"

"I don't know. Something about a suspicious death."

"Hmm. Have Maria seat them in the conference room. Why don't you sit in on the interview. If it doesn't turn out to be something we can help them with, I'll excuse you from the meeting."

"All right. I'll join you in the conference room in five minutes."

Stan nodded and Jodie left. After answering a few phone calls, Stan got up and went to the conference room where he found a large Hispanic woman, her two sons, and three daughters waiting patiently for him. Jodie walked in right behind Stan and they both took a seat.

"Hello. I'm Stan Turner and this is my associate, Jodie Marshall."

The woman, who seemed tired and profoundly sad, forced a smile. "I'm Pandora Alvarez. These are my children—my sons, Ganix and Nehemias, and my daughters, Luz, Jade and Louisa Cervantes. Louisa was just married three weeks ago."

"Oh, congratulations!" Jodie said, smiling at Louisa.

"Yes, that's great news," Stan agreed. "So, what can we do for you?"

Pandora sighed. "It's my husband. He recently died."

"Oh, I'm sorry to hear that. How old a man was he?"

"Fifty-three," Louisa replied. "But his death wasn't by natural causes; he was murdered."

"Murdered? What makes you think that?" Stan asked.

"My father was in perfect health. He didn't drink or smoke and he hadn't taken drugs since he was a teenager."

"Okay, what was the cause of death?"

"The medical examiner ruled it a drug overdose," Pandora replied. "But Louisa is right, Romildo didn't take drugs, so the medical examiner is wrong."

Stan knew the medical examiner wouldn't rule a death as a drug overdose without substantial evidence to that effect. He also knew that family members were often in denial when it came to the habits of parents and spouses, but he didn't say anything.

"So, did your husband have any enemies?" Jodie asked.

"Yes, our boss, Icaro Melendez. My father recently reported him to the Department of Labor. Icaro was livid. He told my father he would pay for his disloyalty."

Stan thought this was an interesting case, but he wondered why the family hadn't taken their suspicions to the police or the Department of Labor. It didn't seem like a civil matter.

"So, what did the police have to say about all this?" Stan asked.

"They say there is no evidence of foul play. They refuse to do anything about it.," Louise replied bitterly.

Stan looked at Jodie and then back at Pandora. He tapped the conference table with his finger nervously. "Well, you may be right about Icaro, but this really sounds like a matter for the police or the FBI. Before we could institute a wrongful death suit, we'd have to conduct a thorough investigation and that would be quite expensive. Right now it sounds like all you have is suspicion and conjecture. We'd have to have a lot more evidence of foul play to take on a case like that. I'm sorry."

Pandora sighed. "I understand. I was afraid you wouldn't take the case, but I tried anyway. So, do you handle probate?"

"Sure, we could probate your husband's will for you."

"While you're probating his will, would you be willing to help us find the evidence we need against Icaro?"

Stan laughed. "Maybe. It depends on what kind of help you're talking about."

"Tell us what kind of evidence you need. There are six of us. We'll find the evidence. Just help us out."

Stan took a deep breath. "Okay, but I'm not promising anything. Our only commitment will be the probate. We'll try to help you find some evidence against Icaro, but no field work—strictly advice and counsel."

"That's all we need," Pandora assured them. "You are very kind."

Stan didn't really think there was a chance in hell anything incriminating would come out of their investigation, but he felt sorry for the family and didn't want to dash their hopes so soon after their father's death. He wondered if there was anything to their suspicions. After they'd left he discussed the case with Jodie.

"So, what do you think, Jodie? Is this a big waste of time?"

She shrugged. "I don't know. I think they all truly believe their father was murdered and, since they all work for Mr. Melendez, they should know as well as anybody what he is capable of."

"Right. Find out as much as you can from each of them about Mr. Alvarez and then I'll talk to the police and the FBI. I wonder if they took a serious look at the case. If they did, we might be able to nudge them into doing something."

"Sounds good. I'll get right on it."

"In the meantime I'll get the will probated and get Pandora approved as independent executrix."

Jodie left and Stan went back into his office. He looked at the clock on his credenza and noticed it was nearly noon. He remembered he'd promised to have lunch with Rebekah so he dropped the legal pad and the papers Pandora had given him on his desk and left for the Black Eyed Pea where he'd promised to meet her. Fortunately, it was only five minutes away so he arrived just as Rebekah was driving up. They walked in together and were seated immediately and given menus.

"How was traffic coming in?" Stan asked as he leafed through the menu.

"Not bad. It only took about twenty minutes," Rebekah responded.

A waitress came over, deposited a basket of rolls, and then flipped open a pad to take their orders.

"I think I'll have the pot roast," Rebekah said. "And a Diet Coke."

Stan closed his menu and smiled up at the cute waitress. "I'm going to have the turkey sandwich and ice tea."

The waitress nodded and left. Rebekah grabbed a roll and began pulling it apart. "This is nice. I can't remember the last time we ate lunch together on a weekday."

"Well, you're free now that Marcia's gone. You can come have lunch with me as often as you like."

"I doubt that. You're usually too busy to eat lunch."

"True, but I'll make time for you, don't worry."

"I don't want to bother you."

Stan sighed. "It's no bother. I enjoy having lunch with you."

Rebekah shrugged. "So, how has your day been so far?"

"Busy. Two interesting clients came in this morning—one of them actually Rollerbladed in all the way from Oak Cliff."

Rebekah frowned. "Why would she do that?"

"Her car was repo'ed."

"Oh, my God. That's terrible. How humiliating."

"I know. But you've got to give her credit. She's determined to overcome all her problems . . . and she's got a string of them."

Stan explained her circumstance in more detail. As they were talking Stan noticed Paula walk in the door. He stood up and waved to her. She saw him and rushed over.

"Hi, Stan . . . Rebekah. I heard you two were having lunch, so I decided to come over and crash the party. I hope you don't mind."

"No," Rebekah said. "Sit down and join us."

"Thank you. I haven't seen you in ages. When I heard you were only five minutes away I couldn't resist."

Rebekah and Paula were good friends now. It hadn't always been that way. At one time Paula had tried to break up their marriage and take Stan away from her. But, Stan stubbornly resisted and eventually Paula married Bart, another attorney working for the Collin County DA's office. Bart had worked for Turner & Waters for a while after he was canned by the Collin County DA's office, but that didn't last long. Bart found he didn't like criminal defense work all that much. He was a prosecutor at heart, so when he was offered a job with the Dallas DA's office he jumped at the opportunity. When Paula got married Rebekah was ecstatic and offered to help with the wedding. Paula appreciated the help since her mother was dead and she didn't have a lot of friends. After that the two of them became close and they'd been good friends ever since.

"I'm glad you decided to join us," Rebekah said. "How have you been?"

"Fine."

"How's Bart?"

"He's very busy. I hardly ever see him. They're working on some big drug prosecution in Amarillo, so he's been gone a lot."

"Oh, that's too bad."

Paula shrugged. "That's the life of an attorney."

"Don't I know it," Rebekah snickered.

"So, how are you holding up now that everyone's left home?"

"I'm miserable. It's so lonely at home. I miss the kids."

"I've suggested she go back to work," Stan interjected.

Rebekah groaned. "I'll never go back to nursing. I never really enjoyed it. I only did it to help Stan get started in his law practice."

"So, what do you do all day?" Paula asked.

"Clean the house, watch TV, do the laundry, iron. There's still plenty to do around the house."

Paula nodded then looked at Stan. "Stan could afford to hire you a maid, you know. You don't have to do housework."

"I've offered to do that," Stan noted.

"I don't want some stranger in my house," Rebekah protested. "Don't worry about me. I'll be fine."

Paula nodded. "So, you won't believe what happened to me today."

"What?" Stan asked.

"Judge Martini tried to appoint me attorney ad litem in a probate case."

"Seriously? What do you know about probate?"

"Nothing. That's what I told him, so he appointed you."

"Me? You've got to be kidding. Did you volunteer me?"

"No, but when I declined he asked if you'd do it. He said it was an important case and he didn't think anybody on his regular panel was up to the job."

"And what makes me up for it?" Stan asked curiously.

"He said something about needing someone stubborn and tenacious," Paula replied.

"That's Stan all right," Rebekah agreed.

Stan stiffened. "Oh, thanks a lot."

As their food was served Stan wondered about the case Judge Martini had handpicked him for. He couldn't imagine why the judge wanted him to be involved. Stan didn't have any special probate experience. He did probate work from time to time but he wasn't board certified and he didn't solicit that type of business. He knew he should be flattered that the judge had specially picked him for the job, but instead he felt uneasy. For some reason he knew he wasn't going to like this new assignment. He just wondered how long it would be before he figured out why.

2
Renegade Son

Jodie Marshall had a unique perspective on the law in that she'd seen it from every angle—as a client, a legal secretary, an investigator, and finally as an attorney. After high school she'd been looking for a job and ran across Stan's ad for a secretary. Stan couldn't afford a seasoned legal secretary, so he opted to hire someone green and train them. Jodie liked the idea of working for an attorney because it would look good on her resume and she'd learn a lot about the law. Before seeing the ad, she hadn't had any particular interest in the law, but as time went on her interest grew.

Shortly before going to work for Stan, Jodie's brother was arrested for DWI and Jodie had helped him through the ordeal. From this experience she learned what it was like to be a client, and the experience made her sensitive to the needs of Stan's clients. She'd often remind Stan of the importance of frequent communication with clients to keep them informed and to relieve their anxieties.

As time went by Stan grew to appreciate Jodie's talents and abilities. He had encouraged her to go to college and allowed her to adjust her hours to fit her academic schedule. After a while she was doing more than secretarial work. Stan noticed she was good with people so he gave her some assignments that normally would have gone to the firm's private investigator. Jodie did so well at this Stan hired a new secretary, so Jodie would have more time to do investigations and paralegal work. When she graduated from college Stan suggested she might want to go to law school. By that time she was very passionate about the law and jumped at the opportunity.

Since she had only recently passed the bar, she hadn't been given her own case yet. She hoped the Romildo Alvarez case might be her first. After their meeting with the family on Monday, Jodie went to the factory owned by Icaro Melendez. She didn't plan on talking to anybody, but just wanted to see the place and get the lay of the land. She wanted to have a mental picture of the plant and Mr. Melendez when she was talking to the family and working on the case.

She stood across the street from the plant, wearing old jeans and a T-shirt rather than her usual business attire. She wasn't sure how she'd get in until she saw a UPS delivery truck drive up. Jodie was disarmingly pretty, so men usually were a little mesmerized when they first met her. Seeing this as an opportunity she walked quickly across the street and intercepted the driver.

"Who's that for?" she asked.

The driver smiled broadly when he saw her and eagerly responded. "Mr. Melendez."

"I'll take it," Jodie said, extending her hands to take the package.

The driver handed her the package without hesitation. Jodie signed for it and then walked into Alliance Fabrications as if she owned the place. A clerk looked up and Jodie smiled at her.

Jodie knew that if she acted like she was just doing her job she'd probably be ignored. She moved quickly, not giving anyone time to question her.

"This is for Mr. Melendez. Is he around?"

The girl nodded and pointed to a doorway. Jodie strolled over to it and stepped inside the big manufacturing facility. It was a good-size workplace—much bigger than she'd expected. She looked around and saw the executive offices to her left but went to the right and walked casually through the busy plant. She noticed the fabrication equipment was old and many machines sat idle in disrepair. There was trash and clutter everywhere, water dripped into buckets from leaks in the roof, and the place smelled of oil and mildew. Hundreds of workers labored at various work stations and along conveyor belts.

From the plant she went out into the yard and looked around until someone stopped her.

"Who are you?" a young Hispanic man in his late twenties asked.

"Oh, I've got a package for Mr. Melendez. Have you seen him?"

"He should be in his office."

"Where's that?" Jodie asked.

"I'll show you," the man said and escorted Jodie back into the plant and took her to the executive offices. He pointed to an office where a tough-looking man sat behind a cluttered desk. He had long black hair, a scar running down his left cheek, and a scowl on his face that gave Jodie a chill. She stared at him for a moment wondering if he was a murderer.

"That's Mr. Melendez," the man advised.

"Oh, very good," Jodie said and handed the package to the man. "Would you give this to him? He looks busy and I'm running late."

"Sure, but I didn't get your name. I'm Ricardo."

"Oh, he doesn't know me. I was out front and the UPS guy just stuck the package in my face and asked me to give it to Mr. Melendez."

"I see. What were you doing in front of the building?"

"Oh, I was meeting someone. I'd been promised a drink."

Ricardo's eyes widened. "Who?"

"Oh, well I just met him yesterday. His name is Ganix."

"Ganix? You don't want to go out with him. He's just a line worker. Why don't you let me take you out for that drink? I'm the boss's son."

"Mr. Melendez is your father?"

"Yes. I'm his youngest son. I just stopped by to get a check for next month's tuition. I'm in college at the University of Dallas."

Jodie's spirits rose as she perceived a great opportunity to get some inside information on Icaro Melendez and Alliance Fabrications.

She pondered the obvious danger in a liaison with Icaro's son. It certainly wasn't the low profile Stan had suggested would be appropriate, but it was just too good an opportunity to pass up.

"Well, okay. Ganix hasn't shown up yet, so I guess it's his loss, right?"

"Absolutely," Ricardo said excitedly. "Don't worry about him. He has no business going out with a woman like you."

Jodie giggled shyly.

"Oh. I still don't know your name."

"Ah, it's Jodie."

"Well, Jodie. I've got to take care of my business with my father. How about I meet you at Fridays on Greenville Avenue for happy hour. It starts at five. Then I'll buy you dinner."

Jodie nodded. "Sounds good. I'll see you at Fridays," she said and made a quick exit. Once she was in her car and driving back to the office she thought about Ricardo and wondered if he knew what went on at his father's plant. She thought about what she had seen there. The place was pretty much how Pandora Alvarez had described it. It was obvious Mr. Melendez was interested more in profit than employee satisfaction or safety. She couldn't imagine having to work in a place like that. The very thought of it gave her gooseflesh.

Late that afternoon Jodie dropped by her apartment to get ready for her date. She wanted to be as disarming as possible so Ricardo would open up to her. After taking a shower, taking pains to make sure her makeup was perfect, and fixing her hair, she picked out a short dress that she knew would be quite distracting. When she was satisfied with her appearance she drove to Fridays, arriving just a little late, so as not to appear anxious. She spotted Ricardo sitting nervously at the bar. He jumped up when he saw her coming.

"There you are. I was afraid you wouldn't come," Ricardo said.

"Why would a girl pass up free drinks and your charming company for the evening?" Jodie asked playfully.

"I don't know. It was just so unexpected meeting you at my father's office. After you left I started thinking you might have agreed to having a drink just to get rid of me. I'm naturally paranoid—something I inherited from my father, I'm afraid. But I glad you're here. What can I get you?"

"Gin and tonic, please."

Ricardo caught the bartender's attention and ordered a gin and tonic for Jodie and a rum and Coke for himself. Then he turned back and smiled at Jodie.

"Meeting someone like you the way I did at my father's sweatshop just seems so . . . so . . . surreal. I half expected to wake up and discover I'd been dreaming."

"Sweatshop?" Jodie repeated. "Do I detect a note of disapproval?"

"You could say that. I'm the maverick in the family if you hadn't already guessed."

"Yes. I was wondering about that."

Ricardo took a deep breath and let it out slowly. "My father is very disappointed that I haven't embraced the family business. Luckily, not so disappointed that's he's cut me off. I think he still has delusions that someday I'll come around. The prodigal son, you know?"

"Right. So, your brothers work in the business?"

"Yes. My eldest brother Rudy is the plant manager and my brother Helio is a salesman."

"What do you make at your plant?"

"Mobile home parts. We supply two major manufacturers."

"Hmm. How many employees do you have?"

"Around a hundred or so. My father doesn't believe in automation, not when you can hire illegal aliens so cheaply."

"Oh, really. I didn't know it was that easy."

"Yes. The illegals are everywhere. If you put out the word that you've got one job twenty-five will show up wanting it."

"So, you don't approve of that?" Jodie asked.

"Not particularly, but I don't want to talk about my father. Tell me something about you."

Jodie looked at Ricardo and wondered if she should lie. If she did it could come back to haunt her later if a wrongful death suit were filed. She decided not to lie, but that didn't mean she had to tell him everything.

"Hmm. Well. I just passed the bar exam after ten years."

"Really? You're an attorney?"

"Barely. I've just been working for a few months. It took me ten years to get through school and pass the bar. I had to work my way through school."

"Wow! That's impressive."

"So, if you don't want to work at your father's plant, what do you want to do?"

"Actually, I'm studying to be an architect or a construction engineer. I've always been fascinated with building things—roads, bridges, buildings."

Jodie and Ricardo continued to talk for another hour or so and then they had dinner. Jodie didn't press for more information about Alliance Fabrications for fear of blowing her cover. She decided it might take a few more dates to get the information she needed from Ricardo without making him suspicious. She liked Ricardo so she didn't mind spending some time with him. She felt a little guilty about deceiving him, but if that's what it took to bring a murderer to justice, she reasoned, she had no choice but to do it.

The next day Jodie met with Nehemias Alvarez, the eldest son of the family, and his brother Ganix. She wondered if Ricardo would say anything to Ganix about her. She decided she had better tell him what she'd done so he wouldn't act surprised if Ricardo said something. Nehemias was a tall, slender, quiet man who, according to Jodie's notes, was twenty-six years old. He wore jeans, a T-shirt, and brown work shoes. Twenty-two-year-old Ganix looked a lot like his brother but was shorter and had a mustache.

"Thanks for coming by," Jodie said.

"No problem. Thank you for taking our case," Nehemias said.

"Well, we're just looking into it for now. It's not going to be easy proving Mr. Melendez murdered your father."

"I know. What can I do to help you prove it?"

"I don't know yet. How long have you two worked at Alliance Fabrications?"

"Since we were twelve years old," Nehemias replied.

"Twelve years old?" Jodie said. "That's not legal, is it? How did Mr. Melendez get around the law?"

"We weren't on the books as employees. The company provides day care for its workers, except the children don't play games, they work."

"Oh, my God! How do they get away with that?"

"Most of the employees are illegal. If they complain they're threatened with deportation. If that doesn't work Mr. Melendez has some men who will keep them in line."

"Why didn't you just quit and find employment elsewhere?"

"Mr. Melendez doesn't allow employees to quit," Nehemias replied.

"What! You've got to be kidding," Jodie said incredulously.

"No. There's no turnover at Alliance Fabrications. As Mr. Melendez likes to tell us, it's the job of a lifetime."

"It sounds like slavery to me," Jodie said.

Nehemias shrugged. "That's what got my father in trouble. He told them he was tired of being their slave and he was going to report them to the Labor Department."

"Hmm. Did they pay you when you started working there at age twelve?"

"Yes, we were paid half the rate as our parents."

"What were your parents paid?"

"Minimum wage."

"How many hours did you have to work?"

"Sixty hours. Ten hours per day, six days a week," Nehemias replied.

"I don't suppose they paid overtime."

Nehemias laughed. "No. Mr. Melendez said we were lucky to be able to work that many hours and shouldn't complain. He said since we were illegal the labor laws didn't apply to us."

"Really? And nobody was in a position to dispute his claim, I suppose."

"No. It would have been too dangerous."

"Do you know the names of the men who Mr. Melendez uses for muscle?"

"You mean the supervisors?"

"Is that what he calls them?"

"Yes. There's Adair Aguirre, Ben Zepeda, and Guido Quesada."

"Have you ever seen them harm an employee?"

"No. They grab you before or after work and take you to a secluded place. There's never any witnesses."

"How do you know this?"

"I've talked to workers after they've been 'reprimanded,' as Mr. Melendez calls it."

"Have you ever been reprimanded?"

"Just once after my father went to the Labor Board."

"What did they do to you?" Jodie asked.

"They roughed me up a bit and then told me that I better keep my father in line or they'd terminate his employment," Nehemias replied.

"Hmm. And since it was a lifetime job, you took that to mean they'd kill them."

"Exactly. And they made good on their threat when he filed his complaint with the Department of Labor."

"Listen," Jodie said. "I went by the plant yesterday just to check it out and I ran into Ricardo Melendez. He asked me why I was there, so I had to make something up."

"Really?" Nehemias said. "What did you tell him?"

"I told him Ganix had promised to take me for a drink."

Ganix looked up in surprise. Jodie smiled. "So, Ganix. If he says anything just go along with it, okay?"

"Sure," Ganix said. "Would you like me to actually buy you a drink?"

"No. It was just the first thing that came to mind. You're a client, so I couldn't go out on a date with you, but Ricardo doesn't know you're my client."

"Okay," Ganix said with a hint of disappointment.

After they'd gone Jodie considered everything she'd learned so far about Alliance Fabrications and Mr. Icaro Melendez. She hadn't realized slavery still existed in America, but now she knew it did and she realized there were probably many other employers just like Alliance Fabrications all over the country. She wondered what her next move should be. After giving it some thought, she decided to go to the courthouse and check the criminal courts' database and see if there were any lawsuits pending against the company.

She checked not only Mr. Melendez's record but also his muscle, Adair Aguirre, Ben Zepeda, and Guido Quesada. There was nothing on Melendez in the criminal records but his three supervisors each had a long list of complaints from burglary to assault and battery. Remarkably, though, nothing had stuck and the three had never gone to jail.

When Jodie checked the civil database a few minutes later she found several lawsuits against the company for breach of contract, unpaid debts, and back sales taxes. After she printed out as much on the cases as she could, she took the material and went back to the office to sort through it. When she was done she took it to Stan and gave him a report of her progress.

Stan laughed. "You just took a tour of the plant on your own?" Stan asked.

"Sure. Why not? The place was so busy nobody paid much attention to me."

"Hmm. So, did you see Mr. Melendez?"

"Yes, from a distance. He looks like a tough hombre. We're going to have to be very careful not to stir him up."

"Well, we'll keep a low profile for now and hopefully get the police or the FBI to do the stirring."

"So, I'm going to meet with Pandora and her daughters tomorrow. After that what should I do?"

"I'll contact a detective friend with the Dallas Police Department. Maybe he can tell us why there was no criminal prosecution. In the meantime you can get an application for appointment of Pandora Alvarez as executrix of the estate."

Jodie nodded and went back to her office. It didn't take her long to put the probate application together. She had done dozens of similar applications for Stan's clients in the past. When she was done, she wondered if there was anything else she could do before meeting with Mrs. Alvarez and her daughters the next day. It occurred to her there might have been a newspaper story on Romildo's death, so she stopped by the Richardson Library after lunch.

She found a small article buried deep in the *Dallas Morning News.*

Worker Found Dead in Vacant Lot

Two children playing in a vacant lot in Oak Cliff Tuesday found the body of Romildo Alvarez, 53, a factory worker for Alliance Fabrications of Dallas, Texas. The medical examiner reported that Mr. Alvarez died of an apparent drug overdose. Fellow workers report that Mr. Alvarez seemed fine on Monday when he was called home early in the afternoon to attend to his sick wife, but never made it there. Mr. Alvarez is survived by his wife, Pandora, and five children.

There has been speculation by persons who desire to remain anonymous that Mr. Alvarez's sudden death was no accident. It's been alleged that Alvarez was killed as a retaliation for a complaint he filed with the Department of Labor alleging Alliance Fabrications had failed to pay overtime and employed underage children. A spokesman for Alliance

Fabrications denied the charges and indicated the Dallas police had investigated them and determined the charges were unfounded. He further stated that Mr. Alvarez had a history of drug addiction and had been observed using illegal drugs in the past.

A spokesman for the Department of Labor declined comment but indicated there was no active investigation of Alliance Fabrications at this time.

Jodie was pretty sure the anonymous source mentioned in the article was Pandora or one of her children. She couldn't believe the Department of Labor hadn't launched an investigation after Romildo's death. Then again the medical examiner's report confirmed a drug overdose and with a history of drug usage, it probably wasn't that surprising that the agency decided an investigation wasn't necessary. She wondered if Melendez had connections in the police department or Department of Labor and paid them to leave him alone. She'd have to quiz Ricardo about that the next time they went out.

3
Ice Pick Widow

Paula Waters had met Stan Turner in law school at SMU in the mid-1970s. They'd been constant companions and best friends. Paula had wanted their relationship to be more than friendship but, much to her despair, Stan was already happily married to Rebekah. Nevertheless Paula was drawn to Stan as he had a propensity for attracting attention and getting himself into interesting predicaments. Before he had even finished law school he had undertaken the task of clearing a friend's name who had allegedly brutally killed his wife and family and then taken his own life. Paula had helped in his crusade and they'd ended up at odds with a powerful Mexican drug cartel. This was the kind of action Paula liked. This was what had attracted her to the legal profession and criminal law in particular. She loved the adrenaline rush of danger and the excitement of living on the edge.

After graduation Stan had gone into private practice and she'd gone to work for the DA. They'd lost touch for a few years until their paths crossed when Stan was defending a teenager accused of DUI and Paula was the prosecuting attorney. This chance encounter rekindled the crush Paula had felt for Stan. It also reminded her of how unhappy she was working petty cases for the DA. She had read with much envy the stories of Stan's exploits in the courtroom defending accused murderers. Stan was living her dream and she couldn't stand it. So she approached Stan with the idea of a partnership. Again, in her mind she hoped it would be more than a legal partnership, but either way she was sure she'd soon be in the spotlight as a premier defense attorney—and she was right.

The partnership of Turner & Waters was an instant success as Paula and Stan embodied the two essential ingredients to the success of any law practice—Stan was a rainmaker and Paula was a capable manager. Whereas Paula lacked Stan's charisma, Stan had no administrative talent. Alone their fortunes were limited, but together they had a bright future—particularly when Paula gave up on her efforts to subvert Stan's marriage and finally settled down with Bart.

Today Paula was bored. She was between murder cases and was relegated to working on a few family law cases she'd reluctantly taken on to keep herself busy. The thing about family law was that it was steady business. There was so much of it you could always pick some up if you wanted it. Usually she referred it out to some of her friends as she hated refereeing petty disputes between angry spouses, but, if there was no other business available, she was practical enough to take it on.

The intercom buzzed and Maria advised Paula that Stan needed her. She dropped what she was doing and headed for his office. Along the way she stepped into the break room and got a cup of coffee. Stan smiled up at her as she walked in and took a seat.

"It's your lucky day," Stan said.

Paula's eyes widened. "Oh, thank God! What's up?"

"You know Maureen Thompson who came in a few days ago on Rollerblades?"

"Yes."

"Well, her husband has been murdered and, of course, Maureen is the prime suspect. She's downtown right now at the city jail."

"Has she been arrested?"

"No, but she's been read her rights. I told her to keep her mouth shut and you'd be right down."

"You don't want this one for yourself?"

William Manchee

Stan laughed. "No, thanks. I'm up to my eyeballs in estate-planning cases."

"You prefer estate planning over a murder case?" Paula asked, incredulous.

"Well, actually, yeah. It's much less stressful."

"Sure, but isn't it boring?"

"No, not really. It's like game of chess. It doesn't look like much fun to the spectator, but there's a lot going on in the minds of the players. In this case the players are the IRS and the taxpayer."

"Oh, okay," Paula said, rolling her eyes.

"You know it's said that paying taxes is voluntary. There are so many loopholes in the Internal Revenue Code that anyone can avoid paying taxes if they are careful how they do business."

"Sure, but the last time I looked tax evasion was illegal," Paula said.

"Sure, but this isn't tax evasion. This is tax avoidance. There's a big difference. One is legal and one is not. I make sure my clients don't do anything that will jeopardize their freedom. After all, a rich man in jail is not much better off than a pauper. . . . Besides, Jodie and I are working on an interesting personal injury case that may mushroom into a major wrongful death suit. I'm going to let her handle it, but I should probably help her out since it's her first big case."

"You think she's ready?" Paula asked.

Stan smiled. "She was born ready. That girl is a snake in the grass. Whoever she's after had better wear their high boots and keep the antivenom handy."

Paula shook her head. "All right. I'd better go see how bad it looks for Maureen. I'm sure she's terrified sitting in the holding cell with a bunch of thugs and drunks."

Stan nodded and Paula went back to her office. She gathered her things together and then called the city jail to advise them she was coming. A familiar voice answered the telephone.

"Molly. This is Paula."

27

"Hey, girl. Where you been? I thought maybe you didn't like me anymore."

"Business is slow. What can I say?"

"Yeah. Yeah. Excuses, excuses."

"Well, thankfully we got a call from a Maureen Thompson."

"Oh. It's your lucky day, then. I think she's being questioned about her husband's murder."

"That's what I heard."

"They're in there now getting acquainted."

"Well, tell them to pull up their pants and get out of there. She's retained my services and I'm on my way."

Molly laughed. "Okay, girl. I'll go tell them the fun's over."

"Thanks, Molly. See ya."

Paula grabbed her purse and briefcase and headed for her car. She'd known Molly Rogers since high school. They hadn't been good friends then, since Molly was a grade ahead of her at Hillcrest High, but they had known each other from the drama club. When Paula started prosecuting for the DA and was questioning suspects at the city jail almost every day, they'd become friends and loved to exchange courthouse gossip. Their friendship hadn't suffered when Paula shifted from prosecution to defense; in fact, the relationship became even stronger and Molly became a valuable source of inside information for Paula. Of course, Molly was always surrounded by other intake personnel, so she couldn't tell Paula anything that others wouldn't hear. Because of that, they'd developed a code that seemed completely innocent to the casual observer but had hidden meaning to Paula and Molly.

Paula parked across the street from the police station and walked up the long stairway from the street to the lobby. She saw Molly behind the long marble intake desk and walked up to her. The waiting room was packed with relatives of inmates waiting for their loved ones to be released.

"Good morning, Molly. Busy day?"

"Every day's a zoo around here," Molly replied. "Your gal's ready to see you. I'll send her to booth six."

"Great. Thanks. We need to do lunch and catch up."

"Promises, promises," Molly said with a grin.

Paula smiled. "Seriously, I'll call you."

Molly nodded and Paula walked over to booth six and pulled open the door. She stepped inside and sat down on the hard bench seat in front of the bulletproof window that separated the visitors from the inmates. A moment later a door opened and Maureen Thompson stepped in, dressed in a black and white striped jumper. Paula sighed at the sight of her, knowing how humiliated she must feel being paraded around in such a demeaning costume. Surely this was cruel and unusual punishment, particularly for someone who hadn't been convicted of anything yet.

"Hi, Maureen. How are you holding up?" Paula asked.

"Not so well. I'm afraid. There are some tough girls in here."

It was obvious Maureen had been crying and was very distraught. Paula felt sorry for her, remembering how she'd felt when she'd been falsely accused of negligent homicide and taken into custody. It was such a helpless feeling to suddenly have your freedom taken away and to be treated like the scum of the earth.

"So, did you tell the detectives anything?"

"No. There was nothing to tell. I had nothing to do with Rod's death."

"How was he killed?" Paula asked.

"They said he was stabbed with an ice pick eleven times."

"Oh, my God!" Paula exclaimed. "Whoever did it must have been in quite a rage."

"That's why they think I did it. You know—being broke, left holding the bag, creditors breathing down my neck, the IRS after me. Actually, though, if it had been me I wouldn't have stopped at eleven."

Paula laughed. "I hope you didn't tell the detectives that."

"No. I kept my mouth shut as instructed."

"Good. So, when did it happen?"

"Last Saturday night, I guess. They asked where I was that night, so I assume he must have died between ten and eleven on February 25th."

"Where were you then?" Paula asked.

"I put the kids to bed at nine and then watched TV until about eleven. Then I went to bed."

"So, you obviously don't have anyone who can verify that you were at home."

"No," Maureen agreed. "The kids were asleep."

"Hmm. So, where do you live?"

"In North Dallas."

"And where was Rod killed?"

"They said he was found in his apartment in Richardson."

"Have you ever been to his apartment?"

"Once or twice to pick up the kids."

"How far is it from your place?"

"About four miles."

Paula sighed. "So, they can prove motive and opportunity, but no eye witnesses."

"No. No eyewitnesses because I didn't do it."

"What about the murder weapon?" Paula asked.

"The ice pick? What about it?"

"Did they find it? Will your prints be on it?"

"I don't know if they found it or not. As for the prints, well . . . I may have used it a week or two ago. The kids were thirsty, so I made some lemonade. The ice had melted and stuck together, so I had to use the ice pick to break it up."

"Was anyone else there besides your husband and the kids?"

"Yes, his girlfriend, Monica. Monica Landers."

"How long has he been with Monica?" Paula asked.

"I don't know. When I discovered they were having an affair and confronted him, that's when he left me."

"So, do you know much about Monica?"

"Not really. Just what I've observed the few times our paths have crossed. I know she's ten years younger than me and only has about half my IQ."

Paula laughed. "Rod wasn't looking for intellectual stimulation, obviously."

"No, just a pretty companion who didn't ask too many questions, didn't talk back, and wasn't too demanding in bed."

"So, he wasn't that good in bed?" Paula asked.

"He thought he was, but now that I've slept around a little, I'd say he was mediocre at best."

"Well, I'm going to have to go talk to your prosecutor and see if they are going to charge you. If so, I'll have to arrange bail. Stan says your financial situation isn't so hot."

"No, thanks to Rod. I have nothing."

"What about your family and friends?"

"My parents are old and living on social security and I don't have time for friends. I have a sister, Elena, but she's a single mom, too."

"Hmm. That's going to make it tough. If they charge you, you may have to sit in jail until your trial. And, of course, there is the matter of my fee. Murder trials are expensive."

"How long will I have to be in jail?"

"Six to nine months."

"Oh, shit! What about my kids? What will become of them?"

"Where are they now?"

"With my sister, Elena, but she's got her hands full with her own three kids."

"Well, don't panic. We'll work something out. Do you have a boyfriend?"

She shook her head. "No. I didn't want a boyfriend after Rod's betrayal."

"Okay. Let me go talk to the prosecutor and I'll get back to you. Just remember to keep your mouth shut. Don't talk about Rod's murder to anyone, particularly cell mates. There are a lot of jailhouse snitches around looking for info they can take to the DA as bargaining chips."

Maureen sighed. "Okay, but I hope you can get me out of here. I can't imagine this place being my home for nine months."

"Actually, if you were in that long they'd take you to county, which is a little better, not much, but a little nicer accommodations."

"Oh, good. That makes me feel so much better," Maureen said sarcastically.

Paula smiled sympathetically and left. She had a bad feeling about getting Maureen out on bond. Given the gruesome nature of the murder, if Maureen's fingerprints were on the murder weapon, Paula questioned whether the judge would even grant bail. He may consider her mentally unstable and a risk to the general public. She was also worried about getting paid. How could this woman on the brink of bankruptcy afford her? She went over to the intake desk and found Molly.

"Have you heard if she's going to be charged yet?" Paula asked.

"Looks that way," Molly replied.

"Who's been assigned to prosecute?"

"Stuart Rawlins, according to the paperwork I've seen."

"Have you seen him around?"

"Check the cafeteria. I saw him and another assistant DA head over that way about five minutes ago."

"All right. Thanks, Molly."

Paula walked to the cafeteria and looked around. She spotted the two assistant DAs walking to a booth with their trays in hand. Paula looked at the menu and grabbed a tray. The food in the cafeteria wasn't too bad. She'd gotten used to it when she worked for the DA's office. After going through the line she walked over to where they were eating.

"Can I join you, gentlemen?" Paula asked.

Stuart looked up and smiled. "Sure, Paula. Have a seat. I haven't seen you around here for a while."

Paula emptied her tray and sat next to Stuart. "Well, I guess we'll be seeing a lot of each other now. I understand you're charging my client."

Stuart's eyes widened. "Oh, you're representing the Ice Pick Widow?"

Paula laughed. "The Ice Pick Widow?"

Stuart picked up the *Dallas Morning News* and unfolded it in front of Paula. The headline read: *Ice Pick Widow Strikes Again?*

"What does it mean, again?" Paula asked warily.

"Didn't you know? Maureen Thompson's previous husband was stabbed to death with an ice pick, too."

"Ah . . . No. She neglected to tell me about that," Paula said as she started to read the article.

Ice Pick Widow Strikes Again?

Rodney Rutherford Thompson, 38, was found dead in his Dallas apartment today by a maintenance worker responding to complaints from tenants of loud music. According to Lance Shepard, he rang Mr. Thompson's bell and when there was no answer he entered the apartment with his service key and found Mr. Thompson on the floor in the kitchen in a pool of blood.

Informed sources report that Mr. Thompson was killed by repeated blows from an ice pick to his heart. The ice pick was not found at the crime scene but was later found by detectives in a dumpster several blocks from the apartment. Thompson is survived by two children, Angela and Michelle, and wife, Maureen Thompson.

Coincidentally, Thompson's estranged wife, Maureen Thompson, escaped conviction for the murder of her first husband, famed guitarist Randy Rhymes, when the jury became hopelessly deadlocked and the judge declared a mistrial. Although the Cameron County District Attorney had promised to retry the then Maureen Rhymes, the case was never re-filed. Ironically, Randy Rhymes was also murdered with an ice pick.

Paula looked up at Stuart. "So, does this mean you're going to oppose bond?"

They all laughed. "Ah. That's a fair assumption."

"Well, I guess it's a moot point. My client's broke and doesn't have any assets to pledge on a bond anyway."

"Then you won't be asking for bond?" Stuart asked.

"Well, I wouldn't go that far. She wasn't convicted of the first murder, so that case is irrelevant to this proceeding."

"We have her prints on the murder weapon," Stuart advised. "She may have gotten away with murder once, but it's not going to happen again."

"I can explain her prints on the ice pick. She chopped up some ice for lemonade last week. Her prints on the ice pick don't mean a thing."

Stuart sighed. "Paula. Give it up. She's guilty. Listen. Get her to confess and I promise I won't ask for the death penalty. Come on. You can save the taxpayers a shitload of money."

"She claims to be innocent and I believe her, so I guess we'll have to let the judge decide. Who did we draw?"

"Sands," Stuart replied.

"Sands?" Paula groaned.

Judge Leon Sands was a cantankerous jurist that everybody hated. He was always at the very bottom of the Dallas Bar Association poll and seemed to take great pride in that accomplishment. Paula felt a wave of depression wash over her.

"All right. When's the arraignment?"

"Two o'clock," Stuart replied.

Paula got up and left the cafeteria. She was feeling a bit ill after the revelation of Maureen's previous murder trial. She walked briskly to the building's exit and as soon as she stepped outside she was mobbed by reporters.

"Paula!" a reporter screamed. "Is it true you're defending the Ice Pick Widow?"

Without breaking stride Paula replied, "If you are referring to Maureen Thompson, the answer is *yes*."

"Do you think there's any chance you can get her off a second time?" another reporter asked.

"Yes, she's innocent, so we'll do whatever it takes to prove it."

"Are you going to ask for bond?" a third reporter said.

"Of course, she's innocent. She shouldn't be locked up for nine months while we prepare for trial."

"But what if she kills again?" the reporter persisted.

Paula shook her head in disgust. "I doubt she'll be getting remarried before the trial, so that shouldn't be a concern. That's all. I have no further comment," she said as she entered the parking garage and almost ran to her car.

She couldn't believe her case had already turned to crap. She was angry and embarrassed. As she drove back to the office she thought of a few choice words for Stan. What was he thinking in taking on this case? Not only was it hopeless but she'd been saddled with a client who couldn't pay—not to mention her inevitable humiliation would be front-page news!

4
Ad Litem

Ever since Paula had advised Stan that Judge Martini wanted him to be an attorney ad litem on a probate case, he'd been very uneasy. He had appeared before the judge many times on routine probate matters, but didn't really know him that well. His appointment had just come in the mail, so he decided he'd better go to the courthouse and review the file. He could have just called the attorneys in the case, but knowing absolutely nothing of the facts he wouldn't even know what questions to ask. When he got to the courthouse he went to the clerk's office and asked for the file. The clerk searched the file drawers and promptly produced it.

He thanked her and then went into an empty courtroom to go through the thick file. As he read through the pleadings he discovered that the decedent, Herbert J. Wolf, had died after a plane crash about a year earlier. According to the application for administration Wolf was survived by a wife, Glenda, but had no children. However, the decedent hadn't died immediately after the plane crash and while he clung to life at Presbyterian Hospital, he told several nurses and a doctor that he had a son, Mitch, that he'd never met and wanted to see before he died.

The problem was nobody had ever heard of Mitch and Wolf wasn't lucid enough to explain how he'd come to father Mitch and where he could be found. Wolf's doctor, however, felt compelled to advise the court of the possibility of an unknown heir, so he wrote the judge a letter explaining what had happened. It was standard procedure to appoint an attorney ad litem for the unknown heirs of an estate during the probate process. Normally the judge would have appointed someone on his ad litem list. It was made up of attorneys who were newly licensed and needed work or semi-retired attorneys and judges looking for supplemental income. But the judge didn't think anybody on his list was qualified to conduct the type of investigation necessary to find Mitch, if he indeed existed. This was particularly true because neither Wolf's spouse nor his two brothers wanted this mystery heir to be found, since he would share in the very generous settlement with the aircraft manufacturer—a tidy sum of 5.5 million dollars.

Stan took notes and when he had all the information he needed, he returned the file to the clerk. As he was driving home he wondered how in the hell he was going to find Mitch. He knew Wolf's family wouldn't help; in fact, they'd try to hinder him. Normally, when Stan had been looking for someone he'd had a last known address, a social security number, driver's license number, former employer, or some other information to get him started. With Mitch he had nothing. He wondered if Paula had been truthful when she said the judge had wanted Stan for the job all along, or if she'd actually volunteered him. It seemed very suspicious how he'd ended up getting this appointment but she'd gotten the news before him. He planned to quiz Paula about it in more depth later.

When he got back to the office Maria said Jodie was anxious to see him, so he went straight to her office. She was on the telephone so he sat in a side chair across from her and waited. A minute later she hung up.

"Stan, you're back. How was court?"

"Oh, I didn't have a hearing or anything. I just had to review the Wolf probate file. As you may have heard I was appointed attorney ad litem for the unknown heirs."

"Oh, so will there be much work involved?"

"I'm afraid so. Apparently there is a son named Mitch, but nobody has ever seen him and, of course, nobody knows where he might be."

Jodie frowned. "Oh. Wow. Good luck with that."

Stan laughed. "My sentiments exactly . . . So, what's up with you?"

"Well, I got lucky and found an inside contact at Alliance Fabrications."

"Oh really? Who?"

"Ricardo Melendez. Icaro's renegade son."

"Renegade?"

"Yeah, the only one who hasn't gone to work for Daddy in the business. He's been a wealth of information."

"Ah. Does he know you're hostile to his father?"

"No. Not exactly, but I haven't lied to him. I told him I was an attorney. I just didn't tell him I was investigating a wrongful death case against his father."

Jodie filled Stan in on the details of her meeting with Ricardo and her unofficial tour of the plant. "That's good work, but I don't want you to see him again. It's much too dangerous and if Ricardo tells his father that you've been milking him for information, he'll probably send one of his goons out to hurt you."

"Okay, but I kinda like Ricardo. I wouldn't mind dating him awhile longer."

"No. He'd probably fall in love with you and that would be a disaster."

Jodie sighed. "All right."

Stan thought about the next step in the investigation. There were a lot of people to question, but once they started interrogating people on the street the word would get to Melendez that someone was after him. When that happened Stan wanted to already have a lawsuit filed. If his investigation took the form of discovery in a lawsuit it would be much less dangerous. Melendez couldn't afford to mess with the state judiciary as it was protected by the county sheriffs, constables, and the Texas Rangers. At least he hoped that was the case.

"Let's put a call in to Detective Besch at the Dallas Police Department."

"Oh, yeah. Bingo Besch?" Jodie said, grinning. "He's a nice guy. I like him."

Stan had met Besch several years earlier when one of Stan's clients went missing. Besch had been assigned to the case and they had become friends. Stan picked up the phone and dialed the number. The dispatcher picked up and put Stan through.

"Besch here," the detective said.

"Detective. This is Stan Turner. How are you?"

"Stan Turner. Boy, that's a name from the past. Where have you been hiding?"

"Oh, I've been off the grid a couple years."

"Oh, right. Sorry about your son's death. What a tragedy."

"Thanks. Listen, we're looking into a possible wrongful death suit against an Icaro Melendez. He's the owner of a sweatshop called Alliance Fabrications. Apparently last year one of his employees, Romildo Alvarez, filed a overtime claim with the Department of Labor and shortly thereafter was murdered."

"Right. I remember hearing about that investigation."

"So, there was an investigation?"

"Yes."

"Well, we were wondering what happened with it and why nobody was charged with the murder."

"I don't remember off the bat. Let me look into it and I'll get back to you."

"Great. I really appreciate your help. I think Mr. Melendez thinks he's God and has the right to strike down anyone who doesn't bow down to him. There have been others who have gone missing."

"Okay. Sounds interesting. Maybe we can work the case together and help each other out like we've done in the past."

"That's what I was thinking. Give me a call after you've had a chance to check it out."

"I will. Nice hearing from you, Stan," Detective Besch said and hung up.

Stan looked at Jodie. "So, sit tight for a day or two and see what Besch comes up with. If he can't help us I know some people at the FBI. Since it was a federal whistle-blower case they may have been involved."

Jodie nodded and stood up. "All right. In the meantime I'll do some more background investigation and talk to some of Romildo's close friends. I'll tell them to keep quiet about the investigation."

Just as Jodie left Maria buzzed in to advise Stan that one of the Wolf family members was on the line. Stan picked up the phone.

"Hello."

"Stan Turner?"

"Yes."

"Hi. This is Walter Wolf, Herb's brother."

"Right. What can I do for you?"

"I just heard you've been appointed attorney ad litem for the estate."

"For the unknown heirs, right."

"So, I was just wondering how long it was going to take you to prepare your report, so we can get on with the final accounting and distribution of the estate."

"Well, I've just been appointed so I can't really say."

"There aren't any children, so it should be pretty cut and dried, right?"

"I don't know. I heard something about a possible child named Mitch."

"That's a load of crap. My brother and I were close and if there had been a child, I promise you, I would have known about it."

"Well, maybe so, but I still have to do a thorough investigation to make sure Mitch isn't out there somewhere."

"I hope this isn't going to drag on for months," Walter moaned.

"It's hard to say. Like I said, I've just been appointed, so I can't really tell you anything right now."

"Well, I can get you a dozen witnesses who will swear that Herb didn't have any children. Just say the word."

"Okay. I may take you up on that down the road. Thanks for calling," Stan said and hung up.

Stan hated when a client died or was near death and all the beloved family members started circling like vultures. It wasn't so bad if it was a first marriage, but if it was a second or third the animosity between the new spouse and children often escalated into outright hatred. He had a feeling this case was going to get ugly, particularly if Mitch turned out to be a real human being. While Stan was contemplating all of this Paula walked in, and she didn't look happy.

Stan frowned. "What's wrong?"

"I'll tell you what's wrong," Paula spat. "Your little Rollerblade princess has done a number on us."

"What do you mean?" Stan asked warily.

"She led you to believe she was the poor abused housewife when she's a cunning little bitch."

"Why do you say that?" Stan asked, feeling confused.

"Because this isn't the first husband who's been murdered," Paula said and dropped the *Dallas Morning News* on Stan's desk. He looked down at the headlines and his mouth fell open.

"The Ice Pick Widow?"

Paula laughed bitterly. "Yeah. The Ice Pick Widow who it looks like I'll be defending pro bono since she's flat-ass broke."

"I'm sorry, Paula. I had no idea. She didn't mention anything to me about her first marriage."

"Yeah, well you ought to check out your clients better."

Stan sighed. "You want me to handle her case? I'll swap her case for the Wolf probate."

Stan filled her in on what he'd learned about the case and relayed his telephone conversation with Walter Wolf.

"No. I don't know a thing about probate or personal injury law. Plus you were appointed ad litem, not me. I'll take care of the Ice Pick Widow. I just wanted you to know there's not likely to be a bonus this quarter."

Stan shrugged. "Well, at least one of us will get paid. Since there's 5.5 million dollars in the Wolf estate, I shouldn't have any trouble collecting my fee."

"Good. I'm sure the search for Mitch will be long and hard, but you've got to do it because it was Herb's last wish, right?"

"Right," Stan agreed. "And I wouldn't want to let the poor bastard son down. He's entitled to his inheritance."

Paula nodded. "Okay, then."

They both laughed, although they knew there wouldn't be a big fee from the Wolf case. At best Stan might get five or ten thousand—not nearly enough to offset the time and expense of a murder trial.

"Listen," Stan said. "Be straight with me about this Wolf appointment. I've been giving it a lot of thought and it doesn't make any sense that Judge Martini, right out of the blue, decides to appoint me as attorney ad litem. So, why don't you tell me what really happened?"

Paula looked away and then sighed. "Okay. I guess this will make us even. I was at the county clerk's office around the corner from the probate court and I overheard two attorneys talking. They were talking about the Wolf case and how the decedent had delayed the settlement of the case by claiming he had a son. For ten minutes I listened to them conspire about how they were going to suggest to the judge that he appoint a certain attorney ad litem on the case. They both agreed that this attorney was lazy and would only do a cursory investigation as to whether Mitch existed or not. They even talked about offering him some inducement to look the other way."

"Are you serious?" Stan said, a little shocked.

"Yes, so I couldn't just sit by and let them get away with a fraud on the court."

"Right. So, what did you do?"

"I went to the judge and told him what I'd overheard."

"What did the judge say?"

"He just rolled his eyes like he'd heard that story a million times. Then he asked me if I'd like to be attorney ad litem on the case, since I'd obviously do a conscientious job."

"Hmm. I can see where this going," Stan said, shaking his head.

"Well, you know a lot more about probate than I do, so I thanked the judge, declined to take the job myself, but suggested the judge appoint you."

Stan smiled. "Okay. That makes more sense. Why didn't you just tell me the truth from the beginning?"

"I don't know. I didn't know how you would react to the appointment, so rather than take a chance on you being mad at me, I left out part of the story."

"Hmm," Stan said. "Well, it's actually turning out to be an interesting case, so I guess I forgive you."

"Good. And, although you were completely derelict in taking Maureen Thompson on as a client, I guess I'll forgive you too since the press is going to be all over this case and you know how much I love to be in the spotlight."

Stan laughed. "Oh, yes. That I do. I suppose you'll need a new wardrobe and a day at the spa to look your best."

"Well, you're right about the wardrobe but I don't have time for the spa, I'm afraid. It is tempting, though."

On the way home Stan thought about Jodie's bold liaison with Melendez's son. He could believe the guts that girl had, but he was worried about her cover being blown and her getting hurt. He hoped she'd take his advice and end the relationship with Ricardo immediately.

Stan thought about Paula, too. He couldn't believe she'd solicited business from Judge Martini. She was a devious one when it came to getting new business. He wondered if there really was a conspiracy between the attorneys for the widow and the two sons, or if that was just a story she concocted to get the judge to offer him the ad litem job. Of course, he didn't really want to know the answer to that question.

When he got home Rebekah advised him that they needed to go to the mall to buy a wedding present for her friend's daughter who was getting married. She said they could eat dinner at one of the restaurants at the mall. Stan was tired and not particularly excited about going shopping but he reluctant agreed to take her. After he'd changed into some jeans and a sport shirt they left for Collin Creek Mall.

Since Marcia had left home Rebekah had been making a point of walking the mall with her friends each morning to try to lose weight. When they got to the mall Stan wanted to eat right away since he was starving, but Rebekah insisted on walking their exercise route with Stan, so he'd appreciate what she was going through to lose weight.

"Okay, you walk all around the top deck and then you walk the bottom deck. That's great. You don't have to show me. I get the picture."

"No. I want you to walk it with me."

Knowing there was no dissuading Rebekah he reluctantly agreed. "All right. Let's get this over with."

Rebekah smiled and they started walking along the upper deck. It was a pleasant enough walk, and had Stan not been so hungry, he probably would have enjoyed it. He was glad Rebekah was taking an interest in physical fitness, as he was worried about her sitting around the house all day with nothing to do. When they got to the end of the upper deck Stan went to the escalator and stepped on. He looked back, expecting Rebekah to walk on, but she just stood there with a frightened look on her face.

"Come on. What are you doing?" Stan yelled back to her.

Rebekah started to step on the escalator but then backed away. She looked around, seeming confused and disoriented. When

Stan got to the bottom level he ran to the stairway and rushed upstairs looking for Rebekah. He found her wandering toward the entrance of J.C. Penney.

"Rebekah! What are you doing?" Stan asked as he rushed up. "Why didn't you come down the escalator?"

"It's too steep. I was afraid I was going to fall."

"What? You've been down escalators hundreds of times. What are you talking about?"

"I don't know. Let's just take the elevator."

Stan sighed. "Okay. Whatever."

Stan was worried. He couldn't understand why Rebekah suddenly was afraid of an escalator. It had never been a problem in the past. They walked into J.C. Penney and found the elevator.

"Were you dizzy?" Stan asked.

"No. Just afraid."

"Maybe you should go see your doctor. It's been a long time since you've had a checkup."

"No. It was nothing. Don't worry about it."

They went to the food court and ordered Chick-fil-A sandwiches. Stan was worried so he quizzed Rebekah about how she was feeling but she assured him she was fine. She asked him about his day, so he told her about the Wolf case and how Paula had conned the judge into appointing him as attorney ad litem. Then he told her about Maureen Thompson.

"You stay away from that woman," Rebekah warned. "What if she did kill her two husbands?"

"Well, she won't be a danger to us either way. We're her only hope of staying out of prison."

"I don't know. What if you don't get her off?"

"Then she'll be in jail, so she won't be a threat."

"Hmm. I don't like you defending people like that."

"What if she's innocent?"

"I doubt it. If it happened twice the same way, she must have done it."

"I hope I don't get many people who think like you on the jury."

Rebekah shrugged. "I bet you do."

Stan thought about that. He thought Rebekah's logic was flawed but he feared many people would come to the same conclusion. Both murders appeared to be vicious crimes of passion and Maureen was the most likely person to harbor that kind of rage against both men. The fact they'd both died by the same type of weapon was even more damning evidence against her.

5
The Tape

Jodie parked her car in the long-term parking lot behind Budget Car Rentals in Richardson, Texas. Then she went inside and rented a car using her dead mother's credit card and her own driver's license that still had her mother's address on it. She'd inherited her mother's house but hadn't tried to sell it yet, so it was vacant. Before her mother had died she'd put Jodie on all her cards and Jodie continued to use them and pay the balances each month. Since her mother had been remarried and had changed her name, this provided her a little anonymity although she knew it wasn't foolproof. She got in the new Nissan Altima but before she got onto Central Expressway she stopped at a 7-11 to get batteries for the small tape recorder she kept in her purse. After she'd installed the new batteries and checked the recorder to be sure it was working properly, she took LBJ to the Dallas North Tollway and headed toward Oak Cliff.

Thirty minutes later she stopped her car in front of the vacant lot where Romildo Alvarez had reportedly been murdered. It was about a mile and a half from the plant and midway between it and Romildo's home. She had learned that Romildo and Ganix usually walked back and forth to work together, but on this occasion Ganix was asked to work late, so his father walked home alone.

Jodie got out and looked around the lot. It was a thinly populated area but she did see one house across the street and down half a block that had a clear view to the lot. She decided to knock on the door and see if anyone there saw anything. A grey-haired Latino man named Ruben Morales answered the door. When Jodie told him who she was, he frowned and looked up and down the street warily.

"Come inside," he said.

Jodie hesitated then stepped inside, hoping she wasn't making a big mistake going into a strange house. He took her into a sitting room and motioned for her to sit down. She sat on an antique chair and looked up at him. He sat on a piano bench across from her.

"What do you want?" Ruben asked irritably.

She told him that she represented the Alvarez family and asked him if he'd seen anything across the street in the lot the day of the murder.

"I didn't hear or see a thing," Ruben insisted, looking away.

"Did you know Romildo Alvarez?" Jodie asked.

"Not formally. But when I saw his picture in the obituaries I recognized him. He and his son walked by here nearly every day."

"Did you see anybody else near the vacant lot on the day of the murder?"

"Sure, there were police and a crime scene unit there most of the night," Ruben replied.

"I mean before the murder," Jodie clarified.

Ruben sighed. "You know, the police asked me all these questions already. Why don't you ask them?"

"We will, but sometimes people are reluctant to talk to the police. Since I work for Mrs. Alvarez, the victim's wife, I thought maybe you might be willing to share something with me that you didn't want to tell the police."

He shook his head. "I didn't see or hear anything," he repeated firmly. "In fact, your coming here has put me and my family in danger. You should go."

"I'm sorry. That certainly wasn't my intent, but there's been a murder and it's important that the persons responsible be brought to justice. I'm sure you don't want murderers lurking around your neighborhood."

Ruben stood up. "One of my sons works at the plant. His boss Guido's been by here already and warned us not to say anything to the police. My son will suffer the same fate as Romildo if I help you."

"Not if nobody knows that you are helping me."

"They already think I'm helping you. You parked your car across the street from the murder scene. Someone may have already taken down your license plate number and reported it to Guido."

"It's a rental car. He won't find anything out."

"Well, you better go anyway before he sends someone here with a camera."

"All right. But if you think of any way you can help me without jeopardizing you or your family, call me."

Jodie handed him her card and then walked to the door. He opened it. She looked back. "What's your son's name?"

"Jesus."

"Well, if my son was working at Alliance, I'd do whatever it took to force them to obey the law and respect the rights of their employees." Halfway to the curb, she turned and said in a loud voice: "If you decide to sell, call me. I'm sure I could move this property in thirty days."

Ruben nodded and closed the door. Jodie walked briskly to her car noticing for the first time a man raking leaves in a property down the street. She got quickly into her car and drove off. She was disappointed that Ruben hadn't offered his help. She couldn't help thinking he might have been a witness to the murder or knew something that could be important. She hoped that in time his conscience would compel him to give her a call.

When she got back to the office there was a phone message that Detective Besch had called from the Dallas Police Department. She immediately returned the call.

"Detective Besch."

"Detective. This is Jodie Marshall returning your call."

"Oh, hi. Yes, I was just getting back to you and Stan about the Alvarez case."

"Yes, what did you find out?"

"Well, I found the case file and went through it. Apparently there were no witnesses and after canvassing the neighborhood, his co-workers at Alliance Fabrications, family and friends, no evidence could be found of foul play. When the medical examiner ruled his death a drug overdose, given his history of drug use, the file was closed."

"His drug history was from when he was a teenager. He hadn't touched drugs for over thirty years."

"I know. I'm just telling you what I found in the file."

"What about the complaint to the Department of Labor?"

"Well, since he was the complainant, when he died the case was closed out."

"They didn't refer the case to the criminal division or the FBI?"

"No. They sent someone out to the plant but the records were clean and nobody was willing to testify to the contrary."

"So, does that mean you can't help us?" Jodie asked.

"No, it's just means we're starting with nothing. If you can get me any evidence of foul play, I can reopen the investigation."

"Okay. I'm working on that right now. I just left a witness who lives across the street from the lot where the murder took place. He denies seeing anything but he did admit that one of the Alliance supervisors, Guido Quesada, came by right after they found Mr. Alvarez and warned them to keep their mouths shut."

"Oh, really? That's interesting."

"Yes, I'm sure either he, Ben Zepeda or Adair Aguirre were responsible for Romildo's death."

Jodie told Detective Besch everything she'd learned so far and he agreed to do some more digging himself. When they hung up Jodie wondered what kind of evidence would be needed to get the case reopened. If she could get some of the employees to talk that might do it, but they were so scared it was doubtful that would happen. Since the Department of Labor had already audited the firm's books and found nothing, Melendez was obviously very good at fictitious bookkeeping. She wondered if he kept a second set of books that were accurate for his eyes only, or had some kind of formula to apply to the regular books to get to real numbers. She decided to ask Stan about it.

"If Melendez is a good businessman, which I think is a given, he probably would have a second set of books. A formula would be too complicated and hard to work with. I'd say probably one of his sons keeps the real books and nobody sees them except those two."

"So, where do you think he keeps the real set of books?" Jodie asked.

"Probably in a safe in his office. I'm sure he keeps a close eye on it."

"After we filed suit we could subpoena it," Jodie suggested, "but they'd probably just deny it existed."

"True, but if we had a witness who knew it did exist, we could file a motion to compel, put the witness on to say he'd seen the second set of books and then they'd have to produce them."

"Right, but if Melendez and his son are the only ones who know about it, who would you get to be a witness?"

"Good point. I'll have to give that some thought," Stan replied.

Jodie left Stan's office and noticed it was almost time for happy hour again. She hadn't told Stan, but she had another date with Ricardo. She had almost broken it off as instructed, but there was so much more information she needed to get from him she couldn't bring herself to do it. After stopping at her apartment to change clothes, she drove to Fridays. Ricardo was at the bar with another man and a woman. She walked over to him warily.

"Oh, Jodie. This is my brother Helio and his friend, Elisha."

Jodie smiled. "Oh, nice to meet you."

"I thought we'd double-date. I hope you don't mind."

Jodie didn't know if she minded or not. She didn't know if Helio was there because Ricardo wanted to show her off, or if Helio was suspicious when he learned of the strange circumstances of their meeting. She could feel her heart pounding as she sat down. Maybe I should have listened to Stan.

Jodie sat on the stool next to Ricardo and he ordered her a drink.

"So, I understand you're a lawyer?" Helio remarked.

"Yes, that's right. Just got my license."

"What kind of law?"

"I've been doing mainly divorces and probates so far. I'm new to the firm so they don't trust me with anything important yet."

Helio nodded. "Well, I'm glad you and my brother bumped into each other. He needs someone with some sense to rein him in."

"Well, we're just friends. I don't know him well enough to tell him how to run his life."

"Yes, but I can tell he's already in love with you, so it will just be a matter of time."

Jodie looked at Ricardo who was smiling broadly. She returned the smile then took a long drink. She wondered what she was going to do. Stan had warned her about letting Ricardo fall in love with her. She decided she needed to get as much information as she could tonight and then break it off with Ricardo the next day.

"So, I understand you're the salesman in the family?"

Helio nodded. "Yes, my father used to handle sales and production but the markets are changing and he's a little old-fashioned. Since I've taken over marketing, our sales have nearly doubled."

"Helio could sell a hairpiece to a hippo," Ricardo joked.

Jodie laughed. "Doubling sales must have put a lot of pressure on your father to boost production."

"Yes. He had to hire a lot of new workers and run a third shift. The plant runs twenty-four hours a day now."

"Really? That must be a strain on him."

"He's got Rudy to help him. Rudy's a good manager and knows how to turn a profit. Dad runs the plant during the day and Ben and Adair cover the swing and the graveyard shifts. They've both been with the family a long time."

"It must be nice to have a successful family business. Keeps everybody close."

"Except Ricardo. You need to help us with him. Dad's going to have to retire one of these days and we're going to need him."

Ricardo turned away. "You know how I feel about that," Ricardo said.

"My brother doesn't approve of some of our business practices," Helio said. "He doesn't realize how difficult it is to run a small business nowadays. He thinks we should pay our employees overtime and pamper them with health insurance and sick time."

Ricardo turned back and glared at Helio. "That's right. It's not fair to treat people the way we do. We take advantage of them because they are illegals."

"How do you get around the Texas Employment Commission and the Department of Labor?" Jodie asked. "Don't they ever audit you?"

"Yes, but we have people who know how to deal with them."

Jodie nodded. She wanted to find out more details on how that worked but she was afraid to press her luck. She looked at Helio. "I guess they could quit if they didn't like the way you treated them."

Ricardo looked at Helio. He hesitated. "Sure, that's right. They're lucky they have a job. Jodie has more sense than you do, Ricardo."

Jodie raised her hands in surrender. "Hey, do what you want, but I'm staying out of the family business. Let's talk about something else."

Helio stood up. "That's all right, Jodie. Sorry we dragged you into our family squabble. I need to get going. It was a pleasure to meet you."

Helio left and Jodie turned to Ricardo. "Hey. I'm sorry I chimed in at the wrong time. It was none of my business. I should have stayed out of it."

"It's all right. You just don't understand. My father works his employees twelve hours a day and only books them for eight. He doesn't give them vacation, sick time or any benefits whatsoever. It makes me sick. I've told them this is America and you can't treat people like that, but he doesn't listen."

"But they could quit if they wanted to, couldn't they?" Jodie asked. "I mean it's a free country. Nobody is forced to work."

Ricardo sighed. "You are so naive. These are illegal aliens. They can't just quit and find another job. If they quit they can't apply for unemployment. They'll either starve or be forced to return to Mexico."

"So, what's wrong with that?" Jodie asked. "Mexico can't be that bad."

"It's nothing but poverty and desperation for most of the population. Once you've lived in America you can never go back. Besides, my father doesn't allow them to quit even if they wanted to."

"What do you mean? How can he stop them?"

"That's Guido's job to keep everyone in line. That's why I could never work for my father. I couldn't sleep at night."

"Where did you get your strong moral conscience?" Jodie asked. "I mean, why aren't you like your brothers?"

Ricardo shrugged. "From my mother. I'm the youngest, so I guess she was more protective of me than my brothers. She is a good woman and she always wanted me to go to college and get away from the family. She said I was better than any of them."

"Well, she must be proud of you, then."

"She is, but I worry about her. My father blames her for the way I turned out. He complains to her all the time about it and treats her worse than dirt sometimes."

After dinner Ricardo suggested they go back to his place for a nightcap, but Jodie artfully excused herself. She felt bad about using Ricardo to gather evidence against his father. The more time she spent with him the more she liked him. When she got home she checked the tape recording and was relieved when she verified that it had worked properly. She wondered if she'd gotten enough to get Besch to reopen the case.

6
Posting Bond

After making peace with Stan, Paula went back to her office to contemplate how to defend Maureen Thompson given the adverse publicity that had already surfaced and the presumption in the media that she was guilty. Her first task was to figure out how to get Maureen out on bond and then to find a way to get paid for defending her. Paula didn't mind a little pro bono work from time to time. In fact she volunteered at the Family Law Clinic once a month, but she wasn't going to handle a high-profile murder case for nothing—that would lead to financial ruin. The firm's overhead was already unbearable and now with Jodie commanding an attorney's salary, it was even worse. She decided to call Maureen's sister Elena and see if she had any ideas.

"Hello. Elena Watson?" Paula inquired.

"Yes," Elena said.

"This is Paula Waters. I'm an attorney representing your sister."

"Oh, good. I'm so glad she found an attorney."

"Yes, she actually retained us for a bankruptcy and then this came up."

"What a shock, huh? Poor Rod. What a way to die."

"Speaking of that. I was a little shocked by the headlines in the *Dallas Morning News* this morning. What can you tell me about the death of your sister's previous spouse?"

"Oh, yes. Well, she didn't kill him, if that's what you mean."

"I hope not, but the MO is the same—the ice pick and all."

"Yes, but Maureen worshiped Randy. She couldn't have killed him."

"I understand there was a hung jury and the case was dropped."

"That's true," Elena replied. "They'd gone on a picnic to the lake and Randy was killed while Maureen was swimming. When she came back she found the mutilated body. Maureen tried desperately to revive him. Of course, she got blood all over her in the process and she'd used the ice pick earlier so her fingerprints were already on it."

"Did Maureen testify?"

"No. Her attorney wouldn't let her."

Paula wondered if that was an indication that her attorney thought she was guilty and would get tripped up on cross-examination. Some attorneys, however, wouldn't ever allow their clients to testify under any circumstances. Paula asked more questions about the previous trial and then got to the matter of the bond.

"I understand your parents can't help with a bond."

"No, they're living on social security."

"Do they have a home?"

"Yes."

"Is it paid for?"

"Yes, but I'd hate for anything to happen to it."

"Do you think your sister would run?"

"No. No. She'd never do that."

"Well, unfortunately you can't pledge your homestead in Texas. Do they have a second home?"

"Ah. No, but they do have a lot at Cedar Creek Lake that they were going to build a home on but never got around to it."

"That might work. Is it a lake front lot?"

"Yes. It's a beautiful lot in a little cove. It cost them twenty grand fifteen years ago."

"Good. Why don't you talk to them and see if they'd be willing to put it up as collateral on a bond. Tell them as long as Maureen shows up for trial they won't lose it."

"Okay. I'll do that."

"The other problem is financing Maureen's legal defense. I know none of you have any extra income, so I'm wondering if you know anything about Thompson Construction."

"Rodney's company? Ah, a little bit. I used to do bookkeeping for him."

"Does the company have any projects in progress?"

"Yes. I believe there are a couple of spec houses nearly complete."

"Who's running the company since Rodney's death?"

"His superintendent, Charlie Hatch."

"Is Maureen capable of running the company?"

Elena laughed. "Are you joking?"

Paula smiled. "How about you? If you were doing the bookkeeping you must know a little about the business."

"I can pay the bills and deal with the lenders."

"Good. Have you seen the corporate papers? Is Maureen an officer?"

"Yes. She was made VP in case of emergency."

"Good. Then Maureen can take temporary control of the company and elect you president. That way with Charlie's help you can finish up the two projects and collect the retainage. Do you know what the houses sell for?"

"They are in the $225,000 range."

"Excellent. So, there should be about $45,000 in retainage then—just about what we need for Maureen's defense."

Elena sighed. "Wow. I guess I'm going into the construction business."

"For a while anyway," Paula agreed, feeling much relieved that she was close to solving one nagging problem.

As soon as Paula got off the phone she called her bondsman, Roger Rand, and had him get a bond ready. She gave him the information on the lake lot so he could do a title check and get an informal appraisal done for his underwriters. If that all checked out, all they'd need would be Maureen's parents' signature on the bond. Paula prayed her parents and Maureen were on good terms.

At quarter to two Paula arrived at the courtroom of the Honorable Leon Sands, Judge of the Criminal District Court #2 of Dallas County. Two reporters accosted her as she walked up.

"Ms. Waters," the first reporter said. "Do you think the judge will grant bond?"

"I should hope so. She's not a flight risk."

"Does your client intend to plead not guilty by reason of insanity?" a second reporter asked.

Paula frowned. "Ah. We haven't really looked into strategy yet, but my client professes her innocence so an insanity defense wouldn't be appropriate."

Paula raised her hand to indicate she was through answering questions then turned and walked into the crowded courtroom looking around for Stuart Rawlins. She spotted him at one of the counsel tables, so she took a seat to wait for the judge to arrive. Right on schedule Judge Sands took the bench and the clerk began calling cases. Paula ran her argument through her mind over and over again until the clerk called the case.

"The State of Texas vs. Maureen Ann Thompson."

Paula stood up and stepped forward.

Rawlins glanced at her then said, "Stuart Rawlins for the State of Texas."

"Paula Waters for the defendant."

"All right, bring in the defendant."

The bailiff led Maureen Thompson over to where Paula was standing. Paula smiled at her warmly.

"Maureen Thompson. You are charged with the murder of your husband, Rodney Rutherford Thompson. How do you plead?" the judge asked.

"Not guilty, Your Honor," Maureen said earnestly.

"All right. Ms. Waters?"

"Your Honor, the defense requests that bail be set in a modest amount. Mrs. Thompson isn't a flight risk. She has two children, a job, and no prior criminal convictions. She has limited income and few assets, so a large bond would be tantamount to denying her bond."

"Mr. Rawlins?"

"Your Honor, Ms. Thompson may not have a criminal record but this isn't the first time she's been on trial for murdering her husband."

"Objection, Your Honor. Allegedly murdering her husband. She's never been convicted and she won't be this time."

"Ms. Waters. This is no time for objections. Let Mr. Rawlins speak. He didn't interrupt you."

"Yes, Your Honor. My apologies."

"You were saying, Mr. Rawlins?"

"Yes, Your Honor. She may not have been found guilty but neither was she exonerated. The state would oppose any bond, Your Honor. We feel her freedom would be an unacceptable risk to the community and, because she has few assets, she would definitely be a flight risk."

"She does own her home, Your Honor," Paula added.

"Yeah, now that her husband is dead," Rawlins retorted.

"Okay. Okay. This is a murder case, Ms. Waters, so I can't set bail too modestly. Bail is set at $200,000."

Paula felt relieved. Two hundred thousand dollars wasn't so bad in a murder case. She felt sure with the lake lot as collateral the bondsman wouldn't have a problem. She just hoped Maureen's parents would be willing to assign it to get their daughter out of jail.

Maureen made eye contact with Paula, and she returned a reassuring smile. Then the bailiff escorted her out of the courtroom. Paula was going to say something to Stuart but he'd made a quick exit, leaving his assistant to handle the rest of the pleas. Feeling a little abandoned, Paula left to make a phone call to Maureen's sister to see if pledging the lake lot was a go.

"Elena?"

"Yes."

"The judge set the bond at $200,000. That's not too bad, actually, for a murder case."

"Oh, really? It sounds like a lot to me."

"It's a fair bond. What did your parents say?"

"They said they'd put the lot up as collateral, but they don't think it's worth more than a hundred grand. They've been trying to sell it for years."

"Oh . . . Well, I guess we'll find out when the appraisal comes back. Do you want me to send the bond paperwork to you or directly to your parents?"

"You can send it directly to them."

"All right. Tell them the bondsman will bring it by or he'll send a messenger who is also a notary, so they can sign it and the messenger can bring it back. If we work quickly Maureen might not have to stay in jail tonight."

"Oh, good. She doesn't do well in jail."

"No, I wouldn't think so. What did you find out about Thompson Construction?"

"I talked to the superintendent and the bank. There's $32,000 in retainage, but they won't release it until the job is finished and there's been a final inspection by the city."

"How long will that be?"

"Ten days, at least."

"What about cash? Is there any money in the bank?"

"Yes, about ten grand."

"Well, you can pay me five thousand now for expenses and another twenty toward my fee when the retainage is paid."

"Do you think it's okay for me to be writing company checks?"

"Yes. I'll have Maureen sign a consent the next time I see her. You can run that by the bank and they'll put you on the signature card. "

"Okay. What about the probate?"

"It will take us about forty-five days to get a probate filed and Maureen approved as independent executrix."

"Don't you think someone might object to Maureen being executor of Rodney's estate?"

"Possibly, but as long as he hasn't divorced her and she hasn't been convicted of his murder, she qualifies to be independent executrix."

"Still, someone in Rodney's family is going to object."

"You're probably right. But, since it's an independent administration, I doubt they can do anything about it. The court lacks jurisdiction. Do you know who the alternate executor is?"

"Rodney's brother, Andrew. You better hope he doesn't end up with the job. He's a real asshole."

"Wonderful. We just gotta make sure that doesn't happen," Paula said, starting to feel a little depressed. Fortunately, she didn't have to worry about that problem—that would be Stan's headache.

When Paula got back to the office she called the bondsman and was distraught to find out the appraiser had only appraised the lake lot at $90,000. Paula's heart sank.

"Is that all?"

"Yes, property values on the lake have dropped quite a bit in the past few years. Dallas growth is strongest to the north, so a lot more people are buying at Lake Lewisville and Lake Texoma rather than Cedar Creek. But, even so, $90,000 is enough. We'll post the bond."

"Oh, thank you, Roger. You're the best."

"Always aim to please. I've got a messenger on the way to Maureen's parents' place. Just as soon as he calls me advising that the paperwork has been signed, I'll run over to the courthouse and file the bond."

"Good. Let me know when I should go pick her up."

Rand agreed and hung up. Paula took a deep breath and leaned back in her chair. It had been a long day, but she'd accomplished a lot and was feeling pretty good until the telephone rang.

"Hello."

"Paula Waters?"

"Yes."

"This is Andrew Thompson. I've just filed papers to be appointed independent executor of my brother's estate. The judge said I had to give you notice in case you wanted to oppose the appointment."

Paula stifled the obscenity that first came to mind, took a deep breath, and replied, "Well, yes. We will definitely be opposing the appointment since Maureen was appointed independent executrix."

"That may be true, but she's not qualified to act. She has a conflict of interest."

"Well, we'll see about that. Be sure and give me notice of the hearing."

"I will, but come on, get real—no judge in his right mind will allow the woman accused of the decedent's murder to handle his estate."

Paula hung up the phone angrily. Andrew had a point, but still, there was a presumption of innocence and if that meant anything, Maureen couldn't be kept from doing her job as executrix. At least, she hoped the judge would see it that way.

7
Unresponsive

On Friday night Stan and Rebekah decided to drive up to Lake Arrowhead Lodge in Oklahoma. They loved the quaint little resort on the lake and made a point to go there at least once each year. On Saturday they ate breakfast in the dining room overlooking the lake, took a swim in the pool, and then checked out and drove to Platt National Park for a picnic dinner. Stan always marveled at the dense Eastern Red Cedar forest that dominated the landscape and nineteen natural springs located in this oasis in the middle of the Oklahoma prairie.

Before they ate they decided to take the leisurely two-mile hike from the ranger station and museum to the natural springs that fed Travertine Creek, which originated from the springs in the park. Rebekah wasn't big on hiking but she had always enjoyed this trip because of the large trees, flowers, and wildlife that often could be seen from the trail.

After they had been hiking for twenty minutes or so, Stan noticed Rebekah was pretty winded, so he suggested she stop and rest on a large fallen log. She didn't argue with him.

"You're out of shape, my love," Stan said teasingly.

"I'm just so tired. I don't know why. We haven't done that much today."

"Maybe you're dehydrated," Stan said and handed Rebekah his canteen.

She accepted it and took a long drink. "Thanks. I'm okay. We can go now."

They continued to hike and by the time they got to the first spring Rebekah was huffing and puffing like she was climbing up a steep hill rather than on a relatively flat trail. Stan watched her with much concern.

"Am I going to have to carry you back?" Stan asked, only partially joking.

"No, I'll be okay. Just let me rest."

They rested a good half hour and then Rebekah announced she was fit to make the return trip. Stan took her hand because she seemed a little unstable and he was afraid she might trip and fall. About halfway back to the camp Stan had to put his arm around Rebekah's waist to make sure she stayed on her feet. After a while they stopped so she could rest. Stan watched her worriedly, wondering if he should stop one of the other hikers on the trail and ask them to get help.

Seeing the concern on Stan's face Rebekah said, "I'm okay. I'm just feeling a little weak today."

"I know. What's wrong with you?"

"Nothing. Just get me back to the car where I can lie down."

Fifteen minutes later, relief washed over Stan as he saw the ranger's station in the distance. Just as he was about to mention it to Rebekah, she collapsed. Stan caught her before she fell and carried her over to a bench near the ranger station.

"I guess I'm going to have to find you a doctor."

"No. I'm not going to some hick doctor out here."

"I'm sure there's a town not too far from here with a hospital emergency room."

"No," Rebekah said. "I'll be fine. Just get me to the car and take me home."

Stan sighed. "Okay, but you need to go to the doctor first thing when we get back. Something is obviously wrong with you."

"It's just menopause. My body is changing."

"I don't think so. I've never heard of menopause causing you to collapse from exhaustion."

"Just take me home," Rebekah repeated firmly.

"Okay."

Stan carried Rebekah through the parking lot to their car and helped her inside. After that they drove straight home, stopping only to get gas and buy a hamburger at Carl's Jr. By the time they got home Rebekah seemed much better and insisted Stan forget anything had happened. Although Stan pressed her, she refused to go to the local emergency clinic which was open on Sundays.

That night as they were getting ready for bed Stan noticed Rebekah looked odd. One side of her body seemed out of kilter. He went over to her and took her limp hand.

"Rebekah! What's wrong?"

"Nothing," Rebekah replied, but Stan could see that something was very wrong.

"Come on. I'm taking you to the emergency room," he said as he put an arm around her and helped her get up.

"No. I'll be all right," she protested.

"You're not all right. Don't give me any crap! You're going to the emergency room."

With much difficulty Stan got Rebekah into the car and drove her to the Plano Hospital Emergency Room. After waiting twenty minutes they were escorted into a treatment room and waited. Rebekah seemed much better now that they were at the hospital. Her face wasn't drooping anymore and she'd regained the strength in her left hand.

"I feel fine. I don't know why you brought me here," she complained.

"Well, we're here, so let them check you out."

A few minutes later a nurse came in and took vitals and asked why they had come in. Stan told her what had happened during the day and about the loss of control over one side of the body.

"Sounds like a TIA."

"TIA?" Stan asked.

"Yeah. A transient ischemic attack. It's kind of like a mini-stroke. A blood vessel in the brain is restricted but only temporarily rather than permanently in the case of a stroke. It's a warning sign that you're in danger of a real stroke."

"Hmm," Stan said. "Isn't that unusual for someone of her age?"

The nurse looked at Rebekah. "How old are you?"

"Forty-six," Rebekah replied.

She shrugged. "Not necessarily. Have you done anything out of the ordinary in the last few days?"

"Well, we just got back from Platt National Park up in Oklahoma," Stan replied.

"Oh, you didn't by chance pick up a tick? A tick can carry Rocky Mountain Spotted Fever. A bite on the arm can cause it to lose strength and cause a general malaise."

"Really?" Stan said.

"Yeah, let me check for tick bites."

"I don't think anything bit me," Rebekah said.

"It's not a bite exactly. They burrow into your skin," the nurse said as she examined Rebekah thoroughly. "I don't see anything. Okay, let me take some blood and then I'll send someone in to do an EKG."

Stan nodded and gave Rebekah a concerned look. The nurse took her blood and then left.

"I feel fine now. Let's just go home."

Stan sighed. "Just relax and let them check you out. We need to find out what's wrong with you."

A few minutes later a tech came in and gave Rebekah an EKG. When it was over and he was about to leave Stan asked, "So, how did it look?"

The tech shrugged. "The doctor will be by in a minute after he's had a chance to read it."

Stan took Rebekah's hand in his and squeezed it gently. "I hope they can figure out what's wrong with you."

"Nothing is wrong with me," Rebekah replied angrily.

"Rebekah! You just don't suddenly become so exhausted that you can't walk."

Rebekah turned away and then a smile came over her face. "You remember when you took Marcia to Indian Princess camp in Oklahoma and you got that tick on your scrotum?"

Stan smiled. "Yeah, how could I forget?"

"That was hysterical!"

"For you, maybe," Stan snickered.

"It's a good thing your—you-know-what—didn't freeze up."

Stan and Rebekah started laughing. The door opened and the doctor came in looking surprised.

He smiled at Rebekah. "So, you must be feeling better."

"I'm fine," Rebekah said. "My husband is a little over dramatic."

"Over dramatic?" Stan protested. "When you suddenly lose control of one side of your body—"

"Yes," the doctor said. "You can't fool around with something like that. You were right to bring her in. However, we've run all the normal tests for this type of thing and can't find anything wrong with you."

"So, what's causing her to be so weak?" Stan asked.

"I don't know. It might be she got dehydrated or overheated."

"It wasn't hot Saturday. We always go to Platt National Park early in the year to avoid the heat. And, I made sure she drank plenty of water."

The doctor shrugged. "Sometimes it's just stress. But you should make an appointment with your primary care physician and tell him what happened. He can do some more investigation and perhaps figure out what caused all of this."

"Thank you, Doctor," Rebekah said. "Let's go, Stan."

The doctor left and Stan helped Rebekah get dressed and then they went home. Stan made Rebekah promise she'd make an appointment with her regular doctor the next day but he knew she wouldn't do it.

On Monday Stan had a telephone appointment with Herbert Wolf's widow in the morning and had made arrangements to visit Herbert's parents in the afternoon at their home. At ten o'clock he made the call.

"Mrs. Wolf?"

"Yes."

"This is Stan Turner?"

"Oh, right."

"How are you?"

"Okay, I guess. Still not over Herb's passing."

"Yes, I'm sorry for your loss."

"Thank you."

"I guess your attorney told you what my job is as ad litem?"

"Yes, he did."

"I just need to know if you have any knowledge of Mitch or any other possible child your husband might have fathered."

"Yes, I am certain there are no children. Herb never mentioned having a child and I'm sure he would have told me something that important in the six years we were married."

"Yes. You would think so. Were you his second wife?"

"Yes. He and his first wife were childhood sweethearts and they got married just before Herb went off to fight in the Vietnam War. He was gone for six years and they were nearly strangers by the time he returned. The marriage only lasted another six months before she filed for divorce. There were no children."

"What was his first wife's name?"

"Angela. Angela Denise, I believe."

"When was the last time your husband saw Angela?"

"Oh, I think four or five years ago," Glenda said.

"Did you ever meet her?"

"Yes, we ran into her at Red Lobster one night and Herb introduced me."

"Did you talk at all?"

"Just for a few moments."

"She didn't mention a child?"

"No. There couldn't have been a child. I don't think there was even any sex after Herb returned. They both realized they'd made a mistake."

Stan nodded. "So, what service was Herb in when he went to Vietnam?"

"He was a pilot in the navy," Glenda replied. "He flew transports mainly. When he got home he got a job as a pilot with Braniff Airlines. When they went out of business he went to work for Continental, based out of Houston."

"Was he piloting the plane that crashed?"

"No, he was a passenger. He'd been scheduled on a flight out of Salt Lake City and was flying there from Dallas to meet it. About the time they arrived a thunderstorm was rolling through. The air traffic controller should have waved them off, but I guess he misjudged the severity of the storm. They got caught in some wind shear and missed the runway."

"Oh, my God!" Stan said.

"Luckily it wasn't a full flight. There were thirty-two fatalities including Herb."

Stan shook his head. "He survived six years flying combat and ends up dying in a thunderstorm on a routine commercial flight."

"Ironic, isn't it?"

"Well, so far I haven't found a shred of evidence that Mitch exists. Do you have any theories as to where your husband came up with the name or why he would claim to have a child?"

Glenda shook her head. "He wanted children and was disappointed that he hadn't had any. I had two miscarriages, unfortunately, which was a bitter disappointment to both of us. We had thrown around names for boys and Mitch was one of them. One of his neurologists suggested that the extensive head injuries that he suffered might have triggered delusions and one of them might have been that he had actually had a child."

Stan thought about that. It was a plausible theory. "Okay. Well, thanks for talking to me. I'll let you know if I find anything out."

"How long do you think your investigation is going to take?" Glenda asked.

Stan hesitated. He knew everyone was anxious to close out the estate and distribute the money, but he couldn't file a report until he was absolutely sure Mitch didn't exist. "I don't know. I've got to talk to Herb's parents and some of his friends. Hopefully another week or so at the most—unless I find something, of course."

Glenda sighed. "All right. Do what you have to do, but please do it expeditiously. I'd like to get this chapter of my life over with."

Stan hung up and thought more about the delusion theory that one of the neurologists had come up with. It made sense to him, but it was just a theory—not enough of a certainty to stop his investigation. He did make a note to talk to each of Herb's doctors to see if any of them could shed light on the situation.

Just as Stan hung up Jodie walked in. "You've got to listen to this tape," she said excitedly.

"What tape?" Stan asked.

"Don't be mad at me, but I taped my conversations with Ricardo and the interview with the landowner across the street from the lot where Romildo was murdered."

"Conversations? I thought you weren't going to see him again."

"Well, I kinda had to go out with him one more time and it was a good thing I did. His brother was there and they got into a little skirmish over Icaro's business practices."

"Really?"

"Yes. You've got to hear this."

Jodie played the tape and Stan listened attentively. When it finished, Stan smiled. "Nice work. Weren't you scared?"

Jodie swallowed hard. "A little, but I don't think I was in danger. There was so much animosity between them, I doubt either one thought much about me."

"I don't know. I'm glad you won't be doing that anymore. . . . We should get this over to Detective Besch. Make a couple of copies. We need one and I'd like to give one to Special Agent Lot at the FBI."

"Will do," Jodie said and left.

Stan shook his head. Jodie was a force to be reckoned with. He hit the intercom button and waited for Maria to answer.

"Yes."

"Maria, get Agent Lot of the FBI on the line, would you?"

"Okay."

Stan wondered if the FBI would be interested in a case like this. It seemed operations like Alliance Fabrications were pretty commonplace and the government hadn't done much to shut them down. They must have known Alliance Fabrications was employing illegal aliens after they investigated Mr. Alvarez's death, yet nothing was done about it. The intercom buzzed and Stan picked up.

"Yes."

"Special Agent Lot is on the line."

"Thank you, Maria," Stan said, pushing the blinking line on his telephone. "Hello, Agent Lot?"

"Yes, Stan. How are you?"

"Oh, not too bad. Overworked and underpaid just like everybody else."

"Well, you've got that right. What can I do for you?"

"Listen, I've been working on a wrongful death suit and I've come across some evidence of labor violations. I've got a tape with some rather glaring admissions from a VP in the company, if you're interested."

"Yes. What's the name of the company?"

"Alliance Fabrications."

"Yes, I've heard of them. There's an opened file, I believe."

73

"Well, I'm about to file the wrongful death suit, but my clients' primary objective is to find out the truth and make the responsible person pay for their father's death."

"Well, that's what they all say, right?"

"True. Often that is the case, but here I think they genuinely want to see Mr. Icaro Melendez behind bars, if he ordered their father's death."

"So, when can I listen to the tape?"

"Well, if you want me to bring it to you, it will have to be tomorrow. I've got to meet with some witnesses this afternoon. I should be back by 4:30, however, if you want to come here."

"I'll come to you. Your office still in the same location?"

"Yes. Nothing's changed."

"All right, see you at 4:30."

Stan hung up and looked at his watch. It was nearly lunchtime, so he grabbed his coat and went to find Paula to see if she wanted to go to lunch. He found her deep into the preparation of a brief.

"You gonna break for lunch?"

Paula looked up. "Yes. I'm famished. Let's go."

Paula got up and they left to run down the street to Dickey's Barbeque. As they were standing in line Stan told Paula about what had happened to Rebekah over the weekend.

"Oh, my God. She just fainted?"

"Well, not exactly. She just seemed to run out of energy until I finally had to carry her to the car. By the time we got home, though, she was fine."

"Wow. That's bizarre. I wonder what would cause something like that."

They made it to the front of the line, Stan paid for both of them, and they found an empty table. As they began to eat, Stan finished the story.

"She had no feeling on her left side?"

"Yeah, for about fifteen minutes and then it slowly came back. By the time we got to the emergency room she was almost back to normal."

"That's strange," Paula said. "So, what are you going to do?"

"I'm trying to get her to go to the doctor, but she won't do it. I know her."

"Hmm. I'm sorry. Do you want me to talk to her?"

"No, that will make her even more intransigent. I'm just hoping she'll get scared and decide to go on her own."

"God, I hope you're right," Paula said, shaking her head.

After lunch Stan drove to Mesquite to meet with Herbert Wolf's parents. They lived in a retirement community near Town East Mall. Stan signed in and then found their apartment on a wall map mounted near the elevators. He went to the third floor and then went left to find apartment 307. He knocked on the door and Eunice Wolf opened it.

"Come in, Mr. Turner. Come right in."

She stepped aside and Stan entered the small but nicely furnished apartment. Mrs. Wolf pointed to the kitchen table and Stan took a seat.

"Arnold will be right with us. He's on the telephone with his stockbroker."

"Oh. All right," Stan replied, wondering if Arnold was trading on margin. He'd had several clients over the years not only lose their life's savings speculating on the market, but also ending up having to file bankruptcy.

"Would you like a glass of ice tea?"

Stan nodded. "Sure, that would be fine."

Mrs. Wolf gave him the tea and sat across from him. A moment later Arnold showed up. "Sorry I'm late. I was just discussing how to invest the five hundred and fifty thousand dollars we'll be getting from the settlement."

"Oh, you're beneficiaries, too?"

"Yes, we agreed to 10 percent. Our attorney thought we should get twenty-five, but rather than go to court we decided 10 percent was enough."

Stan sighed. He wondered if this visit was going to be a waste of his time. If Wolf's parents were getting money, too, they'd have no interest in helping to find another heir to further dilute their interest in the settlement.

"I see. Well, I won't take too much of your time, but I guess you know my job is to make sure there aren't any unknown heirs."

"Yes, well I assure you there aren't," Eunice said.

"So, I understand your son was married twice?"

Eunice nodded. "Yes, his first wife cheated on him not six months after he was deployed to Vietnam. If Herb had have known about it, he'd have divorced her in a minute."

"If she didn't want to be married, why didn't she divorce your son?"

"She liked those government checks coming in. No use having to work if you don't have to."

"Do you know this for a fact, or are you speculating?" Stan asked.

"I know it for a fact. She bragged to Herb about it one time during an argument."

"That's funny, Glenda didn't mention any of this."

"Glenda didn't know anything about it. It was ancient history when she hooked up with Herb. Herb didn't talk much about Vietnam or his first marriage."

"Did Herb have any girlfriends over in Vietnam?" Stan asked.

"No," Glenda said. "He was an honorable man."

Mr. Wolf smiled. "Well, you know men. I'm sure he got a little pussy from time to time while he was on leave."

"Arnold!" Eunice spat. "Just because you did that kind of thing in South Korea doesn't mean Herbert did. You were single, he was married. I'm sure he respected his vows."

Arnold rolled his eyes and winked at Stan. Stan smiled. "So, what unit was he in?"

"VR-2. The Second Naval Transport Squadron operating out of NAS Almeda. He flew a C-130 Hercules to Hawaii and then on to Vietnam."

"Did he belong to any veteran groups?" Stan asked.

"Yes, he went to a reunion in Galveston last year."

"Do you have any information on the unit? I'd like to talk to some of his friends."

"Why on earth for?" Eunice asked.

"Oh, just to verify what went on while he was serving in the war. If his wife wasn't faithful, he might have found out about it and decided the marriage was over. In that case he might have met someone."

"No. He would have told us about that."

"But you said yourself he didn't like talking about the war. There's probably a lot that happened that you know nothing about."

"They sent him a program for the reunion," Arnold said. "I think there's a copy in his personal things we have upstairs."

"He left some things here?" Stan asked.

"No. After he died Glenda said we could come get any of his things that we wanted. She was going to give everything away to Goodwill and throw out whatever they didn't want, so we went over and got a bunch of his stuff."

"That would be great if I could get that brochure. Also, if you don't mind, I'd like to go through his things."

Eunice frowned. "Well, I don't think you'll find anything about children in his things."

"Probably not. But the judge might question my thoroughness if I neglected to, at least, look through his things."

Eunice shrugged. "Okay, but it's mostly junk."

Stan was escorted into a small bedroom that appeared to be used for storage. Over in one corner was a big cedar chest. Mr. Wolf opened it and Stan started going through the contents. Inside the chest were photo albums, letters, memorabilia, medals, and newspaper clippings. Eunice watched him as he worked and answered any questions he had. When Stan was done Arnold gave him the reunion program and he left.

When he got back to the office Agent Lot from the FBI was waiting for him. When Stan walked in the front door he shook his hand and escorted him back to his office. Then he sent for Jodie. After Jodie had joined them Stan played him the tape.

"So, what do you think?" Stan asked.

"Well, that's enough for a search warrant, but from what I understand INS has been through their records before and came up with nothing."

"My clients will testify if they can get some protection."

"That would be good, but since they are related to the victim their veracity might be challenged. What we need are some of the other employees to come forward."

"That's the problem," Jodie said. "They're all too scared for that."

"Well, I might be able to talk my boss into sending in an undercover agent to verify what's on the tape and what your clients will testify to."

"Perfect. If you'll provide protection for my clients, I'll go ahead and file suit for the overtime and child labor violations. That should stir things up a bit, particularly when I notice Mr. Melendez for deposition. They might just get scared enough to make a mistake."

"Yes, and if they make a move on your clients, then we'll have all the proof we need."

After Jodie and Agent Lot had left, Stan called Rebekah to see how she was doing. She said she was fine, but sounded a little tired, so Stan told her they'd order pizza for dinner and not to cook. She didn't put up any argument. Stan spent another half hour cleaning up his desk and answering telephone messages before he left to go home. Just as he was leaving Detective Besch called.

"I listened to the tape you sent over. That was some pretty good work."

"Yes, I told you about Jodie. She's a no-nonsense attorney."

"Well, I think we're going to reopen the case."

Stan told him about his conversation with Agent Lot.

"That's good. We have different agendas, so there shouldn't be any conflict."

Stan hung up the phone feeling pretty good. Before he left he told Jodie about Besch's call. She was elated and told him she had the original petition almost done. Stan promised he'd go over it with her in the morning and then left for home. When he walked in the door he announced in a loud voice that he was home, but Rebekah didn't respond. He went into the kitchen and then the bedroom but didn't find her. Feeling a little panicky, he rushed into the living room and found her on the sofa apparently sound asleep, but when he tried to wake her up she didn't respond.

8
Old Flame

Andrew Thompson's quick application to be appointed executor over his brother's estate upset Paula. She needed access to the money in Thompson Construction for her fee, but if Andrew was appointed executor he would try to block Maureen's control over the corporation. Legally, Maureen owned a one-half undivided interest in the company. More importantly, as vice-president she had the authority to run its day-to-day operations. With Maureen as independent executrix she could do whatever she wanted, but if Andrew became executor he could challenge anything Maureen did since he would control 50 percent of the corporation's voting stock. That was the problem with 50/50 owners in any enterprise—either party could cause a deadlock and virtually destroy the company's ability to do business.

Paula's only hope was that the appointment of an executor would take long enough for Maureen to drain the company of its cash before Andrew could stop her. Ordinarily legal proceedings of this type would drag on for months, but Paula feared somehow Andrew would expedite the process. She thought about it awhile and decided, if she wanted to get paid, she'd have to help Maureen speed up the completion of the houses and push the city to do their final inspections. She figured she only had about ten days.

While she was pondering her strategy, Maria indicated Roger Rand was on the telephone.

"Roger? How'd it go?"

"Your lady is free. She's right here. Do you want to talk to her?"

"Yes. Put her on."

"Paula?"

"Maureen. I'm so glad you're out. How do you feel?"

"Much better now."

"Good. Have Roger drive you to my office. I need you to sign some papers. Rod's brother is trying to get control of the estate and leave you destitute."

"Oh. Please don't let him do that!"

"I'm going to try to stop him, but we've got to move quickly."

"All right. I'll see you in a minute, but I don't want to stay too long. I've got to pick up my kids. I'm sure my sister is sick of them."

"I understand. I'll call her and tell her to pick you up here since you don't have a car. What I need right now won't take long, but I will need to spend some more time with you later in the week. You've got a lot of explaining to do."

"Yeah," Maureen said with a sigh. "I guess I do at that."

Paula hung up and took a deep breath. She could feel the muscles in her neck tightening as she began to worry. Stripping Thompson Construction to pay Maureen's legal expenses would infuriate Andrew and the rest of the family. It might put her in a bad light with the press and the judge too, but she couldn't think of any other option. She'd just have to deal with the backlash when it came at her.

Twenty minutes later Maureen was sitting in her office and Paula was explaining the corporate documents she had prepared.

"We're having a meeting of the board of directors right now. You're the only stockholder at this moment able to vote, so you can elect yourself as president to replace your husband. You and your sister need to go to the bank tomorrow and sign new signature cards. Then you need to get with your superintendent and make sure the houses are finished up in the next few days. I'll contact the city and push them for a final inspection. Once that's done we'll all go to the bank and collect the retainage money. This all has to be done before there is a hearing on Andrew's application for probate. There's no telling what will happen at the hearing and, if Andrew is appointed executor, the assets of the company will be frozen."

"Okay. But what about work?" Maureen asked. "I don't get paid unless I'm working."

"I know," Paula said. "We'll just have to work around all of our schedules."

The door opened and Elena walked in with Maureen's two girls. They ran over to their mother and they embraced.

"Oh, I missed you two so much," Maureen said, trying to hold back her tears. She smiled at Paula. "This is Angela and Michelle."

"Hi, girls," Paula said, smiling broadly. "Did you miss your mommy?"

They both nodded timidly and leaned in closer to their mother.

"Well, you can take her home now," Paula said. "Thank you, Elena, for all your help. I don't know what we would have done without you."

"She's a good sister," Maureen said, still fighting to hold back her tears.

After they'd all left Paula wondered how it would all turn out. Maureen's situation was so desperate. Not only was she on trial for murder, but she was bankrupt, and owed the IRS nearly a hundred grand. As she was lamenting Maureen's situation Stan walked in.

"Just the man I need to see," Paula said.

"Oh, really. Was that Maureen who just left?"

"Yes, she just made bond."

"Congratulations! How did you pull that off? I thought she was broke."

"She is, but her parents had a lake lot that was valuable enough to secure the bond."

"Well, that was fortunate. So, now what?"

"Now I've got her husband's probate to deal with."

She told Stan about Andrew and his application to probate the will. Stan agreed he didn't have a chance as long as Maureen was free on bond and hadn't been convicted of a felony.

"Do you need any help on the probate?" Stan asked.

"No, but I do need you to keep Maureen's creditors at bay while this trial is going on, particularly the IRS. Maureen's going to have enough stress as it is without some revenue officer breathing down her neck."

"That shouldn't be a problem," Stan replied. "If she files an Offer in Compromise it will stop all collection activity for six months or a year while they're considering it. And, if they reject it, I can appeal it and get six more months."

"Good," Paula said, grinning. "Now tell me how I'm going to prove her innocent of murder."

Stan laughed. "Well, Rodney obviously had some problems other than the IRS. I bet if we start digging into his business and personal affairs we'll find other people who wanted him dead."

Paula nodded. "You're probably right. I'll ask Maureen and Elena about that tomorrow. They should know if he had any enemies."

"Once we have a suspect list, then we need to see who on the list would have wanted Maureen's first husband dead as well."

"That makes sense," Paula agreed. "It's just a little hard to imagine who that would be."

"I know, but there has to be a connection between the two murders," Stan argued.

"Not necessarily. The killer may not have had anything to do with Randy Rhymes's murder but only used an ice pick as the murder weapon in order to confuse us and send us down a rabbit trail."

"You may be right. We'll just have to explore all possibilities before we come to any conclusions."

After Stan had left, Paula started to think about how she was going to get the city to expedite its inspection of Thompson

Construction's last few houses. She'd been told that due to personnel cuts it could take as long as seven to ten days to get a final inspection. She knew someone who used to be an assistant city attorney. He had switched years ago to the DA's office to become an assistant DA, but she was sure he'd still have contacts in the building inspection department. They'd been intimate a time or two before she married Bart, so she decided to contact him and see if he might have any suggestions. Looking at her watch, she saw it was after five. She doubted he'd still be in the office, but she remembered he was single and often went to Hooters for dinner or a few drinks after work. She decided to stop by there on the way home and perhaps "accidentally" run into him.

She laughed when she pulled in the Hooters parking lot and recognized Lee Long's big Cadillac parked in a handicapped parking spot. Lee had lost a leg during the Tet Offensive in the Vietnam War. He had a prosthesis and could walk as well as anybody, but he reasoned he was entitled to a lifetime of prime parking spots as a reward for the sacrifice he'd made for his country. To her knowledge nobody had ever argued with him about it.

She went inside and spotted Lee flirting with several of the scantily clad waitresses. She walked his way and then feigned surprise when she saw him.

"Lee? Is that you?" she said, smiling broadly.

Lee looked over at her and then returned the smile. "Paula!"

"Yes. How are you?"

"Fine. What brings you into a Hooters? Are you here alone?"

"Yes. I was on my way home from the courthouse and I got a craving for one of their great ham sandwiches. The guys in the DA's office used to come here all the time to gawk at the waitresses, so unless I wanted to eat alone, I went with them."

"Oh. I see. So, sit down then and join me."

"Thank you, but I don't want to interrupt anything."

"It's all right. I wasn't having much luck luring any of these girls home to my apartment. I guess I'm getting old. It used to be a piece of cake."

"Sorry about that," Paula said sympathetically. "The years do take their toll."

"Well, perhaps I could lure you back to my place. It would be like old times."

"That would definitely be fun, but I'm married now. Bart probably wouldn't approve."

Lee chuckled. "Probably not . . . So, I heard you're defending the Ice Pick Widow."

"Yes, that's right. When I took the case I knew nothing about the first murder."

"Really. She kept that from you?"

"Not intentionally. She'd actually hired us for something else prior to the murder. It's hard to say no to an existing client. But that's water under the bridge. Right now I've got to focus on giving her the best defense possible."

"Of course."

"And, since I've run into you, there is one thing you could help me with."

Lee frowned. "Really, what's that?"

Paula explained her predicament.

"Well, technically the inspections are supposed to take place in the order they are received, but if an inspector wanted to he could pull one out of order and it's unlikely anybody would know the difference."

"So, should I talk to one of the inspectors? Tell them my sad story?"

"No. I doubt they'd want to help your client. Most people think she's guilty. But you're in luck. It just so happens I go fishing with one of the inspectors. I'm sure if I ask him he'll be happy to expedite your inspection, particularly if I picked up the tab for our fishing guide the next time we go striper fishing at Texoma."

"That would be great. The fishing trip is on me."

"Of course, all he's going to do is inspect the property out of order. The property still has to pass inspection on its own merits."

"I understand. That's all we're asking for. The superintendent assures us the property is complete and will pass inspection."

"Good. So, just call me when the inspection requests are filed. I'll take it from there."

"When do I pay for the fishing guide?"

"You don't. That's on me."

"But—"

He put a finger to his lips. "Hush. Just call Bart and tell him you're going to be home late tonight."

"Lee. Come on. I told you, I'm married."

"So you say, but I've read about your indiscretions in the tabloids. Are you telling me they're untrue?"

He was talking about an affair Paula had been lured into with a young security guard. It turned out the security guard was actually a reporter trying to get inside information on a case she was handling. It had been humiliating and had almost destroyed her marriage. But Lee was right, she'd slept with a lot of men, so it didn't matter that much to her. In fact, she thought she'd probably enjoy it if it weren't for Bart. But, if he found out about it, it could be a disaster.

"Can I trust you to keep this to yourself?" Paula asked. "Bart can't find out about it."

"It will be our little secret," Lee said excitedly.

"All right. Let's go. I'll follow you to your place, but I only have a couple of hours."

Lee stood up and motioned to the waitress for the tab. After he paid the bill they left and Paula followed Lee home. A wave of guilt came over her as she followed the big Cadillac through downtown Dallas to Lee's apartment. But she also felt an excitement she hadn't felt in years. She'd always loved being free to sleep with whomever she wanted without guilt or shame. She often lamented her decision to marry Bart. She loved Bart, but she loved her freedom more.

Deadly Defiance

Now she had a compelling excuse to cheat on Bart, and since she had no choice in the matter, she figured she might as well enjoy it. So, as Lee fumbled to unlock the door to his apartment, Paula began kissing him passionately and unbuttoning his shirt. When the door opened they stumbled inside and made a dash for the bedroom, leaving a trail of clothing in their wake.

9
Dangerous Litigation

Jodie's studied her draft of the application for administration. Their strategy was to get Jade Alvarez appointed administrator of Romildo Alvarez's estate. Ordinarily the spouse would apply to be administrator but Pandora wasn't legal, so it would be too dangerous for her to appear in court. Since her daughter Jade was the eldest child and was a natural born citizen of the United States, she would qualify to be administrator and wouldn't have to worry about being deported. Once Jade was appointed administrator, she would then institute the lawsuit to recover Romildo's back pay and overtime that he was due. The question that had yet to be decided was whether to sue for the back pay and overtime for Luz since she was a citizen as well. When the family gathered to sign all the pleadings Jodie brought up the issue.

"We could join Luz in as a plaintiff to recover her back pay and overtime since she's a citizen too, but I don't know if you want to put her at risk. We have convinced the FBI and the Dallas police to reopen their cases, but it could still be dangerous. Melendez is going to be livid when he discovers what's coming down on him. He may still try to retaliate against you."

"Since I'm going to be administrator I might as well join as a plaintiff, too," Jade said.

Jodie nodded. "Yes. You're our designated target, so to speak, so it would make sense for you to be an individual plaintiff. It would probably be a good idea for you to go off the grid while this lawsuit is going on, however. I don't want you ending up like your father."

"Where would I go?"

"Why don't you go to college?"

"College?"

"Yes, that would be perfect. We can find a nice state school somewhere and you can live in a dorm. I'll arrange everything and keep it between you and me. That way there will be no way Melendez or his goons can find you."

"I've always wanted to go to college," Jade admitted. "It's been a dream of mine, but how will I pay for it?"

"My sister is an administrator at a state technical college and works in the student aid office. She says there are a lot of minority scholarships and student loan programs. I don't think it will be a problem getting you financed."

Jade looked at her mother. "Yes, that's a good idea," Pandora agreed, "but what about the rest of the family?"

"Well, the rest of you won't be involved in the lawsuit, but you could still be at risk. Our hope is that with the Dallas police and FBI breathing down Melendez's neck, they wouldn't take a chance at hurting any of you, but there are no guarantees."

"Let's leave Luz out of it," Pandora said. "I don't want her to be a target."

"You're probably right," Jodie agreed. "If we win or settle the case we can probably settle for the rest of you, too. Melendez wouldn't want to go through another lawsuit."

Pandora nodded.

"Okay, tomorrow I'll file the application for appointment of administrator and in a couple weeks we'll go to the court and get Jade's appointment approved. By then we'll have the state court action ready to go and we'll file it immediately. Hopefully during this time the FBI and the Dallas police will come up with enough evidence to start putting some heat on Melendez."

"It's going to be scary going to work after the lawsuit is filed," Ganix noted.

Jodie nodded. "Yes, it will. So, you may want to find another job so Melendez won't be seeing you every day."

"No," Nehemias said. "We can't quit. Guido will kill us if we do that. If we tell him we had nothing to do with the lawsuit I think we'd be better off."

Jodie swallowed hard. "Either way what you are doing is very dangerous. We'll do everything we can to protect you, but there are no guarantees. You don't have to file this lawsuit. You could leave it up to the FBI and Dallas police. They may come through this time with some indictments."

"I doubt that," Ganix said. "They're only taking action now because you and Stan are pushing them."

Jodie nodded. "That's true, so if you really want your father's killers brought to justice, this may be the only way to do it."

"We need to do this," Louisa said. "It's time to put the bastards behind bars."

The debate continued but in the end all agreed Jodie's plan was sound and they should go forward with it. When they'd left she went to talk to Stan about how to proceed. He was on the telephone when she walked in his office, so she sat down and waited. When he hung up the phone he looked at her expectantly.

"Well, they want to proceed the way we discussed," Jodie reported.

Stan sighed. "They've got a lot of guts. I'll say that for them."

"They loved their father and they want to put Melendez behind bars. I'm surprised one of them hasn't just put a bullet in his head."

Stan laughed. "They've probably considered it, but I imagine Melendez doesn't go anywhere without a bodyguard."

"So, what are we going to do to protect them?"

"Maybe I can get Detective Besch to go visit Melendez and warn him to leave the Alvarez family alone. He can be pretty persuasive."

"Good idea. Can I come along? I'd love to see Melendez's face."

"No. You better stay clear of Alliance Fabrications. I wouldn't want you to blow your cover and put you in danger."

"You think they'd come after me?"

Stan nodded. "Yes, our lawsuit is going to cost them a lot of money and they'll figure out pretty fast that we're the ones who stirred up the FBI and the Dallas police."

"Do you think you'll be in danger?"

"Possibly. We'll all have to take extra precautions to protect ourselves and our families."

Jodie shook her head. "I wish there was something I could do. I hate just sitting around waiting."

"Oh. You can go visit Besch. He said he'd let you go through the case file as long as you did it at his office. There might be some information in there that could be useful."

"Sure. I'll go there tomorrow," Jodie said and then stood up to leave.

"All right. Let me know if you find anything good."

As Jodie walked back to her office her cell phone rang. She looked at the screen and saw that it was from Ricardo. She knew she shouldn't take the call but she was curious what he wanted. Her finger lingered over the *talk* button for a long moment, then sighed and pressed it.

"Hello."

"Jodie. This is Ricardo."

"Hey, cowboy. What's up?"

"What are you doing tonight? I thought maybe I could buy you dinner."

"It's a nice thought, but I've only put in eight billable hours today. I've got to log in two or three more or risk the wrath of my boss."

"Your boss sounds like my father. He thinks his employees exist only for his profit."

"Yeah. I guess the difference is, I'm doing it to get ahead. Down the road a few years I'll be a partner and rolling in the big bucks."

"Yes, that's true. My father's employees will die poor."

Jodie felt a surge of guilt. She had an urge to come clean with him and enlist his help voluntarily, but that could be extremely dangerous. Ricardo was a decent guy and she didn't think he'd be anxious to betray his family.

"I'll take a rain check, okay?"

"Just have dinner with me. You've got to eat. I promise it won't take more than an hour and then you can go back to your office and log in another couple of hours."

Jodie sighed and then heard herself say, "Okay, I'll meet you at Macaroni Grill on LBJ near Forest Lane at seven, but I've got to be out of there by eight."

"Excellent. Thank you, Jodie. See you soon."

Jodie looked at her watch and saw it was 5:30 p.m. She wondered if she should go to her apartment and change before dinner. She looked at the stack of telephone messages that needed to be answered and decided Ricardo would have to take her as she was. Besides, maybe if she looked a little tattered he'd lose interest in her and quit calling.

At 6:30 Jodie answered the last phone message and got up to leave. On the way to her car she went to the ladies' room to comb her hair and refresh her makeup. Ten minutes later she was on her way and arrived just a little after seven. Ricardo was in the reception area waiting for her.

"Oh, there you are," Ricardo said as she stepped through the door. I'm so glad you could squeeze me in."

"I'm sorry about that. Didn't anybody warn you about dating an attorney? It can only lead to heartache."

Ricardo shrugged. "That's probably good advice, but I can't help myself. Ever since I met you I can scarcely think of anything else."

Jodie frowned. "Oh, come on. You barely know me. I could be a serial killer for all you know."

"I feel like I've known you for years. Isn't that weird?"

"Yes, very weird. I'm just another girl. There's nothing special about me."

"Oh, but that's not true. You're smart, confident, funny, and caring."

Jodie rolled her eyes. "Well, right now I'm hungry, so let's order some food. You only have me for forty-eight more minutes."

Ricardo motioned to the waitress and she came over to take their orders. He wanted to order a bottle of wine but Jodie protested.

"No wine. It will put me to sleep and then I won't be able to work when I get back to the office."

"Are you really going back to the office? I'd like to show you my apartment."

Jodie laughed. "Yeah. I bet you would."

"The idea doesn't tempt you a little bit?"

Jodie studied Ricardo. The offer did tempt her but she knew she couldn't give in to it. An affair with Ricardo would be incredibly dangerous. Eventually Ricardo would learn the truth about her and if he or his family didn't kill her, she'd probably be disbarred for unethical behavior.

"No. I like you, Ricardo, but my focus is on my career right now and I'm not going to get sidetracked by a relationship. Maybe in a few years my perspective will change, but for now that's the way it's got to be."

He sighed deeply and turned away. Jodie felt bad but knew she was doing the right thing. He turned back to her and smiled. "Have you ever tried the Sausage Salentino?" Ricardo asked.

"No. Is it good?"

After dinner Jodie thanked Ricardo and then left him longing after her. She didn't go back to the office but home to take a bath and lament her decision. He was a good man. She wondered how such a beautiful flower could have grown and blossomed in the Melendez junk heap of a family. She wondered if the flower would wilt when her deceit was revealed.

The next morning Jodie went to see Detective Besch. They drank a cup of coffee together, chatted a few minutes and then, as promised, he left her with the Alvarez file laid out across his desk.

"I've got to go track down a witness, so it may be a while before I get back. If anybody comes in looking for me just tell them I stepped out for a minute and told you to wait for me."

"All right. Thanks, Detective."

Besch left and Jodie began going through the file. She looked at the photos first, shuffling through an array of photos of the body. There were no visible signs of trauma except for the look of horror on Romildo's face. It was uncanny. She could only imagine the fear he must have felt as he watched the assailant inject him with a lethal dose of heroin. She stared at the photo a long minute, letting the anger well within her. She wanted to remember that face, so if her resolve ever faltered, she could just recall that memory to restore it.

Next she read the autopsy report. It confirmed her visual observation that there was no major trauma to the body except for multiple needle marks on his left arm. There was a little bruising to his arms and shoulders that suggested a possible struggle but could just as easily have been the normal bumps and bruises of any common laborer. Pandora and her children had described Romildo as a mild-mannered man, so it was possible when Guido confronted him that he accepted his fate and didn't put up much of a struggle.

Guido Quesada was obviously an expert at killing his victims and making it look like an accident. Jodie wondered how many others Guido had murdered. She wondered if he had done it alone or brought Ben Zepeda or Adair Aguirre along. She found notes in the file from interviews of all three of them, but as would be expected they professed no involvement or knowledge of Romildo's death prior to the reports in the newspapers.

Finally, Jodie looked through a paper bag full of Romildo's personal property. His clothing, pants, and shoes were old and worn and provided no clues as to the events that led to his death, except for a torn sleeve and a missing button—possibly ripped by the assailant as he was preparing to make the fatal injection. As she was stuffing the clothing back in the bag a funny feeling came over her. She looked at the clothing again. Where was the belt? Most men wore belts. And where was Romildo's coat? Surely he wouldn't walk several miles in the cold of winter without a coat.

Jodie made a mental note of these questions and then started going through Romildo's wallet. There was no driver's license, social security card, or voter registration. There were no credit cards, club memberships, or insurance certificates. The only thing in his wallet was $110 in cash and pictures of his family. Jodie thought about how horrible it must be to live in a country where you were expected to be invisible and, on paper, didn't exist. She couldn't imagine not being able to vote, legally drive a car, or open a bank account. But worst of all, she couldn't imagine having to live in fear of Guido Quesada's wrath if you didn't follow the company's rules—or being dragged off by the INS if they suddenly discovered your presence without a green card.

As Jodie was running this through her mind the door opened and Detective Besch walked in with a thin Hispanic man in his mid-twenties. His weather-beaten face and soiled clothing made Jodie think perhaps the man lived on the street.

"Jodie, I want you to meet Rico Toledo. He's been assigned to work undercover at Alliance Fabrications."

Jodie stood up and they shook hands. "Nice to meet you."

"Likewise," Rico replied evenly.

"Ordinarily I wouldn't introduce you to someone working undercover, but since you're dating Ricardo I thought you two should meet. It could be that your paths might cross and you could help each other out."

"Sure," Jodie agreed. "I'm glad you did."

"Anyway. First thing tomorrow morning Rico will arrive with a load of illegals and then he'll be on the inside."

"Good. So what's your objective exactly?"

"Well, we'd like to gather enough evidence to charge Melendez, and whoever he hired to kill Mr. Alvarez, with murder. A secondary objective is to get Alliance Fabrications either in compliance with the labor laws or shut them down. We'll be working with the FBI and the Labor Department on the latter objective."

"Sounds good," Jodie replied.

"Next week after you file suit, Stan and I will go pay Mr. Melendez a visit and warn him against any retaliation. We'll also begin surveillance of Guido Quesada and Mr. Melendez's two sons who work in the business. Hopefully, this will all pay off quickly."

Jodie nodded. "It sounds like a good plan. Let me know if there is anything I can do to help."

"I will," Detective Besch replied.

"Nice to meet you, Rico," Jodie said. "Looking forward to working with you."

"Likewise," Rico replied.

Jodie left Besch's office feeling pretty good. She and Stan had done a good job getting the local police and the federal government back on the ball. Now it would be just a matter of time before they had the evidence they needed to put Melendez and his goons behind bars. At least she hoped that would be the case.

10
The Warning

Stan went to the telephone and called the emergency number in the front of the telephone book. He told the dispatcher he needed an ambulance. She asked for his address and the nature of the emergency.

"I came home and my wife was lying on the sofa unconscious. I managed to wake her but she's very weak and she's not talking clearly."

"Is she awake now?" the dispatcher asked.

"Yes, but she can barely move. She can't even sit up."

"Is she breathing?"

"Yes. She seems to be breathing okay."

"An ambulance is on its way."

"Good."

"Stay on the line until the ambulance arrives," the dispatcher advised.

"Okay. Thanks."

Stan went to the front door and unlocked it. He peered out through the glass but the street was quiet. He went back to Rebekah and knelt next to her.

"I've called for an ambulance, honey. It will be here in a minute."

She shook her head. "No, I'll be all right."

"You're not all right. You can barely move."

"I'm just tired."

"So tired you can't even sit up. Come on. Something is obviously wrong with you and we need to figure out what it is."

Stan heard the sound of big trucks coming to a stop and looked up to see flashing lights through the window. He told the dispatcher the ambulance had arrived and then hung up. As he got to the front door a half dozen firemen were getting out of an ambulance and a big fire truck. Stan opened the door and let them in. They went over to Rebekah and checked her vitals. Stan explained what had happened.

"She seems stable now but she is very weak. Do you want us to take her to the hospital?"

"Yes," Stan said.

"No," Rebekah protested. "I'll be fine."

"Rebekah. Let them take you in and make sure you're okay."

"Your husband is right, ma'am. You should go in and have them check you out. If you blacked out and you're this weak you could have something seriously wrong with you. It could be a mild stroke or a heart attack. If so, proper treatment is critical."

"I know. I'm a nurse. I didn't have a stroke or a heart attack."

"You don't know that," Stan argued. "Just go in and let them check you out."

"No. I just haven't been sleeping well. Just help me to bed."

"So, you don't want us to take you to the hospital?" the paramedic asked.

"No," Rebekah replied. "Thank you for coming out, but I'll be fine."

Stan looked at the paramedic, shaking his head in exasperation. The paramedic shrugged.

"Well, you should go see your doctor tomorrow," the paramedic advised and then began packing up his gear. After they had left Stan helped Rebekah into bed and she went right to sleep. It was too early for Stan to go to bed so he went back into the living room and turned on the TV. He tried to concentrate on the program but his mind kept wandering back to Rebekah. What if she got sicker during the night? What if she quit breathing or had a stroke? He might not even realize it. After a while he couldn't stand it anymore so he went into the bedroom and just sat in the dark listening to Rebekah breathe. As long as he could hear her breathing he figured she must be okay. Eventually he went to bed but he didn't sleep. He just listened to be sure he could hear her breathing.

The next morning Rebekah was much better although she was still weak and Stan had to help her get dressed. After he'd fixed her breakfast she insisted he go to work and promised him she was just fine.

"I'm not doing anything today. I'm just going to sit in front of the TV and watch soap operas all day."

"All right. Maybe I'll come home for lunch," Stan said.

"No. That's too long a drive. Just bring home something for dinner. I'm not sure if I want to cook."

"Sure, I'll bring home KFC. How's that?"

Rebekah nodded. "That will be fine."

They kissed and then Stan left. He felt guilty leaving Rebekah but he had agreed to go with Detective Besch to see Icaro Melendez and warn him not to mess with any of the Alvarez family now that a lawsuit was being filed against Alliance Fabrications. When he got to the office he called Jodie into his office.

"So, is the suit all ready to file?"

"Yes, Jade was approved as administrator yesterday and we've posted her bond and filed her oath."

"Good. Then I guess you can go file it. I'm meeting Detective Besch over at Alliance Fabrications at eleven."

"I wish I could go with you," Jodie said. "I'd love to see Melendez's reaction."

"I'm sorry, but Ricardo may be the only person who will tell the truth if he's interrogated. If your cover is blown he may feel betrayed and clam up."

"He's bound to find out eventually."

"True. Let's just hope eventually is after his father is locked up."

Jodie went back to her office and Stan left to go meet Detective Besch. When he pulled up across the street from the plant he saw Besch leaning against his car studying the place. He got out and walked over to him.

"Morning," Besch said.

"Well, are you ready for this?"

"No. I'm waiting for a little backup in case Mr. Melendez reacts badly to what I have to say to him."

"That's probably a good idea."

"Did you file the lawsuit?"

"Yes. It was filed thirty minutes ago. The process server should be here in a minute."

"Good. We should all go in together."

"What if Melendez isn't there?" Stan asked.

"He's there. Rico reported his arrival at 7:45."

Stan felt nervous. He wasn't used to face-to-face confrontations with his opponents except in the courtroom where there was no danger to life or limb. Before a trial began he would invariably deal with attorneys and battle his adversaries from the periphery. Even though there was still danger he rarely thought about it—out of sight, out of mind. But now he was filing a lawsuit and directly confronting his enemy, an evil exploiter of men and women who obviously felt no moral constraints to his behavior. Stan finally admitted to himself, he wasn't just nervous—he was scared. Even with a police detective and two officers backing him up a lot could go wrong.

"I don't know how you do this for a living," Stan said. "This is scary."

Detective Besch shrugged. "You get used to it. The key is not to get careless or try to be a hero."

"Right."

Stan looked left as he heard a car approaching. It was his process server followed closely by a squad car. The process server got out of his car and walked over to them. Two policemen got out of their car and scanned the scene. Detective Besch went over to the two officers while Stan conferred with the process server. After they had conferred Besch led them into the plant.

The receptionist looked up as the men entered the small reception area. Detective Besch held up his badge. "Detective Besch and Stan Turner here to see Mr. Melendez," Besch barked.

"Do you have an appointment?" the woman asked.

"No. Just tell him we're here."

"What if he runs?" Stan whispered to Besch.

"We've got all the exits covered."

Stan raised his eyebrows. He hadn't seen any other officers. Then he realized serving Melendez was just a diversion. The receptionist got up and left the reception area. A minute later she returned with Mr. Melendez. He looked at his visitors contemptuously.

"What do you want?"

"I'll let Mr. Turner do his business first," Besch said, looking at Stan.

Stan nodded to the process server, and he went over to Mr. Melendez and handed him some papers.

"Icaro Melendez. You've been served!" he said and backed off quickly.

"Served with what?" Melendez said, giving the process server a sour look.

"It's a lawsuit," Stan replied. "You have been sued by the Estate of Romildo Alvarez and Jade Alvarez, individually, for violation of the Fair Labor Standards Act. The specifics are in the lawsuit."

Melendez scowled at Stan then threw the papers onto a desk. "We've already been audited and they found nothing. This is harassment!"

"Now Mr. Melendez," Detective Besch interjected. "I want to make something perfectly clear to you so that there is no misunderstanding. Whether you think the lawsuit has merit or not, it is illegal for you to threaten, intimidate, assault, or injure any party, attorney, or witness to this lawsuit including their employees, friends, and family. Be advised your behavior in responding to this lawsuit will be closely monitored."

"You should hire an attorney," Stan added, "as the suit must be answered by the first Monday following twenty-one days from today's date or a default may be entered."

"Oh. Don't worry. You'll get your answer," Melendez spat, "and I promise you won't like it."

Besch sighed. "What I'm trying to get across to you, Mr. Melendez, is that your only answer to this lawsuit will be to the 14th Judicial District Court. You cannot take any retaliatory action against the plaintiffs. Since you are a corporation you must hire a licensed attorney. You cannot answer the lawsuit yourself. . . . On another note," Besch continued. "I believe the FBI has some business with you."

At that moment Agent Lot strolled in followed by a string of FBI agents.

"Icaro Melendez. We have a warrant to search the premises," Agent Lot said and handed Melendez his search warrant. Immediately the other agents swarmed through the reception area and headed for the executive offices.

Melendez studied the search warrant, shook his head angrily, and then stormed out of the reception area. Detective Besch smiled at Stan.

"Okay. I believe our business is concluded," Besch said. "I suggest we leave and let the FBI do their thing."

"Since the Labor Department has already audited the books and records of the company, why the search warrant now?"

"They're hoping to find the second set of books mentioned in Jodie's tape. If they find that it will prove their case."

"Well, I hope they find it."

Just then a uniformed officer came through the front door with a man in tow. "I caught this guy trying to flee the plant," the officer said.

"Who are you?" Besch asked.

"Pablo Ruiz," the man replied.

"Why did you run, Pablo?"

"Ah. Ah, I haven't got my green card in the mail yet. It's due any day."

"Oh, well. We're not from INS. This is about something else. Since you're here, though, why don't you talk to Mr. Turner. If you're one of his witnesses we can protect you from Mr. Melendez."

"Protect me? Why do I need protection?"

"Because just as soon as we leave here the receptionist over there is going to tell Mr. Melendez that she saw you talking to us. Being a suspicious man, Mr. Melendez is going to draw the conclusion that you're helping us and somehow were responsible for this invasion of his plant."

"Ah, but I didn't—"

"I know that and Stan knows that but it's all a matter of perception. If you want my advice you'll go talk to Stan and become his star witness. The FBI may want to talk to you as well. If you can convince them you'd be a good witness, perhaps they'll let you in their witness protection program."

Pablo gave Besch a painful frown. Stan walked over to him. "Come outside. We shouldn't talk here," Stan said.

Pablo reluctantly followed Stan while glancing back at the receptionist who was eyeing him suspiciously. They walked across the street and got into Stan's car. Stan pulled a notepad out of his briefcase and got all of Pablo's contact information.

"So, how long have you worked at Alliance Fabrications?"

"About two years."

"How did you hear about them?"

"I have a cousin, Carlos, who works here, too. He came about five years ago. He told his mother they had some openings at Alliance Fabrications and she told my mother. To make a long story short I was told to contact a man in Nuevo Laredo and he'd arrange to get me into the United States and then get me to Dallas."

"How did you get into the U.S.?"

"They drove about eight of us in a van to a place in the desert and we just walked across the border in the middle of the night."

"That easy, huh?"

"Well, nobody tried to stop us, if that's what you mean."

"Right. Did it cost you anything?"

"No. I had no money."

"Did they feed you?"

"We got a little food and water each day."

"How long did it take to get to Alliance?"

"I'm not so sure, it seemed like a long time, but in thinking about it, I would say a week maybe."

"So, did you start work immediately?"

"Si. When we arrived they gave us breakfast and we started our first twelve-hour shift."

"What did they tell you about your pay?"

Stan continued to question Pablo and he told pretty much the same story that the Alvarez family had told him and Jodie. Thirty minutes later they got out of the car and rejoined Besch who was talking to Agent Lot.

"Pablo here has an interesting story to tell you, Agent Lot," Stan advised.

"Good. Because we didn't find what we were looking for in Mr. Melendez's office."

Stan frowned. He knew he was talking about the second set of books. "Well, that would have been too easy, right? I'm sure it's stashed somewhere safe after your last visit."

Agent Lot called another agent over and told him to interview Pablo. The agent escorted Pablo over to an FBI van to do the interview.

"So, you didn't find anything at all?" Stan asked.

"No. Apparently they keep the real records of the business off-site."

"Perhaps our man on the inside can figure out where that is," Besch suggested.

Agent Lot nodded. "Stan, we're going to need statements from all of your clients. Their testimony will go a long way to making our case. How many are there?"

"Well, there is Ms. Alvarez's five children. Then there is Pablo, who Detective Besch just recruited."

"That's good. That might be enough, but a few more witnesses unrelated to the Alvarez family would be good and, of course, we need some documentary evidence to go along with it."

"Well, you'll have Jodie and perhaps Melendez's son."

"You think his son would testify?" Agent Lot asked warily.

"I don't know. Maybe if we get him angry enough with his family."

"How would we do that?"

"I don't know. I'll have to give it some thought. In the meantime, what about prosecuting them for income tax evasion?" Stan suggested. "Like they did Al Capone."

Agent Lot frowned. "You want us to bring in the IRS?"

"Well, if they are claiming they are paying minimum wage and overtime but they're not, then they are claiming more deductions on their tax return than they are entitled to. That means they are under reporting their profits and thereby paying less taxes than are actually owed. Since it's being done intentionally, it's criminal fraud, right?"

Agent Lot nodded. "So, what you are saying is if we come up short on proof of the FLSA violations we may still be able to show tax evasion."

"Right," Stan said. "Just a thought."

"Okay. I'll talk to someone over in the criminal fraud division of IRS."

Stan looked at his watch. "Well, it's been an interesting morning, gentlemen, but I've got to check on my wife. She's been a little under the weather the last few days."

"Okay," Besch said. "Give me a call tomorrow so we can brainstorm."

"I will," Stan said as he walked briskly to his car and took off.

As he drove off Stan wondered what Melendez would do once the FBI had left. Would he play by the rules and simply go hire an attorney to defend himself or would he retaliate against everyone who had dared defy him? Stan prayed he'd play by the rules but wasn't optimistic his prayers would be answered.

11
Remorse

Paula didn't go to straight to her apartment after her tumble with Lee. She didn't want to go home in the midst of that sexual glow that she often had after sex. Instead she went to the office and worked until she was exhausted. This also allowed her to make some phone calls and mess up her office so she could back up her cover story that she'd worked at the office all evening.

When she got home there was a note on the kitchen table. She read it with great relief. Bart hadn't waited up for her since he had to be in court early the next morning. She crumpled up the note and thanked God for sparing her from having to face him. In the morning she'd be fine. She was good at forgetting or repressing unwanted memories. Life would be back to normal.

When Bart got up early the next morning she pretended to be sound asleep and didn't stir until he was gone. When she got to the office she called Elena to see if the houses were ready for inspection. Elena advised her they weren't quite ready yet but by the end of the following day they would be.

"You need to have your superintendent make his application for inspection first thing on Thursday morning. The moment they are filed I'll call my contact and make sure they get acted upon immediately. Hopefully the inspections can be done on Friday and Monday we can go to the bank."

"I'll make the call," Elena said. "Just out of curiosity, how did you manage to get the inspections expedited? I've asked some other builders about their experience with getting final inspections and they say it's been taking ten to twelve days."

"Well. It wasn't easy. You just have to know the right people and be willing to give them what they want."

There was a pause on the other end. Finally Elena said, "We went to the bank and signed new signature cards just like you told us."

"Good. When can you bring Maureen back over to my office? We need to have a long conversation."

"How about around three?" Elena suggested.

"That will be fine."

Paula hung up and began going through her messages. She stopped when she found one from Ryan Jones, Randy Rhymes's old agent. She had called him to get some background information on Maureen's ex-husband—the first victim of an ice pick. She dialed the number and got his secretary. The secretary put Jones through.

"Hello."

"Hi. This is Paula Waters. Sorry I missed your call."

"Oh, yes. You called me. What can I do for you?"

"I'm Maureen Thompson's defense counsel. I guess you heard about Rodney Thompson."

"Yes, how is Maureen holding up?"

Paula was surprised by the question and the apparent concern Jones had for Maureen.

"She's holding up pretty well considering everything. I take it you didn't blame her for Randy's death."

"No," Ryan said. "I never thought she was guilty. She's got a hot temper, but she loved Randy too much to kill him."

"That's what other people have told me. Do you have a theory as to who might have wanted Randy dead?"

"Well, Randy had his share of enemies. You know rock stars, they tend to use people and then discard them."

"So, anyone in particular you think I should take a look at?"

"Randy had a falling-out with his financial manager, Robert Brown. He had made some bad investments and cost Randy a bundle.

He'd handled his affairs for over ten years, so the breakup was pretty nasty."

Paula took down the information on Robert Brown but didn't see how there could be a connection between Robert Brown and Rodney Thompson, so she kept asking questions.

"Tell me how Maureen and Randy met."

"They met at a party after one of his concerts," Ryan replied. "Maureen is very pretty as you know and Randy was really taken with her."

"Did Randy have a girlfriend at the time?" Paula asked.

"Not anyone in particular. There were three or four groupies who were always hanging around Randy, hoping he'd take them to bed."

"Hmm. They probably weren't real thrilled when Randy fell for Maureen."

"No. In fact, Maureen ran them off in short order, once Randy made a commitment to her. She wasn't into sharing."

"So, any one of them could have killed Randy and made it look like Maureen had done it."

"It's a possibility. The police questioned them all but apparently they had alibis."

Paula got the information on the three girlfriends anyway, thanked Ryan, and hung up. Jill Johanson, Monica Rogers, and Sandy Watkins had scattered after Randy's death. Jill had moved to Hollywood, Monica to Houston, and Sandy to New York. She sighed. It seemed she'd have to do some traveling.

Paula was now beginning to understand why the jury wrestled with the first murder case. There were several people with more compelling motives to kill Randy than Maureen. She wondered if Maureen had carried insurance on Randy and if she had eventually collected it. She knew that Maureen would collect half a million on Rodney's death if she wasn't convicted for his murder. If she'd collected a sizeable sum on Randy, it would really look bad.

A hour later Elena dropped off Maureen and said she'd be back in a couple of hours. Paula hoped that would be long enough to get the information she needed. She wanted to understand exactly what had happened in both cases. That was the only way she'd have any chance at solving the murders. She took Maureen into the conference room and they sat across from each other.

"All right, Maureen. Let's start at the beginning. Tell me about Randy."

Maureen sighed. "Well, it was kind of a fairy-tale romance. A friend had given me one of Randy's albums for Christmas. I loved it and went out and bought everything he had ever recorded. I became an avid fan and whenever there was a concert anywhere close to Dallas, I was sure to be there.

"It was at a concert in Houston that I got lucky. There was a party after the concert sponsored by a local radio station. Before the concert they had a contest and the prize was a ticket to the after-party. I entered the contest and won a ticket.

"After the concert I went to the party and was introduced to Randy. That was part of the prize. He was very nice and ended up hanging around with me the entire evening. I was ecstatic, particularly when he asked me to stay after everyone else had left."

"So, was it love at first sight?" Paula asked.

"For him it might have been. I don't know. But I'd fallen in love with Randy before I had even met him. Or, I guess I should say, I fell in love with his music, anyway."

"So, I understand there were a few women whose hearts were broken when you and Randy hooked up."

"Oh, yeah. Jill, Monica, and Sandy. They were his unofficial harem and took care of all his sexual appetites."

"So, I heard you ran them off."

She nodded. "Yes. I told Randy I was an old-fashioned girl and would not tolerate any other woman in his life. He said he totally understood and would be absolutely faithful to me."

"Was he?" Paula asked.

"I thought he had been, but the DA in the first trial found some women who claimed to have slept with Randy after we were married. He tried to prove that I'd found out about them and killed him for betraying me. But he couldn't prove his theory because it wasn't true. I never knew about his infidelity."

"So, tell me about Jill, Monica, and Sandy. Did you have any confrontations with them?"

"That was inevitable. They were all very jealous women and didn't want to share Randy, but since he liked them all they had no choice but to tolerate each other. That all changed when I showed up."

"I bet," Paula said.

"Monica was the most outright belligerent. She caught me alone one day before the show and told me she'd slit my throat rather than let me take Randy away from her."

"What did you do?"

"I told her it was Randy's decision who he wanted to be with and that if any of us died he wouldn't sleep until he found out who was responsible. I suggested she might want to stick to traditional seduction techniques and be a good sport if she lost."

"What did she say to that?"

"She delivered a few obscenities I wouldn't want to repeat, but she's a smart girl. I think she knew I was right. If Randy hadn't made a choice between the three of them, it meant only one thing—he didn't love any of them."

"So, you don't think one of them killed Randy and tried to make it look like you'd done it—perhaps to punish him for not loving her and you for destroying what relationship she did have with him?"

"That's what my defense counsel claimed at trial and I think the jury bought into it, but I kinda doubt that's what happened. All three of them have moved on to other musicians. In fact, Jill married Jules Burns."

Jules Burns was a British rock star that Paula had heard of but wasn't familiar with. She assumed from the inflection in Maureen's voice that he was an equal catch to Randy.

"Okay, tell me about Rodney. What happened to make him leave you?"

"His business tanked and he became very distant and depressed. We argued a lot about money and I guess he just couldn't handle it anymore."

"Do you know what specifically happened in the business? From talking to Elena it didn't seem that bad."

"Well, she only told you about his construction management business. I told him just to stick with that but he wanted to go for the big bucks and develop an entire subdivision—Autumn Hills. Unfortunately, the bank pulled his line of credit before he even built the first home."

"Why did they do that?"

"The competition in the homebuilding business is brutal, and one of his competitors opened a subdivision called Park Meadows in the same area as Autumn Hills. The lots in Park Meadows were quite a bit cheaper so Rod had a hard time selling his lots. In fact, he'd only sold one lot in the last six months. Eventually he got behind on his note to the bank and they foreclosed."

"So, this is a different bank than the one we're dealing with on the houses that are being finished up?"

"Yes, but the bank wasn't the problem. Oh, they were getting ready to sue him, but Rod wasn't worried about that. He was worried about his partner."

"His partner? Who was his partner?" Paula asked.

Maureen swallowed hard. "Doc 'the Clock' Mellon."

Doc "the Clock" Mellon was an ex-college football player who ten years earlier had been banned from football when he was convicted of accepting money to influence the outcome of a football game. He was dubbed "the Clock" because he was so big he looked like a giant grandfather clock. During his trial, allegations were made that Mellon and two other players on the team, including the team's quarterback, accepted $10,000 each to "make sure it was a close game" so that a certain gambler with connections to organized crime would win a large bet. One of Mellon's teammates testified that Mellon didn't think it was a big deal since his team could still win the game. Mellon was bitter after the conviction and reportedly turned to friends he had made in organized crime since any chance at a career in the NFL had been dashed.

"Why would Rod do business with the Clock?"

"They went to high school together and were old buddies. When the bank threatened to foreclose the first time the Clock offered to loan Rod $250,000 to buy him the time he needed to get the lots fully developed and sold."

"So, he sounds like a good suspect to me," Paula remarked.

Maureen shrugged. "Maybe. But he and Rod were friends. You think he'd kill a lifelong friend?"

"I don't know. If he's in the mob he might have just considered it *business*. You know, you mess with the Clock, you die. It's a matter of maintaining your reputation."

Maureen didn't say anything.

"So, is there anybody else we should be looking at?" Paula asked.

"The only other major problem that I know about was with the IRS. Many years ago Rod had been referred to a tax preparer out in East Texas who was supposed to be very creative and able to save his clients a bundle on taxes. His name was Ronnie Moses, I think. It turned out his tactics and tricks were illegal and the IRS came down on him and all his clients. Rod had been fighting that battle forever and it just seemed to be getting worse and worse. That's why he had to set up a corporation. The IRS had shut him down personally and even came after me although I had not been involved at all."

"So that would give Rod a reason to kill Ronnie, but that doesn't help us."

"I suppose you're right. That's everyone that I can think of right now."

Paula nodded. "Okay, you've given me a lot to think about. I'll start digging into it and get back to you as new questions pop up."

Maureen left and Paula began sifting through her notes trying to decide what she should check out first. She decided Doc "the Clock" Mellon was her best bet. When she got home that night she decided to elicit help from Bart.

"Honey, what do you know about Doc 'the Clock' Mellon?"

Bart looked up at her. She smiled and began explaining why she was interested. Bart had been a prosecutor for a long time and, even before they were married, had been a great source of inside information.

"The Clock's bad news. Even sniffing around him is dangerous. If you need anything, let me get it for you. They won't mess with an assistant DA, but they'd have no qualms about stepping on you."

"I just need information for now. Where he was on February 25th. What he does to people who don't pay their debts. You know. That kind of stuff."

Bart smiled. "You don't want much, do you?"

Paula shrugged. "Just enough to prove reasonable doubt."

"If you do that you may force the DA into investigating his organization. That won't sit too well with him."

"This is a murder trial. I can't worry about hurting people's feelings for godsakes."

Bart rolled his eyes.

The next day Lee Long called to advise Paula that the three applications for the final inspections had been filed on behalf of Thompson Construction. She thanked him for the heads-up and asked if he'd contacted his inspector friend.

"I'll call him this afternoon after we have lunch."

Paula stiffened. She didn't have time for this nonsense. She hadn't signed on for a long-term affair—just a one-night romp. "Listen,

Lee. The other night was great, but like I told you, I'm not interested in an affair."

"Come on. Just this one time. Then I'll make the call. It will be fun."

Paula shook her head in disgust. "All right. But this is the end of it. The deal is done."

"Sure. Absolutely," Lee promised.

They met at Baby Doe's as the lunch crowd was thinning. Then they went across the freeway to the Anatole where Lee had rented a room. At least he wasn't cheap, Paula thought as they drove into the parking lot.

"Listen," Paula said. "This is a little too public for me. I don't want to be seen here with you. Let's go in separately and meet at the room."

Lee shrugged. "Sure, whatever makes you feel more comfortable."

Paula got out of the car and walked across the parking lot to the hotel entrance. A few minutes later Lee drove up to the hotel entrance and left his car with the valet. Ten minutes later they were together in the room. Paula hated giving in to Lee, but she was stuck. She had been fortunate to get a high-profile case and couldn't stand the thought of giving it up to a court-appointed attorney. She just prayed it would be worth the risk she was taking. Before she left, she made Lee make the phone call. He assured her the job would be inspected the next day.

They left separately as agreed, but on the way out of the hotel Lee was spotted by a friend and was stopped. The old friends chatted awhile while Paula tried to make her escape only to be spotted by a member of media who intercepted her.

"Oh, Paula," Edgar Williams called out. "Paula Waters."

Paula turned and smiled. "Ed. How are you?"

"Fine."

"What brings you to the Anatole?"

"Ah . . . Just meeting a potential witness."

"Oh, really? Who is it?"

Paula smiled "I can't really say, Ed. I don't want to tip off the prosecution on my case."

"Right. How is the investigation coming?"

"Very well, actually. I'm finding a lot of people who had better motives for killing Rodney Thompson than my client."

"Oh, really. Care to give us a name?"

Paula thought a moment. Did she want to try the case in the media? It wasn't usually a good idea, but sometimes letting the media do some of the digging wasn't a bad idea. It certainly could cut down expenses.

"Well, we have no proof of anything but I did learn today that there were three women who were very upset about my client's marriage to Randy Rhymes. One of the things I'm doing now is investigating the possibility that one of these women hated Maureen so much that she killed Randy Rhymes and tried to frame my client for the murder. When that didn't work it's conceivable that she tried again with Rodney knowing it would be tough for my client to beat the rap on the murder of a second husband."

"That *is* interesting," Ed agreed.

"It's just speculation right now," Paula added forcibly. "It may not pan out. Who knows? But this is an example of what I'm doing right now to try to prove Maureen innocent."

Paula ended the interview and then grabbed a cab to take her back to her car. She wondered if she'd been a fool to talk to Ed, but she wanted to take the offensive and not let him focus on what she was doing at the Anatole. When she got home that night her interview had already made the evening news and Paula got some answers to her questions.

"And now it's Ed Williams with the local news. Ed?" Brad Henderson, the anchor, said.

"Thank you, Brad. As you know Maureen Thompson, dubbed the Ice Pick Widow on account of her two husbands both being brutally attacked and killed with an ice pick, was arrested and charged with the murder of her husband, Rodney Thompson, yesterday. Although she avoided conviction for her first husband's murder, Assistant DA Stuart Rawlins assured me today that she will not escape justice a second time. At the bond hearing yesterday, none other than Paula Waters of the firm Turner & Waters, showed up and announced the firm would be representing the young widow.

"What is astonishing is that although Ms. Thompson claims to be broke and in debt due to her husband's financial blunders, she managed to post a $200,000 bond. Later today when I caught Ms. Waters coming out of the Anatole Hotel after meeting with a mystery witness, she told me that there were a lot of persons other than her client who had a motive to kill Rodney Thompson and she would be spending a lot of time trying to prove one of them did it. When I pressed her for names she mentioned three groupies who had been livid when Maureen and her first husband, famed singer-guitarist Randy Rhymes, got married.

"After hearing this angle we contacted investigative reporter John Schmitz who covered the first trial to get his opinion. He said both he and the assistant DA had gone down that road and it led nowhere. So, it sounds like Paula Waters is spinning her wheels as she attempts to come up with some kind of a defense for the Ice Pick Widow. This is Ed Williams reporting."

Paula switched off the TV in disgust. Ed had caught her off guard and managed to make her look bad. She was pissed and now very much determined to prove him wrong. She wasn't quite ready to give up on the three groupies. She had a gut feeling one of them had done it but somehow managed to cover it up. She just hoped she'd be able to figure it all out.

12
Blown Cover

After Jodie filed the civil suit against Alliance Fabrications and Stan had briefed her on the confrontation with Melendez earlier in the day, she went to visit a man who had been a good friend of Romildo Alvarez before his murder. Pandora had indicated he may know more about the murder than he told the police. His name was Juan Salazar. Salazar had worked next to Romildo on the assembly line for over ten years. Juan and his family also lived in the same neighborhood so they often saw each other coming from and going to work.

Jodie had arranged to meet with Salazar in a typing room at the Dallas Public Library as she didn't want their meeting to be observed by anyone working at Alliance and reported back to Melendez. She got to the room a few minutes early and began typing a letter. A few minutes later the door opened and Salazar peered in.

Jodie looked up and smiled. "Mr. Salazar?"

"Yes."

"Come in. Have a seat."

Jodie got up and locked the door so they wouldn't be interrupted.

"Does anyone know you are here?" Jodie asked.

"No. I told my family I was going to get a car wash and run some errands."

"Good. Well, as we discussed over the telephone, I need to talk to you about a few things."

"Sure. I'd like to help the Alvarez family, if I can."

121

"Well, the best way you can help them and everyone else at Alliance is to help prove that Melendez had Romildo killed. Once he and his goons are locked up then we can concentrate on getting you the money they owe you."

"So, what do you want me to do? I told the police everything I knew about Romildo's death."

"Yes, I read your witness interview. As I understand it Mr. Alvarez was called away from the assembly line."

"Yes, they told him his wife was ill and needed him to come home. He was very upset when he heard it because phone messages are only relayed in an emergency."

"I see. So, Romildo left and then what happened?"

"What do you mean?" Juan asked. "That's all I know."

"Isn't it true that when a worker is in trouble they are called away in a similar manner?"

Juan nodded. "That is true."

"So, weren't you suspicious about the summons home? I mean, weren't you a little worried that maybe your friend was in trouble—particularly after he complained to the Labor Department?"

The expression on Juan's face answered the question. He nodded. "Sure, I was afraid he was going to get beat up like we all do from time to time, but not killed."

"But this was more serious, wasn't it? If they just beat him up, it would just add more credence to his complaint with the Department of Labor. Weren't you worried they'd kill him?"

Juan's face dropped and tears began to well in his eyes. "Yes, I was afraid I would never see him again."

"So, what did you do? You must have done something in reaction to what had happened."

"Yes, I went outside and watched Romildo leave. About five minutes later Guido and Ben left in the Jeep. Ben had a gym bag with him."

"A gym bag? Could you describe it?"

"It was blue and grey—a dark blue."

"Had you ever seen the bag before?"

"No."

"Before Ben and Guido left what were they doing?"

"They were in Mr. Melendez's office. All three of them came outside and talked for a while, then Ben and Guido broke off and went to the Jeep. They returned about thirty minutes later."

"How do you know that? Didn't you have to go back on the line?"

"Yes, but the line went down for about fifteen minutes, so I went back outside to see if anything was going on. That's when Guido and Ben returned."

"How did they act?" Jodie asked.

"They were laughing and joking and Ben was wearing Romildo's coat."

"Are you serious? Are you sure it was his coat?"

"Yes, they wanted all of us to know what had happened. It was a message not to talk to the police or the auditors."

"So, you were afraid to tell the police what you had seen?"

"Yes, I'd have ended up like Romildo had I said anything."

"Now, with the FBI involved we might be able to get you into the witness protection program if you testify. If that could be arranged would you tell the FBI what you told me?"

"What about my family?"

"I'm sure they'd put you all in the program."

"Then, si."

Jodie wasn't sure if witness protection could be arranged but she'd tell Special Agent Lot about Juan and see what he said. After Jodie left the library she went back to the office. As she was getting out of her car she heard screeching tires. She turned and saw a Jeep skid to a stop behind her car. Two men jumped out and grabbed her before she could react. She struggled but was no match for the two thugs. Everything turned white as a pillowcase was pulled over her head. Then her arms were tied behind her back and she was thrown onto the floor of the backseat. Pain shot through her arm as it hit the hump between the seats. Doors slammed and she heard the tires squeal again as they drove away.

Jodie's mind raced as she tried to fathom what was happening. Was she about to suffer the same fate as Romildo? She couldn't believe they'd kidnap and kill an attorney. This was America. This couldn't be happening. They must realize they'd never get away with it.

"Where are you taking me?" she demanded.

One of the men responded by kicking her hard in the back. Jodie screamed in pain. "You bastard!"

There was laughter and Jodie decided her best option was to lie still and try to figure out where they were going. In her mind she tried to follow each turn and gauge where they were going. They went over the two speed bumps in the parking lot and then went east onto Banner Drive. They stopped twice, presumably at stop signs, and then turned right onto the access road to LBJ Freeway. A sharp U-turn told Jodie they were going to get onto LBJ going west. Soon they were traveling fast and it was hard for Jodie to judge exactly where they were, but she did the best she could based on her many trips along this same road.

Thirty minutes later the Jeep made a sharp left and a short time later went right. She thought this must be DFW Airport as LBJ was pretty straight until you got to the airport. Then instead of bending south onto Highway 121 they went straight which meant to Jodie that they were heading toward Colleyville. She'd never gone this way before so the trip from that point was a blur. There were a myriad of stops and turns, so she had idea where they had ended up when the vehicle finally stopped.

They dragged her out of the car rudely, got her on her feet, and escorted her into a building of some sort. They were talking in Spanish, so Jodie didn't know what they were saying, but there seemed to be some sort of disagreement as to what to do with her. Finally, someone grabbed her arm and yanked off the pillowcase.

Jodie blinked and then scanned her surroundings. There were three men dressed in casual attire with grim faces. They were in a cluttered office in a warehouse, it appeared. A quick scan of the room revealed half a dozen desks, typewriters, telephones, a fax machine, file cabinets, and a long table along the wall.

"Who are you? Why did you kidnap me?" Jodie demanded.

One of the men slapped her. "Shut up, bitch, if you want to live."

Jodie winced in pain but held back a scream, not wanting to give her assailant the satisfaction of such a reaction.

"Put her in one of the vans. Tie her up and gag her until we need her."

Jodie started to protest when she felt the gag being slipped in place and tightened. She struggled but was powerless to stop it. They dragged her along a corridor and then out into the warehouse. There were a dozen large delivery vans parked in neat rows. They took her to one of them, opened the back, and then lifted her up onto its bed. One of the men hopped up and dragged her against the side panel where they tied her in a sitting position. Jodie mumbled a scream and struggled to free herself, but finally succumbed to her fate and just sat there defeated. The door was pulled shut and there was nothing but darkness.

13
The Note

Stan could have just called Rebekah to see how she was, but he knew she would just tell him she was fine. He wouldn't be satisfied with that, so he raced down Central Expressway toward home. It was midday so the traffic wasn't bad and he made good time. As he drove he wondered what Melendez was doing. He was worried about the Alvarez family and the danger they faced if they continued to work there. He couldn't imagine Alliance would do anything in retaliation for the lawsuit with the police and the FBI watching them so closely. That would be stupid, he rationalized, and they certainly weren't stupid. They couldn't have gotten away with all that they had if they weren't smart and cunning. They knew what battles they could win and those they couldn't.

As Stan neared Plano he saw large cumulus nimbus clouds building to the west and the sky above him began to darken. He drove into his garage and hit the button so the garage door would close behind him. He got out and rushed inside, calling for Rebekah. He found her in the laundry room which he thought was a good sign. If she was doing housework she must be feeling okay.

"Rebekah," Stan said.

"Stan. What are you doing home?" Rebekah asked.

"I told you I would come home for lunch. I'm a man of my word."

"Well, all I have is peanut butter and jelly. I didn't go shopping."

"That's okay. Let's run over to Campisi's and have a meatball sandwich."

"That sounds good. Let me just get this last load of clothes in."

While Rebekah finished up Stan went out and got the mail. He started to glance through it and heard a voice.

"Hey, Stan. What are you doing home at this hour?"

Stan looked over and saw his next door neighbor, John Martin, leaning on a shovel.

"Oh hi, John. Just came home to take Rebekah to lunch. She hasn't been feeling well the past few days so I wanted to check up on her."

"Yes, I saw the ambulance the other day. What's wrong with her?"

"Ah. They don't know for sure. It seems to come and go. It could just be stress, they say."

"Well, you can't be too careful. If we can do anything to help, don't hesitate to call, okay?"

"Thanks," Stan replied. "We appreciate that, but hopefully I won't have to take you up on that offer."

"Well, if you need to, don't hesitate."

Stan thanked John and went back inside. He put the mail on the counter when he saw Rebekah was ready to go.

Rebekah looked at the pile of mail. "Anything interesting?"

"I don't know. Let's go eat. I'm famished. I'll go through it when we get back."

When they got to Campisi's they placed their order and then went inside and found a booth. They had liked this restaurant because it was close by and the meatball sandwiches and pizza were to die for. They had gotten hooked on the place when Stan was at SMU many years earlier. The original store was near the campus and they often stopped for lunch. When they built a second location in Plano, they were ecstatic and often brought the family there.

"So, how did your confrontation go?" Rebekah asked.

"It couldn't have been better. We walked in and served Melendez, Besch warned him not to even think about retaliation or intimidation, then the FBI came in and searched the place. You should have seen the look on Melendez's face."

"I bet he was pissed."

"Outraged is probably more accurate."

"I'm worried about you and Jodie. What if they decide to take their anger out on you?"

Stan shrugged. "That's not likely. That would only help the Department of Labor make their case, and give the Dallas police more incentive to dig into the Alvarez murder."

"Yeah, but you're assuming they'll act rationally and obey the law."

Stan sighed. Rebekah was a worrier and he was used to this lecture. "Well, we'll take precautions. I was planning to call Jake Weston at Excel Security this afternoon and have him provide extra security for the office and each of our homes while this case is going on."

"Good, there are so many crazies in the world and you seem to have a knack for knocking heads with them."

Stan laughed. The waitress came over and put the meatball sandwiches down in front of them. Stan thanked her and then went and got them drinks. When he returned Rebekah was chewing a big bite of her sandwich. Stan felt good. It seemed Rebekah was okay. He couldn't imagine what he would do if something ever happened to her.

On the way home Stan had to put on the headlights as the storm that he'd seen approaching earlier was nearly upon them. Somehow they managed to get home without seeing a drop of rain although they could see lightning in the distance. When they walked in the door Stan went to the bar where he'd dropped the mail. He had just started to pick through it when the telephone rang. It was Maria advising him that one of the veterans who had served with Herb Wolf in the Second Naval Transport Squadron had returned his call. Stan had asked Maria to get a hold of him immediately if any of them called. He wrote down the information on Tom Hooper and called him back immediately.

"Mr. Hooper?" Stan asked.

"Yes, this is Tom Hooper."

"Hi, this is Stan Turner. My secretary told me you had just returned my call?"

"Yes, I did. What can I do for you?"

"I understand you served with Herb Wolf in the Second Naval Transport Squadron during the Vietnam War?"

"Yes, I did. How is Herb these days? Is he coming to the reunion?"

"No. I'm afraid not. He died recently. I'm an attorney and I've been working on his probate."

He sighed. "Damn! Herb was a great guy. We'll miss him."

"I didn't know him, but I've heard he was a good man. Listen, what I called about was his child."

"His child?"

"Yes, on his deathbed he admitted that he had a child named Mitch that he had never told anyone about. Since nobody in his family knows anything about Mitch, I assume he must have been born while he was in the service. Perhaps he had a relationship overseas."

There was silence.

"Mr. Hooper?"

"Yes, I was just thinking. That was a long time ago."

"Did he ever talk about having a child?"

"Well, he joked about it from time to time. He went kind of crazy when he found out his wife had been unfaithful. I think he tried to nail every hooker in Honolulu after he found out."

"So, you took most of your shore leave in Hawaii?" Stan asked.

"Yes, we had leave in Saigon sometimes but it was a pretty dangerous place to hang out. We usually stayed away from the women there. Too many of them were looking for a ticket to America."

"Yes, I bet. So, was there anyone special for Herb in Hawaii?"

"He had a couple of girls he was fond of but I don't know anything about a child. You'd have to talk to one of them."

"Do you know who they were?"

"Mina was one of them. She was a schoolteacher in Honolulu. He met her at a bar."

"Do you remember her last name?"

"Nishi—something."

"Nishi?"

"Ah. Nishihara, I think."

"Okay, what about the other one?"

"Yuzie Gucci or something. I don't know how you spell it."

"He liked Japanese women?"

"Yes, he liked that they were totally devoted to him. They made him feel like a king, he said."

Stan thought of how he could find these two women after so many years. He usually used International Tracing Service but they required a previous address, social security number, date of birth, or previous employer. Without something to start with he could spend ten thousand dollars on a PI and end up with nothing. Then he had an idea.

"Hmm. You don't happen to know anyone in Hawaii, do you? I'm sure the estate would be willing to pay a thousand dollar reward if we can find either of these two women. Five thousand if one of them actually has a child named Mitch."

There was silence for a moment. "Heck yeah. There's two guys who live on the Big Island. I bet between the three of us we could find your gals."

"Good. Why don't you contact them and get started?"

"What about expense money? I'll need to buy a ticket to Hawaii."

Stan chuckled. "You're going to fly over there and help your buddies?"

"Yeah. If there's three of us the search should go faster."

Stan sighed. "Okay, I'll give you five hundred up front for expenses. If you want to spend it on a plane ticket, that will be up to you, but there will be no more payments until you locate one of the women."

"You have yourself a deal, my friend. Can you Western Union me the money? We might as well get started right away."

Stan agreed and they exchanged contact information. Stan shook his head, feeling like he might have just been taken for five hundred bucks, but he had a gut feeling Tom Hooper would be worth the money he was about to fork over. He hung up the telephone and picked up the mail. As was his normal routine he put the junk mail in one pile, the bills in another, and was left with a plain white envelope addressed to Stan but with no postage. *A personal delivery. That's weird.*

He ripped it open and a photo fell out. As he picked it up he was horrified to see a picture of Jodie sitting in a truck with her hands and legs bound and her mouth gagged.

"Oh, shit!" he exclaimed.

Rebekah, who was at the sink, turned and looked at Stan curiously. "What is it?"

"It's Jodie. Someone has Jodie."

Stan unfolded the note that came with the letter and began to read:

If you care about your associate you'll convince your clients to drop the lawsuit and get the FBI and police to back off their investigations. You have 48 hours. No extensions. No excuses. No police or FBI.

"Oh, my God!" Rebekah exclaimed. "What are you going to do?"

Suddenly there was a flash of light and the house was rocked by a deafening clap of thunder. Rebekah jumped and let out a shriek. Stan looked out the window as rain began to pour from the sky, but nothing could distract him from the panic he was feeling after seeing

Jodie bound and gagged. He grabbed the phone and quickly dialed the office number. Maria picked up.

"When was the last time you saw or heard from Jodie?"

"Stan?"

"Yes, where is Jodie?"

"She left a couple of hours ago."

"Where was she going? Did she say?"

"To the library to meet a witness."

"Call the library and see if she is there, or, if not, when she left."

Stan knew she wouldn't be at the library but he wanted to know when the abduction took place. He hung up the phone and then started to call Agent Lot. Before he finished dialing he remembered the note said no police or FBI. He wondered what he should do. Finally he decided he'd have to call the FBI because there was no way he could ever find Jodie on his own and even if he got his clients to drop the lawsuit, Jodie may still be killed. He had to find Jodie before they killed her and he needed all the help he could get. He picked up the phone and dialed.

"Lot here."

"Agent Lot. Somebody has taken Jodie. They left a note in my mailbox with a picture of her tied up and gagged. They want me to drop the suit and get you and the police to back off."

"Oh, Jesus. I'm sorry, Stan. I'll get a team put together and get right over there."

"No. They said no police or FBI, so let's not make it obvious I've violated their demand."

"Well, that's not our usual protocol."

"I know, but what difference does it make? I'll courier the note over to you and we can talk by telephone. Nobody else knows anything. I just talked to Maria. Jodie left the office about two hours ago to meet a client at the Dallas Library. You can send someone over there and follow the trail from there. If you need to talk to Maria, call her. Don't go over there. There may someone watching."

"All right. We'll do it your way for a while, but we may have to come out in the open if we're not making any progress doing it your way."

"That's fine. You know I could dismiss the lawsuit without prejudice. That means we could re-file it later—once Jodie was safe."

"We can't stop you and your client from doing that, but we don't usually recommend dealing with kidnapers. If you let them get away with something like this it just encourages them to use the same tactic in the future."

"What if my clients dropped the suit and refused to aid in your investigations? Would you still go forward?"

"We would try to develop a case without your help, but it would be difficult without witnesses."

"So, you might end up dropping the case."

"Yes, that's a distinct possibility."

Stan sighed. "Oh, shit. I don't know what to do. I never dreamed they'd come after Jodie. One of Melendez's sons must have figured out who she was."

"You're probably right. Once the suit was filed they probably checked out your law firm and realized Jodie worked there."

"I never should have let Jodie go undercover."

"As I recall, she didn't ask your permission," Agent Lot reminded him.

Stan sighed heavily. "True. Okay. I'll let you go so you can get a team put together and start working the case. Call me if you need anything. I'm at home now but I'll be going back to the office and should be there in twenty minutes. I'll have a courier bring over the letter ASAP."

"Put it in a plastic bag in case there's a fingerprint on it or some trace evidence."

"All right," Stan said and hung up.

Stan turned to Rebekah, who was looking a bit shaken. He went over to her and held her for a moment.

"See. I warned you," she moaned.

134

Stan let her go. "I know. You were right. I should have got our security in place sooner. Damn it! I can't believe they came at us so fast."

Stan kissed Rebekah, put the letter in a big ziplock bag, and left for the office. Worry consumed him as he questioned every decision he'd made since the Alvarez case had been thrown in his lap. He'd been reckless in his eagerness to find justice and now someone he loved dearly might die.

Rain continued to pour from the dark sky and by the time he'd gotten out of his neighborhood the gutters along Independence Parkway were overflowing. Stan moved into the center lane to avoid the water rising along the curbs. The traffic around him slowed as driving became more and more treacherous, but Stan scarcely noticed as his mind was frantically searching for a plan, some strategy to extricate Jodie from this most perilous predicament.

14
Getting Paid

Paula sat in the bank lobby, anxiously awaiting Maureen and Elena to show up. They were coming from the City of Dallas Building Inspection Offices with the final inspection approvals on the last four homes built by Thompson Construction. The bank had promised to pay the retainage due just as soon as the final inspections were in hand. Paula was there to make sure she got her promised share of the money, particularly after being forced to violate her marriage vows to get the final inspections expedited. Seeing Maureen and her sister walk through the door greatly relieved her. She got up and walked over to meet them.

"Everything go okay?"

"Yes, the paperwork was all ready for us just like you said it would be," Elena reported.

"Good. Let's get this over with," Paula said.

They walked over to the reception area and saw a sign that directed them to sign a visitor's log that was on a podium. Maureen signed the log indicating they wanted to see Riley Stewart, their loan officer. Then they took a seat and waited. Ten minutes later a secretary went to the log book and inspected it. She looked up and smiled at the three women.

"I'll see if Mr. Stewart is available. Did you have an appointment?"

"No," Elena said. "I called and told him we'd have our final inspections today and he said come by anytime."

The secretary nodded. "Okay, I'll tell him you're here."

She left and Paula let out a deep sigh. "I don't know how anyone can run a business the way banks do. If I left a client in the waiting room for fifteen minutes without asking them what they wanted, I'd be out of business in a week. These bankers are so arrogant. They have no respect for other people's time."

"That's true," Elena agreed. "It was a nightmare getting these loans. You wouldn't believe the documentation they required to approve them and the financial reporting we had to provide every week."

As they were talking the secretary returned and told them Mr. Stewart would see them. They got up and followed the secretary into a small conference room. They sat down and a few minutes later Mr. Stewart walked in. They exchanged greetings and then Elena handed him the final inspection reports.

"So, that was fast. I thought the jobs were just completed the day before yesterday."

"Yes," Paula said. "We asked for an expedited inspection."

"I've never heard of that," Mr. Stewart confessed.

"Well, you know with Mr. Thompson's passing we're anxious to wrap up his business affairs. Can you cut the company a check for the retainage now?"

Stewart cleared his throat. "Well, I'll have to check with the loan committee and perhaps the board. It will take a few days."

"No, no, no," Paula said, exasperated. "That won't do. My client has complied with the loan agreement, so they'd like the retainage *now*."

"I realize you've complied with contract, but due to Mr. Thompson's death the bank is reluctant to release any funds."

"His death is irrelevant," Paula said evenly. "The contract is between Thompson Construction and the bank. We've provided you with a certificate of incumbency showing the current officers of the corporation. There is no reason to delay final funding of the loans."

"Yes, well I'll need to consult with the loan committee."

"Then do it now. We'll wait."

"Well, they don't meet but on Mondays and Thursdays."

"That's your problem. If you have to consult with them, then round them up and do it now. Otherwise cut us the final checks and we'll be out of your hair."

Stewart sighed and stood up. "Give me a minute." He left and walked across the hall to the president's office. He went in and the two men conferred for a few moments. Paula watched them, wishing she could hear what they were saying. Finally, Mr. Stewart turned and returned to the conference room.

"I talked to Mr. Blake and he said he'd have to confer with the bank's legal counsel before authorizing the final checks."

"How long will that take?" Paula asked.

"His secretary is trying to get our attorney on the line right now. If he's in it won't take long, but if he's not available it won't be until tomorrow."

Paula drew in a deep breath. She couldn't believe the crap she was having to go through just to get paid. She glared at Stewart. "You better pray he's in, because if we leave here without a check you're going to wish you never heard the name Paula Waters!"

"Right," Stewart said. "Ah. Let me go check and see if they've found him. I'll be right back."

He had been gone another ten minutes when Paula's patience wore out. She stood up and walked across the hall into the president's office. He looked up at her in astonishment.

"Yes, Ms. Waters. I'm terribly sorry for the delay, but the bank has policies and procedures we have to follow."

Paula shook her head. "Yes, and one of them is to hang on to every dime in your possession as long as possible. If at all possible, use other people's money. I'm very familiar with bank policies."

"No, that's not—"

"Listen, if you don't write a check right now I'll have to assume you intend to breach the contract and I'll be forced to go back to the office and prepare a petition to file tomorrow morning in the district court. Once I do that I'll call a news conference and explain to the press how your bank doesn't honor its contracts."

The president laughed. "We have a dozen lawsuits going at any given time. The press isn't going to be interested in your lawsuit."

"You want to make a bet? I'm a high-profile criminal attorney. I have the media following me everywhere I go. There's probably a reporter or two right outside waiting to stick a microphone in my face the moment I step outside."

The president glanced worriedly out the window.

"You know Becky Collins, the Channel 8 investigative reporter? She's a personal friend of mine and she loves to dig into sleazy business dealings. One phone call and I'll have her contacting all of your construction clients to see if you're treating everyone like this."

"All right, all right," the president said. "We'll write you the checks, but I want your word neither you nor your client will say one negative thing about this bank to the media or anyone for that matter."

Paula smiled, feeling much relieved. "That's fine. We'll put it in writing. We never had a problem with the bank until today. Just give us the checks and we'll be on our way."

Thirty minutes later Paula, Maureen, and Elena left the bank each with their agreed portion of the loan proceeds in cash. The bank had wanted to issue cashier's checks but Paula didn't trust them as she knew that even cashier's checks could be dishonored if the bank chose to do so. Since it wasn't wise to be driving around with a lot of cash, Paula went straight to Gateway Bank, where the firm had an account, and deposited the money.

From the bank she went back to the office, anxious to tell Stan that she'd finally been successful at collecting her fee, but when she stepped into the office she knew something was terribly wrong. Maria was crying.

"What's wrong?" Paula asked urgently.

"It's Jodie. She's been kidnaped. Stan just called. There was a note delivered to his house."

Paula was stunned by the news. She just stared at Maria a moment in disbelief. "What?"

"She's been kidnaped. It just happened a little while ago."

"Who kidnaped her?"

"The note didn't say, but it was obviously Melendez, Stan says."

"Oh, shit! I can't believe this. I thought the police were going to protect us."

"Stan had security arranged, but it doesn't start until tomorrow. We didn't think they'd react so quickly."

"What are we going to do?"

"The note said not to notify the FBI or police, but Stan has talked to them. They're going to work the case but keep their distance."

Paula just sat there in shock for a moment, wondering what to do. She wasn't as close to Jodie as Stan, but she liked Jodie a lot and was outraged that someone had kidnaped her. Her mind raced as she tried to think of a way to find her.

"I wonder if Ricardo had anything to do with the kidnaping?"

"He liked Jodie," Maria replied. "He wouldn't do anything to hurt her."

"Unless he was pissed off that she'd been spying on his family."

"Even so, from what Jodie said he wasn't the type of person that could hurt someone, let alone kidnap them."

Paula considered that. "Okay, if you're right then he's our best bet at finding Jodie."

Maria nodded. "You may be right."

As they were talking the door opened and Stan rushed in, looking rather disheveled.

"Did you hear the news?" Stan asked Paula.

"Yes, Maria was just telling me about it. I can't believe Melendez would do this with police and the FBI watching him so closely. How does he think he can get away with it?"

"Actually, it may have been his only move. We had him so boxed in his only choice was to force us to retreat and to do that he had to have a bargaining chip. I should have realized that and hired bodyguards for all of us."

"It's not your fault, Stan," Paula said. "You brought in the police and the FBI for godsakes. Who would have known Melendez would be so bold?"

"What are we going to do?" Stan moaned.

"I was just telling Maria, I think our best bet is to find Ricardo and get him to help us."

"You think he would?" Stan asked skeptically.

"Yes, from what Jodie said about him. Apparently he is an honorable man and has never approved of his father's business."

"I know, but it's hard to go up against your family."

"Well, it won't hurt to try. All he can do is tell us to go to hell if he doesn't want to help."

"Do we have contact information on him?" Stan asked.

"I'm sure Jodie will have something in the file. I'll go take a look."

While Paula was gone Stan called for a courier. While he was waiting for it to come, he made a copy of the note from the kidnaper and then slipped the original into an envelope. When he was done he gave the package to Maria and told her to have the courier take it to Agent Lot at FBI headquarters.

Paula returned with a file in her hand. "I've got his address and telephone number. How do you think we should handle this?"

Stan considered it a moment. "You should call him. He'll probably respond better to a woman. Feel him out. See if he's in on the kidnaping or not. Just tell him you're Jodie's friend and you're afraid his father has kidnaped her."

"Okay," Paula said nervously. "You better listen in and write down any ideas you get while we're talking."

"Right. Conference me in and then call Ricardo."

Paula nodded and they went into the conference room where there were two phones. Paula connected Stan's extension and then called Ricardo. Stan grabbed a yellow pad and began making a list of questions they needed answered. The phone rang three times before Ricardo answered.

"Hello."

"Ah. Ricardo Melendez?"

"Yeah."

"Ah. This is Paula Waters. You don't know me."

"The lawyer. I've seen you on TV. You're defending the Ice Pick Widow?"

"Right. I'm also a friend of Jodie Marshall. I believe you and she are friends."

"We were until I found out she was just using me to get information on my father. I should have known she wasn't for real. The beautiful ones never are."

"Well, believe it or not, she liked you a lot and felt very bad about what she was doing. In fact, she hadn't planned to see you again after that first meeting because she didn't want to take advantage of you, but you kept calling her."

"I know. I couldn't get her out of my head."

"Yes, she has that effect on men. . . . So, do you know why I'm calling?"

"No. I don't. Let me guess. You want me to testify against my family."

"No. That's not it. You don't know what's happened?"

"I know you brought the police and the FBI down on my father's business and filed a lawsuit."

"True. We did. What else do you know?"

"I know my father is pissed off beyond belief. He called me up and told me his lawyer had checked some law firm directory,

143

Martindale something or other, and found out Jodie worked for Turner & Waters."

"Right."

"I was devastated," Ricardo said. "I still can't believe she could do that to me."

"So, you don't know what's happened to her?" Paula repeated.

"What do you mean?"

"She's been kidnaped."

"Oh, shit! When did that happen?"

"An hour or so ago. She was coming back to the office from the Dallas Library and never made it. Do you think your father would do something like that?"

"No, but the cartel would."

Paula looked at Stan worriedly. Stan just shook his head.

"The cartel? What cartel?" Paula asked.

"I've said too much already. I've got to go and find out what's going on. All I can tell you is you better find her soon because, if you don't, she'll be dead by morning."

"Wait—we have no idea where to look. Help us out here, Ricardo."

"I'm sorry. I can't get involved. I'll talk to my father and try to convince him that kidnaping and murder will only make matters worse, but that's all I can do without risking my own life. I'm sorry."

The phone went dead. Paula reluctantly hung up the phone.

"Well," Stan said. "I should have realized there would be a Mexican drug cartel involved. Smuggling in aliens is probably only a small portion of the business that goes through Alliance. I'd better call Agent Lot and fill him in on what we've found out."

"I'm sorry, Stan. I should have been more persuasive."

"No. You did fine. I think Ricardo will call his father and try to get him to let Jodie go. I doubt he'll be successful, but when he fails he may call us with more useful information. In the meantime I'll call Detective Besch and see if he's heard anything from Rico."

Paula nodded and went back to her office. Depression engulfed her as she contemplated Jodie's desperate situation. She wondered where they'd taken her and if she'd been hurt. Normally, Paula wasn't one to sit around when the shit hit the fan. She was a fighter. But today she felt helpless and was at a loss as to what they could do to find Jodie in the few precious hours that were left before she'd likely be killed.

15
Leverage

Jodie sat in the darkness wondering what her kidnapers were going to do with her. She was shocked they had taken her. It wasn't something she'd even thought was a remote possibility. She wondered how they'd discovered her deception so quickly. After thinking about it awhile she decided they had kidnaped her for one of two reasons. Either they had resigned themselves to the fact that Alliance Fabrications was history and wanted revenge, or they thought that they could use her as leverage to get the police and FBI to back off. Jodie didn't think the FBI or the police would back off, so that meant she would probably die soon, if she wasn't rescued or didn't figure out a way to escape.

She wriggled her wrist and was pleased to find a little play. If she worked at it she might be able to get free. Even if she did get free, however, she doubted it would do her any good since she'd heard them lock the van's door after they'd closed it. She sighed in utter despair. After a while she began to feel sick. It was hot and stuffy and difficult to breathe. She'd never suffered from claustrophobia before but that suddenly changed. Panic overcame her as she struggled to free herself, pulling and wriggling her hands and wrists as hard as she could. A jolt of pain from her wrist forced her to stop. She felt blood oozing out around the rope that bound her wrists.

She stopped to let the pain subside, then she worked the rope again. The blood was acting as a lubricant and it felt like her hands were gradually slipping free. Feeling a ray of hope for the first time, she worked the rope even harder, ignoring the pain and pungent smell of fresh blood. Finally, one hand slipped free. Had there not been a gag in her mouth she'd have let out a triumphant scream. Quickly she freed her other hand and then pulled the gag out of her mouth. Now her only problem was how to get out of a locked van.

In the darkness she felt along the floor and walls looking for some kind of lever or emergency exit door, but found nothing. She tried to lift the back gate but it wouldn't budge. If she couldn't get out of the van then her next strategy would be to surprise whoever came to get her. They would think she was tied up and wouldn't expect to be attacked the moment the door was opened. Such an attack wouldn't be a sure thing, of course. If there were more than one man she'd likely be overpowered, but if only one came to get her she felt she could probably overcome him simply because of the element of surprise. In the darkness she felt for the rope that had bound her. Once she'd found it she took a position near the back gate and waited.

It was difficult for Jodie to keep track of time while she was in captivity. It seemed like she'd been in there for hours, but she wasn't sure. Surely they would bring her food and water soon, unless they'd already decided she must die and wanted her to suffer as much as possible. Eventually she heard footsteps and prepared herself for the fight of her life. She listened intently. Was there one man or two? She couldn't tell for sure, but she thought it was but one. There was a click as the padlock was opened. Then the back door began to go up.

When it was up far enough, Jodie launched herself on the man and pushed him hard into the fender of the truck behind them. As they were falling she looped the rope around the man's neck and pulled it with all her might, trying to choke him. He grabbed the rope with his fingers and tried to pull it out of Jodie's grip, but she held it tightly. He twisted and turned, trying to knock her off his back. She felt a crushing jab to her stomach, knocking the breath out of her, but she was determined not to let go. Finally, the man gave up the fight and collapsed onto the floor. Jodie didn't think he was dead. At least she hoped he wasn't. She had no malice toward him even though he was a thug. She checked for a pulse and was relieved to feel it. After dragging the man behind a forklift where he wouldn't be seen, she scanned the warehouse for an exit.

Hearing voices coming, she quietly made her way toward the back of the warehouse where she could see a fire exit sign glowing intermittently. She prayed it was unlocked and not equipped with an alarm that would be tripped if the door opened. As she got to the door she heard shouting and figured her escape had been detected. Holding her breath, she pushed the door open and slipped out into the yard, closing the door behind her. Relieved that no alarm had sounded, Jodie looked around for a way to escape, but the yard was totally surrounded by a ten-foot chain-link fence with three strands of barbed wire above it. The only exit was through a driveway and parking lot on the north side of the building that led to the main entrance. There'd be guards that way, she was sure.

Frustrated, she searched for another way out. Her eyes fell on a van parked up against the fence behind the building. She wondered if it was operational or a piece of junk. It probably wouldn't have keys in it, but Jodie knew how to hot-wire a car. Her brother had taught her that skill when she'd lost the keys to her own car one time and urgently needed to use it. In fact, it was so easy it was several weeks before she got a new key made.

As she was making her way to the old car, the back door to the warehouse opened and a man stepped outside. Jodie quickly ducked behind the van and froze. Two other men followed the first into the yard and they all began searching for her. Jodie felt another stab of fear as she calculated what to do. A flash of light from the parking lot caught her attention. Suddenly an engine started up and a vehicle tore around the corner of the building and accelerated toward her. The three men stopped their search and watch the approaching vehicle.

As the vehicle approached Jodie found herself bathed in its front headlights. In the spotlight the three men saw her and started to go after her. She ran but the red Jeep Cherokee pulled up between her and her pursuers. The door opened.

"Jodie! Get in! Hurry!"

It was a familiar voice, so Jodie didn't hesitate. She jumped in and the Jeep took off, did a tight U-turn, wheels squealing, and headed back in the direction from which it had come nearly running down the pursuers. Jodie squinted at the man driving.

"Ricardo?"

He looked over and smiled at her. "Heard you were in trouble, so I came as fast as I could."

Jodie just stared at him in shock. She couldn't believe that he'd rescued her after she'd betrayed him. She felt ashamed.

As the Jeep headed for the main gate two men were attempting to close it. Ignoring them, Ricardo gunned the engine and crashed through the gates. Once on the main road he floored it until they made it into Grapevine where they were able to blend into traffic. Once Ricardo thought it was safe he pulled into a Holiday Inn and drove around the back, out of sight, and stopped to talk.

Jodie didn't know what to say. They just looked at each for a long moment then Jodie sighed. "I'm so sorry. I didn't plan to use you to get to your father."

"I know. When I first heard that you worked for Turner & Waters I thought I'd been set up, but when I thought about it, I realized you had just taken advantage of a fortuitous string of events. I'd have probably done the same thing if I'd have been in your shoes."

"So, why did you rescue me? I appreciate that you understand I was just doing my job, but there was no reason for you to stick your neck out for me."

"True. But I couldn't let my father kill you. Not when I could prevent it."

"Right. . . . Thank you. I knew you were a good person from the first day we met. Now I owe you my life," Jodie said sincerely. "But what are you going to do now? Your father doesn't strike me as the type who will be too forgiving."

"No. He'll never forgive me."

"But will he try to kill you?"

"He would if it weren't for my mother. That doesn't mean I'm home free. There will have to be punishment."

Jodie groaned. "You should come with me to the FBI. If you help them prosecute your father they'll put you into a witness protection program."

Ricardo shook his head. "No. I couldn't testify against my father and brothers."

Jodie understood Ricardo's dilemma. Nobody wanted to hurt their own family. She couldn't push him now, she thought, but eventually he'd have no choice. If he wanted to survive, he'd have to testify against them.

"You can stay at my place for a while. My boss has arranged for 24/7 security. That will give you time to decide what to do."

"No. You don't know the people you're up against. They're not going to let a little security cop stop them from getting their revenge. It's a matter of pride and reputation."

"So, what do you think your father's next move will be? Obviously, he's not going to play by the rules."

"No. He's never been one to worry about the rules. My guess is, now that he's been exposed, he'll disappear and set up shop somewhere else."

Jodie thought about that a moment. "What about the plant? He's just going to abandon his business?"

"The fabrication business is just a front. It doesn't make any money. In fact, it loses money. He uses it to provide a way to launder his money from all his illegal ventures."

"Seriously?"

He nodded. "Yes, you wouldn't believe the insane amount of money he makes trafficking in workers and drugs. Half the people who come across the border are mules for his drug inventory in addition to being a lucrative commodity themselves."

Jodie shook her head. "I'd heard a lot about that type of thing, but I never really appreciated how real it was."

Ricardo laughed. "Yeah, you got a nice dose of reality tonight, huh? How are you, by the way? Did they hurt you?"

"No. Just tossed me around like a sack of potatoes, but nobody beat me up or anything."

"You were lucky. I think they took it easy on you because they weren't sure what to do with you. I heard talk they were trying to get the FBI to back off in exchange for letting you go."

"Really? I doubt the FBI would go for that. It would be a bad precedent."

"Yes. That's why I came to get you. I knew they'd kill you the moment they figured out the feds wouldn't go along with their exchange."

"I better call Stan and tell him I'm okay. Would you drop me off at my office?"

"Sure," Ricardo said as he looked longingly into Jodie's eyes. Jodie leaned in and their lips met. They kissed long and hard until Jodie pushed him away.

"We can't do this now. Maybe when this mess is all over."

Ricardo sighed and then started the car. They drove to Highway 121 and took it to I-635. Soon they were closing in on North Dallas and the office building where Turner & Waters was located. Ricardo parked in front of Jodie's car. He got out and they kissed one more time before he left. When he was gone Jodie rushed into the building security office and asked the guard to escort her to her office. The guard was a little surprised by the request but acquiesced. She told him what had happened, so he checked and made sure nobody was waiting for her inside. When all was clear she went to her desk and picked up the telephone to call Stan.

"Stan?"

"Jodie? Where are you?"

"Back at the office. Ricardo rescued me."

"Oh, thank God! I've been so worried about you. The FBI is searching the city for you."

"That's why I called. You can tell them I'm fine."

"They'll want to talk to you."

"I know. I'll wait here for them."

"Are you sure it's safe? I'm sure they're pissed off that you've escaped."

"It's okay. I alerted security and I have a Glock in my bottom drawer. If anybody tries to mess with me, they'll regret it."

"You have a gun in your drawer?"

"Yeah. I had one in my car but the cowards grabbed me before I could get to it."

"All right. I'll call Agent Lot right now. I'm coming, too. I'll see you in twenty minutes."

Jodie hung up the phone and then opened her bottom drawer. She pulled out the Glock 17 and admired it. Once she checked and made sure it was loaded, she fell back into her chair, relaxed, and recalled the evening's events. Her mistake was not having her gun on her person. She vowed never to let that happen again.

There was a knock on the door. She grabbed the gun, stood up, and walked slowly down the hall to where she could get a look at who was knocking. It was Agent Lot, so she rushed over and let him in.

He looked down at her bloody wrists. "Jodie! Are you all right?"

"I am now. It's been a rather rough evening, though."

"Should I take you to the hospital? Those cuts look pretty deep."

Jodie shrugged. "I guess it might not hurt. I don't want to end up with a bunch of ugly scars."

"Okay, let's go. You can tell me what happened on the way."

They left and drove a few blocks to Medical City Hospital. While they waited for a doctor Jodie filled in Agent Lot and his partner on what had happened. Lot asked her if she could remember where she had been held and she gave him rough directions.

"You'll need to ride out there with us to make sure we raid the right warehouse. I'll get a SWAT team assembled while you're being patched up."

Jodie nodded as a nurse came to take her to an examining room. A few minutes later a doctor was examining her wounds.

"How did this happen?" the doctor asked.

Jodie explained how she'd been tied up and had no choice but to do what it took to get loose. The doctor grimaced at her explanation.

"Well, I'm going to have to call in a plastic surgeon. If we're not careful you'll have some pretty ugly scaring. These wounds are quite deep."

"Can you give me a temporary fix for now? I've got to show the FBI where the kidnapers held me."

The doctor frowned. "I suppose, but you better go visit the plastic surgeon in the morning. This isn't something you should put off. We'll clean it up and make sure it doesn't get infected. Then we can put a temporary bandage on it that will do until morning."

Jodie smiled. "Thanks, Doc."

When they finished bandaging her up, Jodie left with Agent Lot and they headed toward Grapevine. Jodie was feeling tired so she closed her eyes.

"I'll get you home just as soon as I can," Agent Lot promised her. He was obviously very concerned about her.

"So, do you have any idea where Ricardo is?"

"No, he's hiding from his family. He didn't say where. He won't help you find them, though. I tried to convince him to, but you can understand why he wouldn't."

"Sure, but if we find him he'll have no choice."

Jodie sighed. "If you do, promise me you won't hurt him. He didn't have anything to do with his family's business."

"It will be up to him, but we will certainly give him every opportunity to cooperate."

They backtracked the route Ricardo had taken after he rescued Jodie. When they rounded a bend in the road Jodie recognized the warehouse where she'd been held.

"There it is!" she exclaimed.

Agent Lot got on his phone and advised his team that they'd identified the location. They all stopped a few blocks away to assess the situation. Fear stabbed at Jodie as she remembered being bound, gagged, and dragged into the warehouse. A shiver went down her spine.

Agents in SWAT gear began pouring out of big vans, quickly surrounding the building. Then the convoy proceeded up to the entrance and stopped in front of the unmanned gate. Agent Lot got out and went to the chain that secured the gate. He motioned to one of his men, and he came over with a thirty-inch bolt cutter. The chain was cut quickly and the vehicles proceeded into the almost empty parking lot. Soon the agents were poised to enter the building and when Agent Lot gave the signal, they swarmed inside.

As Jodie expected, the warehouse was empty. She could imagine the chaos after she'd made her escape. They must have known time was short for an evacuation of the premises. Inside she noticed all the trucks had gone and the place was deserted. Agent Lot walked up to her.

"How many vehicles were in here when you escaped?" he asked.

"Dozens. The warehouse was full of them."

"What kind of trucks were they?"

"Cargo vans and medium-size delivery trucks. The one they put me in was a van, and I memorized the license plate. It was XPT 429."

"Jeez. I can't believe you had the presence of mind to remember a license plate number," Agent Lot said.

"It was an easy license to remember. XPT is the abbreviation I use for *expert witness*. And 4/29 is my mother's birthday."

Agent Lot shook his head. "Okay. Anything that works. I'll get an APB out on that license number and maybe we'll get lucky."

"So, did you find anything inside?" Jodie asked.

"Yes and no. This warehouse was leased by another company out of Kansas—a company unrelated to Alliance Fabrications. Apparently the lease ran out and the owner was getting ready to renovate the property and then put it up for sale. From what we can find out your kidnapers moved in a few weeks ago just like they owned the place. Since the owner was out of state nobody knew they were squatters."

"That's pretty smart. Running your operation out of other people's property so your location can't be traced."

"Perhaps," Agent Lot agreed, "but you'd have to be ready to move on a moment's notice."

"There must be a Realtor or leasing agent involved. I bet the cartel pays them for tips on abandoned properties."

"Could be," Agent Lot said. "I'll have someone look into that possibility."

As they were talking Agent Lot's phone rang. He answered it immediately and talked at length with someone. He grimaced and hung up the phone. "That was Rico. Alliance Fabrications is on fire. Eleven workers including some of your clients were locked inside a storage room so they'd burn to death. Fortunately Rico was able to free them and get them out of the building before they were hurt seriously. It looks like a total loss. I'm afraid Alliance Fabrications is history."

Jodie looked at Agent Lot in dismay. "What about Melendez and the rest of the family?"

"They've fled, apparently. In the excitement of the fire, our surveillance team lost them."

Jodie was shaken. In just a few hours their lawsuit had become moot and they were back to square one in their pursuit of justice for the Alvarez family. She'd underestimated Icaro Melendez and his gang of thugs this round, but that wouldn't happen again. They'd taken her hostage and intended to kill her. Now they'd made it personal! She'd take them down, no matter what it took!

16
A New Strategy

Hearing Jodie's voice was so unexpected Stan nearly dropped the phone. He'd been so distraught over Jodie's abduction that he could hardly think. Now that she had miraculously escaped and he knew she was safe he began to think of all the ramifications of the day's events. Apparently Icaro Melendez had made a decision that it was too risky to hang around and hope the Dallas police and the FBI couldn't make a case against him and Alliance Fabrications. He wondered what had become of the workers at the plant, so he called Pandora Alvarez to see what she knew.

"An entire convoy of vans and trucks came last night and took everyone away. Luckily we got a tip they were coming, so we were able to get away to a safe place."

"It sounds like the warehouse where they kept Jodie last night is where they kept their vehicles for smuggling in undocumented workers. When Jodie was rescued they must have gone straight to the plant."

"Probably."

"Any idea where they went?" Stan asked.

"No. Sorry. When they summon you they don't give you any information. They expect you to blindly follow them."

"Hmm. Was anybody injured in the fire?"

"Not that I heard about."

"I am not sure where this leaves us as far as the lawsuit. We have service on Alliance Fabrications, but with the plant destroyed and without an active business operation, getting a judgment wouldn't do us a lot of good. The only hope is that the building was insured in which case we might be able to garnish the insurance company for the insurance proceeds. Even if there was insurance there may be a lender who is an additional insured and would have priority over us. There's also the possibility the insurance carrier won't pay the claim since it looks like it was a case of arson."

"Isn't there anything we can do?"

"Actually, with what's happened, our case is stronger than it's ever been. Running makes it pretty obvious that Melendez and Alliance were guilty of everything we accused them of and now we can add kidnaping and arson to their list of offenses. What we need to do now is track Melendez down and find Alliance's new operating location. I'm sure the FBI and the Dallas police will put considerable effort into doing just that. Fortunately, Jodie was able to get at least one of the license plate numbers of the transport vehicles. If that truck is spotted the others should be close by."

"What should we do now? We don't have jobs."

Stan grimaced. "I don't know. I'll have to talk to Agent Lot and the representative from the Department of Labor."

Stan promised he'd talk to Agent Lot right away and get back with her. After he hung up Paula walked into his office. She had some news on Maureen's case.

"Bart did some research on Doc Mellon. Apparently he's a well-known loan shark and has a reputation for being intolerant of anyone who can't pay their debts in a timely manner. Bart says there have been several murder investigations that have led investigators to Doc Mellon but they've never been able to pin anything on him. Apparently he contracts out all his dirty work, so he can keep his hands clean. He has a list of competent, well-disciplined enforcers that he hires out as needed. There's never any paperwork or communication that can be traced back to Mellon."

"Did he give you any info on these enforcers?" Stan asked.

"Yes. I've got a list of them with background info and current addresses."

"That could be rather dangerous work checking into that group," Stan noted. "You better farm that out to a PI. I don't want you ending up getting kidnaped like Jodie."

"Okay, I'll find someone to handle that. Either way just being able to talk about Doc Mellon and his enforcers should go a long way to establishing reasonable doubt."

"Absolutely. What about the first murder? Any leads?"

Paula sighed deeply. "You know, that's what sucks about this case. I have to prove Maureen innocent of two murders—not to mention one of them happened nearly five years ago."

Paula knew the judge wouldn't allow any mention of the first murder during the trial since Maureen hadn't been convicted, but she wasn't so naive as to think the jurors wouldn't know about the first murder and hold it against her.

Stan smiled sympathetically. "Yes, that does make your job doubly difficult. Is there anything I can do to help you?"

"Not right now, but I'm sure there will be things that come up that I'll need you to sink your teeth into. You understand business and finance better than me and this case is more about money than anything else."

Stan wondered how he'd have time to do much for Paula with the Alvarez mess and Wolf probate already on his plate, but he didn't want to disappoint Paula. She'd stepped up when Stan was distracted by his son's disappearance and carried the firm for over a year after the funeral when Stan was too depressed to work. "Sure," he said hesitantly. "I'll look into it."

Paula left when the phone rang and Stan indicated it was Detective Besch on the line. "Detective. I guess you heard the good news."

"Yes, that was very fortunate that Ricardo came to the rescue. You don't know where we could find him, do you?"

"No. Apparently he's lying low. He doesn't want any part of your investigation. He's really in a bad spot."

"That's exactly right. If he doesn't help us find his father and convict him of Romildo's murder, then he's likely to go down with him, for obstruction of justice if nothing else."

"Jodie thinks he'll come around if you give him time."

"I've got another problem I need your help with," Besch said.

"What's that?"

"It's Rico. He's disappeared."

Stan thought about that a second. "Well, isn't that to be expected? I'm sure he went along with the rest of the workers when they were relocated."

"Yes, but he should have checked in by now, particularly when there's been a relocation. I'm afraid someone might have seen him report the fire or rescue the trapped workers. They may have put two and two together."

"Hmm. Or maybe Melendez figured out there was a mole in his organization but couldn't figure out who it was. If that's it, he may be keeping everyone incommunicado for a while."

"That's true. But Rico is their newest worker and I would think he'd be the most likely candidate to be the mole."

"I don't think so," Stan said. "There's no reason for them to believe that. I think the blame is going to fall on the Alvarez family and Turner & Waters. That's why Jodie was taken and they left a message in my mailbox."

"I hope you're right. But I'd like to interview the Alvarez family to see if they know anything."

"I don't think they do, but feel free to talk to them. I haven't had time to quiz them in depth about it. It's possible they may know something."

Stan thought about Melendez and his sudden evacuation from the Alliance plant. It was done so quickly and efficiently he thought it must have been planned in advance. Now that Stan thought about it, it made sense to have a contingency plan in the works. But that would mean he must have had a place to go. He thought back to his last dealings with a Mexican drug cartel. They'd set up money laundering operations all over the Southwest. All he'd had to do was follow the money. He laughed, thinking about the gangster movies he'd seen where the advice always given was "follow the money."

In this case it made even more sense, because if he was able to follow the money, not only would he find Melendez, but he might be able to seize some of cash for the Alvarez family. He'd told Jodie to take a few days off, but she had insisted on coming right back to work, so he summoned her into his office. She looked a bit tired and weak, which he thought was understandable.

"What's up?" she asked.

"Have you heard from Ricardo?"

She shook her head. "No. I don't expect to, actually. Not that he doesn't want to talk to me, but he knows I'll try to talk him into turning himself in and cooperating with the police and the FBI."

"You're probably right. In the meantime, I've got an idea how we can find Melendez."

Jodie perked up. "Really? How?"

"There were previous audits of Alliance by the Department of Labor and the IRS. I want you to go through those audits and find me a list of all of Alliance's customers and vendors. I'm pretty sure Alliance's new address will be on one of those lists."

Jodie smiled. "That's right. They would have done business with each other in the past."

"Maybe, but for sure they were laundering their money through the same businesses."

"So, we're looking for a money laundering operation?"

"Yes. And, when we find it, we'll file a garnishment action against them alleging that they owe money to the Alvarez family."

Jodie laughed. "You must have a death wish."

"Well, if I'm going to have to pay for a bodyguard and 24/7 home protection, I might as well get my money's worth."

Jodie sighed. She loved Stan's idea but it scared her. Having just narrowly escaped death, she wasn't anxious to ever feel that kind of terror again. She swallowed hard.

Stan saw the fear on her face. "Listen. Why don't you help Paula on the Thompson case. You've got a conflict with your relationship with Ricardo and I need to hire a new PI anyway. He and I can handle Melendez."

Jodie stiffened. "No. I want to bring that asshole down. Don't worry about me, I'll be fine."

"You sure?" Stan pressed.

"Absolutely. I'll call Agent Lot and get access to the audits right away."

"Good. I'm working on a default judgment now. Just as soon as Alliance blows its answer date, I'll run down to court and get a judgment entered."

"All right. I'll go call Agent Lot."

Stan watched her leave and wondered if he was doing the right thing. Many . . . no, . . . most lawyers would have given up on a case like this once the defendant ceased to exist. Most would cut their losses and move on. That was probably what Melendez was counting on. But Stan wasn't like most lawyers. He had trouble accepting defeat, particularly when he believed in his case and knew a defendant had assets and could afford to pay for their transgressions. This was not particularly good from a business standpoint, particularly when you were handling a case on a contingency basis.

Stan thought about Paula and what she'd gone through to get paid on the Thompson case. She'd confessed to him that she'd broken her marriage vows to get the final inspections done quickly. He knew if she hadn't done that, there wouldn't have been paychecks for anybody that week. He'd eventually get paid for his ad litem work, but the probate courts usually made attorney's wait until the end of the case to get paid. It would likely be six months before the firm saw a dime.

He knew the smart thing to do would be to call the Alvarez family in and tell them to forget about Alliance Fabrications and Icaro Melendez. Just tell them there was nothing that could be done. They would understand and thank them for a valiant effort, particularly Jodie for putting her life on the line for them. Then they'd go on with their lives. Yes, that would be the prudent thing to do, . . . but where would be the justice in that?

Stan knew he needed to hire a private investigator but he was reluctant to do so. Two of his private investigators in the past had been killed working on his hellish cases. Would it be right to put another investigator in jeopardy? Working on either of his current cases would be extremely dangerous. Of course, he would fully disclose to any prospective investigator the risks involved and certainly wouldn't pressure him into taking the job. But he knew from experience no PI worth his salt would turn down a paying job just because it was dangerous. Danger came with the occupation.

Another problem was money. The firm was low on cash and didn't have a lot of resources to be spending on private investigators. He finally decided he had no choice but to hire an investigator for Paula to look into Doc Mellon and his gang. They were Paula's best shot at getting Maureen Thompson off and he certainly didn't want Paula to be at risk snooping around their organization. But he'd have to handle the Melendez investigation himself. Fortunately he would be getting some help from Detective Besch and the FBI, although he wasn't sure how much now that Melendez had disappeared.

While Stan was thinking Maria buzzed him to advise him that Tom Hooper was on the line. Stan picked the phone anxiously.

"Tom. You made it over there."

"Yes, I got here yesterday."

"What did you find out?"

"I found Mina Ishihara quite easily, but I haven't had any luck with Yuzie Gucci."

"Really? What's the problem?"

"She's moved from where she used to live and I can't find her in the telephone book."

"So, what did Mina have to say?"

"She has children but they were all born years after Herb broke up with her."

"Damn!" Stan exclaimed. "I knew this would be too easy. So, what are you going to do now?"

"Well. Stu is at the courthouse going through old marriage and property records and Walt is at the utility company seeing if he can get an old address."

"All right. Well, keep me posted."

"I will, but could you wire us another $500? We've run out of expense money."

Stan sighed. "I told you $500 was all I'd advance."

"I know, but if I remember correctly she had a sister on Maui. If we can find her, she'll know where her sister is. It cost money to get to Maui and I've already spent the $500 you sent me."

Stan stifled a profanity. "All right, but this is it. Don't even bother to ask for more money."

"I won't. I promise," Tom said gleefully.

Stan hung up the phone feeling less than optimistic that Tom would come through for him. He dreaded the thought of having to hire a real PI to find Yuzie Gucci. That would be very expensive. After he'd dropped by Tom Thumb which was a Western Union agent and sent Tom his money, he went home to check on Rebekah.

The house was quiet. So quiet, he thought Rebekah must be asleep. He went into the bedroom but nobody was there. Continuing on into the bathroom he heard water running, saw the shower was on but didn't see Rebekah. Upon closer scrutiny he found her sitting on the floor of the shower propped up against the wall.

"Rebekah! What happened?" he said as he rushed inside, turned off the water and knelt down beside her.

"I fell. I don't know what happened. I just felt dizzy and then fainted, I guess. I haven't had the strength to get up."

"You didn't break anything, did you?"

"No. I don't think so."

Stan helped her up and got her out of the shower. After finding her a robe he made her lie down on the bed so he could examine her.

"Do you feel any pain?"

"No. I'm just so tired."

"Well, you should take a nap. I don't have to go back to the office. I'll stay with you. Perhaps I should take you to the doctor."

"No! No doctors. I'll be fine."

Stan shook his head. He knew arguing with her would be futile. As she slept he went upstairs and got one of her nursing books and started browsing through it. Then he thought of one of Rebekah's nursing friends, Terry Morris. Maybe she could help him out. It was 3:30 p.m. so he figured she'd just be getting home from the morning shift.

"Terry?"

"Yes. Who is this?"

"Stan. Stan Turner."

There was a moment of silence. "What's wrong? Is Rebekah okay?"

"No. That's why I'm calling. She's been having problems of late and you know how she is about going to doctors."

She sighed. "Yes. What are we going to do with that girl?"

"I don't know."

"So, what are her symptoms?" Terry asked.

Stan explained all her symptoms and told her about the trips to the emergency ward and her most recent fainting spell.

"Those symptoms are common to a lot of different diseases. We need to get her to an internist and have a complete physical exam done."

"Good luck with that."

"Let me come over and maybe between the two of us we can convince her."

"That would be great. She's asleep now but she'll probably be awake by the time you get here. If not, I'll wake her."

An hour later Stan answered the door and welcomed Terry into the living room. Terry and Rebekah had worked together in the ER in McKinney and had been friends for over ten years. Terry was divorced and had led a difficult life as a single mother with two kids. She made a decent living as a nurse, but with no child support, the expense of day care, and a son with a learning disability, there was never enough money to pay all the bills. In fact, Stan had put her through bankruptcy right after her divorce to relieve her of the considerable debt her ex-husband had incurred and failed to pay even though the divorce decree ordered him to.

Although Rebekah was angry that Stan had called Terry, Stan knew she wouldn't be rude to her and he was right.

"You didn't need to come over here," Rebekah said, shaking her head.

"I heard you fell in the shower?" Terry said. "I had to come over and make sure you were all right."

"I'm fine. Stan shouldn't have called you."

"I'd have kicked his ass had he not called me," Terry said playfully.

"Something is wrong with you," Stan said, "and we need to figure out what it is."

"That's right," Terry agreed. "I know a doctor over at Baylor who heads up a team of doctors which include specialists in all areas of medicine. What they do is give you a complete physical and do a battery of tests with the results being passed around to everyone in the team. Then they get together and figure out what's going on. It saves you seeing ten different doctors and then not necessarily figuring out what is wrong with you."

Rebekah frowned. "There's nothing wrong with me. You both are overreacting."

"Overreacting!" Stan exclaimed. "You've passed out several times, your left side went numb, you've had no energy, and now you've fallen in the shower. There is something wrong with you and we need to find out what it is."

"Stan is right," Terry said. "At least go see your internist. You know you should do that every few years no matter what."

Rebekah sighed. "Okay. I'll see Dr. Sanders, but he's not going to find anything wrong with me."

"Well. I hope you're right, but I'll sleep better once he's given you a clean bill of health," Terry said.

With that small concession Stan left Rebekah and Terry to catch up. He really liked Terry's suggestion that Rebekah go to the Baylor diagnostic team and wished she'd gone for the idea. It made him angry and frustrated that she so stubbornly refused to listen to reason, but she'd always been that way and he'd learned to live with it over the years. But now it was different; her health was at stake and her irrational behavior could result in her disability or death. He just couldn't sit back and watch her condition deteriorate without doing something. Such a course of conduct was unthinkable and, whether she liked it or not, he wouldn't allow it.

17
Loan Shark

Paula was having difficulty concentrating on her murder case with so much drama going on with Jodie and Rebekah. As concerned as she was for both of them she had to focus on Maureen Thompson. Time wouldn't stand still. The court had set a trial date for June 14, 1995 and it was already the middle of April. Although she had identified several persons with strong motives to kill Rodney Thompson, that alone wouldn't be enough to create reasonable doubt. She had to find evidence of opportunity and ill will. To find this, if it existed, would require a lot of hard work.

Rodney's friendship with Doc Mellon seemed to be her most promising option, but gathering evidence against a high-profile, ex-football star, and known loan shark would be dangerous business. Bart had insisted she let him handle Doc Mellon, but that wasn't really feasible as Bart had his own work to do at the DA's office. When Bart came home that night she asked him about it.

"So, have you dug up anything on Doc Mellon?"

"Not yet. His businesses appear, on the surface, to be legal and there haven't been any formal complaints against him."

"I thought he was a loan shark?"

"Not in the traditional sense. He owns a string of payday loan companies and pawnshops all over Texas. Mostly small loans—less than a thousand dollars. He has a pretty sharp attorney who does the loan documents. On the surface they look quite legal with no more than the 10 to18 percent maximum interest allowed by law. But when you analyze them you can see that he is actually charging over 1000 percent interest. The extra interest comes from loan acquisition fees, late charges, service fees—you name it."

"If it is so obvious what he is doing, how does he get away with it?" Paula asked.

"His customers could file a complaint or sue him for usury, if they dared," Bart replied.

"I see. So, I don't imagine he sues his customers if they don't pay timely?"

Bart laughed. "No. He gets a postdated check and then threatens to criminally prosecute them if the check bounces. It's not legal, but nobody has ever filed a complaint against him for it."

"I wonder if anyone has ever died because they didn't pay a loan back."

Bart shrugged. "Not over a small payday loan, but Mellon's loan to Thompson Construction obviously was in a different class."

"I've read the note," Paula said. "It's got an interest rate of 18 percent, but the kicker is Thompson had to pay a $5,000 per week consulting fee to one of Doc's friends. That made the effective interest rate on the loan 42 percent."

"That's pretty steep but I've heard of worse."

"Of course, it had a ninety-day term and if it wasn't paid timely, it accrued a $100 a day penalty which bumped the effective interest rate to almost 60 percent."

"I wonder what the balance on the loan was on the day Rodney was murdered?"

"I don't know, but I suspect it was nearly half a million."

Paula continued to pick Bart's brain about Doc Mellon and get his advice on how to investigate him without riling him. She finally decided she needed to find some of his victims. They presumably would be willing to provide information as long as they were guaranteed anonymity. To do that she'd research all the lawsuits and Better Business Bureau and Texas Attorney General complaints filed by or against Doc Mellon or his companies, if there were any. If that didn't work, she'd have to put Mellon or some of his underlings under surveillance to find out who they were leaning on.

William Manchee

That afternoon she contacted the Better Business Bureau for each city where Mellon's companies did business and asked if there were any complaints against them. Unfortunately there weren't any active complaints but there were five that had been resolved. Paula asked them if they'd fax her copies of these complaints. They said they would.

After calling the consumer division of the secretary of state's office and finding no disputes, Paula drove to the district clerk's office to search for lawsuits. In Dallas she found two pending lawsuits involving the Clock or his companies and three that had been settled and dismissed. She spent the rest of the afternoon reviewing the trial court's files on each case and making notes. As she drove back to the office, she was pleased; her list of enemies was growing and she still had half a dozen other counties to check on if need be.

Back at the office Paula found the fax from the Better Business Bureau on her desk. There had been complaints about collectors threatening criminal prosecution and wage garnishment, both of which were illegal under Texas law. Each file had a notation of having been resolved. Paula decided to contact each of the complainants. The first two weren't home, so she left messages. The third and fourth refused to talk to her. Finally she hit pay dirt on the last one. Her name was Bessie Burns.

"Mrs. Burns. This is Paula Waters. I'm an attorney and I noticed you filed a complaint against Doc's Payday Loans a few months back."

"Yeah. That was a misunderstanding. They came out and we got the matter resolved."

"How was it resolved?"

"Who did you say you were again?"

"I'm Paula Waters. I'm an attorney for Maureen Thompson and I promise you I won't tell anyone what you tell me. I'm just trying to gather information about Doc's Payday Loans."

"So, what does it matter to you?"

173

"Well, I'll be honest with you. I'm defending a woman accused of murder. I'm certain she didn't do it, so I'm trying to find out who did."

"Oh, I don't want to get involved in any of that."

"I understand. Like I said, I'll keep anything you tell me confidential. I'm just trying to find out if your complaint was legitimate. Did someone really threaten you with garnishment and criminal prosecution?"

"Yes, I've got a letter right here threatening to turn over my check to the DA for prosecution. That's why I filed a complaint with the Better Business Bureau."

"So, how was the matter resolved?"

"The bastards told me if I didn't withdraw the complaint and pay what was owed, I would likely be spending the next few weeks in the hospital."

"Seriously. That's what they told you?"

"That's what someone told me. They called late at night and didn't identify themselves, but I'm not stupid. I only filed one complaint with the Better Business Bureau."

"Did you call the police or the telephone company?"

"No. I'm not crazy. If I complained to anyone about the call I'd probably end up dead."

"Okay. I promise I won't tell anyone what you've told me. You've helped me a lot. I know now I'm on the right track. Thanks a lot."

"No problem. I hope you get your client off and bury Doc Mellon in the process!"

"Oh. One last question," Paula said. "How did you get the money to pay off the debt?" Paula asked.

"I sold my car and got a bus pass," Bessie replied bitterly.

"Oh, my God," Paula gasped. "I'm so sorry."

Paula hung up feeling shocked and angry. She had a strong gut feeling Doc Mellon had something to do with Rodney Thompson's murder. If his people would threaten to beat up a

174

helpless woman and end up forcing her to sell her car to pay them, they were capable of anything. Unfortunately she was no closer to proving Doc Mellon was responsible for Rodney Thompson's murder than when she started. But at least she knew she was on the right track and now it was just a matter of time and hard work to discover the truth.

Before she went home, Paula started reading through some of the lawsuits. One of them was a suit for breach of partnership. Apparently Doc the Clock Enterprises had entered into a partnership with "Dancing Dave" Reynolds, another football player with a payday store location in Waco. Dancing Dave was the plaintiff and he claimed that Doc had promised him an exclusive location in Waco, but when his occupancy permit was denied on the building he'd leased for the operation, Doc wrongfully terminated the partnership and signed a new partnership with a third party. The suit asked for injunctive relief, specific performance, or in lieu of specific performance, damages of $750,000 for loss of expected profits from the operation for the first three years, and attorney's fees.

Paula liked the looks of this suit as Dave Reynolds wasn't somebody Doc Mellon could push around. If she could get him to open up, she might learn a lot from Reynolds. She pondered the question of how to contact him. He wasn't someone you could just call up on the telephone. He had people who managed his affairs and insulated him from the public. That night when she got home, she updated Bart on her day's activities and asked him if he had any ideas.

"I'd call his civil attorney and broach the subject with him. You're going to have to give Reynolds some incentive to help. He's not likely to open up to you just for spite."

"Why not? Judging from the tone of the lawsuit, I think he probably pretty much hates Doc right now."

"True. But Doc has a reputation for violence and he doesn't want to provoke an all-out war."

"Well, I just need information. There's no need for Doc to know anything about it."

"Be sure and tell him that, but you'll still need an angle—some kind of incentive to get him talking."

"How about putting Doc away in the slammer for the rest of his life. Don't you think that would be sufficient incentive?"

"You can't promise that," Bart replied. "The DA won't touch a case against him without rock-solid evidence and you'll never be able to get that."

"I know," Paula said thoughtfully. "Thank you, honey. I think I've got my strategy figured out."

"So, what are you going to do?"

"Well, I may not be able to get the rock-solid evidence necessary to put Doc away, but Reynolds might be able to do it."

Bart smiled. "Now that's an angle. I like it."

The next day Paula put in a call to Dave Reynolds's attorney. She explained that she'd discovered their lawsuit against Doc Mellon and thought maybe they could help each other out. She didn't want to explain too much of her idea to the attorney for fear he wouldn't pass it on to his client or would do a lousy job explaining it. She knew attorneys were often overprotective, arrogant, and controlling. She just had to tell him enough that he'd be obligated to tell his client about it. The attorney was skeptical at first but finally agreed to pass on the information to his client. He said it might take a few days to get back to her as Dancing Dave was a busy man. Paula thanked him and hung up.

Paula got up and went into the break room to get another cup of coffee. Stan was there doing the same thing.

"Great minds think alike?" Paula joked.

Stan looked up. "Right. Or, we could be addicted to caffeine."

Paula laughed. "That's probably more likely."

"So, how's the case going?"

"Slow. I may need to go ahead and hire an investigator for some surveillance work."

"Sure. Whatever you need."

Paula filled Stan in on her investigation of Doc Mellon and her need for some inside information.

"Okay. You can call Jake Weston. He'll arrange whatever you require. I wonder if the police considered Mellon a suspect before they latched on to Maureen?" Stan mused.

"I don't know. I'll ask Bart."

"Yeah, you better. He may have an alibi."

"He probably does," Paula replied. "But he wouldn't have done it himself, anyway. He's got muscle for that. In fact, that's one of the things I need to find out—who handles his dirty work."

"Well, let me know if I can help in any way."

"I've got it covered for now. I think you've got your hands full with Rebekah and Jodie. I'll try to leave you alone."

Stan nodded. "You're right about that. Rebekah's got me totally frustrated. She won't acknowledge that something's wrong with her. Consequently, she's totally uncooperative and somewhat belligerent when it comes to dealing with the problem. And Jodie is like a runaway freight train. There's nothing stopping that girl no matter how dangerous it gets. I worry about her every minute she's out of my sight."

"Well, you've known her since she was a teenager. She's like another daughter to you. I can see that now. I used to think you two had something going on between you, but now I realize you love her like a daughter."

Stan nodded. "I've got to get back to work. Say hi to Jake for me."

Paula said she would and went back to her office. She put her coffee down, picked up the telephone, and called Jake Weston. His secretary put her through and she explained what she wanted. He agreed to put a man on Doc Mellon for a few days and do some research into his entourage. Paula hung up the telephone and wondered if all of this was a waste of time. Money was tight and Jake Weston's services didn't come cheap. She sighed and then put the thought out of her mind. She had no choice. Mellon was her best shot at creating reasonable doubt and she certainly didn't have time to do surveillance work herself.

That night they went to Campisi's on Lovers Lane for dinner. They ordered a large pepperoni pizza and some wine. While they were waiting for their order Paula asked Bart if the police had looked at Doc Mellon as a suspect in Rodney Thompson's murder. It wasn't proper for her to be asking for inside information, but she didn't consider it to be that kind of a request. She was entitled to any evidence, favorable or unfavorable, that the police dug up.

"Sure, he was on the short list, but he was out of town when the murder took place."

"What about his employees? He'd have hired someone else for a job like this."

"No. They didn't look into his employees. There was no evidence to justify that."

"So, they checked his alibi and that was it?"

"As far as I know," Bart replied. "Why do you ask? Have you found some evidence that he was involved?"

"No. Nothing solid, but I know he threatens defenseless women with bodily harm if they don't pay back their piddly payday loans, so you can imagine what he'd do to someone who stiffed him for a quarter million dollars."

Bart nodded. "You want me to look into some of his associates?"

"No. You've helped enough and I don't want to get you in trouble. I've got Jake Weston over at Excel Security looking into it."

"He's a good man."

After they got home Paula took a long bath and thought about Doc Mellon. She wondered why he'd blown an NFL career for a measly $10,000. She guessed for a teenager from the ghetto it must have seemed like a lot of money at the time. From what she had learned he truly was an evil person, someone without a conscience. She knew that was usually the result of serious problems during childhood and wondered what Mellon's story was.

18
Stakeout

Jodie was awakened by the telephone ringing. She had fallen asleep on her sofa while she was watching the ten o'clock news. She wondered who was calling her at such a late hour, praying it wasn't more bad news.

"Jodie?"

"Yes."

"This is Ricardo."

"Oh, thank God," she gasped. "I'm so glad you called. I was worried about you."

"I'm okay," he said. "Don't ask me where I am. Your phones are probably tapped."

Jodie held out the phone and looked at it warily. She put it back to her ear. "Do you really think so?"

"Yes. The people my father does business with are very sophisticated. They must keep up with the latest technology to stay one step ahead of the FBI and the DEA. A phone tap is nothing to them."

"Can they trace your call? Maybe you shouldn't be talking to me."

"No. They'd need more than a phone tap to do that, but you're right, I shouldn't stay on the line too long, just in case."

"Well, I'm glad you're okay. I'll sleep better tonight knowing you're safe. I owe you my life."

"That's right and don't you forget it," he said teasingly.

"Don't worry. I won't. Be safe."

Jodie hung up, making a mental note to have the firm's new PI come in and sweep her line for bugs. It infuriated her to think her phone might be tapped. She needed to be able to talk to Ricardo if she was going to convince him to talk to the FBI, but if her phone was bugged that could never happen.

Feeling a bit uplifted by Ricardo's call, she went into the bathroom and turned on the shower. The hot water pouring over her body began to relax her tight muscles. She lingered, finally beginning to feel safe for the first time in several days. When she was done she examined the plastic surgeons work on her wrists. She'd gone to see him the next morning as directed, not wanting to risk permanent scaring. He'd done a miraculous job and she could barely see where the ropes had cut so deeply into her skin. Satisfied they would heal, she wrapped her wrists again as he had directed her to do and went to bed.

Being incredibly exhausted, she immediately fell asleep. She slept soundly for most of the night, but in the early morning hours began to dream. She saw Ricardo lying on a bed in a nondescript motel room. He was asleep on top of the covers, shirtless but still wearing his jeans. Suddenly there was pounding on the door and screams of thugs demanding to be let in. Ricardo sat up and looked worriedly toward the door just in time to see it burst open. Two men bolted in, pointing their revolvers at Ricardo's bare chest.

Jodie woke up with a start. She sat up breathing heavily, tears running down her checks, and her heart racing. Feeling relief that it had only been a bad dream, she looked at the clock radio which indicated it was 5:03 a.m. Falling back on the bed, she tried to go back to sleep but to no avail. Finally she got up, got dressed, and went to the office. At 8:00 a.m. she called Agent Lot.

"How are you feeling?" he asked.

"Just incredibly tired. I didn't sleep well last night."

She told him about Ricardo's telephone call.

"He didn't tell you where he was?"

"No. He just wanted me to know he was safe."

"He's really got a thing for you, hasn't he?" Agent Lot said.

"Obviously, since he risked his life to save me."

"How do you feel about that?"

"I think it's sweet. He's a great guy and I don't want to see him get hurt. It's not his fault who his father is."

"So, what can I do for you?"

She told him Stan's theory and that he wanted her to go through the audit materials so she could put together a vendor and client list and possibly find Melendez through one of them.

"Well, that's an interesting approach. I'll assign someone to help you with it," Agent Lot said. "We have resources for checking on that kind of thing that, I'm sure, you and Stan wouldn't have."

"That's true. We'd have to do it the old-fashioned way . . . lots of phone calls and visits to each of the vendors."

"You'll still end up doing some of that, but we can probably eliminate a good number of the vendors and clients by running them through our databases."

"Any help would be greatly appreciated," Jodie acknowledged.

That afternoon she went to FBI headquarters and met with Agent Brenda Thomas who had been assigned to help her sort through the audit materials and come up with a vendor and client list. It took most of the afternoon to complete the lists. When they were done Brenda got on the computer and ran the names through the FBI databases. Of the forty-seven vendors, thirty-two were eliminated as being legitimate enterprises. That left fifteen to be checked out. As far as the customers went, there were ninety-four total and fifty-seven of them were eliminated by one criteria or another. That left twenty-seven that needed further investigation.

"How do you think we should approach this?" Jodie said.

"Well, we have surveillance photos of Icaro Melendez, his two sons, and the supervisors. I suggest we start with businesses that have done the most business with Alliance and stake them out. The first time we spot one of them we'll know we're at the right place."

"Unless they've scattered and aren't at just one location."

"That's possible, but either way if we find one of them, we'll be on the right track."

Jodie didn't like Brenda's idea as it seemed like it would take forever, but she couldn't think of a better plan, so she didn't say anything to sidetrack it.

"We should split up so we can cover more ground."

"That's not a bad idea," Brenda agreed. "Most of the vendors are in central Texas so we can work the same general areas. I think half a day surveillance per location will be enough. If we don't see anybody in that time frame they're probably not there."

"How about three hours—just cover the rush hours. That way we can cover all the vendors in seven days."

Brenda looked at Jodie. "You have no patience, girl. It's going to take time to find Melendez."

"In the meantime he might find Ricardo and kill him."

"All right. Three hours per location—six to nine, eleven to two, and four to seven. That will give us time in between to switch locations."

Jodie nodded. Brenda wrote down three names and addresses on a scratch pad and handed the sheet to Jodie.

"I'll call you if I see anybody or, if not, at the end of each shift."

"Sounds good," Brenda said. "Get a good night's sleep and bring plenty of food and water tomorrow. Sometimes it's hard to stay awake and it can get hot in your car if you're sitting in the sun."

Jodie wondered if a good night's sleep was possible. It had been a while since she'd had one. "Don't worry. I'll have my bodyguard with me. Stan won't let me go anywhere without him."

That night Jodie stayed up late hoping Ricardo would call again, but he didn't. That made it almost impossible for her to sleep. When she did get to sleep she had the same dream of thugs breaking into Ricardo's room and shooting him. If it wasn't a dream about Ricardo it was the nightmarish memory of being tied up and locked in the delivery van. When the long night had finally ended, Jodie rolled out of bed and into the shower. Before she was dressed the doorbell rang. With a toothbrush in her mouth she went to the door and peered out the peep hole. It was Brandon, her bodyguard. She yelled through the door that she'd be out in a minute.

Ten minutes later she joined Brandon in his car. He had brought coffee and donuts which Jodie much appreciated as she was famished. She gave him the sheet of paper with their day's work written on it and they headed for their first stakeout.

"Do you do many stakeouts, Brandon?" Jodie asked.

"No. Not really. Usually building security or directing traffic at the church on Sunday."

Jodie gave Brandon a quick once-over. He was in his late twenties, a little overweight, and soft in the stomach. He didn't look one bit intimidating, but he did carry a gun in a holster. She wondered if he'd ever used it.

"So, where did you get your training?"

"The United States Marine Corps. I was an MP."

Jodie raised her eyebrows. "Really. How long were you in?"

"Six years. I enlisted when I was fresh out of high school and reenlisted for a second term."

"So, why did you get out?"

"I went to Saudi Arabia during the Gulf War. I hated it over there, so when my tour was up, I got out."

Jodie nodded. "I can't even imagine what it would be like to be a soldier in battle."

"It's pretty intense. The suicide rate was higher than the number who died in combat."

"Are you serious?"

"Yes, I came close to doing it myself a time or two. You just can't imagine the stress you're under over there."

When they got to the office warehouse of Atlantic Printing and Labeling, Brandon slowly drove by. They turned around and parked across the street in a busy furniture store parking lot. From their vantage point they could see both main entrances to the building. Jodie got out her binoculars and surveyed the scene.

"Looks quiet," she said.

Brandon opened an envelope and pulled out sixteen photographs. They were the surveillance photos of Melendez and five lieutenants plus ten photos of undocumented workers who had been employed at Alliance. Brandon studied them carefully then raised his own binoculars. Employees were starting to come and go as the shift began to change.

Jodie prayed she'd see someone familiar, but it wasn't to be. Two hours later she was beginning to feel sleepy and began to nod off.

"Go ahead and take a nap," Brandon said. "I'll keep an eye out."

Jodie sighed. "I'm sorry. I just haven't been sleeping too well."

"I understand. I'll take a nap at lunch."

Jodie laughed. "Okay. It's a deal."

Jodie slid down and leaned her head against the door. Within a minute she was fast asleep.

Brandon woke her at nine when it was time to move to their new location. She thanked him and called Brenda to tell her they'd come up empty.

"Send Brandon in to take a look around. He can ask them if they have any jobs available."

"Okay."

Jodie told Brandon to go into the offices and snoop around. "If anybody asks you what you're doing, tell them you're looking for a job."

He nodded, walked across the street, and went inside. Ten minutes later he emerged from the building and came back to the car.

"Nothing. Let's go."

They stopped at a Wendy's drive-through and picked up some food for lunch along the way to their next stop. Right at eleven they rolled up in front of their next location, a paint manufacturer named Adam's Paint Supply. Jodie was beginning to get a headache from

being overtired and bored. She struggled to keep her focus. After
eating a double cheeseburger she regained some of her strength and
lifted her binoculars once more.

During their afternoon break Jodie made Brandon stop at a
park where Jodie got out and stretched her legs. She couldn't stand
being cramped in the front seat of the car all day. A wave of pessimism
came over her and she wondered if she wasn't wasting her time. She
couldn't imagine six more days of this. She was glad she hadn't joined
the FBI. If she had to endure much more of this, she'd go crazy.

That night she went to the office to catch up on her mail and
phone messages. Stan was still there, so she stopped by his office to
brief him on the surveillance.

"Sorry, I know it's tedious work, but it's our best shot right
now," Stan said.

"I know. I'm not complaining. If I could only get some sleep,
I'm sure I'd feel much better."

"Why don't you stay at the office tomorrow and let Brandon
do the surveillance alone?"

"No. No. I'm all right. Brandon's never seen Icaro or his sons.
He may not recognize them."

"He's got photos."

"I know, but people often look different in a photograph. I'd
rather be with him."

"Okay."

"How's Rebekah?" Jodie asked.

"I don't know. There's something wrong with her. I just wish
we could figure it out. We tried to get her to go to a diagnostic group,
but she refused. She has agreed to go see her internist. I'm taking her
tomorrow."

"I hope you figure it out. I know it must be weighing on your
mind."

"You got that right. I haven't been sleeping well myself. I lie
awake in the night listening to Rebekah breathe. I don't even mind

her snoring anymore. If I can hear her snoring then I figure she must be okay."

"Maybe you should take a few days off and just be with her."

"I wish I could, but I've got the Thompson probate hearing tomorrow. Andrew Thompson is trying to get appointed independent executor of his brother's estate. I've got to prevent that or he'll find out Maureen has already liquidated the company to pay her legal fees. If that happens the shit will hit the fan."

"Will Paula get in trouble for that?"

"No. Maureen will be criticized, no doubt. But better a little criticism than having to accept appointed counsel when you're on trial for murder."

"Right. Good luck."

Stan gave Jodie a ride home and when she stepped into her apartment she saw the light on her recorder flashing. She picked it up and punched in her code. She listened to a message from a friend and then the dry cleaners. She hit SEVEN after each message so they'd be erased. The third message was from Ricardo.

"Look under the rug at the back door. Can't wait to see you."

Paula hung up the phone and went to the back door. She opened it, bent down, and found a note under the rug. She stood up and read it. It was the address of a restaurant where Ricardo wanted to meet her that evening at nine.

Without a moment's hesitation she took a shower, picked out a suitable dress, and then fixed her hair and makeup as best she could in the short time she had to get ready. Then she wondered how she'd get to the restaurant without being followed. After taking a moment to think, she grabbed her purse and then slipped out the back door. Slowly opening the back gate she ran across the courtyard to her neighbor's and knocked on the door. After a moment the door cracked open.

"Betty. Can I use your phone?"

"Paula?" Betty said, opening the door to let her in. "What's wrong with your phone?"

"I don't know. It's not working. Can I use yours? I need to call a cab."

"Your car won't start?" Betty asked skeptically.

"Yeah," Jodie laughed. "Something like that."

Betty was a good friend and knew better than to ask questions. She nodded and Jodie went to the telephone and called a cab. She told him to pick her up in front of the elementary school two blocks away so anyone watching the apartment wouldn't notice the pickup.

"Thanks, Betty. I'll explain later."

Jodie left and walked to the elementary school, cutting between apartment buildings and staying clear of the street so she wouldn't be seen. The cab was waiting for her when she arrived at the elementary school. She got in and told the driver where she wanted to go.

Several times she turned and looked out the back window to make sure they weren't being followed. She didn't see anyone so she assumed she'd made a clean slip. Twenty minutes later the driver let her off at Texas Land and Cattle in North Dallas. She went inside and scanned the restaurant. The hostess asked if she could help her find someone. She nodded and said she was looking for Ricardo.

"Yes, right this way. He's waiting for you."

The woman led Jodie to a corner booth out of view of most of the patrons. Jodie sat down across from Ricardo and smiled.

"You're a sight for sore eyes," Ricardo said.

"I'm glad you still feel that way."

"Well, you're the last person I should be having dinner with, but unfortunately I can't control my heart."

Jodie laughed. "Isn't that funny how that works? In the end we have no control over our destiny. It's all hormones, body chemistry, and forces we don't understand that ultimately seal our fate."

Ricardo sighed. "Isn't that the truth."

The waitress came and took their orders.

"So, how is your search coming?" Ricardo asked.

"Not so well," Jodie admitted. "We're staking out old vendors and customers hoping to spot your father or brothers. Stan thinks they may have gone to one of them to hold up for a while."

"That's possible. The cartel's businesses are all intertwined. I'm sure they could have absorbed the Alliance workforce pretty easily."

"Any other suggestions?" Jodie asked.

"I have an uncle who operates a handbag manufacturing plant in Waco, Premium Handbag. When I was a kid we would go visit him from time to time. Eduardo Melendez is my uncle's name. He uses a lot of undocumented labor so I'd suggest you add his plant to your list."

"We'll do that," Jodie said appreciatively, "Have you given any thought to cutting a deal with the FBI and going into witness protection?"

"Yes, but I can't do that. It would kill my mother if I betrayed the family. All I've done so far is prevent a murder. She'll forgive me for that, particularly when I tell her I was in love with you."

Jodie swallowed hard. She couldn't see their relationship going anywhere but up in flames. She wondered if there was any way out. Even if Ricardo gave in and accepted witness protection, she wouldn't want to go with him. She was quite happy at Turner & Waters and her future was bright. She couldn't imagine giving that up, but she was pulled to Ricardo as well. She could see herself with him and being happy.

The waitress showed up with their food and placed it all before them. Jodie was hungry as it had been a long time since they'd stopped at Wendy's for lunch. There was a lull in the conversation while they ate and made small talk. Then the conversation got serious.

"So, how are you staying clear of the cartel?" Jodie asked.

"Moving around, living on cash, not staying in any one place more than a night."

"Yeah. But how long can you do that?"

"For a while. I guess eventually I'll have to relocate somewhere."

"You should do that now. Don't hang around here for me. I don't want to be responsible for your death."

Ricardo leaned forward. "I was hoping you'd come with me."

Jodie's stomach tightened. Running off with Ricardo wasn't an option, but she didn't want to hurt his feelings after he'd forsaken his family for her and saved her life. The situation was unbearable.

"You know I can't do that. I never led you on about our relationship. I tried to discourage you but you wouldn't give up."

"I wouldn't give up because you never told me to get lost like most women have done in the past. I could see in your eyes that we had a future and was sure in time you'd come around."

"Well, you may have been right under normal circumstances, but the situation is impossible for us now. You need to be realistic and accept that."

"I'll never accept that," Ricardo replied stubbornly. "I love you and I won't settle for anything less than to be at your side for the rest of my life."

A tear welled in Jodie's eye. She turned away in frustration. Ricardo leaned forward and took her hands in his.

"I'm going to hang around until we figure this thing out. Maybe if you catch my father and brothers, things will calm down and I can come out of hiding. You never know."

Jodie shook her head in disbelief. Ricardo was a hopeless romantic and she feared that would be his undoing.

19
The Worlds Worst Patient

Dr. Michael Sanders was in his sixties and reminded Stan of one of his professors at UCLA. He was definitely the scholarly type, taking voracious notes and ordering a long list of tests. Rebekah wasn't happy about any of it. She hated being x-rayed, couldn't pee on demand for a urine sample, and hated having her blood drawn. She was the world's worst patient as far as Stan was concerned and he was embarrassed taking her to the doctor.

"Well, when we get all these tests back perhaps we'll understand better what's going on with you," Dr. Sanders said. "Your blood pressure is okay and there wasn't anything unusual with your EKG, so I can't tell you much right now. I'll need to see you next week to go over your test results with you."

"I have to come back?" Rebekah complained. "Can't you just call me and tell me what you find over the phone?"

"I could, but I'll probably want to discuss treatment options or refer you to a specialist depending on what the test results show. Is that a problem?"

"No," Stan said, frowning at Rebekah. "We'll see you next week."

Rebekah was noticeably quiet all the way home. This was normal behavior when she was angry. Stan didn't understand why she was mad at him but didn't have time to drag it out of her. He had stayed home and accompanied Rebekah to the doctor because he was afraid she wouldn't have gone had he not taken her. Perhaps that was why she was mad, but he couldn't think about that now. He had clients waiting for him at the office, urgent matters that had to be attended to, and a probate hearing in the afternoon that he had to attend.

When he got to his office a client was waiting for him with a new bankruptcy. He took her in immediately and started working on her case. After a while he took her into the conference room where Maria sat down with her to ask her questions about her assets and liabilities. When Stan got back to his desk Jodie was waiting for him. He shut the door.

"I saw Ricardo last night," Jodie said.

"Really? How did that happen?"

Jodie explained everything except the more intimate moments between her and Ricardo. Stan thought about it a minute.

"Well, I guess we need to let the FBI know. We don't have to tell them where we got the lead. I'm sure the Waco location is on one of your lists. If not, you can add it to one of them. Nobody will know any better."

"Thanks. I don't want it to get out that Ricardo is helping us."

Stan nodded. "No. That would just make the cartel search harder for him."

"So, how should we handle this?"

"Tomorrow you and Brandon go to Waco to do your morning stakeout. If you don't see anything in the morning stay on until after lunch just to be sure. Then, if you come up empty, have a vendor lined up between Waco and here for your afternoon stakeout."

"All right, but how will I explain the deviation from our plan?"

"You know," Stan said thoughtfully. "I was noticing on your list there was one of our old clients down in Waco."

"Really? Who is that?"

"The Party House Strip Club."

"What? You have a strip club for a client?"

"Yeah. I put them through Chapter 11," Stan said, smiling wryly. "Took my fee in kind."

Jodie's mouth dropped.

"No—just kidding. I did it as a favor to a friend down there. Anyway, if there is anything illegal going on in Waco, Arnold Moses will know about it. Just tell Agent Lot I'm going to see Arnold and you're meeting me there for lunch."

"Okay. What if he wants to meet with Arnold, too?"

"Tell him he's an old client and will open up to me, but not to a federal agent. Tell him we'll call him immediately if anything turns up."

Jodie agreed and left. Stan thought about Arnold Moses. At the time Stan had been excited about having an excuse to hang out with the girls at the club, but after he had met them and spent some time with Arnold he lost his appetite for the place. Most of the girls smoked, were on drugs, and made their real money after hours. A few of them were pretty but many of them were much too old for what they were doing and had to put on layers upon layers of makeup to cover up their age, bruising, or poor physical condition. After a while Stan quit making trips to Waco and made Arnold come to him. When the case was finally confirmed, Stan vowed never to represent a strip club owner again.

After lunch Stan drove to downtown Dallas to the records building where the probate court was located. He wasn't looking forward to the hearing as he detested family disputes. Everyone was always so emotional. It was almost as bad as family court. Maureen Thompson was sitting on a bench in the front of the courtroom when he walked in. Andrew Thompson and his lawyer were standing in front of the door to the courtroom talking.

"Hi, Maureen," Stan said.

"Hi, Stan. How is Rebekah? Paula told me she wasn't feeling well."

"She's okay. Thanks for asking."

"So, what's going to happen today?"

"Well, there are two applications for administration of Rodney's estate—yours and Andrew's. The court has to consider both of them and then make a decision as to which one of you to appoint as administrator. Usually, a wife would have priority but since you were separated and are charged with Rodney's murder, it's going to be a toss-up as to who is appointed."

"I don't want Andrew handling the estate. He's an asshole."

"Well, you're going to have to convince the judge you can handle the job. Andrew's attorney will try to rile you and get you to lose your temper. Just stay cool."

"Okay. I'll try but I hate Andrew."

"Don't say that to the judge. Andrew is one of the beneficiaries of the estate and you will be representing his interests, too, if you get appointed."

The bailiff stepped out of the courtroom and motioned for them to come in. When everyone was seated in the gallery the constable said something into his intercom and then stood up. A moment later the door behind the bench opened and the judge stepped out. Everyone got to their feet as the judge took the bench.

"Okay. The Estate of Rodney Thompson, Application for Appointment of Administrator filed by Andrew Thompson and Application for Appointment of Administratrix filed by Maureen Thompson. Since Mr. Thompson filed his motion first we'll start with his argument."

Andrew Thompson's attorney stood. "Your Honor. I'm Paula Bracken, attorney for Andrew Thompson, brother of the decedent. Although we concede that Maureen Thompson has a superior right under Probate Code §77, as the wife of the decedent, to be appointed administratrix of the estate, it is our position that she is disqualified to so act. As the court probably is aware Ms. Thompson has been charged with the murder of her husband and is currently out on bond. Although she has yet to be convicted, she will be quite busy defending herself and will not have the requisite time to handle the responsibilities of the job. Further, if she is convicted she will no longer qualify to be administratrix under Probate Code §78 and the court will be forced to appoint someone to replace her. Also, if she is convicted she will lose any right of inheritance of her husband's estate and likely be incarcerated. Finally, it is no secret that the decedent had left Ms. Thompson, they were no longer living together, and a divorce was in the works.

"Your Honor. Under Texas Probate Code §78 the court has the discretion to disqualify any applicant if he or she is *unsuitable* in the discretion of the court. We think it is obvious that Ms. Thompson is *unsuitable* and therefore her application should be denied."

"Thank you, Ms. Bracken," the judge said. "Mr. Turner. What do you have to say about this?"

Bracken sat down and Stan stood up. "Your Honor. As counsel admitted, Maureen Thompson has the clear right to be appointed administratrix. The fact that she has been charged with her husband's murder means nothing since there is a presumption of innocence which the court is bound to respect. The speculation about a divorce is, just that, speculation and of no legal force or effect. Ms. Thompson is clearly the proper person to administer this estate and we request her application be accepted and an order to that effect be signed."

"Thank you, Mr. Turner."

The judge took a deep breath. "Mr. Turner's arguments are correct. There is nothing technically blocking Ms. Thompson's appointment as administratrix; however, this court would be remiss if it were to ignore an indictment for murder. This is why the state legislature wisely gave the court discretion to disqualify a person from serving in a fiduciary capacity if in the court's discretion such person was *unsuitable*. In making this decision I must consider what's best for the beneficiaries and the creditors of the estate. In this regard I think it unwise to appoint someone who may in time have a conflict of interest with the other beneficiaries and the creditors of the estate as long as someone else has come forward and is qualified to do the job without any potential conflict. Therefore, I am denying Maureen's Thompson's application and appointing Andrew Thompson as administrator of the estate subject to qualifying and posting bond."

"Thank you, Your Honor," Bracken said.

"I'll need to set a bond amount. How much do you estimate the personal property of the estate to be worth?" the judge asked.

"That's hard to say, Your Honor," Bracken replied. "With the economy as bad as it is business was at a standstill. I doubt the company's had any market value."

"Then what is the approximate liquidation value of each of the companies?"

"I'm not sure, Your Honor," Bracken admitted. "We'd have to do an inventory."

The judge turned to Maureen. "Ms. Thompson. Are you familiar with your husband's estate? I assume you are since you also applied to be administratrix."

"Yes. I'm very familiar. We have done a recent inventory."

"So, what's the liquidation value of the various companies your husband owned?"

"There is cash of about $2,000, accounts receivable of $88,000, materials of $3,000, tools and equipment of about $50,000, and three trucks and two trailers worth about $30,000."

"That's market value rather than cost?"

"Yes," Maureen replied.

"How did you make your valuations?" the judge asked.

"I had an appraiser give me a preliminary estimate."

The judge nodded. "And is it true there is no income at this time?"

"Correct. Everything is at a standstill right now."

"Then I'll set bond at $173,000."

The judge made a note on his docket sheet. "Thank you. Is there anything else?"

Bracken looked at Andrew Thompson. Thompson started to open his mouth to say something and then closed it. Stan grabbed Maureen's arm and escorted her out of the courtroom.

"Sorry about that. You can't really blame the judge for his ruling. He'd have probably taken a lot of heat had he found in your favor."

"What about the money we took from the company?"

"Ah. Don't worry about that. You had a right to take it. You were in charge of the company as VP and it was your profit from all those jobs. Besides, it will take Andrew months or years to figure out what happened. If we don't get you off by then it won't make any difference anyway."

Despite his assurances to Maureen, Stan was very worried about the discovery of their raid on the company's assets. Although it was technically legal since there was no court proceeding pending at the time and all the vendors had been paid, the court still might try to set aside the transaction and have the money be restored and administered as part of the estate. If that happened the firm would be in trouble since much of the money had already been spent. Stan prayed it would never come to that.

20
Enforcers

When Paula walked in her office she saw a thick envelope on her desk. She opened it and discovered it was Excel Security's background report on Doc Mellon. According to the report Mellon had two associates who worked with him on a daily basis. Rich Ralston was his business manager who supervised his various enterprises and investments, and Arch Lang handled security. Ralston had an MBA from the University of Dallas and Lang was an ex-cop from Waco.

The report went on to say that Lang had been fired from the Waco Police Department for use of excessive force in the arrest of a college girl for underage drinking. After cuffing the girl her boyfriend became angry and made some disparaging remarks about Lang. In response, he pushed the boyfriend and when he pushed back, Lang began hitting him repeatedly with his billy club. He eventually arrested the boyfriend for disorderly conduct. Unfortunately for Lang, the boyfriend sustained a broken arm and extensive bruising on his arms, shoulders, and back. Witnesses at the scene uniformly agreed the beating was unprovoked and totally out of line.

Rich Ralston had no criminal history according to the report but had been sued for his alleged involvement in an oil and gas scam. The suit claimed Ralston fabricated drilling reports and prepared a fraudulent financial statement which was sent to investors. The suit was still pending and no trial date had been set. Paula closed the report and set it back on the desk. Next she picked up a surveillance report on Ralston and began reading it.

The report indicated a driver had picked Ralston up at his home in the White Rock Lake area of Dallas at 8:30 a.m. The home had a value of $322,000, according to the Dallas Central Appraisal District, which was a conservative value. They stopped at Denny's at 9:10 a.m. where they met a second man identified as Rex Russo. Russo was another former football player, a tight end, from Mellon's alma mater, Texas Tech. From there they went to Mellon's office where they stayed until 12:30. In the afternoon, Ralston and Russo stayed at the offices but Lang picked up a man named Simon Smith and together they visited a long list of residential addresses and small businesses.

Simon Smith was described as a white, dark-haired male, thirty-five years of age, 6' 2", approximately 280 pounds, with several visible tattoos on his arms and neck. According to the report he was arrested and convicted of assaulting an officer, burglary, DUI, and possession of a controlled substance. He served thirty days in the Dallas County Jail for the assault charge and two years for the burglary and possession charges. He did 1000 hours community service for the DUI. He was currently on probation for another year on the DUI.

Attached to the report was a list of the businesses and individuals who were visited by Lang and Smith. Paula knew what the visits were about. These were collection calls or visits to encourage people to pay their debts in a timely fashion. The fact that there were businesses on the list interested Paula. These were not payday customers. They were most likely larger borrowers like Rodney Thompson. She decided she needed to pay them a visit. There were seven names on the list stretching from Grand Prairie to Mesquite. She started with Grand Prairie, stopping at a café called the Mid-Cities Grille. It was a single-story structure that at one time housed a Denny's. When Denny's lease was up, Art Anderson leased the building to fulfill a lifelong dream of owning his own restaurant. Paula took a seat at the counter and ordered a cup of coffee. After she'd been served she asked the waitress if Mr. Anderson was around. The waitress nodded and went to the kitchen to get him. A moment later a tall, grey-haired, fair-skinned man dressed in white pants, shirt, and apron walked out. Anderson was the owner as well as the cook, it appeared. He introduced himself and Paula gave him her card.

"An attorney?" Anderson said, frowning. "What did I do now?"

Paula laughed. "No. I'm not after you. I'm actually hoping to get your help."

Anderson looked at her warily. "What kind of help?"

"You do business with Doc Mellon?"

Anderson stiffened. "Yeah. The biggest mistake of my life. I was a fan, thought it would be cool to be associated with the Clock. Now I know he's nothing but a cocksucker."

Paula nodded. "That's what I've been told. Maybe you can help bring him down."

He shook his head. "No. I don't have a death wish."

Anderson explained how he'd started his business by draining his 401K plan that he'd accumulated over twenty years working at the GM assembly plant in Arlington. Unfortunately, he'd underestimated the startup costs of the business and was about $50,000 short. That's when someone he met at a sports bar mentioned Mellon's name.

"The bastard probably got a nice referral fee for hooking me into the scam," Anderson moaned. "Now I owe $100,000 and—"

"And what?" Paula pressed.

"And, nothing. I just don't want anything to do with that bastard. You need to leave."

Paula stared at him. "What's he threatened to do if you don't pay?"

"Like I said. I can't be involved in this. I'm going to get him paid and be done with it."

"Did you know there's a way to legally get out of the debt entirely?" Paula said, hoping to get him curious.

Anderson's expression didn't change. "If he finds out I've been talking to you—"

"What will he do?"

201

Anderson just shook his head. "This conversation is over."

"Don't you understand? Unless you win the lottery you'll never pay off this debt. You'll be working twelve hours a day for him for the rest of your life. I'm offering you a way out."

Anderson put up his hand, turned, and walked back into the kitchen. Paula stared at the swinging door in frustration. Finally, she paid her bill and left.

The next business on Paula's list, a dry cleaners, was locked up as tight as a drum. There was a sign on the door stating that the landlord had locked the tenant out for failure to pay rent. There was a telephone number where customers could call to make arrangements to pick up their laundry. Paula called the number.

"Hello," a female voice said.

"Hi. I was just bringing my laundry to be cleaned and read your sign. What happened?"

"Oh, my uncle, Jo An, died unexpectedly. We had to shut down the business."

"How did he die?" Paula asked.

"Car accident. Uncle Jo ran into a telephone pole. I guess he had too much to drink."

"Do you know anything about his business?"

"No. I'm a student. I'm on break and just trying to help out."

"Well, sorry about your loss. Thanks."

Paula didn't want to talk about Mr. Jo's business over the telephone, but she made a note to look into it. She wondered if it had anything to do with the Mellon loan. She pulled out her list and set off for the next business. Unfortunately, the owner wasn't in, so she put a check mark by the name to remind her to come back later. Then she went to the fourth location. It was a paint and body shop. The owner's name was Margie Lewis. Paula introduced herself and explained why she had stopped by.

"Oh, sorry. I can't help you. I don't discuss my business affairs with strangers."

"I understand, but this is a matter of life or death."

"Exactly," the woman replied. "That's why I keep my mouth shut."

Paula sighed and handed the woman her card. "Well, if you change your mind call me. I'm sure we could help each other out."

"Uh-huh. Sure," the woman said and then turned away.

Paula left feeling frustrated and angry. Why wouldn't people let her help them? She couldn't understand it. The last one on the list was Sammy Lee in Mesquite. She was in Carrollton, so she took Midway Road to LBJ Freeway and went east. About thirty minutes later she was in a strip shopping center near Town East Mall. The sign on the marquee outside read: DON'T TRUST YOUR MONEY TO A BANK, BUY A SAFE. Paula wasn't sure about the wisdom of that, but figured the owner would have some strong arguments to back it up if anyone asked. A bell alerted her entry into the establishment. A short Asian male came out from the back room with a name tag that read: Don Lee.

"Hi. Can I help you?" he asked looking at Paula expectantly.

"Hi. I'm Paula Waters. I'm an attorney and I'd like to talk to you about Doc Mellon."

The expression on the man darkened. "I don't know anything about him."

"Didn't you borrow some money from him?"

Lee didn't answer. "What's this about? He going to sue me, too?"

"No. I don't represent Mr. Mellon. I represent a woman accused of murder, Maureen Thompson. You may have heard about her on the news."

"The Ice Pick Widow?"

"Yes."

"What's that got to do with Doc Mellon?"

"Like you, the victim was one of Mr. Mellon's customers."

Lee's face stiffened. "I know nothing."

"I understand. Let me assure you our conversation today is strictly confidential. Doc Mellon will never know we talked unless you tell him, and I wouldn't recommend that."

"So, what you want?"

"How much did you borrow from him?"

"Twenty grand. I had fire and no insurance. Had to rebuild."

"What was the cause of the fire?"

"Don't know. Fire inspector couldn't figure it out."

"Hmm. So, what are your payments?"

"Thousand a week."

"For how long?"

"One year."

"Fifty-two thousand repayment on a $20,000 debt."

"Nobody else would lend me the money."

"So, have you ever gotten behind?"

"Yes. Business is sometimes slow."

"Is that why you were paid a visit by Simon Smith and Arch Lang?"

Don Lee nodded dejectedly.

"What did they have to say?"

Don lifted his shirt to reveal several nasty-looking bruises to his side and back. Paula cringed at the sight.

"Oh, my God! Did you go to the doctor?"

"No. No way. It's okay."

"Listen," Paula said. "If there was a way to get rid of Doc Mellon and his collectors, would you be interested?"

"No. Too dangerous."

"It wouldn't be dangerous," Paula lied. "The police would be involved, maybe even the FBI. You would be protected and Don Mellon and his goons would be sent to jail."

Don didn't answer.

"I know it would be scary and it won't happen unless you want to do it."

Don looked around nervously.

William Manchee

"It's all right," Paula said. "You don't have to make a decision now. But I know a way you can get rid of the debt right now and I'd be happy to help you do it. At the same time we'll put Doc Mellon and his *associates* behind bars where they belong."

"I don't know," Don finally said. "Very dangerous. Let me talk to wife. I call you."

Paula nodded and handed Don her card. He took it, and for the first time, smiled. Paula shook his hand and then left. As she drove away she wondered if he'd have the guts to stand up to Mellon. She knew he must be incredibly scared after the beatings he'd endured. Realistically, it was unlikely he'd do it, but at least she had planted a seed, and either way she had a witness she could subpoena for trial.

21
First Arrest

Jodie and her bodyguard left at five so they'd be sure to get to Waco by 7:00 a.m. for the arrival of the early shift at Premium Handbag. The drive had been pleasant as they had beat the rush-hour traffic. The plant had been built in a strip shopping center that had previously been the home of a Safeway grocery store. It was situated right along the freeway and there was a huge parking lot in front. This forced Jodie to park in a high-traffic location near the front door. In order to explain their presence Jodie acted as if she was the wife of a worker, waiting for him to get off work. While she was sitting on the hood of her car talking to passersby, Brandon took down the license tags of all the cars in the parking lot. When he was asked what he was doing he simply told them he was looking for unauthorized vehicles.

By 9:30 a.m. they had yet to discover a person of interest, so Brandon took a walk inside the plant. Nobody paid any attention to him, perhaps because they'd seen him working outside, so he headed for a sign that read BREAK ROOM. As he was entering the break room a man leaving caught his attention. He was sure it was one of Melendez's supervisors but he couldn't remember his name. He asked a man drinking a cup of coffee who the person who'd just left was.

"Oh, that's Ben Zepeda."

"He's new, isn't he?" Brandon asked. "I haven't seen him around."

"Yeah. He just started this week."

"It seems like there are a lot of new faces around here lately."

"That's because they started a third shift."

"Oh, right. I forgot about that."

Brandon bought a Coke from the vending machine and then went back outside to report to Jodie his sighting of Ben Zepeda.

"Fantastic. I'll call Brenda and let her know. Then we're supposed to meet Stan at the Party House."

Jodie called Agent Thomas and told her about spotting Ben Zepeda. She said she'd have someone from the FBI's Waco office check it out.

"You'll need to stay here and wait for the FBI. I'll go meet with Stan and Arnold Moses. I'll come back and pick you up when I'm done."

"I'm not supposed to let you out of my sight," Brandon complained.

"I know. Don't worry about it. You'll need to help the FBI find Zepeda. I'll be fine. Nobody even knows I'm in Waco."

Jodie left and drove across town to the Party House Strip Club. It was located in a single-story light blue and white stucco building with a big neon sign on the roof. There was a driveway in front with valet parking and a fenced-in parking lot in the back. Jodie parked across the street, walked over to the building, and went inside.

It was just opening and the staff was still setting up the lunch buffet. A topless waitress gave Jodie a once-over as she walked in. "The dressing room is in the back, honey," she advised.

Jodie laughed. "No. I'm here to see Arnold Moses."

"Oh. Arnie's in the office in the back, but he's got a visitor."

"I know. That's my boss, Stan Turner."

"Oh. Okay. Go on back, then, sweetie."

Jodie thanked her and went back in the direction she had pointed. As she walked she passed a dancer on stage slowly wrapping herself around the silver pole that rose to the ceiling. Several beer-bellied admirers stared at her with their mouths open.

She heard Stan's voice and quickened her pace toward the back office. She knocked.

"Come in," Arnie said.

Jodie pushed the door open and stepped in.

"Oh. Jodie. Come on in and meet Arnie. We've just been catching up."

"Wow! Look at you," Arnie said, giving Jodie the once-over. . . . "Boy, you know how to hire them, Stan. You want a job, honey?"

Jodie smiled politely. "Ah. Thanks, but probably not."

"You ought to consider it. You'd make a fortune."

"Hey. Quit trying to recruit my employees," Stan said jokingly.

Arnie shrugged. "I'm sorry, already. You can't blame me for trying."

Arnie extended his hand and Jodie shook it firmly. Then she sat down next to Stan.

"Any luck?" Stan asked.

"We found Ben Zepeda," Jodie said.

"Really? That's great!" Stan exclaimed. "Did you contact Agent Lot?"

"No. I called Brenda. She's my contact. I figured she'd like to tell Agent Lot the news."

"She'll appreciate that."

"Brandon's waiting at the plant for some agents from the local FBI office."

"Good. I hope Zepeda sticks around until they get there. He could be a valuable source of information."

"I doubt he'll talk," Arnie said. "The punishment for cartel members who talk to the feds is a bullet in the forehead."

"Well, he could go down for the Alvarez murder, so maybe he'll talk in exchange for a spot in the witness protection program," Jodie suggested.

"You never know," Stan said. "Anyway, I was just telling Arnie about Melendez packing up his operation in the middle of the night and then setting the building on fire."

Jodie nodded. "Right."

"So, Arnie. What's the scoop on Premium Handbag these days?"

209

"It's got a big contract with JT Hooper's department stores. I heard they got more orders than they can handle."

"How are they keeping up?"

"They got an influx of illegals and added a third shift to accommodate them," Arnie replied.

"That could mean some of the employees from Alliance made it down here," Jodie said.

"Well, I'm sure the FBI will check into that when they pick up Zepeda," Stan said.

"Where did you hear about the influx of labor?" Jodie asked.

"Eduardo comes here at least twice a week. He talks to the girls and they pass on the info to me. I think he mentioned it to them last week."

"So, has he talked about our lawsuit or the FBI's investigation?"

"No. He just said things were heating up in Dallas so his brother left town."

"Any idea where his brother Icaro ended up?" Jodie asked.

"No. He paid Eduardo a visit but, as I understand it, he didn't stay long."

Stan stood up. "Keep your ears open, Arnie. Let me know if you hear anything interesting, okay?"

"Yeah, right. I have better things to do than spy for you."

Stan grinned. "I know. You don't work for nothing. Don't worry. I'll pay if it's good intel."

Arnie shook Jodie's hand again. "If you get tired of working for this old slave driver, come see me. I'll take good care of you."

Jodie rolled her eyes. "I'll remember that."

They left the Party House and Stan drove them back to Premium Handbag. They found Brandon pacing out in front of the plant. They parked and walked over to him.

"So, what's happening?" Stan asked.

"They're inside right now. I gave them the photo and told them where I last saw him."

Suddenly Zepeda came running out a side door with an agent in pursuit. He ran through the parking lot to his car and jumped in. Not liking what was unfolding before his eyes, Stan got in his car and started the engine. The agent was thirty yards from Zepeda's car when he started the engine and drove straight at the agent. Stan pushed the accelerator hard, peeling rubber as he sped to cut off Zepeda. The agent stood his ground and fired a round at Zepeda but the car kept coming. Just before Zepeda's car struck the FBI special agent, Stan's slammed into it from the side, driving it into a row of parked cars. Both cars came to an abrupt halt.

The agent jumped to his feet and rushed over to Zepeda's car. He ripped open the door and stuck a gun in his face. Jodie ran over to Stan's car, worried that he'd been hurt. She opened the door and found Stan slumped over.

"Stan! Are you all right?" she exclaimed as she pulled him off the steering wheel. Stan looked up at her groggily.

"Did we get him?" Stan asked.

Jodie shook her head. "Yeah, we got him. Do you have a death wish? You scared the shit out of me."

Stan shrugged.

"Well, Agent Lot never would have forgiven me if I let one of his agents get killed."

The agent walked over with a handcuffed Zepeda in tow. "You must be Stan Turner," he said.

"Yeah."

"Thanks. I don't know what would have happened had you not shown up."

"Don't give it another thought. What's your name?"

"Rogers. Special Agent Tom Rogers."

"Well, Tom. I'd like to be there when you interrogate Ben here."

Zepeda glared at Stan. "Don't waste your time. I'm not talking."

"Hmm. Are you sure about that?" Stan asked. "You don't want to take the rap for Romildo Alvarez's murder, do you?"

"I didn't kill him!" Zepeda spat.

"Well, if you didn't, you know who did?" Stan said.

Zepeda shook his head. "*No estoy diciendo nada quiero un abogado.*"

Stan didn't speak Spanish but he knew what *un abogado* was. Zepeda wanted a lawyer.

Two more FBI cars drove up and four agents got out. They inspected the wreckage and asked Rogers what had gone down. One of the agents took Zepeda and secured him in the backseat of his vehicle. When Agent Rogers was finished at the crime scene, he drove Stan and Jodie to FBI headquarters. Brandon stayed back to help the remaining agents sweep the plant for any of the old Alliance workers. He told them he'd join them at FBI headquarters when he was done.

"So, if Zepeda doesn't talk we've got a serious problem," Jodie said.

"How's that?" Stan asked.

"Melendez will hear about what happened and just get even harder to find."

"Maybe we can do something about that," Stan said thoughtfully.

Jodie looked over at him. "What are you thinking?"

"How many customers did you come up with from your review of the audit?"

"Twenty-seven or so," Jodie replied.

"What if we garnished each and every one of them?" Stan asked.

"Ah. That would certainly piss them off, if nothing else."

"That it would. But it would also totally disrupt their money laundering operation and force them out in the open."

"I was right. You do have a death wish," Jodie said.

Stan smiled. "No. I have confidence that the FBI can protect us. If Alliance's receivables are garnished, they'll have to make an appearance in court or lose their money. I wonder how much we could capture."

"A lot, I'm sure," Jodie said. "Hundreds of thousands, I bet."

"I think you're right. It's a win-win situation. If they try to stop us and make an appearance in court the FBI can arrest them. If they don't make an appearance the courts will award us the money."

"Sounds like a good strategy, if we live long enough to implement it."

"I know it's risky, but it's either that or just drop the case and forget about it."

Jodie sighed. "No. We can't do that. I guess we better get back to the office and get to work."

When they got to FBI headquarters Agent Rogers advised Stan he'd have to give a statement because of his involvement in Zepeda's arrest. Stan agreed and met for over an hour with another agent. When he was finished Jodie and Brandon were waiting to head back to Dallas, They informed Stan that Zepeda was still refusing to say anything, so there wasn't going to be any interrogation. Disappointed, they piled in Brandon's car and headed back to Dallas.

"So, what are you going to do without a car, Mr. Hero?" Jodie asked.

Stan shrugged. "I don't know. I don't suppose my insurance company will pay for the damages since I intentionally rammed Zepeda's car."

"Probably not," Jodie agreed. "Maybe the FBI will pick up the tab since you saved an FBI agent."

"Maybe, but knowing our beloved government, I'm not going to hold my breath."

When Jodie got home her recorder was blinking again. She checked her messages and found another one from Ricardo. This time he told her to look in her purse. He told her that at their last meeting he'd slipped a note in there with directions to another place they could make contact. She read the note. It gave her directions to a nearby convenience store with instructions to look under the pay phone for a number written on masking tape. He told her to call the number and then destroy the tape. She left out her back door again and walked to the convenience store. She found the tape just as Ricardo had promised and called the number.

"I feel like I'm a CIA operative," Jodie said.

Ricardo laughed. "You can't be too careful when it comes to the cartel. How's the hunt going?"

She told him about the stakeout, Stan's heroics, and Zepeda's arrest.

"Well, that's a start. If you could get him to talk, that would be great."

"I don't think that's too likely," Jodie said dejectedly. "He's already got an attorney."

"That figures. You know, I was trying to piece together bits and pieces of conversations I've heard over the years. The family has tried to keep me in the dark, but it was inevitable that I'd overhear some things."

"Uh-huh."

"Well, have you ever heard of a town called Boerne? It stuck out to me because it sounded like the name of a person. It was only recently that I drove past it and realized it was a town."

"Right. It's down near San Antonio, isn't it?"

"Uh-huh. Anyway, my father and brothers were always talking about shipping stuff to 'Bernie.' I thought it was one of their friends. Now I realize there must be a manufacturing plant in Boerne. If you could find it, it wouldn't surprise me if some more of Dad's workers ended up there."

"And this manufacturer probably owes Alliance a lot of money."

"True. I'm sure they pay Alliance a ton of money."

"Thanks. I've got a list of customers. I'll see if any of them are located in Boerne."

"I'm getting bored lying low," Ricardo said. "If I sneak over to your place will you keep the window open for me?"

Jodie laughed. "No. I wouldn't advise it. You're liable to end up getting shot—if not by my bodyguards I'd probably shoot you thinking you were a cartel hit man."

"Hmm. There's a Harvey Hotel on Central and Park Blvd. You could catch a cab and meet me there. We could keep each other company during the night and then you could sneak back into your apartment early in the morning and the cartel and your bodyguards would never be the wiser."

Jodie thought about it. Deep down she knew it was a bad idea, but she really wanted to see him. "I don't know, Ricardo. I'd like to, but it could really hurt our case. Maybe when all of this is over."

"You promise?" Ricardo asked. "Or are you just placating me so I'll keep feeding you information?"

"No! I'm serious. I really like you and would love to meet you at the hotel if it wouldn't compromise my work. I couldn't do anything that reckless. It would really hurt the firm and Stan and Paula have been very good to me. I couldn't do anything to hurt them."

"All right. I'll sleep alone, but I'm not going to forget your promise."

"I don't want you to. If we get through this mess somehow, I want to spend time with you. I'm not promising anything permanent, but I'll give you the opportunity to make me fall in love with you."

"That's all I ask. Just give me a chance."

"I will, but you've got to promise me to stay out of sight no matter how bored you get."

Ricardo sighed. "All right. As long as we can talk each night."

"Will this number be good tomorrow?"

"Yes, but call me from a pay phone. Don't use your cell or office phone."

"What about a throwaway phone?"

"Yeah, as long as you don't use it near your apartment or your office. I'm sure they'll be monitoring cell phone traffic from there."

"Do you really think so? I can't imagine they'd dedicate that many resources to keeping track of me."

"Don't underestimate them. You and Stan have brought the feds down on them and forced them to run, but more importantly, you've humiliated them and they can't let you get away with it."

Jodie swallowed hard. She wondered if she should tell him about Stan's plan to garnish all their customers and disrupt their money laundering operation. She almost did but then thought better of it. She didn't want him worrying any more about her than he already was. It would be cruel and wouldn't serve any purpose.

They said good night and hung up. As Jodie was about to leave the convenience store she noticed a car parked out front with two men sitting in the front seat. She waited awhile hoping they'd go away, but when they didn't she called Brandon.

"Hello."

"Brandon. Can you call your guy watching my apartment and have him come pick me up?"

"Huh? Aren't you in the apartment?"

"No. I needed some milk so I walked to the convenience store. I didn't think anybody would notice I'd left, but there are a couple of guys out front and I'm afraid they may work for the cartel."

"Okay. Sit tight. Stay in the store. I'll call Toby and tell him to go pick you up."

"Thanks," Jodie said and hung up.

Jodie smiled at the store clerk who was giving her a suspicious look. She wondered if he kept a gun behind the counter in case the two men came inside. She picked up the phone again and pretended to make another call. When she turned to look at the two men she gasped. They weren't sitting in the car anymore. Frantically, she looked around searching for them. She spotted them walking toward the front door.

"Do you have a bathroom?" she asked the clerk.

He pointed toward the back of the store. Jodie rushed in that direction until she found a small family room. She went inside and

216

locked the door. Afraid they might fire at her through the door, she huddled in a corner behind a large metal trash can. After a moment there was a knock on the door.

"Sorry. I'm sick. I may be a while," she said in a loud voice.

There was another knock. Harder this time. Her stomach twisted as she feared they would soon be breaking down the door.

"I've called the police. You better leave," she warned.

The knocking turned to hard kicks. The door shook violently but the lock held. Jodie looked around for a weapon should the door give way, but there was nothing. Not even a towel rack she could pull out of the wall. Then she heard voices.

"Get away from the door! Reach for that gun and you'll regret it."

Then she heard a siren. She breathed a sigh of relief. The police had arrived.

"Drop the weapon!" a voice said.

"No problem. I'm a security officer. I was just responding to a distress call from my client. Jodie, you can come out now. It's safe."

Jodie unlocked the door and peered out. Two police officers had their guns on a man she assumed to be Toby. She'd never actually met him since he worked the night shift when she was asleep.

"Are you okay, ma'am?" one of the officers asked.

"Yes, now that Toby and you are here. What happened to the two men?"

"They ran when the police got here," Toby said.

Jodie rubbed her forehead. Suddenly she felt exhausted. She put her hand on the doorjamb to steady herself.

"Are you all right?" Toby asked.

"No. Can you take me home? I'm not feeling so hot."

Toby looked at the two officers.

"Do you want to file a complaint against the two men?" one of the officers asked.

"No. I didn't get a good look at them and they didn't harm me, thanks to Toby's prompt response."

The officers holstered their weapons and moved out of the way so Toby could take Jodie out to his car. Without looking back they got in and drove off. Toby drove Jodie home and checked the apartment to make sure nobody was lurking inside. After he'd left Jodie went straight to bed. Before she fell asleep she questioned her decision to become an attorney. She loved the job but the stress was unreal. She cringed at the thought of how bad it would get when Stan really put the heat on Melendez and the cartel with his garnishment campaign. She wondered if Agent Lot would consider loaning her a bulletproof vest.

22
Default Judgment

The following Tuesday morning Stan had taken Rebekah to breakfast since she had a doctor's appointment at ten. She was angry about having to go see the doctor again, so Stan figured if she had a nice breakfast she might be in a better mood. The strategy had worked and Rebekah seemed to be in good spirits when they walked into Dr. Sanders's office. Unfortunately the reception room was packed with patients and they had to wait nearly an hour before they were summoned into an examination room.

"This is ridiculous. You're missing work just so the doctor can tell us there's nothing wrong with me."

"Yeah, but there *is* something wrong. You just don't pass out or lose the strength in one side of your body routinely. There has to be something causing it."

"It's just stress."

"Stress from what? Your life is a hell of a lot simpler now than it used to be with four kids running around."

"Yes, but I still have you to worry about. Who knows when some thug might put a bullet in your head?"

"Oh, come on. It's not that bad."

"Tell that to Jodie. I doubt she's sleeping too well these days."

Stan didn't have a comeback for that one. He tried to imagine if the tables were turned. He'd certainly be worried about Rebekah if she were a lawyer and up against criminal elements, but would it cause symptoms like Rebekah was experiencing? He didn't think so.

"You know if you volunteered or got a part-time job it might take your mind off me and the kids. It would probably be good for you."

"I don't want to go to work. I told you that already."

"All right. Just a thought."

The door to the examination room opened and the nurse came in. She took Rebekah's blood pressure and temperature and had her stand on a scale to be weighed. She left and a few moments later Dr. Sanders walked in with her chart in his hand.

He wrote something in the chart and then looked up. "Hello, Rebekah, Stan."

Rebekah forced a smile. "Hi."

"How are you feeling today?"

"Fine," Rebekah replied coldly.

Dr. Sanders gave Rebekah a once-over and then said, "Well, let me do an examination and then we'll talk about your test results."

Rebekah nodded and Dr. Sanders began listening to her heart and lungs. He then checked her reflexes and the strength of her arms and legs. When he was done he sat down and opened his chart.

"Well, your vitamin D and B12 levels are very low. You've got high PTH and calcium levels. We'll need to do a bone density scan to make sure there hasn't been any damage to them. You could have osteoporosis. I'm going to refer you to an endocrinologist for that. You should also see a cardiologist and a neurologist."

"What?" Rebekah protested. "You can't handle this yourself?"

"No. You'll need a specialist in each of these areas. There are many different things that could cause these abnormalities in your blood work."

Stan cringed at the thought of getting Rebekah to see three more doctors. Rebekah's eyes glazed over. Stan could imagine what she was thinking. On the way home, he didn't broach the subject of seeing three more doctors as he knew what she'd say—no way. After letting Rebekah off at home, Stan went to the office.

When he walked in he noticed Jodie and Maria in the conference room with papers spread out everywhere. He walked in to see what was going on. Jodie looked up. She told him about the skirmish with two cartel goons at the convenience store.

"When I got back to my apartment I couldn't sleep so I got up early, came to the office, and started working on our garnishments."

"How's it coming?"

"I started with Foremost Mobile Homes of Boerne. Ricardo told me Alliance did a lot of business with them, so I'm using them to create my master garnishment petition. Once it's done it will be easy to put the other twenty-six together."

"Right," Stan said.

"It's a lot of work since I have to find each one's registered agent. And I'll need eight grand for the filing fees."

"Okay, good work," Stan said, obviously impressed with Jodie's fast start. "I guess I better get a default judgment entered and figure out how to dig up the filing fees."

"How long will that take?" Jodie asked.

"The answer date has passed, so I just need to take our witnesses down to the court and prove up the default."

"So, you'll need Jade Alvarez to prove it up?"

"Right. Just for a few hours."

"Let me know when you need her and I'll contact her at school and arrange it."

"Okay, but be careful how you contact her. We don't want the cartel finding out where she is."

Jodie nodded and Stan went to his office. When he went through his messages he came across one from Glenda Wolf. He picked up the phone and called her.

"Just checking to see if you've finished your report yet. Everyone is anxious to finalize the estate," Glenda said.

"Right. Well, I'm not quite done yet. I've found some old girlfriends who may have mothered his child. I'm checking that out."

"That's not possible. Herb would have told me if he'd knocked anyone up. There wouldn't have been any reason for him to hide something like that from me."

"Unless he didn't know he'd done it. The boy may have just recently begun searching for his father."

Glenda sighed. "Well, I'm sure you're wrong. Herb didn't have any children."

"I'm hoping to hear something soon from my contacts in Hawaii. Just as soon as I find something out, one way or the other, I'll finish my report and send it to the court."

"Thanks. Just hurry, would you? This thing has been dragging on too long."

Stan hung up and thought about Tom Hooper. He hadn't heard from him for a few days and wondered if they'd had any luck finding Yuzie Gucci. Unfortunately Tom hadn't given him a number in Hawaii to contact him, so Stan decided to call his home number and leave a message. Unfortunately his recorder was full and couldn't take any more messages. Stan decided he'd just have to wait and hope Tom would eventually call him. His only other option would be to travel to Hawaii and he obviously didn't have time to do that.

On the following Monday, Stan and Jodie met with Agents Lot and Thomas to talk to them about their garnishment strategy and the impact it would have on the cartel.

"You're playing a dangerous game, Stan," Agent Lot advised.

"I know, but that's the only way to get their attention. So far they've just ignored us. If we cut off their cash flow they'll either have to appear and file a motion for a new trial or lose the cash. If they appear then Melendez and his sons will have to reveal their locations and submit to discovery."

"They won't make an appearance. They'll do something dramatic to force you to back down—another kidnaping or an assassination would be my guess."

"True. But this time you guys will be ready. If anyone comes after us you'll have agents close by to protect us and take them down."

"As hard as we will try to anticipate every way they might come after you, nobody thinks of everything," Agent Lot warned.

"I have confidence in you," Stan said.

Agent Lot sighed. "I hope you're not expecting too much."

When Stan got back to the office he started flipping through his phone messages. He saw one from Andrew Thompson's attorney. His heart sank. He knew Andrew would be wanting access to Thompson Construction's books and records and it wouldn't be long before he realized all the cash had been cleaned out. He didn't want to even think about the ramifications of that discovery. Reluctantly he returned the call.

"This is Stan Turner."

"Hi, Stan. This is Paula Bracken, Andrew Thompson's attorney."

"Right. We met at the hearing the other day."

"Yes, well I'm a little embarrassed having to make this call."

Stan perked up. Why would she be embarrassed? he wondered. "What do you mean?"

"Well, at the hearing Andrew was a little surprised to learn he had to post a bond. I had mentioned it to him, but I guess it didn't sink in. Anyway, when he went to apply for the bond he was turned down. Apparently he's got some credit issues."

Relief washed over Stan. He couldn't believe their good fortune. "Is that right? I'm so sorry," he lied.

"I know. We had the hearing for nothing. Anyway, I'll be withdrawing Andrew's application to be appointed administrator of Rodney Thompson's estate. I'm sorry for any inconvenience this has caused you."

"No problem. Don't worry about it," Stan said smiling broadly. "We'll keep you apprised of what's going on."

Stan hung up and immediately called Paula to give her the good news. She was elated as she'd been expecting a firestorm when Andrew discovered what they had done. She thanked Stan and suggested God must be smiling down on them.

On Tuesday Stan met Jade and a forensic accountant at the Dallas County Courthouse in front of the courtroom of the 14th District Court. After Stan had gone over their testimony with them, they entered the courtroom. Jade and the accountant took a seat in the gallery and Stan checked in with the bailiff. The bailiff told him he was the eleventh case on the docket, so he went back and took a seat next to Jade.

A few moments later Judge John Brock took the bench and began calling the docket. At this early morning docket the court heard simple discovery motions, summary judgments, and defaults. Forty-five minutes later the court called their case.

"The Estate of Romildo Alvarez and Jade Alvarez v. Alliance Fabrications, Inc.," the judge said.

Stan knew Judge Brock from SMU Law School. They'd been classmates but hadn't been friends. Stan didn't have many friends in law school since he was working full-time and involved in politics at the time. Judge Brock knew of Stan, however, since Stan had attracted considerable media attention since law school.

Stan and Jade stood up and approached the bench. The judge was studying the file when they arrived in front of the bench. He looked up and smiled.

"So, you put the fear of God in your defendant, I hear. They just packed up and left town rather than face the mighty Stan Turner."

Stan laughed. "No. I think it was the Dallas police and the FBI that scared them."

"Yes. Pretty resourceful to get them involved."

"It probably wouldn't have been prudent to take them on alone."

"No. You're probably right about that. So, you want to take a default?"

"Yes. They've defaulted and we're here to prove up our case and take a judgment if the court is willing."

"Well, according to the record they were properly served. Bailiff, check the hall to be sure no one is here for Alliance Fabrications."

The bailiff got up and went out into the hallway. He called the case but nobody answered. A moment later he came back in. "No response, Your Honor."

"All right, then. Call your first witness."

"Jade Alvarez," Stan announced, turning toward Jade.

"Ms. Alvarez, do you swear to tell the truth, the whole truth, and nothing but the truth?"

"I do," Jade replied.

"Go on, counsel."

"Ms. Alvarez. Are you the duly appointed administratrix of the Estate of Romildo Alvarez?"

"Yes."

Stan had her identify her letters of administration and they were admitted into evidence.

"Have you and your father worked for Alliance Fabrications, Inc. over the years?"

"Yes."

Stan had Jade provide the dates and normal hours of employment for both her and her father. She explained how they worked twelve-hour shifts six days a week at minimum wage but without overtime. She told them about the poor working conditions, the intimidation, verbal abuse, and lack of breaks, sick pay, or vacations. Her story of the day her father went missing brought dead silence to the courtroom. Stan looked back and saw two reporters sitting in the back row taking notes. He had hoped to avoid the press so the cartel wouldn't be tipped off to the fact that he was up to something, but it appeared he'd have no such luck. When he was finished with Jade he called up his forensic accountant, Larry Stone.

"Mr. Stone. Now, you've heard the testimony of Jade Alvarez regarding the periods of employment and hours of work, is that right?"

"Yes."

Deadly Defiance

"And prior to today have you had a chance to determine what amount of pay should have been paid these two employees had they complied with the federal wage and hour laws?"

"Yes."

"How much should Ms. Alvarez have been paid for her years of service?"

"Well, the minimum wage currently is $4.25. It has changed over the years, so taking into consideration those changes, the base rate for eight hours comes out to $86,944. When you add in overtime at time and a half, that number doubles to $191,268."

"What about Romildo Alvarez?"

"He worked almost twice as long as his daughter, but the minimum wage was lower in the earlier years. His base rate actually paid was $148,720. Again, if you take into consideration overtime at time and a half, he should have been paid $326,634."

Stone provided charts and documentation for his calculation of damages and the interest that was lost. When he was done Stan addressed the court.

"Your Honor. We have also alleged causes of action for fraud, breach of contract, false imprisonment, and an assortment of other torts. The conduct of the defendant was obviously willful, intentional, and malicious and designed to thwart the laws of the United States of America. Accordingly we're asking for punitive damages of one million dollars each for both Jade and Romildo Alvarez. Thank you."

"All right. It seems there could be a statute of limitations as well as other possible defenses, but since there is no one here to raise them I'll consider them waived; the motion for default judgment is therefore granted and the court awards damages as requested. Do you have a judgment prepared?"

"I do, Your Honor," Stan said and handed it to the judge.

The judge signed the order and returned it to Stan. "You understand if I get a motion for a new trial, I'll probably be inclined to grant it, assuming the defendant has a half-decent excuse for not answering."

226

"I understand. Thank you, Your Honor."

"Good luck trying to collect it," the judge said, rolling his eyes.

"Thank you. May we be excused?"

"Yes. Have a good day."

Stan and his witnesses went out into the hallway where Jodie was waiting. Stan thanked Larry Stone and he left. The two reporters walked over to them.

"Nice judgment you got," one of the reporters said.

"Right, but like the judge said, good luck collecting it."

"So why bother, then?"

"Well, the FBI is still looking for Icaro Melendez and his sons. If they find him they may find some assets we can attach."

"Do you have any leads on any of them?"

"Well, just the Ben Zepeda arrest, but he's not talking. We haven't given up, though."

"So, has the FBI bought you a new car yet for saving their special agent?"

"No. It would be nice if they did, though. I'm still driving a rental."

"Thank you, Mr. Turner."

Stan nodded and the two reporters left. Stan looked at Jodie. "Are you ready?"

"Yes, sir. I've got all twenty-seven garnishments ready to file."

"Okay. Let's do it."

Stan went to the court clerk's office and got a conformed copy of the judgment. Technically the judgment was not final for thirty days, but he felt it was unlikely Melendez would appeal it. If they did and the garnishment was defeated, his clients had no non-exempt assets at risk so it was no big deal. He felt he could have gotten a pre-judgment garnishment anyway, but he would have had to persuade the court to allow it. This way he had the right to file the garnishments and didn't have to get anyone's permission.

Jodie took the judgment to the district clerk's office and filed the twenty-seven garnishment actions and arranged for service. Stan went to the abstract department and got eighteen abstracts of judgment for filing in each of the counties involved just in case Alliance owned any real estate there. Stan knew it could take weeks for all the garnishments to get served, but at least the process had been started. He knew it wouldn't be long before the cartel felt the impact of what had been done. Then they'd likely come after them like a hive of angry bees.

23
The Sting

Paula stared at her computer screen. She was putting the final touches on her trial outline, witness and evidence lists. She liked to have her game plan in mind well in advance of trial. There was just one thing left to do and she had to enlist Detective Besch's help in doing it. She called him and invited him to lunch. They met at Ojeda's, a Mexican café which she often frequented. She ordered a burrito dinner and a margarita. Besch got beef fajitas and a beer.

"So, counselor. It's nice of you to buy me lunch, but what's the occasion?"

"Well, you've been so much help to Stan and Jodie here lately, I wanted to do something nice for you."

"Oh, well you know Stan and I go way back, so it's no big deal."

"Yes, it is, and I wanted to show my appreciation by offering you up a high-profile criminal on a silver platter."

Besch stopped eating and looked intently at Paula. "Okay, I'm listening."

"You know Doc Mellon, right?"

"Doc 'the Clock,' sure."

"Well, I've been investigating him as a suspect in the Rodney Thompson murder."

Besch's eyes lit up. "Oh, I see where this is going. You want me to nail Mellon for Thompson's death so your client will be off the hook."

"Well, that could be the result. You never know."

Besch laughed. "You said something about a 'silver platter.'"

229

Deadly Defiance

She explained to Besch how Doc Mellon operated his payday loan business and got around the Texas usury laws.

"He also makes loans to small business owners who have bad credit or don't have collateral. The loans look legitimate on their face but there are other strings attached—consulting fees, kickbacks, commissions, you name it. His customers are soon his slaves and can't do a damn thing about it or they'll risk Mellon's wrath. A guy named Simon Smith dishes out the punishment but the man calling the shots is Mellon's security chief Arch Lang. I'm sure there are more players, but those are the only ones I've identified."

Besch raised his eyebrows. "Well, it sounds like this is someone who we need to get off the streets, no matter how it affects your client. How can I help?"

Paula explained her plan in detail and Besch promised to run it by his superiors to see if they'd go along with it. She stressed the importance of protecting the witnesses as she'd promised them they'd be kept out of harms way. He assured her they wouldn't get hurt, if the brass gave the go-ahead for the operation. They finished their lunch; Paula thanked Besch and went back to the office and immediately went to see Stan and update him on the situation in case Besch called him.

That night Paula couldn't sleep as something was bothering her. Maureen Thompson's first murder trial had gotten a lot of press, so it wasn't a stretch to assume the murderer used an ice pick as the murder weapon, so it would appear like Maureen's handiwork. But if Doc Mellon was behind Rodney Thompson's murder, who killed Maureen's first husband? Obviously, it wasn't Doc Mellon. Or, could it have been? Paula pondered that possibility. Could Randy Rhymes have borrowed money from Doc Mellon or one of his companies? That was something she'd have to check out, she decided before taking a sleeping pill and going back to bed.

The next day Paula got to the office early, grabbed a cup of coffee, and began sorting through the previous day's mail. As she was working she remembered the possible connection between Mellon and Rhymes that had come to her in the night. She wondered who she could call to confirm that connection. After looking through her witness list, her eyes fell on the name of Ryan Jones, Randy's ex-agent. She figured if anybody would know about a connection, it would be him.

"I'm not sure if he borrowed anything from Doc Mellon," Jones said. "Randy didn't mention a loan to me. If there was a loan, I would imagine his manager Bob Brown was responsible for it. Bob was getting pretty reckless there at the end. The women, the booze, and the gambling finally did him in."

"So, where is Bob Brown these days?"

"I have no idea. When Randy found out he'd been embezzling and the money was gone, he hired some goons to beat the crap out of him and he hasn't been seen since."

Paula took a deep breath. She couldn't believe her luck. The location of the only person who could link the two murders was unknown. Now what was she going to do?

"Was there a criminal prosecution for the embezzlement?"

"No. Like I said. He had disappeared so there wasn't much point prosecuting a ghost."

As Paula listened, the pieces of the puzzle began to fall into place. All she needed was a few bits of hard evidence to tie it all together. But without this evidence all she had was speculation. She thanked Jones and hung up. While she was contemplating the situation Maria came over the intercom and advised her Bart was on the line.

"Hey, I'm in the neighborhood. You want to have lunch?" Bart asked.

"Yes, I'm starving. Thank you. I'd have probably skipped lunch had you not called."

"Good. Meet me at Dickey's on Forest Lane in ten minutes."

"All right. I'm on my way."

It was unusual for Bart to take her out to lunch. She wondered if he was really just in the neighborhood or there was something on his mind. She stood up, grabbed her purse, and made a quick trip to the ladies' room. When she looked in the mirror she saw dark circles under her eyes. She hadn't been getting enough sleep. Digging into her purse, she dug out her emergency cosmetics and made the dark shadows disappear. Then she put on fresh lipstick and headed for the rendezvous with her husband. He was sitting on a bench by the cash register when she walked in. He got up and they embraced.

"Boy, this is a nice surprise," Paula said.

He nodded guiltily. "Well, actually I'm here on official business."

"Hmm. I figured as much," Paula confessed.

They went through the line. Paula got ribs and Bart a three-meat platter. They both got a Coors Light to wash it down. After they'd found a table and started eating, Bart explained the purpose of the meeting.

"The DA found out about your proposed sting operation against Doc Mellon. He doesn't think Mellon had anything to do with Rodney Thompson's murder, but he's been trying to build a case against Mellon for years."

"Oh, really?"

"So, he's approved the plan but with no guarantees. If they take Mellon down, but you don't find the evidence to clear your client, then it's just like it never happened. You won't get any favors when Maureen's trial comes up."

"That's fine," Paula said. "I know it's a gamble, but I'm sure Mellon was behind the murder—I'll do anything to prove it."

"Okay, then. Tell me your plan. I've been assigned to be your liaison."

Paula smiled. "Oh, that's great. It will be like old times, working together on a murder case."

Paula was referring to the one case they had worked together several years earlier as co-counsel after Bart had lost his job at the Collin County DA's office, and temporarily worked for Turner &

Waters. Their client had been accused of setting a fire that killed an entire family. It had seemed like a hopeless case at the outset, but they dug into it, worked hard, and ended up getting their client off. They loved working together, but Bart had a problem switching from prosecutor to defense counsel. Consequently, it was their one and only case as Bart soon got a job with the Dallas DA's office.

That night Paula explained to Bart the details of her plan. The next day he ran it by his superiors and got the go-ahead. A few days later Detective Besch, Bart, and Don Lee met in the conference room of Turner & Waters. Mr. Lee was extremely nervous and Paula was trying to calm him.

"You don't have to do a thing except take this original petition to the justice of the peace court. You won't be in any danger because Doc Mellon won't be served for several days," Paula assured him.

"From the moment you file the petition with the JP court you'll have 24/7 police protection. Someone will be watching you at every moment," Detective Besch said. "We won't let anything happen to you."

"Now what this is," Paula continued, "is a petition alleging usury. That means you are suing Mr. Mellon and his company for charging excessive interest. If you win, which I assure you, you will, the interest and principal balance of the loan will be forfeited and you'll owe him nothing."

"Sure, but if he shoots me or my wife, what good will that do?"

"That won't happen," Detective Besch replied. "The moment they make any move against you we'll arrest them."

"What if they come in, shoot me, and don't ask questions? You not have time to stop them."

"Well, that's possible," Paula said, "but not likely. They are going to try to convince you to drop the lawsuit first. You see, if they just walk in and kill you it would be too obvious that they were the killers. They'll want to make you back down first."

"Okay, but I hope you know what you're doing."

Paula felt a cringe of guilt as she worked to convince Don Lee to play his role in the sting. She wondered if she was doing the right thing. If she got Don Lee killed, what would she tell his widow? She came close to aborting the plan but couldn't bring herself to do it. She had a gut feeling it would all work out in the end.

Don Lee signed the complaint and Paula drove him to the JP court in Garland so he could file it. Paula followed him at a distance into the auxiliary courthouse to be sure it got filed properly. He went up to the window and handed the petition and two copies to the woman.

"What you got there, honey?" the clerk asked.

"I want to sue Doc Mellon."

The clerk raised her eyebrows. The name Doc Mellon was familiar. Doc's Payday Loans, Inc. filed a lot of criminal complaints for bad checks. They never let them go to trial as they knew the judge would throw them out, but the threat of criminal prosecution was all that they were after. The clerk read the petition.

"You suing him for usury. Do you even know what that is, honey?"

Don nodded.

"You a lawyer?" she asked.

"No. My son took business law in school. He read about usury."

"Huh. Well, we don't usually get suits like this in this court. You know, don't you, that you can only get $5,000 damages in this court?"

"Not want damages. Just want to cancel interest and debt. Please file petition."

The clerk shook her head. "All right. Everything looks in order. I'll need $110 if you want it served."

"Yes, I do. Thank you," Don said, handing the woman a check.

She took the check, file stamped the petition, and gave Don one of the copies back. Don thanked her and turned to leave. She put a hand on one of his arms to stop him.

"You own a gun, honey?" she asked.

He shook his head. "No. No gun."

"You may want to think about getting one," she warned.

Don Lee swallowed hard then turned and left the courthouse. Paula came up beside him and asked him how it went.

"No problem."

"What did the clerk say to you when you were leaving?"

"She said I should buy a gun."

Paula winced. She looked back at the courthouse nervously. "Okay, remember that the police will be watching you every minute until this is all over. Just act normal—business as usual. There are cameras covering every inch of your store and home, mics in your car in case they stop you on the road, and tracking chips in your shoes in case somehow you get separated from us. So don't worry."

Lee looked at her skeptically and then got in the car. She drove him back to his shop and then left. She saw Detective Besch in a car down the street and rolled up next to him. He rolled down the window.

"He's really scared," Paula said. "I am, too."

Besch smiled sympathetically. "He'll be all right. We've got tails on Mellon and his men. The moment they make a move we'll pounce on him like a leopard."

"All right. Keep me posted," Paula said and drove off.

Nothing happened that night, but that wasn't unexpected. It would take a while for Mellon and his men to be served or learn of the lawsuit through the grapevine. They figured something would come down the second or third day.

The next morning when Paula got to work she got a message that Mellon had been served. She sat nervously in her office for the next few hours, unable to concentrate on anything for more than two minutes. She was just getting up to get her third cup of coffee when the phone rang. It was Besch.

"Lang and Smith are on the move and heading toward Lee's place."

"All right. I'm on my way."

Paula hung up the phone and ran to her car. She got onto LBJ Freeway and was nearing Town East Mall within ten minutes of Besch's call. She drove slowly down the street in front of Lee's store. Then she spotted Besch's car down the street. She parked, walked back to him, and got in the passenger seat.

"You made it here fast," Besch said.

"It's not that far if there's no traffic."

"They're due here in the next few minutes. There are two Mesquite police officers in the alley who can be inside the shop in twenty seconds. That bum over there with the shopping basket is an undercover agent. I've got audio and video right here in the squad car so we can watch what goes down."

Besch's radio squawked. "Suspects are coming around the corner," a voice said.

Besch picked up the radio. "Roger that. Everybody, heads up!"

A silver Dodge Ram pickup turned the corner and parked in front of the store. Arch Lang got out of the passenger seat with a scowl on his face. He was clutching the citation and petition in his hand like he was trying to crush them. Simon Smith stepped out with a grin on his face and cup in his hand. He spit into the cup, set it on top of the dash and shut the door. He nodded at Lang and they entered the store.

Paula and Detective Besch looked down at the small monitor. They saw Lang and Smith pass in front of the camera and approach Lee, who looked terrified. Lang threw the paper on the counter in front of Lee.

"What's this, you little fucker?"

"Ah. That's usury suit. My son say you charge too much interest. Not legal."

Lang shook his head in disbelief. Smith leaned over, grabbed Lee by the shirt, and pulled him across the counter. He fell hard onto the ground. Smith knelt down, grabbed Lee's ear, and pulled it hard. Lee let out a scream.

"Listen, you little piece of shit. You're going to go back to the JP court and withdraw this complaint or I'm going to put a bullet in your head and then go looking for your wife."

"No! No, Please. I'll—" Lee wailed as two officers burst into the room from the back and a third from the front door.

"Police! Put your hands in the air," one of the officers screamed.

The two men backed up and put their hands in the air. They were quickly cuffed and escorted outside. Paula and Detective Besch came running in the store. Lee was staggering to his feet. Paula rushed over to him.

"Are you okay, Mr. Lee?" she asked, praying he wasn't hurt.

He stroked his ear. "I think so. He tried to pull my ear off, but it's on pretty good."

Paula laughed. "Thank God for that," she said, putting an arm around him to steady him. "I was really worried about you."

Besch looked back at her and smiled. "Mission accomplished. Now let's just hope we can get one of them to turn on Doc Mellon."

Paula nodded. "Yeah, I hope we can for Maureen's sake."

Paula followed Besch to the Mesquite Police Department where they had taken Arch Lang and Simon Smith. She felt relieved that so far her plan had worked out. Now it was up to Detective Besch to get Lang or Simon to turn on Doc Mellon. She wondered if there was any chance in hell that would happen. She parked in the lot adjacent to the station and went inside. Besch was waiting for her.

"Come with me," he said, motioning with his hand.

Paula followed Besch down a long hallway, took a right, and went through a bullpen area adjacent to three interrogation rooms.

"They've got Mellon in room 1. He just lawyered up—won't say a word."

"Well, that was expected," Paula replied. "What about Lang and Smith?"

"They've just been set up in rooms 2 and 3. I'm going to start with Smith. I think he's our weakest link."

Paula nodded. "I think you're probably right."

Besch rolled up his sleeves, grabbed two cups of coffee, and entered the interrogation room. He set a cup of coffee in front of Simon Smith. He had a scowl on his face and was shifting around in his chair nervously.

"Mr. Smith. I'm Detective Besch of the Dallas Police Department. I believe you've been advised of your rights."

"Uh-uh. I don't have to talk to you."

"True, so don't say anything yet. Let me explain a few things before you make a decision on whether to talk or not."

Smith nodded.

"I was one of the officers running the joint sting operation with the Mesquite Police Department against your operation. I guess you know we've got the entire exchange on audio/video."

Smith shrugged. "So? That doesn't prove a thing."

"Oh, quite to the contrary. It proves assault and battery, extortion, usury, witness intimidation, not to mention murder."

"Murder?"

"Yes, one of your customers was a man named Rodney Thompson. Do you remember him?"

Smith didn't respond.

"Well, he was a customer. Your company loaned him $250,000. Now you've probably read in the newspapers that he was murdered with an ice pick and his wife is on trial for that murder."

"I read something about that."

"So, is it a coincidence that Mr. Thompson defaults on his loan from your company and then ends up dead?"

"Coincidences happen. The wife did it before. Now she did it again."

"I don't think so," Besch said. "I think your boss Doc Mellon ordered you to kill Thompson and you thought it would be cute to kill him with an ice pick so everyone would think his new bride did it.

"Anyway, I can see that you're wondering why you should finger the Clock for the murder. What's in it for me?"

Smith nodded.

"Well, let me put it this way. If you were just following orders, well, the brunt of the blame will fall on Doc. We'll put a good word into the DA and tell him to go easy on you. What do you think?"

"I want full immunity."

Besch shook his head. "You're not going to get a free ride on this one. We can talk the DA into knocking the charges down some—take the death penalty off the table, maybe get the possibility of parole in ten, fifteen years. We can help you out, but there's no free ride."

"I want a lawyer."

Besch sighed. "Come on. You don't want to end up on death row. That's what's going to happen if you don't cooperate."

Smith shrugged. "I'll take my chances. Just get me a lawyer."

Besch stood up, shook his head, and left the room. He looked at Paula and shrugged. "Sorry, I thought maybe he'd go for it, but he's not as dumb as he looks."

"It's okay. It was a gamble. At least we got them on extortion and the other charges. That will put them out of business for a while."

"Yes. Thank you setting that up for us. If you think of any way I can help you prove Ms. Thompson innocent, let me know."

"Won't the DA be angry with you if you help me?"

"I don't care about that. Mellon is obviously the killer. It's the only thing that makes sense. I don't want to see an innocent woman go to jail any more than you do."

Paula smiled. "I'm glad to hear that. I'll definitely let you know if anything comes up where I could use your help."

They shook hands and Paula left to go back to the office. As she drove back on LBJ Freeway, a wave of depression came over her.

She had gambled and lost. She could still try to convince the jury that Doc Mellon was the killer, but they weren't likely to buy it without more proof. Her head began to throb and she could feel the muscles in her neck and shoulders tightening. She needed a bath and good massage. She hoped Bart was up to it.

24
Eye Witness

While Jodie was waiting for the garnishments to be served, she thought about the man who lived across the street from the vacant lot where Romildo Alvarez had been murdered. She wondered if he was still there or had relocated to be near his son. If he was still there, she thought perhaps he might know something. She and Brandon decided to drive over there and find out. When they knocked on the door Ruben Morales opened it slowly. Jodie gasped when she saw him. He was pale, unshaven, and looked like he hadn't slept in days.

"Mr. Morales? Are you all right?"

"No. I'm not. My son Jesus is dead."

"What?" Jodie gasped. "Who told you that?"

"Someone from the Travis County Sheriff's Office."

Jodie swallowed hard. "How did it happen?"

"They don't know. They found his body in a ditch south of Austin."

"Oh, my God! I'm so sorry."

Ruben turned and walked into the living room. Jodie and Brandon took that as an invitation, stepped in, and closed the door. Ruben fell back into a stuffed chair. Jodie and Brandon sat across from him on a brown leather sofa.

"Did you even know he was leaving Dallas?"

"No. He just didn't show up one night, so I walked to the plant and saw it had burned. I was beside myself because I didn't know if he was alive or dead. Fortunately, a fireman still on the scene told me there hadn't been any fatalities."

"So, you have no idea what happened to Jesus?"

"No."

Jodie told Ruben everything she knew about the evacuation of the Alliance workers. She told him about Zepeda's arrest and the garnishments that were under way which they hoped would flush out Melendez and his sons.

"Listen. I know the last time we met you said you didn't know anything about Romildo Alvarez's death. I know at that time you were reluctant to say anything because your son was still working for Alliance. Now the situation is different. In light of that, did you see anything the night of Romildo's murder?"

Ruben sighed. "Yes. I'm sorry. I should have told the police what I saw. I know that now."

"Well, I don't blame you for not talking, but now you have nothing to lose. If you help the police they can protect you."

"I don't care about myself. I want Melendez to pay for killing my Jesus."

"Good. Tell me what happened."

"I was at home sitting on the front porch reading a magazine when I saw Romildo walking up the sidewalk across the street. It was early for him to be going home so I wondered what had happened. Was he sick? Had he done something wrong and been sent home?"

"Uh-huh."

"Then I saw Guido's car coming. I knew that was trouble, so I went inside and closed the blinds. Luckily he didn't see me and didn't realize I was watching."

"What did you see?"

"Guido and Ben got out of the car and started walking on each side of Romildo. He tried to get away but they grabbed him by both arms and dragged him across the vacant lot to the alley where they pinned him on the ground. Then Ben stuck something in his arm. After a few moments Romildo went limp and they stood there and watched him for a while. Every few minutes Guido would check his pulse. I guess to make sure he was dead."

"Are you absolutely sure it was Guido and Ben?"

"Yes, it was them. There is no doubt."

"Can I call Detective Besch and have him come by? Will you tell him what you just told me?"

Ruben nodded.

Jodie borrowed Ruben's phone and made the call. Twenty minutes later Besch and his partner drove up. Ruben retold the story and Besch had him go across the street and show them exactly how it all went down.

"Well, now we can get a search warrant for Melendez's home," Besch said.

"Maybe Ben Zepeda will talk now, too, if you give him some incentive," Jodie suggested.

"What do you mean?"

"Well, maybe if you promise not to seek the death penalty, he'll turn on Melendez. That's about the only way you'll be able to prove Melendez ordered the hit."

"That's up to the DA. First we've got to find him and get him in custody."

"If he heard about Zepeda's arrest he may have left the country. If so, you may never find him."

Besch shrugged. "It won't be easy for him to walk away from everything he's built over the last twenty years. I think he's still in the U.S."

"I hope you're right."

"I'm still counting on Rico to surface one of these days and tell us where he is."

"You think he could still be alive?" Jodie asked.

"I don't know. If he were dead we'd have probably found the body by now. No, I think he's alive but for some reason can't contact us. When the time is right, he'll call us."

That afternoon Besch got a search warrant and led a team to Melendez's home in Highland Park. Not surprisingly, the place had been cleaned out, so they found no incriminating evidence nor any clues to Melendez's whereabouts. Besch was also able to get a warrant to search Ben Zepeda's and Guido Quesada's homes. At Quesada's place they got lucky. Not only did they find Romildo's jacket but they also found a trash can that hadn't been emptied for a while. In it they found discarded syringes and empty bottles of the drug that had killed Romildo.

When Jodie got back to the office she called the civil division of the Kendall County Sheriff's Office to see if her garnishment had been served. She was referred to Deputy Hanson.

"Hello."

"Hi. This is Jodie Marshall. I was told they assigned my paper to you for service."

"Oh. Okay. Who's the defendant?"

"Foremost Mobile Homes."

"Oh, yeah. I served them this morning. They were not happy."

"What did they say to you?"

"They asked me what the lawsuit meant. I told them to call their attorney, but if they owed any money to Alliance Fabrications or had any of Alliance's property in their possession they needed to hold on to it until the court decided who it belonged to. I explained that your clients now had a lien on anything that was owed to or belonged to Alliance and if they turned loose of it, you could collect whatever they gave away from them."

"How did they react to that?" Jodie asked.

"They said if they didn't send Alliance the money they owed it, they'd probably end up dead."

"Really. Did you ask them to elaborate?"

"Yes, but someone got through to their attorney and apparently he told them not to talk to me."

" I see. Well, that's good news. I hope they take your advice. Thanks for your help."

"No problem. If they don't take my advice and you end up with a judgment against them, let me handle the execution. I know how you can collect it."

"How's that?"

"I'm always thinking ahead, you know. You've got to do that to be successful. So, I followed one of their trucks one day and it went to a huge warehouse about five miles from the plant. There must be 500,000 square feet of merchandise, parts, supplies there—you name it."

"That's not so unusual, is it?"

"It wouldn't be, except Foremost builds mobile homes and there is nothing in this warehouse that is remotely related to that business. What's even stranger is that this warehouse has been empty for over five years. Then suddenly last week trucks start pouring in and overnight it's filled to the rafters and staffed by at least fifty warehouse workers."

Jodie perked up. Had Deputy Hanson stumbled across Icaro Melendez's new hideout? Could they have finally caught a break? She wondered if she should say anything about her suspicions to Hanson or not. If she did he might tell the sheriff about it and there was no telling what they would do. Finally, she decided to play it cool for now.

"Well, I'll definitely take you up on that if they are foolish enough to ignore the garnishment. Where exactly is that warehouse?"

Hanson gave her directions.

"Great. Thanks again for your help and the info. I'll definitely be in touch."

"No problem."

Jodie hung up and immediately went looking for Stan. She found him in the library and told him what she had found out. He agreed the warehouse looked promising so they called Agent Lot.

"All right. I'll get our San Antonio office to put it under surveillance. If we spot any of our suspects there we'll get a SWAT team out there."

"Great. I'll sleep a lot better knowing Melendez and his gang are behind bars," Stan confessed.

"You and me both," Jodie agreed.

"You've had a good day, Jodie. I heard you uncovered an eyewitness in the Alvarez murder."

"Yes. Ruben Morales. I had talked to him before and felt he knew more than he'd admitted to. His son worked for Alliance and he'd been warned to keep his mouth shut. It just suddenly occurred to me that his son might be missing, too, in which case he might feel like opening up a bit. But he wasn't just missing—they'd found him dead in a ditch."

"Jeez," Agent Lot said. "That would be hard to take."

"Yes. He was devastated and anxious to get a little revenge, I think."

"Well, I'll let you know if I hear anything," Agent Lot said.

"Thanks," Stan said and disconnected.

Jodie waited around the office awhile hoping someone would call, but when six o'clock rolled around she went home. When she walked in the door she noticed the recorder blinking. She rushed over and listened to her messages. The last one was from Ricardo. He didn't leave a message but she knew how to contact him. After checking her purse to be sure she had her disposable cell phone, she went back outside and walked over to Brandon's car. He looked up at her expectantly.

"I feel like a drive," she said, holding up her cell phone.

"Sure, hop in."

Jodie got in the backseat and Brandon drove off. While she was waiting for him to get far enough away from the neighborhood to safely make the call, she wondered if she should tell Ricardo about the warehouse. There was a very slim possibility that he might alert his father if he knew the FBI was about to nab him. She didn't think he would, but there was no reason to take that risk. After a while she flipped on the phone and dialed his number.

"Ricardo?"

"Oh, I'm so glad you called. The cartel nearly found me."

"Oh, my God!" Jodie exclaimed. "What happened?"

"It was just by chance that I left my room to get a candy bar. When I came back I saw two men trying to break into my room. I don't know how they tracked me down, but I've been on the run all day."

"Oh, Ricardo. I'm so sorry. Are you all right?"

"No. I lost my clothes and everything that was in my luggage. Fortunately I had my wallet and cell phone in my pocket."

"Listen, Ricardo. It's too dangerous for you out there now. It's time to come in and talk to the FBI. Things are coming to a head. You need to come in and make a deal with them while you can. Time is running out."

"Why do you say that? What's happened?"

"I can't go into any detail, but a witness has come forward who saw Ben and Guido kill Romildo Alvarez. Ben has already been arrested. If Ben cuts a deal with the FBI they may not need your help anymore and you'll lose any chance of getting into the witness protection program."

Ricardo thought about this for a long moment. "But if I go into the witness protection program I'll never see you again."

"I know, but at least you'd be alive. Your father and brothers might eventually forgive you for rescuing me, but the cartel won't. You have to get into witness protection or you're going to end up dead."

Ricardo sighed. "You're probably right. I'm really scared and I'm tired of running."

"We'll come and get you right now," Jodie said. "Where are you?"

Ricardo told her where he was and said he'd wait to be picked up. She hung up feeling much relieved that he'd finally seen the light. After telling Brandon where they needed to go she called Agent Lot to give him the good news and find out where she should take him. Unfortunately he wasn't in and she had to leave a message. When they got to the north entrance of Northpark Mall, the rendezvous point Ricardo had given her, he wasn't there.

"This is where he said he'd be," Jodie said.

"He probably didn't want to sit out in the open. I bet he's inside the mall. Go on in and check it out."

Jodie nodded and got out of the car. She looked around anxiously and then proceeded up the stairs and through the revolving doors that led to the mall. When she got inside she felt a tug on her arm. She spun around and was relieved to see Ricardo's smiling face. They embraced.

"Oh, Ricardo. You scared me. When we drove up and you weren't there—"

"I know. I'm sorry, but I didn't want to sit out in the open. I figured you'd come inside."

Jodie's cell phone rang. She pulled it out of her purse and hit the TALK button. "Hello."

"Jodie. This is Agent Lot."

"Oh, perfect timing," she said, smiling at Ricardo. "I've got Ricardo here with me. He's ready to come in."

"Excellent. Good work. Where are you?"

"Inside the north entrance to Northpark Mall. Brandon's outside waiting for us in his car."

"Okay. Sit tight. I'm not but ten minutes away."

"Good, see you in a minute."

Jodie turned to Ricardo. "Agent Lot's coming here. We should go tell Brandon what's going on. Come on."

Ricardo nodded and followed Jodie through the revolving doors. When he emerged she took his hand and led him down the half flight of stairs leading to the street. As they were stepping down the last stair they heard screeching tires. Looking up they were horrified to see a sky blue Chevy Malibu speeding past them. Two armed men leaned out of open windows and began firing at them. Brandon jumped out of the car and fired at the fleeing vehicle, knocking out the rear window. When he looked back at Jodie and Ricardo his heart sank. Ricardo was down and Jodie was covered in blood.

25
The Arrest

Stan brought Kentucky Fried Chicken home for supper since he figured Rebekah wouldn't be in the mood to cook. She'd been very depressed after getting her test results from Dr. Sanders. The thought of having to see three more doctors and endure all the testing that would follow worried her immensely.

"What if they find something terrible—something that will make life unbearable?" she moaned. "What if it's cancer?"

"It's not. Don't worry. Whatever it is, there'll be a treatment for it. They just need to figure out what it is. Once they do, you'll probably be back to normal in no time."

Rebekah wasn't satisfied, but she dropped the subject and concentrated on eating her dinner. After they were done and settled in for a quiet night of TV watching, the phone rang. It was Tom Hooper. Stan perked up.

"I wondered if you'd ever bother to call me," he complained mildly.

"Yeah, well. We've been combing the islands trying to find Yuzie Gucci and not having much luck. It turns out we were spelling the name wrong. It's *Yuzu Eguchi*."

Stan laughed. "Well, that would make a difference."

"Anyway, we found her and she does have a son."

"Really? Is he the right age?"

"Yes, I think so."

What's his name?"

"Michio."

Stan thought about it. "Right—Mich for short. It sounds like Mitch. So, have you talked to Yuzu?"

"No. We thought it best to leave that up to you."

"Right. Good work. I guess you've earned your fee. I'll wire you what was agreed."

"Thanks. This was actually a blast. If you ever need us to find someone again, let me know."

"I'll do that," Stan said and then went over the information about Yuzu Eguchi and Michio one more time before hanging up. Rebekah looked at him expectantly. He explained to her what had happened.

"Oh, great! Now you've made a half dozen new enemies. If the cartel doesn't rub you out someone in the Wolf family surely will."

Stan laughed. "No they won't. They may be upset at first but there's plenty of money to go around. They'll get over it. In time they might even thank me for finding their lost heir."

"Don't hold your breath," Rebekah said bitterly.

Stan just looked at her. He wondered where all the anger and resentment had come from. Was this something that had been simmering for many years and suddenly was boiling over, or was this another symptom of the unknown ailment that had suddenly manifested itself? His thoughts were interrupted by another telephone call. This time it was Agent Lot. He said he was calling from Presbyterian Hospital.

"Jodie's okay, but I'm afraid Ricardo is dead."

Stan felt relief and then a profound sadness. Poor Ricardo was dead. He couldn't believe it.

"Who did it?"

"We're pretty sure it was assassins sent by the cartel. Your guy Brandon put a few rounds through the back window of the car so hopefully he hit one of them. If he did they'll have to take their wounded somewhere to get medical attention."

"Well, if he got them through the back window it would likely be a head shot, don't you think? If so, they won't need medical attention, they'll need a coffin."

"Possibly, but we're checking all hospitals and medical clinics just in case."

"Should I come down there?"

"No. Brandon is taking Jodie home. She just needs rest. But we may need you to come down to Boerne tomorrow. One of the Melendez sons has been spotted at the warehouse we've been staking out."

"Oh, that's great news. Are you going to grab him?"

"No. We've got someone following him. Hopefully he'll lead us to his father."

"So, why do you need me down there?"

"Apparently your clients have a lien on everything in the warehouse on account of your garnishment. We'll need to sort that all out. Any contraband we'll have to seize, but what's left over you can have to satisfy your judgment. From what I've been told some of the stuff is pretty valuable."

Stan was elated by the news and thanked Agent Lot for his cooperation and generosity. Stan knew if Agent Lot had wanted to he could have seized everything in the warehouse, declared it contraband, and left his clients high and dry. Now maybe the Alvarez family might come out okay. When he turned to tell Rebekah the exciting news he gasped at the sight. She was pale and struggling to breathe.

"Rebekah! What's wrong?"

She mumbled something and then became limp in his arms. Dialing with one hand and holding her with the other, he dialed 911. Within minutes an ambulance and a big fire truck came rumbling down the cul-de-sac. Stan let the paramedics in and then watched anxiously as they took Rebekah's vitals, put her on oxygen, and then transported her to the waiting ambulance. Soon, Stan was following the ambulance to Plano Hospital. This time Rebekah only spent a few minutes in the emergency room; after a quick examination they sent her directly to intensive care. Stan called the family and then went to the waiting room in shock.

The first one on the scene was Stan's daughter Marcia. She was on spring break and had been staying with a friend in McKinney when she got Stan's call. Stan rushed over to her when she walked in the room. They embraced.

"How is she?"

"I don't know. They took her to intensive care. Apparently her blood pressure is sky-high."

"Really? She's never had high blood pressure before."

"I know. Something else must have caused it, I guess. It's really weird."

"So, none of the doctors she's been going to have found anything wrong?"

"No. Only osteoporosis, but that's probably unrelated to this."

"Right. I can't believe they don't know what's wrong with her."

"I know."

As they were talking Terry Morris walked in and joined them.

"I talked to the nurse, and the doctors have ordered a cranial CAT scan."

"They think something is wrong with her brain?" Marcia asked.

"They don't know but that's a possibility. Since she has no history of hypertension they're trying to figure out what caused her blood pressure to spike. It's a good thing you called 911 right away. If you hadn't she'd probably be dead."

Tears welled in Stan's eyes and he turned away, trying to keep his composure. Marcia grabbed his hand and squeezed it. "They'll figure it out, Dad. Don't worry."

Stan forced a smile and wiped a tear from his eye. The door opened and Reggie walked in with his girlfriend, Angela. Mark came in a few moments later with Rebekah's parents. In the next hour Jodie and Paula called to see how Rebekah was doing but Stan had nothing to tell them. The doctors had yet to find out the cause of Rebekah's episode, or whatever it was.

As the hour got later the waiting room thinned. The staff doctor had reported that Rebekah was stable and not in any danger, so most everyone left for the night. Marcia, however, stubbornly lingered until after midnight when Stan finally convinced her to go home and get some rest. She agreed only on the promise that she could spell Stan at dawn so he could go home and have breakfast and take a nap.

Stan tried to sleep on the sofa but found it impossible. Nor could he focus enough to read a magazine or the local newspaper someone had given him. Most of the time he found himself daydreaming about his life with Rebekah and all that they had been through together. He wondered if Rebekah would ever get better and their life return to normal. He prayed that would happen and promised God that if Rebekah's health was restored he'd spend more time with her and not take her for granted. He got no response, of course, but he knew God had heard him and felt better having made the commitment.

He woke with a start when Marcia shook his shoulder at 6:00 a.m. "Dad. I'm back. Go home and get some sleep. I talked to the nurse and there's been no change."

Stan sat up and yawned. "Okay. You sure she's okay?"

"Yes. Nothing is going to happen in the next four hours, so go home and come back at 10:00. They have her scheduled for some new tests then."

Stan nodded, hugged Marcia, and left. When he got home he took a shower and then set the alarm for 9:30 a.m. Soon he was fast asleep. Moments later the telephone rang. Stan fumbled for the phone and knocked it onto the floor. Finally he picked it up and put it to his ear.

"Yeah."

"Stan, this is Agent Lot."

"Oh, hi."

"Sorry to wake you, but they've arrested Melendez."

Stan sat up quickly. "That's wonderful. Did he put up a fight?"

"No. We didn't give him the chance."

"What about Rudy and Helio?"

"They're still at large. Word is they've gone back to Mexico. Apparently they tried to get their father to come, too, but he was too proud to admit defeat."

"That sounds about right. Any word on Rico?"

"No. He's still missing."

Stan swallowed hard. "I hope he's okay."

"You and me both, but it's not looking good. If he was okay he would have surfaced by now."

"I'm sorry," Stan said.

"So, can you come down here and help us sort through this warehouse?"

"I wish I could, but my wife's in the hospital."

Stan explained what had happened.

"Gee, I'm so sorry. I hope she's going to be all right."

"Yeah. Maybe later in the week she'll be better and I can sneak down. I'd ask Jodie but she's been through a lot."

"No. You're right. We should let her have a few days to recuperate from the trauma of seeing Ricardo murdered."

"Oh. Speaking of that, did Melendez have anything to say about his son's execution?"

"No. He lawyered up immediately, but judging by the look on his face when we mentioned it, he knew nothing about it."

"I don't doubt it. I think he was just a local administrator. Higher-ups made the decision to kill Ricardo when he rescued Jodie."

"Probably so. I'll let you go. Tell Rebekah to get well."

"I will. Thanks."

Stan hung up the phone and tried to fall back to sleep but with little success. He tossed and turned, trying to clear his mind so he could drop off, but he couldn't stop thinking about Rebekah and what was wrong with her. Finally, he got up and fixed himself something to eat. He was famished and felt better after downing some scrambled eggs and coffee. Soon he was on his way back to the hospital. When he got there Reggie and Terry had returned.

"The doctor said you could visit Rebekah. She's awake now," Terry said.

"Oh, really? How is she?"

"She seems fine. Come on. They've moved her. I'll show you where she is."

Stan followed Terry into the ICU. Rebekah was in the far corner of the eight-bed unit staffed by a crew of nurses. It reminded Stan of the cockpit of an airliner, there were so many instruments and monitors surrounding every bed. Rebekah smiled when she saw Stan.

"How do you feel, honey?" Stan asked.

"Fine. When can I get out of this place?"

Stan looked at Terry and shook his head.

"Well, when they figure out what's wrong with you."

"All the tests were negative, so there must not be anything wrong with me."

"Except your blood pressure," Terry corrected.

Rebekah shrugged. "I guess I was nervous over Jodie and this cartel mess."

"That's not what caused this," Stan protested.

"Well, it doesn't matter. I feel fine now, so take me home."

"Ah. You're still in intensive care," Stan reminded her.

"Not for long," Terry said. "They're taking her down to a regular room in a few minutes."

Stan shrugged. "That's good. Have you talked to the doctor?"

"Yes. They still don't know what's wrong with me. That's because there is nothing wrong with me."

"They still have more tests to run," Terry said.

"What kind of tests?" Stan asked.

"An MRI, an EEG and some others," Terry replied. "They're going to keep doing tests until they come up with something."

"I don't want any more tests. Just let me go home."

"You can go home when the doctor releases you. You're a nurse. You know the drill."

Rebekah gave Stan a dirty look. Stan laughed. "Hey. It's not my fault you're sick."

Despite Rebekah's protest the doctors continued to run tests for the next two days but still couldn't figure out what had caused Rebekah's blood pressure to spike. Eventually they gave in to Rebekah's relentless campaign to be released and let her come home. Stan was glad to have her home as the hospital routine was brutal, but he noticed the stay had weakened her dramatically. Terry told him that was not unusual and that she would regain her strength, but he wasn't so sure. It seemed the life was slowing draining out of her and he couldn't do anything to stop it. He felt scared and helpless.

The next day Terry agreed to stay with Rebekah so Stan could go down to South Texas and deal with the garnishment and the warehouse the feds had seized. Jodie was feeling better so she decided to come along and help out. Before they left they went to the office and sorted through the mail and phone messages that had stacked up. They soon discovered they'd hit pay dirt on several of the other garnishments as well. There were many phone calls from lawyers representing other garnishees who wanted to talk.

They felt like much of the danger had passed with Melendez behind bars, but they brought Brandon along just in case. They met Agent Lot and Deputy Hanson at the warehouse and were given a tour of the huge building.

"Apparently most of this stuff was legally obtained, so your garnishment lien is good," Deputy Hanson advised. "So, if you like I'll post it for sale."

The problem with a sheriff's sale, like any other auction, is that one would be lucky to get ten cents on the dollar. You could bid at the sale yourself to try to increase your return, but if you weren't careful you might end up being the top bidder and buying everything yourself. Stan had consulted the Alvarez family about this and they all agreed they didn't want the goods and wanted him to just get as much cash from the sale as he could.

"Yes," Stan replied. "When will the sale take place?"

"In about thirty days. We have to give proper notice and publicize the sale."

"Is there anything I can do to help draw bidders?"

"Yes. If you want to draw bidders outside of this area, to drive up the price, you'll need to publicize the sale. That, of course, will require some cash."

"How much?"

"That depends on how much publicity you want. I can give you a list of the newspapers where these types of sales are advertised and you can work directly with them."

"Okay," Stan said.

"I'll also give you a list of past customers in case you want to do a direct mailing."

"I'll take care of the direct mailing," Jodie volunteered. "I do it all the time for Junior League projects."

"Great. I'll contact the newspapers and see what their rates are. I might be able to trade some advertising for an exclusive interview on the case," Stan said, turning to Jodie. "Would you be willing to be interviewed about your kidnaping?"

Jodie gave Stan a troubled look. She didn't relish the idea of revealing her inner feelings about what had happened to a stranger and then seeing it in print for all the world to see. But, if it would help her clients, how could she refuse? Her face relaxed. "Sure, why not? It would probably be therapeutic to talk about it, anyway."

"Cheaper than a shrink, that's for sure," Stan agreed.

With the details of the sheriff's sale resolved, Agent Lot drove them to FBI headquarters for a briefing and conference on the case. Two other agents sat in on the briefing. One of them was Agent Brenda Thomas who had been working with Jodie on the case in Dallas. She explained that she had traveled down for the Melendez arrest and interrogation.

"It's great to see you," Jodie said, a few moments before the meeting started.

"So, how are you holding up after Ricardo's murder?" Brenda asked. "That must have been pretty traumatic for you to see him gunned down that way."

Jodie nodded. "Yes. I still can't believe it happened. It was all my fault, too."

"How do you figure?" Brenda asked.

"Well, in retrospect, we probably led the goons right to Ricardo. It didn't occur to me that they'd be following us when we drove to Northpark. I was just so excited that he had finally agreed to come in that I let my guard down."

"Well, wasn't that Brandon's responsibility? He was providing security?"

Stan walked in, nodded at Brenda, and sat down.

"Right. But in my enthusiasm I probably distracted him. He swears there wasn't anyone following us, though."

"You can't blame yourself for his murder. You did everything you could to protect him."

"Didn't Ricardo say the cartel was pretty sophisticated in their electronic surveillance?" Stan interjected.

Jodie nodded. "He did say that."

"I wonder if Brandon swept his vehicle for a tracking device? They probably saw that you often let him drive you around. It would have been pretty clever to put a tracking device on his car."

Jodie's eyes went wide. "You don't think—?"

"Call Brandon and have him check it out."

Jodie excused herself to go call Brandon. He'd gone back to Dallas when Agent Lot had asked them to come to FBI headquarters.

"So, it looks like we're making some headway," Stan said.

"Yes," Brenda agreed. "Thanks to you and Jodie. I've never seen such a take-no-prisoner approach to litigation."

Stan laughed. "Well, it was obvious dealing with the cartel that normal litigation strategy wouldn't work. We had to hit them hard and hit them quick."

"You're lucky you're both still alive. Weren't you worried about the cartel coming after you?"

Stan shrugged. "You can't worry about that kind of thing. In the past I've let fear stop me from doing what I knew was right and I've always regretted it. If you let it govern your actions you'll end up doing a pitiful job or doing nothing at all."

"I understand what you are saying, but the risks you two take are staggering."

Stan laughed. "Look who's talking! You get in the face of criminals and thugs every day."

"Right, but we're armed and trained to deal with them—plus we have the support of the federal government."

"So do we. We have you and Agent Lot."

Brenda laughed as Agent Lot and a third agent entered the conference room.

"What's so funny?" Agent Lot asked.

"Oh, nothing. Stan and I are just having a little philosophical discussion."

"Oh. Okay. Where's Jodie?"

Just as the words were asked, Jodie walked back into the room. "You were right, Stan. There was a tracking device affixed to Brandon's bumper."

Brenda shook her head in dismay. "Brandon should have inspected his vehicle."

"He swears he inspects his car every morning. He thinks they must have attached it while he was at a coffee shop for lunch."

"All right," Agent Lot said. "I've just been informed by Detective Besch that Rico has surfaced."

"Where is he?" Jodie asked excitedly.

"In El Paso, it seems. He's managed to work himself into a handler position. He's hoping to gather enough evidence so we can take down some higher-ups in the cartel."

"Isn't he a little out of his jurisdiction being a Dallas cop?"

"True, so we've made this a joint operation with the Dallas Police Department. You have to take advantage of opportunities like this."

"What's the timetable on this?" Stan asked.

"Apparently there is a meeting of some of the higher-ups in the cartel tomorrow afternoon. He's going to try to give us a time and location as soon as he finds it out."

"How is he going to get that kind of intel?" Brenda asked.

"I guess he's gotten tight with one of the participants in the meeting. He's going to be his driver."

"Yeah, but if they are careful they won't tell him where they are going until he gets in the car."

Agent Lot shrugged. "That's true."

"So, let's turn the tables on them," Stan said. "Slip a tracking device to Rico so he can attach it to the car he's driving just before they leave."

Agent Lot smiled. "Good thinking, counselor. That's exactly what we'll do."

After the meeting Stan went back to Dallas to be with Rebekah but Jodie stayed behind. Agent Thomas had invited her to go to El Paso with them to witness the takedown of whoever showed up for the big cartel meeting. Ordinarily they didn't invite civilians to this type of operation, but considering the contribution she'd made to the investigation and what she had been through, they made an exception. Jodie was excited about the invitation and prayed to God this would be the end of the Alvarez matter as she was ready for her life to get back to normal.

26
Making the Connection

Paula couldn't believe the trial was less than two weeks away and she still couldn't link Doc Mellon to the two ice pick murders. She knew he was responsible for the murders but couldn't come up with the evidence to prove it. If she didn't put it together soon, Maureen Thompson would likely be convicted and spend the rest of her life behind bars. She couldn't let that happen.

She knew there was a way to make the connection. In fact, for a moment she thought she had it, then it slipped away. She wracked her brain trying to rekindle the thought that was eluding her. There was somebody who could help her make the connection, but who was it? She got out her notes and began reviewing them but nothing stood out. Then she ran across the name Bob Brown. Brown was Randy Rhymes's business manager. *If anyone had borrowed money from Mellon it would have been him.* The more she thought about it the more she knew she was on the right track. *Brown had mismanaged Randy's accounts and must have been desperately short on cash. He couldn't tell Randy about what he'd done, so when he got desperate enough, he must have gone looking for quick cash and was referred to Doc Mellon.* Now the only problem was finding Bob Brown to confirm her theory. There was a last-known phone number next to his name that Ryan Jones had given her. She called the number.

"I'm sorry but Mr. Brown doesn't work here anymore," a female voice advised.

"Do you know where I might find him?"

"I think he said he was moving back home. He'd had it with the big city."

"Where's home?"

"Lubbock. He was born and raised there. I think he was going to set up a new practice in the suburbs."

Paula thanked the woman and called information in Lubbock. There was no listing for a Robert or Bob Brown. Frustrated, she hung up the phone. As she was thinking of what to do next, Stan walked in.

"How's it going?" he asked.

Paula shook her head. "I need to locate a CPA named Robert Brown. Supposedly he's in the process of setting up a practice in Lubbock."

"Did you try the chamber of commerce? If he's looking for new accounts that's the first place he'll probably go to meet people."

"That's an idea."

"If you have a local address you could also go by his post office and see if he left a forwarding address."

"All right. I'll give those ideas a try."

"If that doesn't work, call Jake and have him do a skip-trace. It will take a couple of days, but I'm sure he'll find him."

Paula nodded. "I wonder who has Randy Rhymes's records. There might be some documentation of the Mellon note there."

"The executor of his estate should have them. You can probably call the probate clerk and get that information."

"Good idea," Paula said, digging into her drawer.

Stan excused himself and left her to work. She pulled out a sheet of paper with all the court telephone numbers on it, found the probate court's number, and began dialing. A clerk answered and within a few minutes she had Randy's executor's name and telephone. She called him immediately and his secretary put her through.

"I'm sorry. I was never able to get those records. I think Bobby shredded everything when he realized Randy was onto him."

"So, how did you handle his estate?"

"There wasn't much to handle. Everything had been lost. I collected on a few insurance policies that hadn't lapsed. There was just barely enough cash to pay the funeral expenses."

"Boy, what did Brown do with all the money?"

"Gambling, drugs, loans to friends, bad investments, you name it."

"Did you find any evidence of a loan from Doc Mellon or DMI, Doc Mellon Investments?"

"No, but I have a vague recollection of someone from DMI calling me shortly after Randy died. They wanted to know if there was anything left in the estate to pay creditors. I told them the estate was insolvent and not to bother filing a proof of claim. They weren't happy to hear that, but I never heard from them again."

"You're sure it was DMI?"

"I believe so."

"But you don't have anything in writing from them?"

"No. They took my advice and didn't file a proof of claim."

"So, did this person mention the name 'Doc Mellon'?"

"No. I don't think so, but DMI rings a bell."

"Did they mention how much they were owed?"

"I seem to remember him mentioning they were out a couple hundred grand."

Paula thanked him and hung up. Although it was a little shaky, she now had confirmation that there had been a loan from Mellon to Randy Rhymes. She found it hard to believe that Mellon would kill the customers who couldn't pay him. That didn't seem like a good business practice to her, but the evidence seemed to point to that conclusion. Then Paula had a horrible thought. What if Mellon made his customers take out life insurance policies as additional security for the loans? That was a pretty common practice with banks, so why not for DMI, too? They certainly had an insurable interest. That would also explain why they wanted it to look like Maureen Thompson was the murderer.

Paula got up and went into Stan's office. She knew he used to be a life insurance agent, so she figured he might know how to find out if there had been insurance policies taken out by Doc Mellon on Randy Rhymes and Rodney Thompson.

"Yes," Stan said. "As a matter of fact, I know an underwriter over at Cosmopolitan Life. He's helped me in the past research that type of information. I'll give him a call and get him working on it."

"Fantastic!" Paula said. "I can't wait to find out. This will give me the connection I need to prove Doc Mellon is the murderer and clear Maureen."

Stan smiled. "Good work! You may have just saved her life."

"Hurry up. Make the call. I can't wait!" Paula urged.

"All right, but it will take him a day or two to research it, I'm sure."

"Okay, but just get him working on it. I'm running out of time."

Stan picked up the phone and called Cosmopolitan Life. He talked to his friend Ned Baily and told him what he needed.

"If the decedents were murdered, there would have been investigations to be sure the beneficiaries were not responsible. I'll call the firm that usually handles them and see if they were hired for the Rhymes or Thompson murders."

"Thanks. I appreciate your help."

Stan hung up the phone. "Okay. I'll let you know the minute I hear anything."

Paula nodded and went back to her office to call the Lubbock Chamber of Commerce. Unfortunately, nobody there had heard of Bob Brown. Frustrated, Paula went to the post office that serviced Bob Brown's old address. Miraculously, he had left a forwarding address but it wasn't to an address in Lubbock. It was to an attorney's office in Dallas. Paula looked up the number and called the attorney.

"Yes. I am receiving the mail. I'm handling Mr. Brown's probate."

"Oh, no. Robert Brown is dead?"

"Yes, I'm afraid so. He suffered a massive coronary about a month ago."

"Do you have any of Randy Rhymes's records? Brown had managed his affairs for some time."

"No. I don't know what happened to those records. I presumed Randy Rhymes's estate must have picked them up."

"No. They seem to be missing. There's even unconfirmed reports that he shredded everything. Do you have any knowledge of that?"

"No, but if it is true, that would explain a lot."

Paula thanked him and hung up. She was running out of options. Then she suddenly realized she hadn't thought of the most obvious place to look for the policies. Doc Mellon surely had copies of them, if he or his company was the beneficiary. She picked up the telephone and called Detective Besch. He wasn't available then, but he called her back within ten minutes.

"Have you guys confiscated all of Doc Mellon's records?"

"Yes, everything we could find," Besch replied.

"I need to look through them. I know there is a file for Rodney Thompson but I believe there should be one for Randy Rhymes as well."

"What makes you think that?"

"His business manager was pretty desperate and may have borrowed some money from Doc Mellon to keep afloat for a while longer. If so, I'm wondering if Mellon required a life insurance policy as a condition of making the loan. That's a pretty standard practice in the banking world."

"That's a pretty interesting theory. I'll go take a look straightaway and let you know."

"Thanks. I'm getting desperate. Randy Rhymes didn't have any financial records when he died; Bob Brown is dead and apparently he shredded all his records before he died. We're trying to track down the policies through one of Stan's friends but that's just a crapshoot. The policies should be in Doc Mellon's records. I hope you find them."

"If they're there, I'll find them," Besch assured her. "I'll call you in a few hours."

"Thanks. You're a lifesaver."

Paula hung up and then sat back in her chair. She was starting to feel the panic that invariably set in when a trial date was getting close. No matter how diligent she was there never seemed to be enough hours in the day to properly prepare for trial. She needed to nail down her evidence soon, so she could have some time to plan her presentation to the judge and jury. While she was waiting to hear back from Besch, she started working on her trial outline. As the prosecutor, Stuart Rawlins would put on his case first. That would mean the jury would hear all the evidence against Maureen Thompson before Paula could open her mouth. This was a tremendous advantage as many jurists made up their minds on the defendant's innocence or guilt within the first few hours. She could give an opening statement right after Rawlins, but that usually wasn't a great idea because the jury wouldn't hear from her again for several days. She usually liked to wait and give her full presentation at one time, after the prosecution was done. During her voir dire she'd ask the jury to listen carefully to the evidence and not to draw any conclusions until the trial was over. She hoped they'd listen and take her advice. Finally, late in the afternoon, Besch called her back.

"I've got good news and bad news."

"What's the good news?" Paula asked.

"I found a file on Robert Brown. Mellon loaned him and Rhymes $200,000, but there was no mention of an insurance policy."

Paula felt a surge of hope wash over her. That was the critical connection she needed to link the two murders. The fact that there wasn't any mention of an insurance policy was disappointing, but not fatal. She may not be able to fully explain what went down, but she sure could stir up a lot of doubt as to Maureen's guilt.

"What about the general accounting records—any premium payments to insurance companies?"

"We don't have those records. An accountant named Ronnie Moses has them and we haven't been able to locate him yet. He's on vacation or something."

"That's the same accountant who got Rodney in trouble with the IRS. I wonder how much they paid him to get lost."

"I don't know that there was time to warn him. I think we took Doc Mellon by surprise."

"Unless he had standing orders in the event of an arrest," Paula suggested.

"It's possible, I guess," Besch admitted.

"What about his insurance agent? Whoever handles their insurance would have a copy of the policy and know who was insured."

"Apparently Rich Ralston had an insurance license and handled all of the company's insurance."

"So, did you search his home?"

"Yes, but there were no business records there."

Paula thought about that. She wondered where they would keep sensitive records like that—a safety deposit box, perhaps? That would be logical but probably a little too obvious. She remembered one of Stan's old clients who kept a stash of money in a private safety deposit box so no one would ever find it.

"Can you see if he had a safety deposit box at his bank?"

"Sure, I'll have someone check it out."

"I wonder if he rents out safety deposit boxes at any of his pawnshops. If so, he might keep all his sensitive documents there."

"Good idea," Besch agreed. "I'll see if there are any boxes and if so, get a warrant to search them."

"You're a pretty handy guy to have around, Detective," Paula teased.

"Well, I want the asshole put away as much as you do. Plus, we wouldn't even have a case against him had it not been for you. So, it's the least I could do."

Paula hung up and leaned back in her chair. She was tired and hungry. It was time to go home. Unfortunately, when she looked out the window she saw it was raining hard. She hated to drive in bad weather. The traffic was a nightmare and nobody in Texas knew how to drive in inclement weather. She'd be lucky if she made it home alive. She called Bart and asked what he wanted to do for dinner. He said he'd pick up a pizza and a bottle of wine on the way home. She told him she'd be needing a massage, too. He told her if there was a big tip in it for him, it was no problem. She smiled in anticipation of the evening ahead.

27
Bar Hopping

Jodie had cried for hours after Brandon dropped her off at home. She blamed herself for Ricardo's death. She cursed herself for using him to get information on his father. Over the weeks her feelings for him had grown despite her attempts to keep herself aloof. He was a kind and gentle man who had fallen in love with her the first day they had met. She wished she'd taken Stan's advice and not seen him again, but realized now impossible that would have been since she too had fallen in love.

For several days she was incapacitated. She had no appetite and it was difficult to even get out of bed each day. Fortunately, Stan and Agent Thomas had called her and asked her if she was up to going to El Paso. She wanted to tell them no, but her grief was beginning to turn to anger. Anger toward Icaro Melendez. *How could a father put out a hit on his own flesh and blood?* No. She wouldn't be sitting around feeling sorry for herself. She'd be doing everything in her power to put Icaro Melendez and his gang of thugs six feet under!

On Thursday Jodie flew to El Paso and the FBI put her up in a Holiday Inn near downtown. The motel was adjacent to a strip club called the Regency Club. Rico had mentioned that the guys from the cartel often hung out there in the evenings. He suggested it would be a place they could make contact with him before the meeting. The meeting was scheduled for the following day at noon at an undisclosed location. Brenda met Jodie at the motel bar late Thursday afternoon to brief her on the operation and discuss their strategy.

269

"We've got one problem," Brenda advised.

"What's that?" Jodie asked.

"Since Rico checked in we haven't been able to get him the tracking device. We were expecting him to show up at the strip club next door last night, but he didn't make it. If he doesn't show up tonight, we'll have a problem."

"Well, I'm sure he'll do everything humanly possible to come tonight."

"I hope so. I don't know what we'll do if he doesn't show."

"Are there other clubs in town? His crew may have decided to go somewhere else. Rico wouldn't have been able to object too strenuously about it without calling attention to himself."

"Unfortunately, there are about six clubs in town similar to this one. We don't have the manpower to cover them all."

"I know what Rico looks like. Perhaps I could go clubbing tonight. I might get lucky and spot him. Do you have a spare tracking device?"

"Sure, we've got several of them with us, but Helio Melendez knows you and Rudy may have seen photos of you. If you ran into one of them it would be a disaster."

"Helio only met me once. He may not recognize me, particularly if I change my hair color and wear colored contacts."

"That might work, but it's still very dangerous. You've already nearly been killed twice."

"I'm not going to be doing anything other than sitting at the bar and flirting with a few guys. If I see Rico I'll make sure I catch him alone."

"Still, a lot of things could go wrong."

"Well, it's up to you. I'm just trying to help out."

Brenda nodded. "I know. I'll run it by Agent Lot and see what he says."

Brenda left, indicating she'd be back in an hour or so. Jodie was excited about the idea of doing some undercover work. She had always enjoyed her undercover jobs for Turner & Waters. As a child she had wanted to be an actress and had taken as much drama in school as she could get. Unfortunately, her acting career had never gotten off the ground for one reason or another—mainly due to money issues and the need to work. When Stan and Paula began giving her undercover assignments for Turner & Waters it allowed her to utilize her dramatic talents which delighted her to no end.

After Brenda left, Jodie went down the street to Walgreens and bought what she needed to disguise her appearance, including a pair of thick-rimmed glasses. She hadn't brought proper clothing for barhopping, so she stopped at a small dress shop and purchased a modest cocktail dress and high heels. It wasn't her usual look, but she didn't want to attract too much attention or she'd be fighting off men all night.

A little after six Brenda stopped by Jodie's room. She had gotten the go-ahead on Jodie's undercover gig and had brought the tracking device. She showed Jodie how it worked just for her own edification as Rico would already know what to do with it. They discussed various approaches for Jodie to deliver the package to Rico depending on the situation. Jodie assured her she'd have no trouble.

"Listen. If anything doesn't look right or you don't think you can isolate Rico enough to deliver the package, just forget about it, okay?"

"Okay. Don't worry. I don't have a death wish. I'll be careful."

"You've got my number. If you see him, call me. There'll be someone less than ten minutes away from you at all times. Wait for them to get there before you make a move if you can."

"All right. Where will you be?"

"I'm going to be here at the Regency. That's where Rico's supposed to be."

"Do you have a list of the other clubs?"

"Yes," Brenda said as she dug into her purse. She pulled out a piece of paper and handed it to Jodie. "We're covering the first three clubs. They are the closest to this location. If you would go to the others—spend maybe thirty minutes at each one and then move on. If we haven't located him by then you can go back and start over."

After Brenda had left, Jodie spent an hour changing her hair color, putting on her new contacts, and applying makeup. When she was done she got dressed, put on her glasses, and looked in the mirror. A smile came over her face as she barely recognized herself. She looked at her watch and saw it was 7:15 p.m. It was time to go, so she called the front desk and asked them to call her a cab. Ten minutes later she was on her way to Platinum Show Girls.

The cab pulled up the driveway of the single-story white stucco building. A big neon sign with pink letters spelling NUDE illuminated the entryway. Jodie paid the driver and got out of the cab. As the cab pulled away she programmed the cab's telephone number into her cell phone so she'd have it when it was time for her to move on.

As she approached the front door a young man opened it for her. She smiled and walked into a small crowded reception area. Music spilled out of two black leather doors as customers entered the club. Jodie walked through the door and observed a square grey bar with pink soda-fountain seats straight ahead. To her left there was a large stage with a silver pole running from the floor up to the ceiling. A girl in a pink bikini and white cowboy boots was just beginning to dance. Jodie went to the bar and took a seat at the far end. A topless barmaid came over and she ordered a gin and tonic.

From her vantage point she could see both sides of the bar and the front door. The barmaid deposited her drink and Jodie dropped a five-dollar bill on the counter. As she sipped her drink she scanned the room but didn't see Rico or any other familiar faces. The girl in the pink bikini slipped off her top to the delight of the men who surrounded her.

Much to Jodie's chagrin a middle-aged man came over and sat next to her. She ignored him as best she could until he got the hint and went away. A dancer came by and offered her a lap dance. Jodie politely declined but slipped a five-dollar bill in the girl's bikini bottom just to be a good sport and keep the management happy. After thirty minutes she pulled out her cell phone and called a cab. It was waiting for her when she stepped outside.

The next club on her list was the Chit Chat Club. It was laid out like a theater with a stage at one end, two bars on each wall, and tables in the middle. Colored lights cast an erotic red glow over the club. Rather than single dancers they had a troop of girls do a routine and then mingle with the crowd at its conclusion. There were doors on each side that led to private areas for more intimate encounters or private parties. Jodie took a seat at a table in the corner of the room. It wasn't a great vantage point but it was the best that was available the way the club was laid out. Almost immediately a young man took the seat next to her. He wasn't bad-looking so Jodie smiled.

"Do you mind?" he asked.

"No. Have a seat."

"Can I buy you a drink?"

"Sure. Gin and tonic," Jodie replied distantly.

Jodie figured it wouldn't hurt to have a drink or two with the man. It would make her less conspicuous and she could talk while she kept an eye on the door and watched the club.

"So, you from El Paso?"

"No. Just passing through on my way home to Dallas. How about you?"

"Oh. I'm from Houston. I'm here on business."

"What do you do?"

They talked for a half hour then Jodie excused herself to go to the bathroom. From the bathroom she called a cab and then slipped out of the club. The next one on her list was the Blue Diamond Club. The cab drove up and she disappeared inside and took a seat. After telling the cabbie where to go, she let out a big sigh. Her undercover work hadn't been as much fun as she had imagined it would be, and she wished she could go back to her motel and crash. Before she got to the Blue Diamond Club she called Brenda to report in.

"Any luck?" Brenda asked.

"No. How about you?"

"Nothing. There are a lot of college kids from UT coming and going but very few Mexicans. I'm starting to get discouraged."

"So, what will we do if Rico doesn't show up?"

"Pack it up and go home, I guess, until we hear from him again."

"What if something happened to him? What if his cover was blown?"

"Let's hope that hasn't happened, but if it did he's probably dead by now."

Jodie hung up as the cab approached a huge blue diamond ten feet high rotating above a white brick building that appeared to have once been a warehouse. The interior had been gutted and reconstructed in a modern, almost space-age decor. As Jodie walked inside she headed for a strategic place near the door and ordered a gin and tonic. Again she was plagued with suitors and dancers vying for her attention.

After another forty-five grueling minutes had passed and she hadn't seen anybody who remotely resembled Rico, her eyes fell upon a familiar face. She didn't know his name, but she had seen him on TV in Dallas. He was some kind of a public official. What was odd about the man was his company—two burly Mexicans who appeared to be his bodyguards. Jodie wondered who this mysterious man was and if he was in town for the big cartel meeting. She decided to find out.

He was in the middle of a lap dance so she waited until the dancer moved on, then she walked in his direction and stopped abruptly in front on him.

"You look familiar. Have we met?" she asked.

The two bodyguards shifted in their seats and gazed at Jodie warily. The man looked at her and shrugged. "I don't think so . . . but we can certainly remedy that."

Jodie gave him a pensive look and then burst out, "On TV. Haven't I seen you on TV? Dallas. You live in Dallas, right?"

"Yes, I do and occasionally I'm interviewed by the media. I'm Lee Long, Assistant District Attorney."

"Oh, Virginia Lee. Pleased to meet you," she lied.

"Can I buy you a drink?" he asked politely.

"Oh, thank you. You're so kind, but I was just about to call it a night. I'm leaving in the morning to go back to Dallas. I've been watching you for thirty minutes wondering where I'd seen you and I just couldn't go home until I figured it out."

"Well, I'm glad you came over and introduced yourself. It's nice to run into a friendly neighbor when you're out on the road." Lee stuck his hand in his pocket, pulled out a card, and handed it to Jodie. "Call me sometime when you get back home. I'd love to buy you a drink."

Jodie set down her purse precariously on the table and studied the card. She smiled broadly. "Wonderful. I'll do that," she said as she reached for her purse, clumsily knocking it to the ground. The contents spilled onto the floor. She bent down and grabbed her wallet. The two bodyguards helped her pick up her lipstick, eyeliner, Kleenex, cell phone, and lip balm. She apologized for her clumsiness and left.

When she got outside she called a cab and then dialed Brenda's number.

"Hello."

"Any luck?" Jodie asked.

"No. It's almost eleven and there's still no sign of him."

"Well, I may have stumbled across something."

Brenda perked up. "What's that?"

"I spotted someone who looked familiar—someone I'd seen on TV in Dallas. It turns out he's an assistant DA. What I found odd was the company he was keeping—two Mexican bodyguard types. I'm just wondering if he isn't here for the big meeting."

"Well, that *is* interesting. What's his name?"

"Lee Long."

"Did you ask him what he was doing in town?"

"No. I didn't want to hang around too long and make him suspicious. I just said a quick hello and got out of there."

"Well, nothing's going on here, so I'm on my way. What club are you at?"

"The Blue Diamond."

"All right. I'll be there in ten. Don't let him leave before we get there."

"Yeah, right. How am I supposed to do that?"

"I don't know. At least get his license number."

Jodie agreed and then hung up the phone as her cab drove up. She got in and told the driver she was waiting for someone so he should park across the street until he came.

"I can't just sit around, lady," he complained.

"Keep the meter running. It will only be five or ten minutes and I'll pay you for your time and give you a nice tip."

The driver shrugged and pulled into a parking space across the street. It was a perfect spot for Jodie to watch the front door. For the first few minutes it was quiet then the door swung open and Lee Long and his entourage stepped out.

"Shit!" Jodie said under her breath.

The men were laughing and kidding around as they headed for a big limousine parked up the street. Jodie looked down the road anxiously, hoping to see Brenda's FBI vehicle approaching but the road was quiet. Looking back she saw the light flash on and the doors slam. Quickly she fumbled in her purse for the tracking device. It had a strong magnet so all she needed to do was stick it on a metal surface in an inconspicuous spot on the vehicle. As the limo started toward her she stumbled out of her car.

Just as the limo reached the cab she ran out in front of it. The driver slammed on the brakes but not before Jodie was knocked to the ground. As she struggled to her feet she stuck the tracking device under the front bumper. Then she walked away from the car, grasping at her hip and moaning in pain. Lee Long jumped out of the limo, ran up to her, and grabbed her arm.

"Are you okay?" he asked. "I'm so sorry. The driver didn't you see us?"

Jodie looked up at him. "Huh? No. Where did you come from?"

"Should I call an ambulance?"

"No. No. I think I'm okay," Jodie said, struggling to her feet. "Nothing is broken. I guess it was my fault for not looking both ways. I'm glad my mother wasn't here to scold me."

Lee laughed. "You sure you're okay? I've got insurance. You want my insurance information?"

"No. No. That's not necessary. I'm so embarrassed."

"It's okay. I'm just glad you weren't hurt. I'd hang around awhile but I've got to meet someone. You've got my card. If you need to see a doctor, go ahead. My insurance will cover it. Be sure and call me for that drink, okay?"

"I will. Thanks," Jodie said as Lee and his friends got into the limo and drove off.

Five minutes later Brenda and Agent Lot showed up with two other agents. She explained that Lee Long had left.

"Damn it. You couldn't stall him?"

"No, but I did manage to attach the tracking device to his bumper."

Brenda laughed. "You're something else, girl."

"Yeah. Good work," Agent Lot agreed.

"I aim to please," Jodie said, handing her purse to Brenda.

"What's this?" Brenda asked.

"If you have your lab crew check out the contents of my purse they'll find the fingerprints of the two thugs that were with Mr. Long."

Brenda took the purse and looked inside. "Seriously?"

"Yes, I 'accidentally' dumped everything out on the floor and they were quite the gentlemen to help me pick everything up."

Brenda laughed. "Why don't you go back to the motel and get some sleep? We'll pick you up at seven for breakfast. Then we'll see where Mr. Long leads us."

"Sounds like a plan," Jodie said, yawning. "I could use some sleep, actually."

When Jodie got back to the hotel she called Stan to fill him in on what was happening and find out how Rebekah was doing. When she mentioned Lee Long, Stan became alarmed.

"You sure it was Lee Long?"

"Yes."

"That was one of Paula's old boyfriends. In fact, she mentioned that he helped her get the building inspections expedited for Thompson Construction. She's not going to be happy if it turns out Lee is connected to a Mexican cartel."

"Well, I may be wrong about him. We'll know for sure in the morning. I'm sure the FBI will have identified his two bodyguards by then."

"I hope he's not involved. If he is, it could cause us some serious problems," Stan said.

"I can't believe the cartel could buy off an assistant DA," Jodie said. "It doesn't seem possible."

"Money can buy just about anything. Long probably had a lot to do with the DA's decision to drop the Alvarez murder investigation."

"You're probably right. Having someone on the inside would definitely have its advantages."

After Jodie hung up she removed her contacts and all her makeup, washed the color out of her hair, and then took a shower. She felt much better when she finally crawled into bed at 11:27 p.m. It had been an exciting day, a little scary at times, but she'd loved every minute of it. She wondered if she ought to consider applying for a job with the FBI. Then she remembered, government employees didn't get paid all that much, so what she had with Turner & Waters was a better deal in the long run.

28
Specialists

When Stan returned from South Texas he took the day off and spent it with Rebekah. He was concerned that her strength hadn't returned and she was having trouble walking by herself. He went to the pharmacy and bought her a cane, but it pained him that she had to use it. He finally put his foot down.

"We better start visiting those specialists Dr. Sanders referred us to."

Rebekah frowned. "That's a waste of time."

"Maybe, but I'm not going to sit idly by and let you wither away."

"I'm feeling better. Don't worry."

Stan went into his office and found the notepad with the list of doctors they were supposed to see. There was a neurologist, cardiologist, endocrinologist, and possibly an oncologist. The task of getting Rebekah to go to that many doctors was daunting. Stan wondered which one he should take her to first. He called Terry to get her advice.

"I don't know. I doubt she's got heart issues. She has no history of that. It could be neurological. Perhaps you should start there. The endocrinologist would be next. I don't think she has cancer."

"All right," Stan said. "I'll call the neurologist although I don't think they found anything on her CAT scan."

"Well, she had symptoms characteristic of a seizure. That's why I think you should see a neurologist first."

"Okay. This just seems like such an inefficient way to figure out what's wrong with her. There should be someplace we can go where all the specialists work together."

"There are places like that, but Rebekah would have to check in and stay there for a few days."

"Right. Good luck with that."

Terry laughed.

"What does the endocrinologist do?" Stan asked.

"Oh, he deals with hormones, glands, and body chemistry—that kind of thing. They treat people with diabetes, thyroid disorders, pituitary gland issues, and so on."

"I'll call that doctor, too, I guess. We'll see who we can get an appointment with first."

Stan hung up and called the neurologist. The earliest appointment he could get was in ten days. That seemed like such a long time to wait when Rebekah's condition was so precarious. Next he called the endocrinologist and got more bad news: the next available appointment there was in three weeks. Stan chewed on a nail as he pondered the situation. He felt so helpless.

That night Stan got a telephone call from Jodie. She had gone barhopping hoping to run into Rico. She hadn't found him but had seen someone she recognized—Assistant DA Lee Long. Stan knew Lee Long was one of Paula's old flames and he'd helped her get some building inspections expedited recently. This wasn't a good situation if it turned out Lee Long had a connection to the cartel. If the connection between Paula and Lee Long came out, it could be embarrassing and taint the firm's image. Stan called Paula to alert her to this new development.

"He's in El Paso?" Paula asked.

"Yes, Jodie thinks he's going to the big cartel meeting tomorrow."

"I can't believe he'd be involved with a drug cartel. Jodie must be mistaken."

"Why would he have two Mexican bodyguards?"

"I don't know. There must be some explanation."

"So, worst-case scenario, do we have a problem?"

"Hell, yes. If he finds out I led the FBI to him, he'll be pissed off and out for my blood."

"So, what he did for you isn't a big deal, is it?" Stan questioned.

"The press would make it into a big deal—getting special treatment. I could have a problem with the bar association if they found out sleeping with him was part of the deal. It was the only way he'd agree to help. What I didn't count on was his insistence I sleep with him a second time."

"Well, there's nothing we can do about it now, so we'll just have to keep our fingers crossed that it doesn't come up."

"Now I'm not going to be able to sleep," Paula moaned. "God dammit! Wouldn't it be my luck if Lee Long turns out to be a spy for the cartel. I can't believe this."

"It's too bad you can't get Bart's help on this. He could talk to Lee and make sure he doesn't mention any of this."

"Yeah, right. I'm going to tell Bart I slept with Lee so he'd help me expedite a building inspection."

"I know you can't. It was just a thought."

Stan hated dumping this problem on Paula when she was up to her elbows in a murder case, but he had to do it so she wouldn't be blindsided by the press or the police down the road. He figured given some time, she'd come up with a strategy to deal with the situation. At least he hoped so.

29
Opening Statement

An incredible depression came over Paula. Besch had just called and told her he hadn't been able to find any records kept by Rich Ralston nor did they find a safety deposit box at the bank or any of the company's pawnshops. Stan had promised to keep looking for proof of the insurance, but Stan had his hands full with Rebekah and Jodie. She doubted he'd have the time to pull a miracle out of his hat. She was at the point where she'd have to face the reality that she had all the evidence she was going to get on Doc Mellon. Now the big question was, would that be enough to create reasonable doubt?

It was Friday and the trial was scheduled on the following Monday. Paula worked hard all weekend finalizing her trial outline, witness questions, and going through the evidence. She felt she was ready but not confident of victory. She felt sick. She hated to lose, but it was looking more and more like that might happen and there wasn't a damn thing she could do about it.

On Monday she avoided the press by entering through a back door of the district clerk's office that led into the building's stairwell. That meant she had to climb nine flights of stairs, but that was preferable to being mobbed by reporters. When she reached the ninth floor she took the back hallway behind the courtrooms and stuck her head into the clerk's office.

"Hi, Cecilia," she said to Judge Sands's clerk.

"Oh hi, Paula."

"So, everything on schedule?"

"As far as I know. You're still number one."

283

"Good. It's time to get this over with."

"Boy, ain't that the truth. I've must have had twenty calls already this morning from reporters."

"Tell me about it. It's a media circus."

Paula peeked in the back door and saw Maureen Thompson seated at the counsel table. She walked over to the table and sat down.

"Well, now it all begins," Paula said to Maureen.

Maureen took a nervous breath. "How do you think it looks?"

"Well, we've got a great alternate theory as we've talked about, but we can't absolutely prove it. We don't have to prove it, necessarily, to create reasonable doubt, but I'd feel better if we could prove there were insurance policies on Rod's and Randy's lives."

"I wish I could help you, but I don't have any idea."

"I know. You didn't get involved in the business side of things. Don't worry, Stan is still out beating the bushes for some kind of proof of it."

"I asked Charlie Hatch about it, but he didn't know anything about financing. He was just responsible for day-to-day operations."

"Right," Paula said dejectedly.

The judge walked in the back door and said something to the bailiff. The bailiff nodded and then said, "All rise for the Honorable Judge Leon Sands."

The judge took the bench and sat down. After looking at his docket he opened a file and said, "The State of Texas vs. Maureen Ann Thompson. Can I have appearances?"

"Stuart Rawlins for the State," Rawlins replied.

"Paula Waters for the defendant," Paula said.

The judge nodded. "All right. Is everyone ready?"

"Yes, Your Honor," Rawlins advised.

"The defendant is ready, Your Honor," Paula agreed.

The judge looked at the clerk. "Would the clerk give counsels their jury packets?"

The clerk stood up and brought an envelope to Paula and Rawlins. Each of them opened them and started looking over the material.

"I'll give you about thirty minutes to look the information over and then we'll begin picking the jury. You'll each have six strikes. Any questions?"

"No, Your Honor," they both said.

The judge left the bench and went back to his office. Rawlins and his assistant began going through the jury list. Paula and Maureen got up and went into a conference room so they'd have privacy. Twenty minutes later everyone was back in the courtroom and jury selection began. It took the rest of the day to select the jury of five men and seven women who would decide Maureen's fate. Three alternates were also selected in case anyone got sick, died, or became disqualified during the trial. When the selection was completed and the jury was seated, the judge recessed the trial for the afternoon. He told Rawlins to be ready to give his opening statement first thing.

Bart was there when they broke for the day. He wanted to help Paula deal with the press and take her to dinner to get her mind off the trial. They were mobbed by reporters as they left the courtroom. Elena and Maureen went out the back door and down the stairs to avoid the reporters entirely. This had been agreed upon ahead of time because Maureen had been so viciously attacked by the press and had received death threats.

"Ms. Waters. Are you satisfied with the jury?" a reporter asked.

"Yes," Paula replied as Bart pushed a path through the crowd. "They seem to be a fine cross section of the community. We have no complaints."

"Ms. Waters. How are you going to overcome the overwhelming evidence against your client?"

Paula looked at the reporter. "We have a good explanation for every piece of evidence the prosecution will introduce. They have nothing but circumstantial evidence."

The elevator door opened and Bart pulled Paula inside. He then spread his arms, barring anyone else from entering the elevator.

"Sorry, this elevator is full."

Paula pushed the CLOSE button and the door slid shut. The three people already on the elevator when Bart and Paula got on gave them a puzzled look.

Bart smiled. "The press. They just won't leave us alone."

One of the passengers nodded and rolled his eyes. When they got to the first floor, they got out and faced yet another mob of media. Bart groaned before pushing another path through the frantic reporters.

"Ms. Waters? Is it true that you assisted the police in making a case against Doc 'the Clock' Mellon?"

"Yes. That's true. In the investigation of this case I came across certain information against Mr. Mellon that I passed on to the police."

"Is there any connection between his arrest and Maureen Thompson?"

Paula looked at the man. He was the first one who had made the connection between the two cases. She wondered if she should acknowledge the connection. After a few seconds' reflection she decided to tell the truth as she had nothing to lose and could use some help from the press. If they thought there was a new angle to investigate, they'd be on it like a fox on a rabbit.

"Yes. We believe so. When I give my opening statement it will all become clear."

"Ms. Waters. Can you tell us more about the connection now?"

"No. Sorry," Paula said, shaking her head. "You'll have to wait."

They finally made it through the crowd and headed across Commerce Street to the West End. They liked the Palm Restaurant and Bart had made them reservations there. Once inside they were escorted to a corner booth and given the wine list. Bart got them a

William Manchee

bottle of Au Bon Climat and then placed their orders. Paula got the filet and lobster and Bart got a T-bone steak. They ate silently until they were well into their meal before Paula couldn't stand the silence anymore.

"So, what's the scuttlebutt at the office?"

"Ah. Well, you know, everyone's pretty confident they are going to get a conviction."

"Even though they know Mellon's a scumbag and probably the real killer?"

"They'll admit he's a scumbag, but they don't think he had anything to do with Rodney Thompson's death. Unless you have something you haven't shared with them, you don't have much proof of that."

Paula sighed. "We're still working on it."

Bart smiled gently. "Don't think about the trial. Just enjoy your food. When we're done, I'll take you home and you can take a bath. Then I'll give you a massage."

"Hmm. Dinner, a bath, and a massage. You really know how to spoil a girl."

"Of course. Isn't that why you married me?"

"That and so I'd have a spy at the DA's office."

They both laughed and didn't bring up the trial again that evening. When they got home Bart made good on his promises. Then they went to bed early, so Paula would be well rested when Rawlins put on the state's case the following morning.

Paula felt rested and relaxed the next morning. She got up, ate breakfast, and then spent a half hour putting on makeup and getting dressed. She couldn't decide what to wear. Should she dress conservatively or flash it up a bit? Finally she decided a little distraction would be good during Rawlins's opening, so she wore a red linen-look suit with matching shoes. She felt good but that soon changed when Stan called at just after eight.

He told her he hadn't had any luck yet finding the insurance policies but was planning to go out to East Texas to track down

287

Mellon's accountant. He promised her he'd still keep digging and assured her that he hadn't given up. She knew he was stubborn and would diligently search for the policies, but in reality she'd pretty much given up on him finding them. She had resigned herself to the fact that she'd have to create reasonable doubt with what she had.

Bart escorted her to the courthouse and helped her through the throng of reporters as he had done the day before. Then he left her to go to work. Maureen Thompson was at the counsel table when she arrived. She went over to her and took a seat.

"Good morning," Paula said. "How are you doing today?"

"Okay," Maureen said, but her smile looked forced.

Paula leaned in close. "Anything going on yet?"

"No," she replied softly. "It's been quiet. Rawlins has been studying his notes and his associate has been organizing evidence."

Paula gazed around the packed courtroom. People were standing against the side and back walls. Paula wondered if the judge would allow that during the trial. She saw Elena and waved to her. Then she spotted Detective Besch talking to Linda Samuelson, Stuart Rawlins's assistant. Paula heard a loud conversation behind her. She turned and saw the judge entering the courtroom.

The bailiff stood up. "All rise for the Honorable Leon Sands!"

The room quieted and everyone stood up. The judge motioned for everyone to be seated. "All right. Mr. Rawlins. You may read the indictment."

"Yes, Your Honor."

"In the name and by the authority of the State of Texas: The Grand Jury of Dallas County, State of Texas, duly organized at the August Term A.D., 1995 of the 14th Judicial District Court, Dallas County, in said court at said term, do present that one Maureen Thompson, defendant, on or about the 25th day of February 1995, in the County and said State, did intentionally or knowingly cause the death of her husband, Rodney Rutherford Thompson, by stabbing him with an ice pick until he was dead, such act being against the peace and

William Manchee

dignity of the State of Texas. "

"Very good, Mr. Rawlins. You may proceed with your opening statement."

"Thank you. Your Honor, ladies and gentlemen of the jury. In the course of this trial the state will show, beyond any reasonable doubt, that on the evening of February 25, 1995 the defendant, Maureen Thompson, did enter into the apartment rented by her husband and located in the Regency West Apartment complex, for the purpose of murdering her husband, Rodney Thompson.

"The motivation for this murder was anger, jealousy, revenge, and a $500,000 insurance policy. Mr. Thompson had just left the defendant and took up residence with another woman. To make matters worse he left Ms. Thompson penniless, massively in debt, and in a home that was about to be foreclosed. Her anger and jealousy was understandable, but it did not give her the right to kill her husband to collect the insurance.

"The body was discovered by Lance Shepard, a maintenance man living at the Regency West Apartments. Mr. Shepard will testify that on the evening of February 25, 1995 he was contacted by the manager to check on a report of loud music coming from apartment 247, occupied by the decedent, Rodney Thompson. When he arrived at the apartment he quickly understood why the neighbors were complaining. Someone in apartment 247 had turned the stereo up so loud it could be clearly heard outside the apartment. He knocked on the door but there was no answer, so he peered into the front window and saw an overturned lamp. Fearing that Mr. Thompson may have had a medical emergency, he used his master key to enter the apartment.

"Once inside, he proceeded into the living room observing the overturned lamp, a broken vase on the hardwood floor, and magazines and newspapers scattered about. There was also such an odor in the apartment that he had to hold his nose to keep from gagging. The stench seemed to be coming from the kitchen, so he went there to investigate. That's where he found the decedent, Rodney Thompson, on the floor, naked from the waist up, and with an ice pick stuck in his chest.

"Upon discovery of the body, Mr. Shepard immediately called 911. Several minutes later Detective Leonard Gossett and two patrol officers arrived and secured the crime scene. Detective Gossett will testify that he found the murder weapon, a nine-inch Johnson-Rose chrome-plated ice pick sticking out of the body. He called the paramedics who arrived about eight minutes later. They checked the victim, determined he was dead, and called the medical examiner.

"The medical examiner will testify that when he arrived he examined the body and found ten additional wounds from the ice pick in close proximity to the victim's heart. He subsequently calculated that the murder took place between ten and eleven p.m. that evening.

"Paul Robb from the forensic analysis unit will testify that there were two sets of fingerprints on the ice pick—the victim's and the defendant, Maureen Thompson.

"Detective Gossett will also testify that after securing the crime scene he went to the defendant's house located only four miles from the crime scene. There he questioned her and she denied any knowledge or involvement in the homicide but could not provide a verifiable alibi. She also revealed that her husband had recently left her for another woman, allowed her car to be repossessed, and refused to support her or their children.

"Friends and family will testify that Maureen pleaded with her husband not to abandon them, but he was under a lot of stress from a failing business and became so depressed that he was unable to face, let alone deal with his problems. Although we cannot probe the defendant's mind it is quite likely she came to the conclusion that the insurance policy on her husband's life was more likely to solve her problems than pleas to the husband.

"So, it is not surprising that on the night of February 25, 1995, after she had put her two children to bed, she put on her

Rollerblades and skated over to her husband's apartment to kill him. We know that was her intent because she turned up the volume of the music so that the ensuing struggle would not be heard by the neighbors. Then she went to the Waterford crystal ice bucket that they had been given as a wedding present, picked up the ice pick, and proceeded to violently stab Rodney Thompson, not once or twice but eleven times in the heart.

"This tells us that this was a crime of passion, a premeditated, calculated murder in retaliation for Mr. Thompson's infidelity, abandonment of the family, and destruction of the marriage."

This is where Rawlins would have noted that Maureen Thompson had collected on her first husband's insurance policy despite the fact that he had also been hacked to death with an ice pick. Fortunately for Maureen, Judge Sands had ruled that the first murder trial would not be mentioned as it was irrelevant since she hadn't been convicted. Rawlins had protested the ruling strenuously but Paula had argued that any mention of that trial would be extremely prejudicial to the defendant's case and the judge agreed.

As a practical matter every juror knew of the previous murder trial and the accusations made against Ms. Thompson from all the media reports within hours of the murder, but the judge had instructed them to disregard those reports and not consider any evidence other than what was presented to them by counsel during trial. So, Rawlins bit his tongue and concluded his statement.

"So, I'm confident you will do your duty as jurors to carefully weigh the overwhelming evidence we will present to you and find the defendant guilty of the murder of Rodney Rutherford Thompson."

"Thank you," Judge Sands said. "Ms. Waters. Would you like to make an opening statement now?"

Paula wondered what she should do. She feared if she didn't make a strong opening statement the jury might make up their minds before she got a chance to put on her case. She had to somehow make them keep from drawing any conclusions until all the evidence was in. The dilemma that she faced was that she didn't want to lay out a defense she couldn't prove. The jury would be unforgiving if she suggested Doc Mellon was responsible for the murders and then couldn't prove it or at least make it appear more likely that Doc Mellon was the murderer.

The judge cleared his throat. "Ms. Waters."

Paula stood up. "Ah. Yes, Your Honor. I think I will make an opening statement now."

It was a gamble, but Paula finally decided she had to take it. If she lay back and simply tried to argue that Rawlins hadn't proven his case, whether he had or hadn't, she'd lose. There was just too much circumstantial evidence of Maureen's guilt. She had to put forward her alternate theory and pray to God that Stan could find the insurance policy that would prove Doc Mellon was the murderer.

"All right, then," the judge said. "You may proceed."

Paula took a deep breath, nodded to the judge, and then turned to the jury. "Your Honor, ladies and gentlemen of the jury. I know you are all wondering what I could possibly say to contradict or nullify the conclusions Mr. Rawlins has drawn from the evidence he has promised to provide you during the course of this trial. I will admit his arguments seem persuasive, but that's because you won't know the whole story until we put on Maureen's case. So, I would suggest you not put the noose around Maureen Thompson's neck quite yet. You see, I intend to call witnesses who will provide a dramatically different explanation for what occurred the night of February 25, 1995.

"Specifically, Maureen's sister will testify that she and the defendant went to Rod's apartment the weekend before the murder to drop off the kids and she personally saw Maureen chipping ice for lemonade. So, it's no big surprise that the defendant's fingerprints were found on the murder weapon.

"You'll also hear from Charlie Hatch, the superintendent for Thompson Construction. He'll testify that Thompson Construction was in serious financial trouble and owed $250,000 plus interest to someone you all have probably heard of—Doc 'the Clock' Mellon, the former football star. He'll tell you that Mellon wasn't the type of man who would write off a debt. In fact, you may have heard that Mr. Mellon has recently been arrested on charges of assault and battery and extortion among other charges.

"In the course of the trial I'll put on expert witnesses who will explain Doc Mellon's methods of doing business which include threats, intimidation, and bodily harm. We may not be able to prove absolutely that Doc Mellon killed Rodney Thompson but I'm sure we will be able to convince you that it is much more likely that he is the murderer.

"While you are listening to this testimony, I want you to remember the prosecution has to prove their case beyond all reasonable doubt. As Mr. Rawlins has already told you there are no eye witnesses. All the prosecution's evidence is circumstantial including the defendant's fingerprints on the murder weapon which, as I said, got there quite innocently. All the defense has to do is create reasonable doubt as to Maureen's Thompson's guilt. If we do that you must acquit her.

"Maureen and I want to thank you all in advance for your jury service. I know what an inconvenience it is to have to serve on a jury, particularly for a long case like this one, but I want you to know you are rendering a great service to the community and we appreciate it very much.

"One last reminder, and I know I've said it already but it's so important I'm going to say it again. You have an obligation to listen to all the evidence before you make up your minds. Keep an open mind until the last witness sits down. This is a complicated case and it's going to take your complete attention and concentration to effectively digest all the facts, sift through the evidence, and come to a just decision.

"But I know you can do it, and I'm confident when the dust settles you'll find Maureen Thompson innocent. Thank you."

Paula smiled and walked back to the counsel table. Maureen gave her a nervous smile. She felt relieved. Now at least she knew what she had to do and didn't have to hold back.

The judge looked at his watch. "All right, we'll take a twenty-minute recess and then Mr. Rawlins, you can call your first witness."

"Very good, Your Honor," Rawlins said.

The judge stood up and left the bench. The courtroom broke into excited chatter. Paula stood up and watched the jury file out of the jury box. She wondered what they were thinking. Had she piqued their curiosity? Would they keep an open mind as she had asked them to? She thought she saw the last juror smile at her, or was it her imagination? She prayed they'd do the right thing.

30
Confrontation

As promised Brenda picked Jodie up at seven and took her to IHOP for breakfast. On the way Brenda filled her in on the latest developments.

"We identified the two bodyguards. They do have cartel connections, so I think Mr. Long must be involved with the cartel in some fashion."

"Do you know where he is?"

"Yes, he ended up at the Hilton last night. He's still there right now. As soon as he leaves we'll follow him to the meeting."

"So, you never heard from Rico?"

"No. I don't know what happened to him. Hopefully he'll be at the meeting."

When they got to IHOP Agent Lot was already there drinking a cup of coffee. He stood up when they walked in and waved them over.

"So, any idea what this meeting is about?" Jodie asked.

"Yes, we think it's about your garnishments," Agent Lot replied. "The cartel has to decide how to deal with the situation. You've put the squeeze on their money laundering machine and they have to do something about it. It's also probably about our arrest of Melendez and his men."

"So, how are you going to handle the meeting? Are you going to shut it down and arrest everybody?"

"No. We have to have a good cause to do that. We'll just have to play it by ear and hope we can ID some of the participants. If we see

Rudy or Helio, of course, we'll go in immediately and arrest them. They'll probably put up a fight and that will legally allow us to arrest the whole lot of them. How long we can hold them will depend on who and what we find on the premises."

The waitress came over and took their orders. Agent Lot had banana nut pancakes, Brenda a vegetarian omelet, and Jodie an International Passport Breakfast with Swedish pancakes. She poured them all coffee before she left.

"So, what do you think they'll do about the garnishments?" Jodie asked.

"That may be why Lee Long is here," Lot replied. "They need advice on how to deal with the legalities of the garnishments. There are too many of them to deal with in a traditional manner."

"Traditional?" Jodie asked.

"Bribery, intimidation, and murder. You and Stan are too heavily guarded, the Alvarez family is out of reach, too; so they may be forced to hire attorneys to protect their interests. The question under discussion, I believe, will be whether to hire attorneys to appeal the judgment and quash all the garnishments, or abandon everything you've captured."

"What do you think they will decide to do?"

"I don't know. Hopefully Rico can fill us in on their plans."

"If he's even at the meeting," Brenda said.

"Let's hope he is," Lot replied.

Agent Lot's phone buzzed. He answered it and listened intently for thirty seconds and then hung it up. "Okay, time to roll. The limo is on the move."

They got up quickly, paid the bill, and left. Agent Lot pointed to his vehicle and suggested they all go with him. He gunned the engine before Jodie had even buckled her seatbelt.

They drove several miles toward the outskirts of town until they found themselves in an industrial district. The reek of oil filled the air. Agent Lot pulled over in a convenience store parking lot and killed the engine.

"They'll be driving by here in a couple of minutes. We're to wait here for further instructions."

Brenda nodded and Jodie took a deep breath.

"You guys do this a lot?" Jodie asked.

"All the time," Brenda replied, smiling. "Most of the time it's pretty boring, but I have a feeling today might be different."

Jodie realized she had a knot in her stomach. She was usually pretty cool under pressure but all the talk of the cartel focusing all of their attention on Stan and her had her worried. Perhaps they'd been a bit too aggressive in their approach to the case. She realized Stan's philosophy of ignoring the nature of your enemy and relying on the government for protection was a bit reckless in hindsight. Flashbacks of Ricardo's assassination jolted her. She began to sweat and shake slightly. Brenda looked at her intently.

"You okay?" Brenda asked.

Jodie sat up straight and smiled. "Yeah. I'm fine. This is just a little nerve-racking."

"Maybe you should have stayed back at the motel."

"No way!" Jodie protested. "I wouldn't miss this for the world."

Brenda nodded and turned away. Agent Lot's phone buzzed. He picked it up, listened a moment, and then started the engine.

"They're almost here. We're to cover the back of a warehouse about half a mile from here."

Jodie looked out her window and saw the limo coming down the street. It passed along with several other FBI vehicles following at a safe distance. As soon as they were out of sight Agent Lot took them to their assigned spot on the perimeter of a big office-warehouse complex. Agent Lot picked up a radio on the seat next to him and held down the TALK button.

"South team in position."

"Roger. The limo has parked in front. There's already a half dozen vehicles in the parking lot. Seven occupants are getting out—Long and his two bodyguards, two Hispanic males, a woman and the driver is . . . Rico. Yes, it's definitely Rico."

They all let out a collective sigh of relief. Jodie looked at Brenda and smiled.

"So, at least we'll find out what they plan to do," Jodie observed.

"Hopefully," Brenda said. "Rico is just the driver. They may not let him into the meeting."

"Oh," Jodie moaned. "That's true."

"From what I heard about Rico, he'll figure a way to hear what's going on."

"I wonder why he didn't contact us last night?" Jodie mused.

"They must have had him out of pocket somehow," Lot replied.

The radio crackled. "Another vehicle approaching—black Escalade license 2ST 872. Three men getting out, one staying in the vehicle. Vehicle driving off. It looks like he's parking the Escalade across the street. He's opening the door. There's a rifle lying across the front seat. He's pulling out binoculars. Everyone be sure you're out of view.

"All right. Another vehicle approaching. A Blue Ford F-350 club cab, license TT5 552. Three men and a woman occupying the vehicle. They are parking and now leaving the vehicle. It appears one of them may be Helio Melendez. Can we get Ms. Marshall's confirmation? I'll send over a photo."

"Roger that," Agent Lot replied.

Brenda looked at Jodie. Jodie raised her eyebrows. A few moments later a car drove up and an agent brought over a Polaroid of the suspect. Jodie took it and looked at it intently. A surge of adrenaline washed over her. She took a deep breath. "That's him. That's Helio Melendez."

Agent Lot took the photo and handed it back to the agent who took it and jumped back into his car. They drove off and Agent

Lot picked up the radio. "That's an affirmative on the ID. It's Helio Melendez."

Brenda smiled at Jodie. "Now the fun begins."

Jodie smiled back nervously. "Can't wait."

"You stay in the car while this goes down. Keep your head down if any bullets start flying. These windows are not bulletproof."

Jodie nodded as the radio crackled again. "SWAT teams in position."

"Hold your ground," Agent Lot said. "Let them have their meeting. We'll nail them as they're leaving. "

"Why wait?" a voice protested.

"We may get some valuable intel if we let them talk awhile. We've got the perimeter covered. Nobody's going to get away."

"But they could spot us at any time," the voice argued.

"Everyone keep out of view. If anything looks awry, we'll go in immediately," Agent Lot assured him.

"On your command," the voice conceded.

Thirty minutes later the radio crackled. "There's movement at the front door. It looks like someone is leaving."

"All right," Agent Lot said. "Let's move in. SWAT, are you ready?"

"Roger. SWAT standing by."

"Okay. Let's move," Agent Lot commanded.

Simultaneously, SWAT teams swarmed in toward all four entrances to the building. Agent Lot and Agent Thomas followed the team through the back loading docks into the warehouse. Although they encountered no resistance, gunfire could be heard from the front of the building. The team continued to sweep the warehouse when a door burst open in front of them. Three men came running through with guns held high. For a moment they contemplated taking on the three SWAT members confronting them and then thought better of it.

"FBI! Drop your weapons! Down on your knees."

The three men reluctantly dropped their weapons and hit the floor. The agents ran over quickly, cuffed them, and turned them over to Agent Lot and Agent Thomas. Another man slammed through the door. Seeing all the agents, he made a quick turn to the right and ran behind a row of pallets stacked high. Two of the SWAT team ran after him. Jodie watched with great interest as he slipped out a back door and jumped off the dock to the pavement. As instructed, she ducked down out of view, hoping the man wouldn't see her. Suddenly the car shook as the man hurled himself over the hood and ducked down for cover. He looked inside to see if the keys were in the ignition. They weren't, but he noticed Jodie hiding in the backseat. He pointed his gun at her.

"Get out of the car!" he demanded.

"I don't think so," Jodie said, kicking the door open hard. The door hit the man, knocking him backward. As he tried to maintain his balance a bullet hit him in the shoulder. He went down hard, losing his gun in the process. Jodie opened the opposite door and ran to the safety of the SWAT team.

"Nice move," the man said.

"Nice shooting," Jodie replied.

"Thanks. It was like shooting a wounded duck. Not a major challenge."

Agent Lot rushed over. "I told you to stay in the car."

"Sorry about that, but when he pointed his gun at me I decided saving my ass was more important."

Agent Lot chuckled. "All right. I'm glad you're okay."

"How's it going inside?"

"We've taken Rudy Melendez into custody along with everyone else at the meeting. Rico is safe. They took him in with cuffs on just in case he needs to go back in play later."

"Good. What about Lee Long?"

Agent Lot shook his head. "Some of the cartel members put up a fight and I'm afraid Mr. Long got caught in the cross fire. A bullet struck him in the head. He died before he hit the ground."

Jodie's mouth dropped. "Oh, my God!"

"Yeah. It's a real shame. We were anxious to talk to him."

"So, what now?" Jodie asked.

"Let's get you to the airport. I think you've had enough excitement for one weekend."

Jodie didn't argue. She was tired, shaken, and ready for a nice quiet flight home. Although she'd stared down the barrel of a revolver once again, it had all worked out. With most of the cartel members in custody she felt safe for the first time in months. Now the firm could prosecute their garnishment claims, liquidate the assets they'd captured, and give the Alvarez family a nice fat check. And with all the evidence the FBI had gathered it was quite likely Icaro Melendez would soon be on death row along with Ben Zepeda and Guido Quesada. Although it had seemed an impossible task when Pandora Alvarez had first walked in the door, somehow they'd managed to obtain justice. Jodie felt proud as the big Southwest jet took off into clear blue skies on its way to Dallas Love Field.

31
Obstruction of Justice

Maria's voice came over the intercom announcing that Stan had a call from Ned Baily of Cosmopolitan Life. Stan picked up the telephone eagerly as Ned was working on finding out if Doc Mellon had purchased insurance policies on Randy Rhymes and Rodney Thompson.

"We can't find any investigations on either of your guys, sorry."

"Really?" Stan said, incredulous. He was certain Paula had been right and there would have been investigations. "Are you sure there are no other firms that might have done the investigation?"

"No. There are a few others, but I called all of them. Nobody did an investigation of an insurance claim on the lives of Rodney Thompson or Randy Rhymes. And since there is zero chance that a claim would be paid without an investigation, I'd conclude there were no insurance policies on them."

"Damn. I can't believe it," Stan moaned. "Well thanks, Ned. I appreciate your help."

"Sorry I didn't have better news."

"Well, it's not your fault. The facts are what they are."

Stan set down the phone, feeling extremely depressed. He couldn't go back to Paula and tell her there were no insurance policies, but that's what it looked like. He tried to think of a scenario that would explain why Doc Mellon would want Randy and Rodney dead. Perhaps it was just a message to his other customers that the penalty for default was death, but he doubted that. Mellon wouldn't be willing to write off that kind of money and his business would dry up in a hurry if people realized the stakes were that high. No, there had to be insurance policies. He couldn't quit looking quite yet.

The company's accounting records would be the obvious place to find the missing insurance policies, but they were with the accountant who was missing. Stan decided it was time to find Ronnie Moses. Not having time to mess around, he called the State Board of Accountancy and got business and home addresses in Tyler, Texas. It was about a two-hour drive to Tyler, so he told Maria he'd probably be gone most of the day. She said she'd reschedule his appointments.

He knew if he found Moses, he couldn't just barge into his office and demand to see the records. He'd have to have a court order authorizing him to review them and make copies of anything he wanted. He told Paula his plans and she called the court clerk and asked that a subpoena duces tecum be issued for the records. Stan picked it up on his way to Tyler.

Stan loved the drive out to Tyler. East Texas got a lot of rain so there were lots of trees and foliage. Bluebonnets were plentiful too along the medium of I-20 which connected the two cities. He felt relaxed as he turned off the freeway and took Highway 67 into the city. Moses had an office in the old downtown area near the federal courthouse. Stan parked in the lot in front of the three-story office building and went inside. After consulting the directory for a suite number he took the elevator to the third floor. Much to his shock and dismay he found the door locked.

Dispirited, he went to the office next door and inquired as to whether anyone knew where Ronnie Moses might be. The receptionist said she hadn't seen him in several days but she'd ask around the office and see if anyone else had seen him. She came back a moment later and reported that no one else had seen him, either.

"Isn't it unusual to have his office closed during regular business hours?" Stan asked.

The girl shrugged. "Not for Ronnie. He doesn't have any employees, so if he has to leave the office he just locks it up."

"Hmm," Stan said, pulling out a card. "If you see him would you call me? It's a matter of life or death. I've got to talk to him."

The receptionist took Stan's card and agreed to call him if Moses showed up. Stan went back to his car and looked at the map to see how to get to Moses's home. Once he had the route in his head he started out of the parking lot. As he was pulling out onto the street a man in a station wagon drove past him. Stan stopped and looked back at the man. He'd never met Moses but he'd been given a general description. The man got out of the station wagon and walked into the building. Stan pulled into the nearest parking spot and followed him back in. The elevator was closing as Stan approached it, so he rushed to the stairs and ascended them quickly. The door to Moses's office was closing as Stan rushed out of the stairwell. He got to the door and tried to open it but it was still locked.

The door was glass, but it was dark and Stan could only see a few feet into the office. He knocked on the door and waited. There was no answer so he knocked again, harder this time. A minute went by and Stan knocked again.

"Mr. Moses. I know you are in there. Open the door. I need to talk to you."

Stan heard a door slam and wondered where the noise had come from. He walked down the hallway and realized there was a back entrance to Ronnie Moses's office. He'd made a quick exit when he heard Stan knocking on his door. Stan rushed back to the lobby and saw Moses getting back in his car and driving away. By the time Stan got to his car and started the engine, it was too late. Ronnie Moses had disappeared.

Assuming that Moses was going home, Stan resumed the route he had previously mapped out. Twenty minutes later he was driving down a country road looking for the address he had written down back at the office. When he found the two-story ranch-style structure, he passed it and parked down the street so Moses wouldn't see him if he looked out his front window.

Moses's station wagon was nowhere to be seen, but Stan figured he may have parked it in the garage, so he went up to the front door and knocked. Much to his surprise the door swung open and a teenage boy gave him a once-over.

"What do you want?" he asked.

"I'm looking for Ronnie Moses," Stan replied.

"My dad's not at home right now."

"When do you expect him?"

"I don't know. He doesn't have a regular schedule."

"Is your mother here?"

"No. It's just me and my dad."

"So, he'll be home for supper for sure, huh?"

"Maybe."

"You don't have dinner together?"

"Not usually. I fix myself something or get some fast food."

Stan sighed and handed the kid a card. "Have him call me when he comes in, okay?"

The kid nodded, put the card in his pocket, and shut the door. Stan turned and looked around. He didn't know what to do. If Moses didn't want to cooperate he'd have to go to the sheriff's office and get a deputy to come with him. But if Moses wasn't around the sheriff's deputy wouldn't be able to do anything, either. Then Stan had a idea. He got in his car and drove away, but not too far. Just as he expected, the station wagon drove up a few minutes later. Before Ronnie Moses could react Stan raced back and parked right behind the station wagon, penning it in.

Moses looked at Stan like a deer caught in headlights. He didn't quite know what to do. Stan jumped out of the car and approached him. Moses tried to back away but Stan caught him by the arm.

"Wait a minute. I've got a subpoena for Doc Mellon's records."

Stan shoved the subpoena in Moses's face. Moses took a deep breath and took the paper. He studied it a moment and then looked back at Stan with a look of reluctant acquiescence.

"Okay. I've got them in my office."

"Back downtown?" Stan asked.

"No. My office in back," he said, pointing to what appeared to be a guesthouse. "Wait here. I'll go get them for you."

Stan wondered if he shouldn't go with Moses to the office, but he didn't figure he had any place to run. There was no way he could get back to his car without passing Stan, so he figured he was safe. A few moments later Moses came back with a big box and set it down. Stan knelt down and opened the box. He looked at the collection of old phone books and frowned. Just as he was about to ask for an explanation he smelled smoke and noticed that the guesthouse was on fire!

"Fuck! What did you do?" Stan yelled as he ran over to the house. He looked around for a hose but there wasn't one in sight. He opened the front door but the fire was too intense for him to go inside. When he looked back Ronnie Moses was gone.

Stan watched the house burn until the fire department arrived. He explained what had happened and told the fire inspector that he thought Ronnie Moses had set the fire.

"Well, it's his house, so I guess if he wants to burn it down, he can."

"Not when it's full of records under subpoena. I think that's called obstruction of justice."

"I wouldn't know," the fire inspector said. "You'll have to take that up with the sheriff."

Stan knew he was right so he headed to the sheriff's office. He didn't want Moses to get away with destroying critical evidence. After filing a formal complaint against Moses the sheriff took his statement. Two hours later he was on his way back to Dallas feeling very depressed and dejected. Now what was he going to do?

On the way back to his office he tried to think what other ways there might be to find out if there were insurance policies on Rhymes and Thompson. The only thing he could come up with were banking records. The bank would have all of Mellon's bank statements. If he could get those statements from the bank's archives he might find a check made out to an insurance company. If so, the check would likely have a policy number on it. Once he had the carrier's name and a policy number he could get copies of the policies from the insurance company. He remembered that Mellon banked at the First National Bank of Terrell, Texas so he stopped there on the way home.

The receptionist referred him to Mellon's account manager. Although Stan didn't have a subpoena for the bank, he showed him the one to Ronnie Moses as an example of what he could get. The account manager said once he had a subpoena made out to the bank he would be glad to order the copies, but that it would take thirty days to get those records.

"That's not going to cut it. We need those records right now. The case has gone to trial. We're running out of time."

"I'm sorry, but our archives are kept in Houston at our regional warehouse. When we get an order for old records we submit it to the warehouse and they have to research the microfiche to get the copies you're requesting."

"What if I go to Houston? Can I help do the research myself?"

"No, but if you want to pay for expedited service, they'll put your request at the front of the line."

"How much?"

"Well, we usually charge $25 per hour, but it's $75 for expedited services."

"Fine. I'll fly down there right now. What are their hours?"

"Eight to four, Monday through Friday."

"Okay. You tell them I'll be there bright and early tomorrow at eight a.m. Unless we get very lucky, I'm going to need someone to work on it all day—maybe two days."

"Don't forget your subpoena. It's not your account, so they won't give you the time of day without it."

Stan nodded and left. It was after seven when he got home. Rebekah was watching TV and smiled when he walked in.

"So, how was your trip?"

"A waste of time. I didn't get a look at a single record."

"Oh, no. What happened?"

He summarized his dismal day for her. She shook her head sympathetically then got up and walked toward the kitchen.

"I've got supper ready. It's in the oven keeping warm."

Stan got up and followed her into the kitchen. She served them and then they ate in silence for a few moments until Stan put the day's events out of his head.

"So, how are you feeling?" he asked.

Rebekah didn't smile. "Oh, I don't know. I've been very lethargic today. I wanted to scrub the kitchen floor but I just couldn't get up the energy."

"You don't need to be scrubbing floors. We should get Maid Brigade to come in twice a week."

"Nonsense. What else do I have to do all day?"

Stan didn't say anything. They'd had this discussion before and he didn't want to repeat it.

"I'm going to have to get up very early tomorrow," Stan said. "I've got an eight o'clock appointment in Houston."

"Oh, crap. I was hoping you could stay in bed with me tomorrow."

Stan laughed. "I wish I could, but Paula's got a murder trial going and I'm her only hope at tying up the loose ends."

"Good luck with that. Most of the news commentators think Maureen Thompson is as good as convicted. They don't think Paula will be able to overcome the overwhelming evidence against her."

"That's because Paula hasn't put her case on yet. The DA's evidence is all circumstantial. Nobody saw Maureen kill her husband and that's because she didn't do it."

Rebekah raised her eyebrows. "Well, I hope you find what you're looking for."

Stan was a little hurt and disappointed at Rebekah's attitude. She'd already convicted Maureen, just like the media and the police had done. That wasn't like her. Usually she would be on Stan's side, providing support and encouragement. But ever since she'd been ill, her personality had changed. She didn't seem to care what Stan was doing and had trouble focusing on anything. Stan was very worried and didn't know what to do. If he brought it up she'd just get angry and run off and sulk.

They went to bed early that night and when Stan left early in the morning Rebekah didn't wake up. Stan could hear her breathing normally, so he let her sleep. He was worried about her, though, as he drove to the office on the way to Love Field for the fifty-minute flight to Houston Hobby airport. He had to find out what was wrong with her. He had never felt so helpless about something in his life.

Maria had promised to have the subpoena he needed on his desk. She'd also mapped out the route from the airport to the bank warehouse carefully for him. He didn't want to get there late and give them any excuse for further delay. At five minutes to eight he was standing at the front entrance of FNB Regional Data Center with briefcase in hand. He walked inside the moment the doors were unlocked and handed the subpoena to the receptionist.

"I think they are expecting me," he advised.

The receptionist looked at a list on the desk and then picked up the telephone and told someone Stan was there. A few moments later a woman came down the hall and approached Stan.

"Mr. Turner?"

Stan nodded. "Hi."

"I'm Ruth Bowers. We've been expecting you. Come this way."

Stan followed the woman down the hall to a small workroom with a half dozen microfilm viewers. She motioned for Stan to take a seat.

"So, why don't you tell me what you're looking for and then we can figure out the easiest way to find it."

"Sure," Stan replied. "I need to cover calendar year 1994. We're looking for any check payable to a life insurance company. Specifically, we are trying to find out if any premiums were paid on an insurance policy on the life of Rodney Thompson. We also need to look at calendar years 1989–1990. In these years we're looking for the same thing, payments to an insurance company for a policy on the life of Randy Rhymes, but also for large deposits—$100,000 or better. Rhymes died in March 1990 and his beneficiary would have received the proceeds of the life insurance later that year."

"All right. There were two accounts, so I'll take one and you can take the other. All the check images for 1994 are on the spools. When we're done, I'll have to go get 1989–1990. Do you know how to use these viewers?"

"Yes," Stan said. "It looks like the same system they use in the Dallas County Clerk's office for the deed records."

Ruth handed one box of reels to Stan and took the other one over to a reader. They both loaded up the first reels and started reviewing each check. There were about 250 checks in each statement so it was tedious work.

"Here's a check to State Farm for $212.00," Ruth said.

Stan made a note on a legal pad. "Okay. Any reference or memo?"

"Fire & EC McKinney office."

"Nope. We're just looking for life insurance," Stan said, turning back to his viewer.

In the next hour they covered about three months and only found three checks to insurance companies, two to State Farm and one to Gibraltar Life Insurance Company. The State Farm checks were more payments on casualty insurance policies but the Gibraltar Life had possibilities. Unfortunately it did not name the insured, just a policy number. Stan noted the information on his legal pad and they continued to work. By noon they had finished and identified twenty-

311

seven checks to insurance companies. Seven of these were to life insurance companies but none of them identified the insured. While Stan left to get a hamburger at a McDonald's down the street, Ruth went to get the 1989–1990 spools.

The afternoon session was more tedious as they had to review two years of individual checks and deposits. Fortunately, Stan was getting better at skimming the material and working the equipment more efficiently. He was determined to finish that day and get home to Dallas and find out if their hard work would pay off. At 4:30 p.m. they finished with another list of insurance company names. Unfortunately, they didn't find any large deposits. This did not depress Stan too much as he doubted Doc Mellon would deposit a large check into his operating account. He no doubt had other, less public places to keep large sums of money.

Stan thanked Ruth and went back to the airport. He called the office and gave Maria the information so she could start getting contact information on each insurance company. He asked her how Paula's trial was coming.

"The prosecution is still putting on its case but is expected to rest soon."

"Shit. I need to get this information to her soon. Call each company and get their contact information. They'll probably need a subpoena before they'll release any information, so start working on that. I should be back in Dallas by seven."

Maria said she'd start working on it immediately. Stan felt optimistic that they'd now find the checks they were looking for. He rushed to the gate, not wanting to miss his flight. Unfortunately, it didn't matter: the flight had been canceled!

32
Overwhelming Evidence

Paula watched the jury file back into the courtroom. She wondered how Stan's search was going. She'd hoped and prayed he'd stroll into the courtroom, insurance policies in hand, but that hadn't happened and she had to assume it wouldn't. She sighed and looked at Rawlins who stood confidently, anxious to get started.

When the last juror was seated the judge nodded to Rawlins. "You may call your first witness."

"The state calls Detective Leonard Gossett."

Leonard Gossett stood up, his thick salt-and-pepper hair glistening in the fluorescent light. He was a ruggedly handsome man who obviously spent a lot of time outdoors. As he approached the witness stand he pulled out a notepad, set it on the railing in front of him, and took the stand.

Rawlins smiled. "Mr. Gossett. Would you please identify yourself?"

Gossett revealed that he was a twenty-year veteran of the Dallas Police Department, that he'd been a detective for seven years, and had received several decorations for valor in the line of duty. Rawlins took him through the events of the evening of February 25, 1995 and he testified just as Rawlins had predicted he would in his opening statement. When he was finished Paula took him on cross.

"Mr. Gossett. You testified that you spoke to Maureen Thompson on the night of the murder, is that correct?"

"Yes."

"How did you even know where Ms. Thompson lived?"

"The apartment manager had her address on file and gave it to us."

"So, you went to the manager and asked if she knew where Maureen Thompson lived?"

"Well, she actually came to the crime scene and we asked her if she knew where Ms. Thompson lived."

"What made you want to talk to Ms. Thompson?"

"We questioned the manager, maintenance man, and several neighbors who advised us that Mr. Thompson was estranged from his wife and there was bad blood between them."

"So, this information made you put Maureen Thompson on your person-of-interest list?"

"No. A spouse is always on the list. This information just confirmed that we needed to talk to her immediately."

"What time was it when this interview took place?"

"It was about 11:15 p.m."

"How did she appear to you?"

"What do you mean?" Detective Gossett asked.

"Was she dressed when she opened the door?"

"No, she was in a robe."

"Did she say she had been in bed when you rang the bell?"

"I believe she did say that."

"Did she look sleepy?"

Gossett shrugged. "I don't remember her looking sleepy."

"Was her hair wet?"

"Ah. No. I don't recall it being wet."

"Did you smell any kind of body odor from her?"

"What? . . . Body odor? No, not that I can remember."

"Was she sweaty?"

"Sweaty? No. I don't recall that."

"In your interviews with the manager and friends did you learn that Ms. Thompson's car had been repossessed?"

"Yes, that was mentioned."

"So, you knew that her only mode of transportation was by Rollerblades?"

"Well, someone mentioned that, but I don't know that for a fact."

"Assuming it is true, don't you think if Maureen Thompson had skated over to Rodney Thompson's apartment that she would have worked up a sweat?"

Gossett shrugged. "I suppose."

"Yet her hair wasn't wet, which it would been if she had taken a shower or, if she hadn't taken a shower she would have been sweating and probably smelled, wouldn't you agree?"

"Not necessarily. She could have taken a shower and blow-dried her hair."

"Do you know how long it takes to get from Maureen's house to Rodney's apartment on Rollerblades?"

"No. I haven't clocked it."

"Well, I have and it took about forty-five minutes. Does that seem reasonable to you?"

"That's about right."

"Do you know what the time of death was?"

"It's been estimated to be between ten and eleven o'clock."

"So, assuming it was ten o'clock. The earliest Maureen Thompson could have gotten home would have been 10:45 p.m., is that right?"

"That's correct."

"So, that would have given her thirty minutes to take a shower and blow-dry her hair before you arrived, right?"

"Right."

"Admittedly, that might have been enough time, but if the time of death was 10:15 or later it's not likely Maureen would have had time to skate home, take a shower, and blow-dry her hair before you got there to question her."

"None of these times are certain. They're just estimates."

"I suppose Ms. Thompson could have taken a cab to the apartment," Paula admitted.

"Actually, no. We checked all the cab companies and she didn't get there by cab."

"Okay, then—Rollerblades it is. How did Maureen react when you told her Rodney was dead?"

"She acted surprised."

"Did she cry?"

"Yes."

"Did it look genuine?"

He shrugged again. "I don't know. She may have been acting. Who knows?" Gossett replied irritably.

"Did you read Ms. Thompson her rights before you arrested her?"

"Of course, that's standard procedure."

"When was that done?"

"After we talked to her for a while and she could not provide us with an alibi, we read her rights to her."

"So, you questioned her for a while without explaining to her that she was a suspect in her husband's murder."

"Yes, but—"

"No explanation is necessary. It's clear what you were trying to do," Paula spat.

"Objection!" Rawlins yelled. "Argumentative."

"Withdrawn," Paula said. "No further questions."

Rawlins next quizzed Lance Shepard, the manager who had discovered Rodney Thompson's body. He reiterated what Detective Gossett had testified to and confirmed that he had told the detective about the Thompsons' marital difficulties. The most damaging result of the testimony were statements allegedly made by Maureen.

"Mr. Shepard. Did Maureen Thompson ever threaten her husband?"

"Sure. She told him once he would pay dearly for abandoning her and the children."

William Manchee

"Objection, hearsay," Paula said.

"Your Honor," Rawlins replied. "These are admissions against interests plus we have another witness who actually heard these threats made by the defendant."

"And that would be?" the judge asked.

"Mr. Thompson's brother. I'll be calling him shortly."

"Very well, objection overruled."

Rawlins turned back to the witness. "So, did you hear about any other threats?"

"Yes, I heard another time she suggested he was a worthless piece of shit and ought to jump off a bridge so she could collect his insurance."

There was laughter from the gallery. The judge looked up and glared at the spectators.

"Thank you, Mr. Shepard. Pass the witness."

Paula got to her feet and took the witness on cross-examination.

"Mr. Shepard. How did you acquire your knowledge of the Thompsons' marriage?"

"From Rodney. He came to me after he moved in to get an alarm system. I guess he felt compelled to explain why he needed the extra security."

"Did he say he was afraid of his wife?"

"No. Mainly he was concerned about her coming in and taking stuff."

"So, he just didn't want her in the apartment alone, right?"

"That was my impression."

"So, other than what Mr. Thompson told you, you have no knowledge of what went on in the marriage?"

"That's true."

"Do you know a man named Doc Mellon?"

"The Clock?"

"Right."

"Sure. I was a fan."

"Did you ever see the Clock at Mr. Thompson's apartment?"

"Ah, as a matter of fact, I did. Several times."

"Objection, Your Honor," Rawlins said. "This question lacks foundation and is irrelevant."

"It's not irrelevant, Your Honor, but I can wait to interrogate this witness when I present our case, if the court prefers. I just thought it might be more convenient for the witness if I ask him questions relevant to the defense while he's on the stand."

"Mr. Rawlins. If you insist, I'll make the witness come back and answer Ms. Waters's questions after you've presented your case, but I'm always in favor of making life easier for witnesses, if possible."

Rawlins frowned. "If there aren't going to be a lot of questions, I'll withdraw my objection, assuming Ms. Waters can show the relevance of the testimony."

Paula nodded. "Yes, I only have a few questions and they are relevant to the defense's alternate theory of what happened in this case as outlined in my opening statement."

The judge looked at Rawlins. "All right, objection withdrawn," Rawlins said.

The judge looked at the witness. "You may answer the question."

"What was the question?" Shepard asked.

"Did you ever see Doc 'the Clock' Mellon at Mr. Thompson's apartment?"

"Yes."

"Did you have an occasion to talk to him on any of those occasions that you saw him?"

"Yes. I shook his hand and told him I was a big fan the first time he came over."

"Do you know what his relationship was with the decedent?"

"He said he was a long-time friend, and I know they were business partners."

"How do you know that?"

"On one occasion I noticed them in the pool area and went over to say hello. In our conversation they asked when I thought the real estate market would turn around."

"Your Honor? This is more than a few questions," Rawlins complained.

"I'm almost done," Paula replied.

"Very well. Let's move it along."

"So, did you notice or sense any tension or animosity between them during that encounter?"

Shepard shrugged. "Actually, the Clock did seem a little impatient."

"So, there was some tension between them?"

"Yes, that was pretty obvious but I don't know why."

"Fair enough. Did you see Mr. Mellon on the day of the murder?"

"No. Not on the day of the murder, but the day before I did."

Rawlins stood up. "Your Honor?"

The judge glared at Paula. "Are you about done, counselor?"

"Yes. One more question. Then I'm done with this witness."

The judge nodded, and Paula continued. "Tell us what you observed Mr. Mellon do on the day before the murder."

"I saw him pull up in the parking lot. He got out of his car and walked briskly to Mr. Thompson's apartment. I followed him, hoping I'd get a chance to say hello. When I got to the apartment he was already inside. I was about to turn around and go back to the office when I heard them arguing."

"Could you hear what they were saying?"

"No. Not until the door opened and Mr. Mellon stormed out."

Rawlins looked at the judge and shook his head. The judge ignored him.

"What did he say then?"

"The only thing I heard was Mr. Mellon saying that time was running out."

"Time was running out?" Paula repeated. "Do you know what that meant?"

"No, but it was a threat of some sort—that much was obvious."

"Thank you, Your Honor. No further questions of this witness at this time."

"Mr. Rawlins. Any redirect?" the judge asked.

"Yes. Mr. Shepard. You have no personal knowledge of what was going on between the decedent and Mr. Mellon, do you?"

"That's true."

"No further questions, Your Honor," Rawlins said.

Rawlins next put on a string of witnesses including the medical examiner, a forensics expert, and Rodney's brother. Rodney's brother testified as to the disintegration of the marriage between Maureen and Rodney, his brother's financial problems, Maureen's complaints, and thinly veiled threats made on account of Rodney's inability to support her. Paula took Thompson on cross to get clarification on those alleged threats.

"So, it's your testimony that Maureen Thompson said that Rodney would regret abandoning her and the children?"

"That's right."

"Could she have meant that he would have regretted not seeing the children as much?"

Thompson shrugged. "No. She was talking about something different."

"But that was just your interpretation, wasn't it?"

"Well, you had to be there to appreciate it. It wasn't about the children."

"Okay. So, you also testified that Ms. Thompson suggested her husband ought to do the family a favor and jump off a bridge, so she could collect his life insurance."

"Yes, that's what Rodney told me she said after he went over to apologize about her car being repossessed."

"So. She had good reason to be upset on that occasion?"

"I suppose, but she didn't have a right to kill Rodney."

"Objection, nonresponsive," Paula said.

"Sustained. Mr. Thompson, just answer the questions. Don't comment on them."

"Sorry, Your Honor."

"No further questions, Your Honor," Paula said.

"Mr. Rawlins, redirect?" the judge asked.

"No, Your Honor."

The judge looked at his watch and then looked up. "It's nearly five o'clock. We'll convene at 10:00 a.m. tomorrow morning," he said and left the bench. Paula stood up and began gathering her things together.

"So, what do you think so far?" Maureen asked.

"Oh, there hasn't been anything unexpected. We knew Rawlins had a lot of circumstantial evidence against you. There's nothing we can do about that. It's all going to come down to how the jury reacts to what we have on Doc Mellon."

Maureen sighed. "So, has Stan found the insurance policy yet?"

"Well he's not here, so I guess not."

"What if he doesn't find it?"

Paula didn't want to say it out loud, but she knew it would be unlikely the jury would buy their defense if they couldn't prove a strong motive for Doc Mellon to kill Rodney Thompson.

"Don't worry. Even if he doesn't find it, I think we can still show reasonable doubt," Paula assured her.

Maureen didn't looked convinced but she didn't say anything. Elena walked up and escorted Maureen out of the courtroom. As Paula packed her briefcase she wondered why Stan hadn't contacted her. Even if he hadn't found the insurance policy she figured he ought to keep her updated on his progress. As her anger welled Bart walked up.

"Ready to make your escape?" he asked.

She smiled at him and nodded. "Yes, get me out of here. I'm exhausted."

Bart took her hand, led her out the back door of the courtroom, down the hall, and into the stairwell where they made their escape unnoticed. As they scampered across the street to the parking garage, Paula glanced over at the crowd of reporters hanging around the entrance to the courthouse. She felt greatly relieved that she had successfully eluded them as she wasn't in the mood to face anybody right then.

After stopping at Black Eyed Pea for a quick dinner, they went to their apartment where Bart gave her a massage and drew her a bath. He was good that way, appreciating the tremendous stress she was under and trying to relax her and get her mind off the trial. As she soaked in the hot bath she wondered if there was any chance in hell she could get Maureen off. The more she thought about it, the more depressed she became. *Damn it, Stan! Where the hell are you?*

33
Bad Dream

It was after seven when Stan got home. He'd tried to call Rebekah but she hadn't answered. This worried him as it was unusual for her to go out in the evenings when he wasn't home. He had called Terry as well to see if she was with her but again got no answer. He opened the door and rushed inside.

"Rebekah? I'm home."

He glanced in the kitchen but she wasn't there, so he headed for the family room. Relief washed over him as he spotted Rebekah on the sofa watching TV. He rushed over to her only to have his spirits dashed when he saw her flushed face and eyes glazed over.

"Rebekah! What's wrong?"

She tried to speak but no words came out. He felt her forehead and was alarmed by how hot she felt.

"Jesus. You're burning up."

Rebekah tried to smile. "I'm okay. Just a little fever."

"The hell you are! Come on. I'm taking you to the emergency room."

"No," she protested.

"Bullshit. You're coming."

Stan pulled on her arms but got no response, so he put his arms under hers and lifted her to her feet. She was dead weight in his arms and it became obvious he wasn't going to be able to go very far without her help, so he put her back down on the sofa.

"I'm calling an ambulance."

"No! I'll be okay."

Deadly Defiance

Stan ignored her and went to the phone and called 911. Ten minutes later a fire truck and an ambulance pulled up in front of the house. The paramedics came in and Stan explained how he'd found her. They took her vitals, determined she was in no immediate danger, and loaded her into the ambulance. Stan followed them to the hospital.

The emergency room waiting area was two-thirds full when Stan walked in. He looked around then walked up to a nurse at the front desk.

"An ambulance just brought my wife in," he explained.

She looked up without emotion. "What's her name?"

"Rebekah Turner."

The nurse grabbed a clipboard and handed it to Stan.

"Fill this out. I'll need a driver's license and insurance information."

"What about my wife? Can I go back and see her?"

"They'll call you when they have her in a room."

Stan sighed and took the clipboard. "Okay," he said and walked over to the nearest vacant chair. He stared at the blank form without seeing it. *What could be wrong with her? She seemed fine when I left her.* Finally he regained his focus, completed the form, and took it back to the nurse. She gave him back his license and insurance card and reassured him they'd call him once she was in a room. He went back to his chair, wondering if he should start calling the family. Before he'd made a decision a door swung open and another nurse stepped out.

"Mr. Turner?" she said.

Stan got up and rushed over to her. "Yes. Is she in a room?"

"Ah. No. They've taken her to ICU."

Stan's mouth dropped. "Why?"

"Her blood pressure is very high—220/115. They've got to figure out what's causing it. In the meantime there is danger of a stroke so they need to treat the hypertension aggressively."

"Oh. Okay. So—"

324

"You should go to the ICU waiting room on the sixth floor. The doctor will call and give you an update after they've stabilized her. It will be a while, though, so if you need to call anyone you've got time."

Stan nodded. "Thanks."

Stan turned and headed for the elevator. When he got to the waiting room he found a phone and called Terry. She said she'd be right over. Then he called Reggie and the rest of the kids to explain what was happening. Finally, he called Paula.

"Stan. I was hoping you'd call."

"How's the trial going?"

"So-so. Any luck on finding an insurance policy?"

"No. I've struck out so far, but I did pick up a few leads from the bank records we reviewed."

"Good. We've got to find that insurance policy."

"I know. Unfortunately, there's a complication that has come up."

"What's that?"

He told her about Rebekah and the current situation.

"Oh, I'm so sorry. Don't worry about the insurance policy. Maria can call the insurance companies and follow up on the leads."

"No. No. I've got plenty of time. I'm just sitting around worrying. It will be good to have something to do."

Paula sighed. "I should come over there."

"No. You need to stay focused on the trial. I'm sorry to burden you with this, but I thought you should know I'm a little distracted right now."

"It's all right. What can you do?"

Stan hung up feeling like he'd let Paula down. He was sure there was an insurance policy out there somewhere but was beginning to think he'd never find it. When he turned to go back to his seat Terry walked in.

"Hi, Stan. I'm sorry I missed your call earlier but I went out to dinner with a friend."

"It's okay. I didn't mean to spoil your evening, but I thought you'd want to know about Rebekah."

"Of course. I'd have been really pissed had you not called me. So, what's the situation?"

"Her blood pressure is through the roof again. They don't know what's causing it, so they're just trying to bring it down right now and stabilize her."

"Damn. I hate that they can't figure out what's wrong with her. If they could identify the problem they could treat it and we'd be done with this nonsense."

"I know. It's so frustrating."

"So, have you seen her yet?"

"No. They said the doctor would come out and give us a report after they got her stabilized."

"Yeah. That could take hours. Come on. Let's just go see her right now."

Stan hesitated. "But—"

"Trust me. The nurses won't care if we go in and take a peek at her."

Stan reluctantly followed Terry into the ICU. It was an eerie scene in the dark of night with the constant humming, rhythmic beeping, and flashing lights. The nurses looked up as they walked in but didn't say anything. Terry walked deliberately past each station looking for Rebekah. When she found her she motioned to Stan.

"Here she is."

Stan walked up and gasped at the sight of her. He'd never seen her so pale and fragile. He looked up at the monitor and noted that her blood pressure was still high—202/111—with a pulse of 130. She had a temperature, too—101.8.

"They're giving her an antibiotic," Terry noted. "She must have an infection of some sort. I hope it's not pneumonia."

"Pneumonia? How would she get that?"

"I don't know, but it's pretty common."

"How long will it take the antibiotic to bring her temperature down?"

"It's hard to say, but I bet by morning it will be gone."

They watched her for a while until one of the nurses hinted that they should leave. When they got back to the waiting room Reggie and Mark were there. After they filled them in on the situation they all found a seat and waited. When the doctor finally showed up an hour later he had very little to say and couldn't tell them what had caused the hypertension attack or the fever. He promised in the morning he'd have some answers.

The next morning the doctor reported that the fever had come down and Rebekah's blood pressure was much better, but he still had no explanation as to what had caused it all. He promised some test results would soon be in that would clarify things. Stan got the impression he was clueless as to what was wrong with her and doubted anything would change after the blood work came back.

After the doctor had left Stan turned his attention to the insurance leads he had to check out. After he called Maria and got the contact information he began making phone calls. Unfortunately, none of the leads panned out. The checks had been for life insurance policies but not on the life of Rodney Thompson or Randy Rhymes.

Frustrated, he ripped up his notes and threw them in a trash can. As he was lamenting his bad luck, a nurse approached him.

"Mr. Turner."

"Yes."

"They're taking your wife to a room. She's out of danger so she won't need to stay in ICU today."

"Good. What room?"

The nurse told him and Stan went to search for Reggie and Mark who he thought had gone to the cafeteria to get breakfast. When he got there he saw them sitting at a table. He went over and joined them.

"Well, they're taking your mother to a room. I guess she's out of danger."

"Good," Reggie said. "Do they know what's wrong with her yet?"

"No. They're running more tests."

"I can't believe they can't figure it out," Mark complained.

Stan shook his head dejectedly. "You and me both. This has been going on for months."

"Why don't you find a new doctor?" Reggie suggested.

"These are new doctors. The hospital has their own staff, so they're doing new tests and considering every possibility."

"Yeah, in the meantime Mom may die."

"No. They said she wasn't in any danger right now. We should give them time to figure it out, I suppose," Stan said grudgingly. "Listen. You guys don't need to hang around here all day. I'll call you if anything changes. I'm sure you have things to do. Come back tonight during visiting hours."

Mark and Reggie protested but eventually left. After they'd gone Stan went up to Rebekah's room. She was asleep when he got there, so he just sat in a chair and watched her, wondering if she'd ever recover. For the first time the thought that she might die crept into his mind. He really didn't see how it could happen but the continued inability of the doctors to diagnose Rebekah's problem was unsettling.

After he'd been sitting there for an hour or so he began to doze off. He hadn't slept all night and his weariness was catching up with him. As he fell into a shallow slumber he began to dream. He was at a funeral home looking down at his dear Rebekah laid out in a coffin. He felt empty inside like all of his life had been siphoned away. His attention was drawn away from Rebekah's corpse by a man in a blue suit. He was asking Stan a question.

"How many death certificates will you need?" the man asked.

Tears began to well in Stan's eyes. His beloved Rebekah was dead! It couldn't be! She couldn't be dead. "No! No!"

"Mr. Turner. Wake up. You're dreaming," the nurse said.

"Huh?" Stan said with a start. "What?"

"You were dreaming."

"Oh, right. Sorry," Stan said as he thought about the dream. . . . "Oh, my God! . . . That's it," Stan said, leaping to his feet. "I've got to go. I'll be back in a few hours."

"Okay," the nurse said. "We'll take good care of her while you're gone."

"Thank you," Stan said excitedly. "I'll be right back."

Stan knew the nurses must have thought he was crazy leaving the way he did, but he didn't have time to explain to them why he was so excited. They wouldn't have appreciated the fact that he'd just figured out how to prove Maureen Thompson was innocent of two murders.

34
Closing Arguments

Bart's pampering had done wonders for Paula and she felt refreshed and eager to get on with the trial. During breakfast she went over her closing argument with Bart as it was likely Rawlins would finish up early in the morning and she'd be putting on her case most of the day. She didn't expect her case to take more than a day to put on, so it was possible she'd have to make a closing argument if the judge decided to push the case to a conclusion. She'd had cases in the past when the judge had made them stay until 10:00 p.m. because the docket was so full and he wanted to move on to the next case.

When they arrived at the courthouse it was obvious there would be no avoiding the press as they had all the entrances blocked, even the back entrance through the district clerk's office. As they approached the main entrance, reporters surrounded them.

"Ms. Waters," a reporter said. "Do you think there is any way you can overcome the prosecution's strong case against your client?"

Paula laughed. "Yes, absolutely. You heard our opening statement. Maureen Thompson isn't the only one who had a motive to kill Rodney Thompson."

Bart cleared a path and pulled Paula through it.

"Ms. Waters," another reporter said. "Have you prepared your client for a possible adverse verdict?"

Paula glared at the reporter. "I'm not her priest."

Bart opened the door and they entered the courthouse. Two bailiffs came to their rescue and helped push a path through the crowd of reporters and curious spectators.

"Ms. Waters," a third reporter said. "Where is your partner, Stan Turner? Why hasn't he been here to help with the case?"

Paula stopped and looked at the reporter. "Stan's wife is ill, so he's busy taking care of her."

"What's wrong with her?" the reporter asked.

Paula shrugged. "They are not sure, but I've been told she's out of danger and her condition is stable."

"Will you ask for a continuance?"

"No. I'm lead counsel, so the court wouldn't consider such a motion."

The elevator door opened and Bart and Paula stepped inside. The two bailiffs blocked the door, preventing anyone else from getting aboard. When they finally got to the courtroom Maureen Thompson was already at the defense table and the courtroom was nearly full. Rawlins looked over at her and nodded. Paula smiled and started unpacking her briefcase. A few moments later the back door to the courtroom opened and Judge Sands appeared and took the bench.

"All rise," the bailiff bellowed.

Everyone got to their feet. "Be seated," the judge said. "Mr. Rawlins, call your next witness."

"Yes, Your Honor. The defense calls Tony Bartos."

A well-dressed, middle-aged Hispanic man stood up and walked to the witness stand. He was sworn in and Rawlins began questioning him.

"Mr. Bartos. What is your occupation?"

"I'm an agent with State Farm Insurance Company."

"And did you know the decedent, Rodney Thompson?"

"Yes. I handled all of his insurance requirements."

"And did he have an occasion to buy a life insurance policy from you?"

"Yes, he did. A $500,000 twenty-year term policy."

"And who was the beneficiary?"

"Maureen Thompson."

The crowd stirred at the revelation. Maureen swallowed hard.

"When was this policy taken out?" Rawlins asked.

"Just after they were married—October 7, 1991."

"Who paid the premiums on this policy?"

"We got a check each month for $127.52 from Maureen Thompson."

"Even after the real estate market crashed and they were struggling financially?"

"Yes. It came in every month like clockwork."

"So, has a claim been made on the policy?"

"No. Not as yet. Ms. Thompson wanted to file one, but I advised her to wait until this trial was over. The company won't consider an application while she's under indictment for murdering the insured under the policy."

"I see. A prudent policy, I'm sure. Pass the witness."

The judge nodded. "Ms. Waters, your witness."

"Thank you, Your Honor," Paula said. "Mr. Bartos. Is it unusual for a man to buy an insurance policy shortly after he gets married?"

"No. Not at all."

"Is $500,000 an unusually high amount considering Mr. Thompson's situation as a small business owner?"

"No. In fact, I had recommended a million, but he didn't think he could afford that much premium."

"In fact, isn't it true that $500,000 wouldn't even replace half the income Mr. Thompson was generating for the family?"

"Exactly, that's why I suggested a million-dollar policy."

"Now. You seem to suggest that there is something wrong with Ms. Thompson making sure the life insurance premiums were paid when times got bad?"

"No. I didn't mean to—"

"It's all right. Let me ask you something."

"Sure."

"The Thompsons had small children, isn't that right?"

"Yes."

"So, wouldn't it have been irresponsible for Ms. Thompson to let the insurance policy lapse?"

"That's true. Life insurance is important."

"In fact, without this life insurance the children will be penniless."

"I don't know for sure, but you may be right."

"You said if Ms. Thompson is acquitted she'll get the $500,000, is that right?"

"Yes."

"And if she is convicted who gets the money?"

"The children are the contingent beneficiaries."

"So, do you think Ms. Thompson did the right thing in paying these premiums at great personal sacrifice to herself?"

"Objection, Your Honor. Asked and answered."

"Sustained. Ms. Waters, you've made your point. Let's move on."

The back door to the courtroom opened and Stan rushed in. Paula saw him coming and turned to the judge.

"Your Honor. Can we take a ten-minute break so I can confer with my partner?"

The judge looked at the clock and saw it was 10:15. Very well. We'll reconvene at 10:30."

Stan hurriedly explained what he'd discovered and then left to go back to the hospital. Paula reviewed the new evidence with cautious excitement but wondered how she should present it. When the trial had been recessed she was about to pass the witness. Now she decided to utilize the witness's knowledge to lay a predicate for later testimony. The back door opened and the judge strolled in.

"All rise," the bailiff said.

"Be seated. Bailiff, bring in the jury."

After the jury was seated Paula continued her questioning. "Mr. Bartos, you testified that Ms. Thompson tried to file a death claim after Mr. Thompson's death."

"That's correct."

"What is required to file an insurance death claim?"

"Ah. Well, there's a claim form that must be filled out and signed. Of course you have to have the original policy or sign a lost policy affidavit."

"Is that all?"

"No. You also have to get a death certificate and submit that as well."

"I see. And all these things are mandatory for every insurance claim?"

"Yes. They are required before a claim can be considered."

"Thank you, Mr. Bartos. Pass the witness."

Rawlins stood. "No further questions. The prosecution rests."

The judge nodded. "Thank you, Mr. Rawlins . . . Ms. Waters, call your first witness."

"Thank you, Your Honor. The defense calls Elena Watson."

Elena stood up and walked to the witness stand. Paula smiled at her and then began asking questions. Elena identified herself as Maureen's sister and then explained that they had worked in the decedent's business and was familiar with their business and personal lives.

"Ms. Watson, the prosecution has introduced forensic evidence that established that her fingerprints were found on the ice pick. Do you have an explanation for that?"

"Yes. The weekend before the murder I drove Maureen to take the kids to Rodney's apartment since her car had been repossessed. We didn't stay long but before we left I know Maureen chopped some ice with the ice pick for the kids' drinks."

"I see. So, you're not surprised her fingerprints were found on the murder weapon?"

"No. Not at all."

"You've testified that you were a regular visitor to the Thompson house before they split up?"

"Yes. I was part of the family. I must have been over there once or twice a week to babysit or just hang out."

"So, how would you characterize their marriage?"

"They were very happy until the real estate market crashed and Rodney's business began going south."

"What happened when the business began to fail?"

"Rodney started to become irritable and short-tempered. This resulted in many arguments and hurt feelings."

"Do you know a man named Doc Mellon?"

"Yes. He was one of Rodney's friends and a business partner."

"Do you know how much he invested in Rodney's business?"

"Yes. I believe it was $250,000."

"How do you know that?"

"I did the company's bookkeeping. I deposited the check."

"I see. So, what was Mr. Mellon supposed to get in return for his investment?"

"Rodney said it was really a loan but it was booked as equity so he could make a better return on his investment."

"So, what kind of a return was he looking for?"

"Objection!" Rawlins spat. "She would not have any direct knowledge of that so whatever she says will either be hearsay or speculation."

"Sustained," the judge ruled.

"Your Honor. I would respectfully ask that you let me ask the question and rule on each question. Also, I would like to be heard before you rule on an objection."

The judge glared at Paula. "Very well. Ask your questions. The witness will not answer the questions, however, until a ruling has been made."

"Thank you, Your Honor. Ms. Watson, do you know what kind of an investment return Mr. Mellon was expecting? All I'm looking for is a yes or no response."

"Yes."

"How do you know this?"

"I overheard him talking to Rodney about it."

"Objection, Your Honor. This is irrelevant."

"Your Honor, it's not irrelevant. It goes to Mr. Mellon's strong motive to kill Mr. Thompson."

"Objection! Your Honor, Mr. Mellon isn't on trial here."

"True, but I have a right to prove someone else killed Mr. Thompson."

"That's enough. Overruled," the judge said.

"Thank you. Ms. Watson, so you overhead Mr. Mellon and your brother-in-law talking about what return on investment was expected?"

"Yes. Mr. Mellon was bragging about how he tripled his money every year in his payday loan business, so he expected to at least double his investment with Rodney."

"Did Mr. Mellon ever discuss what happened to customers who didn't pay their debts?"

"No, but he bragged about the fact that he never wrote off a debt."

"What if someone filed bankruptcy?"

"I asked him that very question and he said his customers knew better than to hide behind a bankruptcy."

"Did you ask him to expand on that?"

"No. I didn't think it was prudent."

"Thank you. Pass the witness."

Rawlins got to his feet. The judge nodded for him to begin.

"Ms. Watson. You love your sister, don't you?"

"Of course."

"So, you'd say anything to protect her, wouldn't you?"

"No. I wouldn't lie for her. Everything I've said is the truth."

"Right," Rawlins said, rolling his eyes. "Now other than what you think you overheard in a few conversations between Mr.

Thompson and Mr. Mellon, you know nothing about Mr. Mellon's businesses?"

"That's correct."

"Pass the witness," Rawlins said.

The judge looked at Paula. "Any redirect?"

"No, Your Honor."

"Very well, call your next witness."

"The defense calls Doc Mellon."

The courtroom stirred in anticipation of Doc Mellon's testimony. Mellon stood up and strutted up to the witness stand, smiling and waving to a smattering of fans in the gallery. Paula waited for the commotion to stop and then asked him about his background and relationship to Rodney Thompson.

"Now, in conjunction with the investment in Thompson Construction, did you require a life insurance policy?"

Mellon shifted in his seat nervously and then said, "On advice of counsel, I take the Fifth."

A man stood up and addressed the court. "Your Honor, I'm Mr. Mellon's attorney. May I approach the bench?"

The judge waved him forward and Rawlins and Paula joined him at the bench.

"Your Honor. My client is currently under indictment and whereas these cases are not obviously connected to each other, there may be connections that I am unaware. Consequently I have advised my client not to testify here today."

The judge rubbed his forehead. "Counsel, why don't you listen to the questions and evaluate them individually before you make a recommendation to your client. He doesn't have a right to refuse to answer questions that do not incriminate him."

"That would be too dangerous, particularly in light of the fact that Ms. Waters was instrumental in my client being indicted."

"Your Honor," Paula interjected. "I'm entitled to ask the witness any relevant question I want and, if he wants to take the Fifth, he can."

"Your Honor," Rawlins protested. "That would be highly prejudicial. The jury will assume Mr. Mellon has something to do with Mr. Thompson's murder when that's not the case at all."

The judge sighed. "There's merit to all of your positions, so I'm going to allow Ms. Waters a few questions. Let's say, ten questions and I'll instruct the jury that they shouldn't make any assumptions simply due to the fact that Mr. Mellon is taking the Fifth."

"Objection, Your Honor," Rawlins said.

"So noted," the judge replied.

"That's fine with me," Paula said.

"All right. Let's take a break," the judge said, looking at the clock. "Actually, it's nearly time for lunch. Let's break for lunch and come back at 1:30. That will give Ms. Waters a chance to formulate her ten questions. Go back to your seats so I can announce a recess."

Everyone went back to their seats. The judge cleared his throat. "We're going to recess for lunch. Court will resume at 1:30."

The judge got up and everyone rose. When he was gone the court erupted in excited chatter. Paula looked at Maureen and shook her head. "This is where it's going to get dicey."

Maureen nodded. "Don't you think all of this will really confuse the jury?"

"That's my intention. If we talk enough about Doc Mellon, one of the jurors is sure to be convinced he's responsible for Rodney's murder."

"God, I hope so. . . . What did Stan bring you?" Maureen asked.

Paula smiled wryly. "Oh, something that Doc Mellon will have a lot of trouble explaining."

As they were talking Bart walked up and put his hand on Paula's shoulder.

"Boy, I don't know what you did, but you got Rawlins really riled up," Bart said.

"Did I?" Paula asked. "Well, he hasn't seen anything yet."

Bart gave her a quizzical look. "You should stick around for my next witness," Paula suggested.

"Okay. Maybe I will."

"Have you heard about Rebekah?"

"No. Not since last night."

"Stan dropped by and said she was out of ICU."

"That's good."

"They still don't know what's wrong with her."

"Hmm. What do you want for lunch?"

"Oh, I don't think I have time to go out. Take Maureen and bring me back a sandwich. I'll be in the attorney's conference room working on my ten questions."

"Ten questions?"

"Don't ask. You guys better go. I'm running out of time."

Bart and Maureen left and Paula took her things into the attorney's conference room. Deciding which questions she should ask wasn't easy to do. There was a lot of ground to cover. She looked at the eighty-eight questions she had previously prepared. In practice, those eighty-eight questions would have likely mushroomed into two hundred or more questions as many answers suggested new questions. Finally, she began by crossing out questions that were obviously not important. That got her list down to about fifty. Then she decided to scratch anything that didn't relate to an insurance policy on Rodney or what the consequences would be if Rodney didn't pay back the loan. Paula jumped when someone pounded on the conference room door.

"Come in," she said.

The door opened and Bart walked in with a sandwich and Coke in hand.

"Oh, thanks. I'm starving."

He set the food down and took a seat across from her. She began eating voraciously while she explained the situation to Bart.

"So, did you get your questions set?"

"Uh-huh. Take a look and let me know what you think."

Bart took up the sheet of paper and read the questions. He nodded. "That about covers it."

There was another knock on the door and the bailiff stuck in his head. "The judge is about to take the bench."

"Oh, thanks," Paula said, getting up.

"I'll take care of this," Bart said and waved Paula on.

Paula walked quickly to the defense table and sat just as the bailiff ordered everyone to rise. The judge took the bench and told the bailiff to bring the witness back in. When the witness had been reseated he nodded to Paula.

"Ms. Waters. You may continue."

"Thank you. Permission to treat the witness as hostile?"

"Permission granted," the judge said.

"Mr. Mellon. Is it true that you lent Rodney Thompson the sum of $250,000?"

Mellon looked down at an index card and read what was written. "On advice of counsel, as is my right under the Constitutions of the United States and the State of Texas, I respectfully decline to answer the question on the grounds it might incriminate me."

The judge looked over at the jury. "You are instructed that no inferences should necessarily be drawn by this witness's exercise of his Fifth Amendment rights. It's common knowledge that Mr. Mellon is under indictment in another criminal case pending in another court. It is possible that his refusal to testify relates to that case rather than this one, although only the witness knows for sure. I know this is confusing, but this is an unusual case and it can't be helped. Ms. Waters, you may continue."

Paula nodded. "Mr. Mellon. Is it true that as additional security for the $250,000 loan to Mr. Thompson, you took out an insurance policy on his life?"

Mellon looked down at his index card again.

"Ah. You can just say, 'I take the Fifth' if you want," Paula said. "We'll understand."

"Okay. I'm taking the Fifth," Mellon said.

"Very well. Is it true that in your payday loan and pawnshop businesses you often employ threats, intimidation, and bodily harm as a collection technique?"

Mellon sighed. "I take the Fifth."

"Is it true that you often brag to your family and friends that you have a 100 percent collection record?"

Mellon smiled. "Like I said. I take the Fifth."

"So, since Rodney Thompson was broke and there was no chance you could collect from him, you decided you wanted to collect on his insurance policy, right?"

Mellon's smiled faded. "I take the Fifth."

"That meant you had to kill Rodney Thompson, right?"

Mellon swallowed hard and looked away. "I take the Fifth."

"But if you were tied in any way to the murder, you wouldn't be able to collect on the policy, right?"

Mellon coughed. "I take the Fifth."

"And since you had to make sure someone else was convicted for Rodney Thompson's murder, who better than an estranged wife who had already been charged for allegedly murdering her first husband. Have I gotten it right so far?"

Mellon gave Paula an icy stare. "I take the Fifth."

"Is it true you had someone use an ice pick to kill Rodney Thompson so it would appear Maureen Thompson was the killer?"

"I take the Fifth."

"Is it also true that you were also responsible for other murders, including the murder of Maureen Thompson's first husband, Randy Rhymes?"

"I take the Fifth."

"Objection, Your Honor. This is ridiculous! The next thing Ms. Waters is going to say is that Doc Mellon is responsible for the Kennedy assassinations!"

"Withdraw the question. This is my last question, Mr. Mellon. You can probably go ahead and answer it. It's a simple question and I can bring in another witness to establish it if need be.

But since you're already on the stand I'm going to ask you: Is Simon Smith one of your employees?"

Mellon looked over at his attorney who nodded.

"Yes. He works for one of my companies."

"Great. I'm done with this witness, Your Honor."

"All right. Mr. Rawlins, your witness."

"No questions, Your Honor."

"Ms. Waters. Call your next witness," the judge said.

"The defense calls Roy Wells."

A tall, thin man in a dress shirt and tie walked up to the witness box. The judge swore him in.

"Mr. Wells. How are you employed?"

"I'm a clerk at the Dallas Health Department."

"And what is your job there?"

"Vital statistics—birth and death certificates."

"And did someone from my office visit you yesterday in conjunction with Rodney Thompson's death certificate?"

"Yes. He wanted to know who had ordered and received copies of the death certificate."

"So, it is your job to keep a record of every death certificate issued in Dallas?"

"Yes. We have to account for the fees charged so we always give out a receipt."

"And who has obtained Mr. Thompson's death certificate since his death?"

"Ms. Thompson, Eternal Rest Funeral Home, and Simon Smith."

There was a buzz of excitement in the courtroom. The bailiff stood up and glared out at the crowd and the noise subsided.

"Simon Smith? Mr. Mellon's employee?"

"Apparently."

"So, why would Simon Smith want Mr. Thompson's death certificate?"

343

Wells shrugged. "The only reason I can think of is he wanted to file a death claim against an insurance policy."

The gallery erupted in excited chatter. This time the bailiff's glare didn't faze the crowd. The judge banged his gavel. "I'll have order in the courtroom."

The room went quiet.

"Thank you, Mr. Wells. Pass the witness."

Rawlins looked at the witness and started to say something but stopped.

"Mr. Rawlins. Do you have any questions for this witness?"

"Ah . . . Well . . . I guess not, Your Honor."

"All right. The witness may stand down. Call your next witness, Ms. Waters."

"The defense would recall Tony Bartos."

The judge looked at the bailiff. "Find Mr. Bartos and get him back in here."

"Yes, Your Honor," the bailiff replied.

A few minutes later Mr. Bartos took the stand and Paula began questioning him.

"Mr. Bartos. Do you know of any other life insurance policy on the life of Rodney Thompson other than the one they took out with State Farm?"

"No. I don't. If there is one it must have been taken out after the State Farm Policy because the application requires the disclosures of all policies in force on an insured."

"Now you testified that in order to file a death claim it was necessary to procure a death certificate, is that correct?"

"Yes. The insurance company wants to be sure the insured is dead and looks to the cause of death on the certificate to determine how much to pay or if payment should be made at all."

"I see. Now you said that to file a claim it was necessary to surrender the original policy or sign a lost policy affidavit, is that correct?"

"That's right."

"So, do you know if Maureen Thompson had the original policy?"

"No. She didn't. Apparently she'd lost it."

"More likely Rodney lost it or gave it to someone, right?"

"Objection," Rawlins said. "Calls for speculation."

"Sustained," the judge ruled.

"You don't know where the original policy is, do you?"

"No."

"If someone were to assign the policy as collateral on a loan, how would that be documented?"

"There's a form that would have to be filled out and it would be sent to the insurance company along with the original policy."

"So, let's say Doc Mellon insisted he have the policy as collateral for his investment in Thompson Construction. To accomplish that Rodney would fill out the collateral assignment form and give it to him along with the original policy?"

"That's correct."

"So, that would explain why Ms. Thompson couldn't find the policy?"

"Objection!" Rawlins said. "This is all speculation, Your Honor."

"Your Honor. It's not speculation. It's a plausible theory particularly in light of the fact that we know Doc Mellon obtained a death certificate."

"I'll allow it," the judge said.

"Speaking of the death certificate. Can you think of any reason why Doc Mellon would need Rodney Thompson's death certificate other than to file a death claim?"

"No," Bartos replied. "I really can't."

"Thank you. Pass the witness."

"Mr. Rawlins. Your witness."

"Yes, Your Honor. Mr. Bartos. You don't have a death claim from Mr. Mellon, do you?"

"No. We don't."

"So, if Doc Mellon had taken the policy as collateral, don't you think you would have at least received the collateral assignment by now so it could be reported to the company?"

"That would be the expected procedure."

"No further questions."

"Ms. Waters, redirect?" the judge asked.

"Yes, your honor. Mr. Bartos. If Doc Mellon had processed a collateral assignment then it would have been obvious that Maureen Thompson lacked a financial motive for killing her husband."

"Yes. Whatever had been owed to Doc Mellon would have had to be paid out first, so she would have only collected the difference, if any."

"Is there any requirement that a collateral assignment be processed with the insurance company within a certain period of time?"

"No. As long as it is filed before a claim is paid on the policy it would still be effective."

"So, if Doc Mellon wanted Maureen Thompson to take the fall for her husband's murder, he could simply hold onto the policy and the assignment until after she was convicted."

"Objection! Your, honor," Rawlins exclaimed. "Calls for speculation."

"Withdrawn," Paula said. "Plaintiff rests."

The judge looked at Rawlins. "Mr. Rawlins. Do you have any further questions of this witness?"

"No, your honor."

"Any rebuttal witnesses?"

"No. The prosecution closes," Rawlins advised.

"Ms. Waters?"

"The defense closes, Your Honor."

"Very well, we'll take a twenty-minute recess and then you can give closing arguments."

After the judge left, several reporters approached Paula for a statement. Being pressed for time, she declined any comment and went into the attorney's conference room where she'd have privacy while she worked on her closing argument. She felt good about how everything had gone. Somehow Stan had come through with the critical pieces of the puzzle despite the distraction of Rebekah's hospitalization.

She read through the closing statement she had written earlier and made a few changes based on the evidence that had just been produced. Then she read it over several times so it would come out natural when she delivered it. She felt confident when the case reconvened.

"Ladies and gentlemen of the jury. I want to thank you for your attentiveness throughout this trial. I know a trial like this can be quite tedious at times. If you will remember at the beginning of the trial I told you that according to the law Maureen Thompson was presumed to be innocent. In order to overcome that presumption, Mr. Rawlins would have to prove beyond any reasonable doubt that Maureen Thompson caused the death of her husband by stabbing him repeatedly with an ice pick.

"As you know, Mr. Rawlins did not produce anyone who saw Maureen Thompson murder her husband. All he established was a possible motive and a fifteen-minute window of opportunity. This clearly isn't sufficient to establish beyond all reasonable doubt that Maureen Thompson killed her husband. Do you really think Maureen Thompson put on her Rollerblades and skated over to her husband's apartment and killed him? We know she didn't take a cab, walk, or hop on a bus. None of those means of transportation would have gotten her there in time. It's true she might have gotten a ride or rented a car, but the prosecution introduced no evidence of this.

"On the other hand we introduced evidence of a $250,000 loan from Doc Mellon to the decedent, Rodney Thompson. Not a conventional loan but one that had to be disguised as an equity purchase so that Mellon could get the 100 percent interest rate that he insisted on having.

"You heard about the collapse of the real estate market that put Rodney Thompson in dire straits causing him to default on many of his obligations and effectively shut down his business. I asked Doc Mellon if it was his practice to use violence and intimidation to collect his delinquent accounts and he took the Fifth Amendment because he is currently under indictment for that very thing. You can bet he was livid when he realized he'd have to write off the loan to Rodney Thompson. Then he got a great idea. Since the loan was in default he had a right to ask for more security, so he told Rodney he wanted his insurance policy as additional collateral. Since Doc Mellon refused to testify we couldn't ask him to confirm this, but we know this is true since the policy is missing and he took the trouble to obtain a copy of Rodney's death certificate.

"So, where is the insurance policy now? Well, obviously Doc Mellon couldn't file a death claim until after Maureen Thompson's trial was over. If he'd have filed it before the trial he would have become a suspect, but after Maureen Thompson had been convicted the insurance company would have had to honor the assignment of the policy to him and pay the death claim.

"It was a brilliant plan but fortunately my law partner used to be a life insurance agent and figured out what had happened. So, I think, at the very least, you all will agree we have proven there is reasonable doubt as to whether the defendant, Maureen Thompson, had anything to do with her husband's death. In fact, I think you may well agree that the prosecution has put the wrong person on trial.

"Thank you again for your service as jurors. I know it is a very difficult job, but I am confident you will do the right thing and find Maureen Thompson not guilty."

Paula smiled then returned to her seat. The judge looked at Rawlins.

"Mr. Rawlins. You can make your closing statement."

"Yes, Your Honor," Rawlins said and then turned to the jury and shook his head. "Well, I've got to give Ms. Waters credit, she's spins a good yarn. Unfortunately for her, it's all speculation and guesswork. A missing insurance policy and a death certificate is supposed to prove that Doc Mellon killed Rodney Thompson. I don't think so. You heard the judge. You can't assume anything by the fact that Doc Mellon elected to exercise his right under the Constitution not to testify. I know Ms. Waters tried to make it appear that Doc Mellon was responsible for the Second World War, but the fact is that whole line of questioning was just theatrics. It meant nothing.

"We all know what happened here. It's a fairly common scenario. Rodney Thompson fell on bad times which created unbearable stress on the marriage. Eventually it got so bad he left his wife. Maureen Thompson was understandably upset and felt abandoned. She told Rodney to his face that he was more valuable to her dead than alive. Of course, we'll never know what was the final trigger that made her take matters into her own hands, but that's clearly what happened. Whether she Rollerbladed over or asked a friend to give her a ride, she somehow got to Rodney's apartment, found the ice pick she'd used the week before, and got her revenge.

"You heard the testimony of the medical examiner. This was a crime of passion, perpetrated by someone who was filled with anger and rage. This was the act of an abandoned wife who had been betrayed by the man she thought loved her. Whether this was a murder for profit, revenge, or simply out of anger, it makes no difference. Maureen Thompson intentionally caused the death of her husband and you must do your duty and find her guilty of murder.

"Thank you."

The judge sat up and looked out over the jury. "All right. This concludes the evidentiary phase of the trial. Now after I give you some instructions, you will withdraw to the jury room to deliberate and come up with a verdict."

The judge gave the jury its instructions and then directed the bailiff to escort them to the jury room. When they were gone he recessed the trial until they had completed their deliberations.

"How long do you think it will take the jury to make a decision?" Maureen asked.

"I don't know. It could be a while. I'm sure it won't be today. Stay close to home, though. The bailiff will call me when the jury has completed its deliberation and we'll be expected to return within an hour or so."

"Okay. I'll be at Elena's place. I don't want to be alone."

"That's probably wise," Paula agreed. "I know this is a scary time for you."

"Actually, I feel better than I expected. You did a good job of pointing the finger at Doc Mellon."

"Well, the son of a bitch deserved it. He's a damn loan shark for godsakes."

"What will happen if I lose?" Maureen asked.

Paula sighed. "Well, they'll take you into custody right away. Then down the road a few days they'll have a sentencing hearing."

"Oh, God. I can't go to jail, Paula. I didn't kill Rodney."

"I know. Just keep your chin up. I'm sure it will all work out."

Elena came and took Maureen away. Then Bart arrived. "Nice job. I heard the closing arguments. You convinced me."

"Yeah. Well, you're prejudiced."

"True. But aside from that I'm serious. You were very convincing."

"Thank you."

"I see Stan came through for you," Bart said.

"Yeah. Just in the nick of time. We should go visit Rebekah now that we've got a break in the action."

"Okay, we can go pay her and Stan a visit and then go out to dinner."

Paula nodded and then began packing up her briefcase. As she was working a reporter came over.

"Ms. Waters. How did you think the trial went?"

Paula smiled. "You tell me. It's hard to get a good perspective when you're in the thick of battle."

"You did a good job. I think it's going to be a tough call for the jury. You definitely made Doc Mellon look bad but I'm not sure the jury will understand the insurance angle. It was pretty complicated."

The reporter's comments worried Paula. She wondered if he was right and they wouldn't understand the implications of Doc Mellon requiring a collateral assignment on his insurance policy. It seemed fairly obvious to her, but maybe it wouldn't be so obvious to a jury. A sick feeling came over her. Had she failed to provide an adequate explanation to the jury? Had her theory gone right over their heads?

35

Diagnosis

After Stan had returned from his trip to the health department where he discovered the critical evidence proving that Doc Mellon had obtained Rodney Thompson's death certificate, he was aghast to find Rebekah's room empty. He rushed up to the nurses' station.

"Where's my wife?"

The startled charge nurse looked up. "Oh. Ah. They took her for a test."

"What test?"

"They think she has hyperparathyroidism."

"What's that?"

"Ah. Well. Let me read you the description in one of my textbooks. After they took her away for the test I was curious, so I looked it up." She opened a big brown book. "

'Hyperparathyroidism is an excess of parathyroid hormone in the bloodstream due to overactivity of one or more of the body's four parathyroid glands. These oval, grain-of-rice-size glands are located in the neck. The parathyroid glands produce parathyroid hormone, which helps maintain an appropriate balance of calcium in the bloodstream and in tissues that depend on calcium for proper functioning.' The doctor said if the test was positive they'd need to do surgery."

"Surgery?"

"Yes. Often it's caused by a tumor. If so, it will have to be removed."

"Can she live without the parathyroid glands?"

"I asked the doctor that and he said that usually only one or two will be affected. As long as at least one remains functional, she'll be all right."

"So, when will she be back?" Stan asked.

"Probably a half hour or so."

"All right. I'll just wait in her room."

"That will be fine."

Stan went into Rebekah's room and stretched out on the bench seat in front of the window. He was tired and fought off an urge to go to sleep. Finally, the door opened and an orderly rolled Rebekah back into the room.

Stan got up and went over to her. "So, how did the test come out?" Stan noticed Rebekah's eyes were red. He took her hand and squeezed it. "What's wrong?"

"The test came out positive. They're going to have to operate."

"Oh. I'm so sorry, honey. But at least they found out what is wrong with you. Now they can fix it and life can get back to normal."

"What if I don't make it?"

"Nonsense. You're going to get through it fine."

"I don't know."

The orderly left and closed the door. Stan leaned over the bed and kissed Rebekah. "I really got scared when I came in here a while ago and you weren't here."

She smiled faintly. "You'll miss me when I die."

"Cut it out. You're not going to die."

She sighed. "They're going to do it tomorrow morning at six a.m."

"That early?"

"They said it would take one to three hours depending on what they found once they cut me open."

"I'm sorry you have to go through this, but it's going to be okay. It will just be like going to bed at night and waking up in the morning."

"Okay, why don't you do it for me?" Rebekah suggested.

William Manchee

He laughed. "I would if I could, believe me."

"You better go tell the kids. Give me the phone and I'll call my mother."

Stan gave Rebekah the telephone and then went out to the waiting room to call the kids and fill them in on the situation. While he was talking to them Paula and Bart walked in.

"Stan! How's Rebekah?" Paula asked.

"Oh. She's okay. They finally found out what was wrong with her."

"Oh, thank God!"

Stan brought her and Bart up to speed then he asked her about the trial.

"The jury is out. I think it went pretty well, but you never know. Juries are funny. They don't always see things the way we do."

"Maybe we should have hired a jury consultant."

"We didn't have the money," Paula reminded him.

"True. I doubt it would have made a difference anyway. You did a great job. Maureen was lucky to have you as her legal counsel. I seriously doubt a court-appointed attorney would have gone after Doc Mellon the way you did."

"You got that right. They would have made her plead out, I'm sure."

As they were talking Jodie walked in. Paula raised her eyebrows and Bart smiled.

"Jodie! You're back," Stan said. "How did your undercover operation go?"

"The FBI took Icaro Melendez into custody. They made a lot of other arrests, too. There was one casualty, though."

"Who was that?" Paula asked warily.

"I'm sorry, Paula. Your friend Lee Long was gunned down."

"What?" Paula said, feeling incredible relief. "Gee. That's too bad. Poor Lee."

Paula looked at Stan, restraining a smile. Bart frowned.

"So, did they ever figure out why Lee was even there?" Stan asked.

"No. Not yet." Jodie replied. "But I didn't come here to talk about Melendez. How's Rebekah?"

"She's going to be okay. She's going to have surgery in the morning and I'm sure she'll be fine after that. There are four very small glands that have been causing all of her problems. As long as they can save at least one of them she'll be okay."

"That's good. How long will she have to stay in the hospital?"

"Just a few more days."

The next day, bright and early, Rebekah had her surgery and the surgeon removed a walnut-size tumor from her parathyroid. Fortunately there was a good gland left to allow Rebekah to function normally in the future. In fact, within minutes of the surgery her blood work showed marked improvement. Stan was waiting for her when they brought her into the recovery room. She was wrapped in layers and layers of blankets.

"I'm so cold," Rebekah said.

"I can see that," Stan replied. "You're shivering. Other than cold, how do you feel?"

"Tired. Take me home so I can sleep in my own bed."

"I will. Just as soon as the doctor says it's okay."

Stan stayed with Rebekah until they took her back to her room. He talked to the doctor and was told she'd probably sleep all day after the stress of the surgery, but if everything looked normal in the morning he could take her home. While Rebekah was sleeping Stan decided to call Paula and see if the jury had come in yet.

"Yes, the court coordinator called a few minutes ago. I'm getting ready to go to the courthouse."

"Rebekah is sleeping, so I think I'll come down there, too."

"Good. See you in a few minutes."

Stan found Reggie and told him he was going to the courthouse to hear the verdict in the Maureen Thompson murder case. Reggie promised he'd stay with his mother until Stan got back.

There were press vans parked all around the courthouse when
Stan emerged from the parking garage. He walked across the street
and walked in the front entrance. Someone in a crowd of reporters
spotted him and rushed over.

"Stan. Where have you been? We thought you'd be second
chair in the Maureen Thompson case," a reporter asked.

"Ah. Well. We were a little short on personnel so I had to
track down a few witnesses and locate some evidence that was
needed."

"Was it you who found out that Doc Mellon had ordered
Rodney Thompson's death certificate?"

"Right. We've been looking for that link for some time. We
finally got lucky and found it."

"So, what do you think the verdict will be?"

"I'd never bet against Paula Waters. Unfortunately, I didn't
see much of her in action, but I heard she did a great job."

Stan finally made it to the elevators and up to the ninth floor.
As he walked into the courtroom he noticed the jury was filing in. He
continued on and took a seat next to Paula.

"You made it," Paula whispered.

"Yes. I wouldn't miss this for the world."

The bailiff looked over at them and frowned. Stan sat up
straight and smiled.

The judge cleared his throat. "Ladies and gentlemen of the
jury, have you reached a verdict?"

The jury foreman stood up. "Yes, Your Honor. We have."

"The defendant will rise," the judge ordered.

Stan, Paula, and Maureen stood up. Paula took Maureen's
hand and held it tightly. The court clerk took a folded piece of paper
from the jury foreman and took it to the judge. The courtroom was
still as the judge read the verdict then returned it to the clerk.

"Please read the verdict," the judge said.

"On the count of knowingly and intentionally causing the death of her husband, Rodney Rutherford Thompson, we find the defendant . . . not guilty."

The courtroom burst out in general bedlam. The judge banged his gavel. "I'll have order."

The room quieted and everyone took their seats. Then the judge turned to the jury.

"I want to thank the jury for its hard work and dedicated service. You are discharged." The judge then turned to the defendant. "Ms. Thompson, you are free to go. Court dismissed!"

When the judge had left the bench Maureen hugged Paula and then Stan. "Thank you so much," she said. "I can't believe this nightmare is over."

"I know. Isn't it a wonderful relief?" Paula agreed.

Maureen turned to Stan, tears flowing down her cheeks. "Thank you for not giving up on me. I know you had to leave your sick wife to track down that death certificate. I will always be in your debt."

"Nonsense. Paula did all the hard work. She's the one you owe your life to."

Maureen nodded as Elena came over and gave her a hug. Then Bart showed up and advised them the press wanted to interview Maureen.

"It's up to her," Paula said, looking at Maureen.

Maureen shrugged. "Why not."

"Well, I've got to get back to the hospital," Stan said. "Nice job, Paula. I'll see you tomorrow."

Paula waved as Stan made his exit. He felt elated that everything had gone so well. As the elevator took him to the ground floor he wondered what Doc Mellon was thinking. *His* nightmare was just beginning. That thought made him feel good. Perhaps there was justice after all.

36
Unknown Heir

A few weeks after the surgery, Stan decided he and Rebekah needed a vacation. The obvious destination was Hawaii as Stan had a little business he needed to do there and he didn't want to leave Rebekah at home. They flew to San Francisco and spent a few days relaxing and enjoying the sights and then flew on to Honolulu. They'd booked a cruise but had a few days before it began, so they took that time to look up Yuzu Eguchi and her son Michio.

They lived on Maui so Stan and Rebekah took a plane and landed at Kahulu Airport on the north side of the island. It was a gorgeous day, so the flight was spectacular. Since they weren't planning to stay on the island they hired a cab to take them to Pukalani where Yuzu Eguchi and her son were supposed to live. Before they left they had called her and told her they were coming by. They didn't want to fly all the way there and not find them home. Yuzu wanted to know what the visit was about, but Stan didn't want to tell her over the telephone, so he just told her it was about her old friend Herbert Wolf. That got her attention.

When the cab left them off at her door she came out to greet them. A young man in his early twenties stood in the doorway watching them curiously.

"Aloha," she said.

"Aloha," Stan replied. "You must be Yuzu."

"Yes."

"Nice to meet you. This is my wife, Rebekah."

Yuzu bowed slightly and extended her hand.

359

"Come inside. Meet Michio."

Michio stepped forward and shook Stan's hand. "Aloha," he said.

They went inside and were seated in a small living area. Yuzu asked them if they wanted tea and cookies.

"Sure, that would be nice," Rebekah said. "Your home is very beautiful."

"Our family has lived here for over a hundred years. It's been destroyed twice by hurricanes, but each time we rebuilt it."

"Wow. We don't get hurricanes in Dallas but a lot of people lose their homes to tornadoes."

"Yes, I've heard about your tornadoes," Yuzu said as she served them both a cup of tea.

"Thank you," Rebekah said. "I love this china. This is a very exquisite design. I've never seen it before."

"It's very old. My grandmother gave it to us."

"So, I guess you're curious as to why we came to see you," Stan said.

"Yes. How can we help you?"

"Well, as I told you over the phone Herbert Wolf has died."

"Yes. That is so sad. He was a good man."

"How long has it been since you've seen him?"

"Twenty-two years, I'm afraid."

"So, I understand you two were quite close while he was stationed here during the war."

"That's true. We were young and in love, but you know what happens to wartime romances."

"Yes. It must have been devastating for you when he left."

"It was. I was heartbroken. It took me years to recover."

"So, why didn't you come to the mainland to be with Herbert?"

"Like I said, my family has lived here for over a hundred years. I didn't want to leave. I begged Herb to stay and live on Maui, but he wouldn't do it. He said his future was back in Dallas."

"Have you had any contact with Herbert in the last few years?"

"No."

"Really? No telephone calls, letters, or anything?"

She shook her head. "I wrote him quite often for about a year after he left, but he never wrote me back. I figured he had moved on and didn't want to have to think about me."

"I'm so sorry," Rebekah said. "Men can be so thoughtless sometimes."

"Yes, they can," Yuzu agreed. "So is this about Michio?"

"Yes. Is he Herbert's son?"

She nodded sadly, a tear welling in her eye. "I found out I was pregnant after he left. I wrote him and told him I was going to have his child but, like I said, he never wrote me back."

"Did you write him after your delivery? Somehow he found out your son's name."

"Yes, I continued to write him. After a while, I figured he wanted no part of us."

"So, why didn't you go to court and try to get child support? It must have been hard for you to raise Michio all by yourself."

"I'm not by myself. I have a big family and we take care of each other. Michio has not wanted for anything."

"Well, that's good to hear," Stan said. "Anyway, Herb left quite a large estate and, if we can prove Michio is his son, he'd be entitled to a good portion of it."

"I don't want his money," Yuzu replied.

"Well, it's not your decision. It's up to Michio. He's over eighteen."

Michio, who hadn't said a word the entire time suddenly perked up. "How much money?"

Stan smiled. "Quite a lot. Hundreds of thousands, maybe more."

Michio looked at his mother. "I should take the money for the family. We could use it."

"No. I don't want his money. The bastard left me and deserted his son."

"He may have abandoned you," Stan said, "but you don't know for sure he ever read your letters. My mother had a similar experience. Her first husband served in the Korean War. When she got married her parents didn't approve and they did everything possible to torpedo the marriage, including intercepting and hiding every letter that her husband had written to her while he was overseas."

Yuzu frowned. "You mean you don't think Herbert got my letters?"

"That wouldn't surprise me from what I've learned. He never mentioned Michio until recently. Perhaps he found your letters long after you sent them, when it was too late to respond to them."

Yuzu thought about that for a moment. "So, what do you think we should do?"

"I think Michio should claim his inheritance. He's entitled to it and apparently Herbert wanted him to have it, since he brought up Michio's name on his deathbed."

"He did?" Yuzu asked.

"Well, he called him Mich, but I'm sure he meant Michio."

Yuzu suddenly became choked up. Tears began pouring out of her eyes.

"What's wrong?" Rebekah asked.

"We had talked of children and I told him I liked the name Michio. He said he did too and it was a good name for a mixed couple because his nickname could be Mich and it wouldn't offend either of our families. His parents' friends would think it was short for Mitchell or Michael and my parents' friends would know it was short for Michio."

"So, it sounds like his family kept you two apart and he was as heartbroken as you were," Stan said.

"I hate it when parents try to run their children's lives. It's not right," Rebekah complained.

Yuzu sighed. "So, how does this work?"

"Well, Rebekah and I are going to be here cruising around the islands for a week. If you like, Michio could come back with us and I'll report to the court that I've found him. They'll probably have to be some medical tests done to prove he is Herbert's son, but the whole thing shouldn't take but a week or two. He can stay with Rebekah and me. We have a big house and all our children have grown up and gone away to school, so we have lots of room."

"Oh, that is so nice of you," Yuzu said.

"Rebekah will enjoy the company, won't you, honey?"

Rebekah nodded. "Yes, it's so quiet with all the kids gone. I'd love to have a guest for a few weeks. Have you ever been to Texas?"

"No," Michio replied. "I have never even been to the mainland."

"Well, we'll give you the grand tour. I'm sure we'll have plenty of time."

"So, do I have any other family?" Michio asked.

Stan looked at him. He hadn't thought of the emotional impact all of this would have on Michio. "Yes, you do, but don't expect them to accept you with open arms. They don't know you and your sudden appearance will decrease their share of the estate. But, in time, I'm sure things will work out."

They continued to talk and Yuzu promised to have Michio ready to leave in a week. They agreed she'd put him on a plane to Honolulu and then they'd travel together to Dallas. When Stan and Rebekah finally left they felt good. After all this time poor Michio would finally get something from the father he'd never known.

About the Author

William Manchee makes a living as a consumer lawyer practicing in Dallas, Texas with his son Jim. Originally from southern California, he lives now in Plano, Texas. Writing is his passion in life and his novels are in the genres of mystery, science fiction, and suspense. He is the author of the Stan Turner Mystery series, the Rich Coleman Novels and the Tarizon Saga.

THE STAN TURNER MYSTERIES
by William Manchee

Undaunted (1997)
Disillusioned (2010)
Brash Endeavor (1998)
Second Chair (2000)
Cash Call (2002)
Deadly Distractions (2004)
Black Monday (2005)
Cactus Island (2006)
Act Normal (2007)
Deadly Defiance (2011)
Deadly Dining (2014)
Deadly Blood (2018)

Printed in the USA
CPSIA information can be obtained
at www.ICGtesting.com
JSHW021251100324
58652JS00005B/63/J